Botolph

by

D.S. Pepper

This is the First Edition of "Botolph".
It was published in Great Britain in December 2010
by Earlsgate Publishing
Post Office Box 721
FOLKESTONE
CT20 9EY.

ISBN 978-0-9567508-0-8

Typeset in Book Antiqua / Papyrus.

To my dear wife, Zina.

If you require a further copy of this book,

please send your cheque for

£8.99 plus £3 p&p to

Earlsgate Publishing,
PO Box 721,
Folkestone,
CT20 9EY.

*Please note: there is a comprehensive Glossary
at the back of the book.*

Acknowledgements.

I would like to thank all those who have encouraged me in this venture.   Zina, particularly, gave me much-needed support to get the project underway. Subsequently she has continued to support me by coping with my obsessive relationship with Botolph and accompanying me on visits to sites in East Anglia and further afield in research for this book.

I have also had a lot of support from my family and friends in the proof-reading of the book, namely: my son Tom and his partner Sara, my step-daughters Lorna and Gorgina, and my friends Duncan Hopkin, Ray Beaglehole, Patricia Taylor and Paul Kemsley.

Also, during my research, Charles Evans was very helpful as agent for Lord Radnor's Estate, as was Paul Fox who lives on the site of Eanswythe's Nunnery.

Many members of the Rotary Club of Folkestone Channel have had to endure my enthusiasm at our weekly meetings and the organisers of "A Town Unearthed" (Folkestone's Lottery-funded Roman Villa excavation project) and Folkestone Book Festival were very helpful in giving me encouragement as publication day drew near.

My thanks also to Jeremy Hodgkinson of the Wealden Iron Research Group who kindly checked the manuscript for "Ironworks howlers"; Martin Lloyd, who helped me unravel some mysteries of the publishing world; Nicholas Reed, Eamonn Rooney, and Andy Linklater who guided me through some historical minefields.

Æ (Known as an "ash"). In the interests of simplicity, I have sometimes chosen to reduce this to a simple "E" as from Æthelbert to Ethelbert and sometimes I have favoured the "A".

Ce In Anglo-Saxon pronunciation (as in modern Italian) where "C" is followed by an "e" or an "i", the "C" is pronounced as "Ch". Thus, for example, Ceolbert is pronounced "Cholbert" and Ceaster (as in Hrofsceaster, the Anglo-Saxon for Rochester) is pronounced "Chaster".

List of Figures

Page

Contents

Characters

Adulph	Botolph's elder brother
Anna	King of East Anglia 636 - 654.
Atheran	Husband of Botolph's sister, Matild.
Augustine	Saint sent from Rome in 597 AD to re-introduce Christianity to England. Founded the abbey at Cantwarebury.
Audomar	Saint and Bishop of Sithiu 637- 670. Also known as Saint Omer.
Bertha	King Ethelbert's Queen and Eanswythe's grandmother. Bertin Monk at Sithiu who met Botolph and Luka on their arrival.
Betta	Torrel's wife at Cnobersburg.
Blue-Eyes	Captain of Sigeberht of East Anglia's guard.
Botolph	Central character of this book and, during the latter years of his life, reputed to be the wisest and holiest man in England. (See next section).
Burgundo-Fara	Abbess of Faremoutiers 620 - 655.
Caelin	Master-at-arms at Burgh Castle.
Ceolbert	Travelling monk, based at Cantwarebury.
Chagneric	Burgundo-Fara's father.
Chagnoald	Bishop Faro's and Burgundo-Fara's brother.
Chlothar I	French king 511- 561. Son of Clovis I and great grandfather of Dagobert. Husband of Arnegunde.
Clovis I	King of Gaul 466-510. Became King of all the Franks.
Clovis II	Younger son of Dagobert. King of Neustria and Burgundia 639-657.
Dagobert I	603-638. Father of Sigebert III and Clovis II.
Denis	Third century saint. Bishop of Lutetia and Meaux.
Ebertram	Monk at Sithiu.
Ecci	Boatman near the Bloomery.
Eanfled	Daughter of Aunt Ethelburga. Married King Oswiu.
Eanswythe	618-640. Abbess of Folcanstane. Daughter of Eadbald and granddaughter of King Ethelbert.
Eadbald	King of Cantium 616-640. Eanswythe's father. .
Ecberht	King of East Anglia.
Eligius	King Dagobert's counsellor. Also known as Saint Eloi.
Eormenred	The elder of Eanswythe's two brothers.
Eorcenberht	Younger brother of Eanswythe. Succeeded Eadbald as King of Kent.
Ethelbert	560-616. First Bretwalda-king of all England. Eanswythe's grandfather.

Ethelburga	Abbess of Liminge. Eanswythe's Aunt.
Faro	Bishop of Meaux. Burgundo-Fara's brother.
Fursey	Irish saint and Abbot of Cnobersburg.
Guberna	Head of the Bloomery.
Hansa	Boatman's son on Rumniae Marsh.
Hessa	Carter who took the boys to Gippeswic.
Honorius	Archbishop of Canterbury 630-653.
Hwanna	Young Clovis II's wet nurse.
Ivan	Monk in Cantwarebury Scriptorium.
Kera	Botolph's mother.
Leofric	Botolph's father.
Luka	Central but fictional character. Botolph's friend.
Marcus	Capellanu to Dagobert.
Markan	Tall monk-teacher at Cantwarebury.
Martha	Wife of Folcanstane fisherman and daughter-in-law to Eric.
Martin	Saint who gave half his cloak to a beggar at Samarobriva.
Matild	Botolph's elder sister.
Matthew	Prior of Cnobersburg.
Modegisile	Bishop of Tours. Keeper of the key of Saint Martin's Cloak.
Montey	Measurer at the Bloomery.
Mosel	Farmer from Apuldre.
Mummolin	Brother at Sithiu who became Abbot.
Nanthild	Dagobert's second wife. Mother of Clovis II.
Penda	King of Mercia.
Radingus	Irish Bishop / Eveqcomte of Caesaromagus.
Richbert	"Lanky-Boots" trainee monk at Cnobersburg.
Sigebert III	Young King of Austrasia 534-655. Son of Dagobert.
Sigeberht	King of East Anglia who became a monk.
Theudebert	Eanswythe's maternal grandfather and friend of Burgundo-Fara's father.
Torrel	Sailing master at Cnobersburg.
Uffa	Eadbald's chief cook.
Ymme	Eanswythe's mother.

Saint Botolph
(620 - 680 A.D.)

Botolph was a real person who was renowned for his mildness and kind disposition.

He was born at a very exciting time, only twenty-three years after Saint Augustine had been sent by Pope Gregory I to revitalise Christianity in England. Like many of his countrymen, Botolph saw hope and love embodied in the new religion and he was inspired to spread this spirit of optimism throughout his known world. As a result he became one of the greatest of the seventh century English missionaries.

Most Benedictine monks lived a static life confined in their monastery. Botolph however was allowed to satisfy his desire to travel, and thus became revered as the patron saint of travellers from the time of his life until later medieval times when he was supplanted by Saint Christopher. Nevertheless there remain many edifices which give testament to his renown. The four gates of London each had churches dedicated to Saint Botolph and three of these still remain.

There are nearly seventy other churches in England which bear his title and the name of the town of Boston in Lincolnshire is believed to be a corruption of "Botolph's Town".

His name even features on the sign of a Public House on Romney Marsh in Kent called "Botolph's Bridge Inn" ... but more of Botolph's Bridge in a later book, although mention must be made here of another Botolph's Bridge in Peterborough. Societies of Saint Botolph have come and gone throughout the centuries and one is still loosely alive based in the church in the little village of Botolph (53 inhabitants) in West Sussex. I hope that the publication of this book may see its resurgence.

His travels and fame spread across to the continent, not only to France but also to Denmark where the festival of Botolph's Mass is still held each June.

Comparatively little is known about his life because of the destruction of records by later raiding parties. Many historians and writers have simply copied and followed the guesswork of their predecessors. There are, however, sufficient historical facts that give us a skeleton of Botolph's life; imagination and surmise flesh out the rest.

There is a suggestion that he was the son of a wealthy family and born in East Anglia but this may be merely conjecture. I have chosen to have him come from humble beginnings, the son of an iron worker living on the Kent/Sussex border.

His name is written variously as "Botulph, Botolf, Botwulf" etc; (my gardener, Norman, insists on calling him "Bolt-off"!). I have elected to retain the second "o" because I think the enunciation of the word flows better than it would with a "u". Although normally an advocate of simplicity, I find that retention of the "ph" does justice to its owner by giving the name a more holy and noble appearance than the hard, primitive and rugged "f"!

Botolph was, I believe, a very special person living at a very special time. Although the tales of his activities are liberally dramatised, I have done my best to ensure that they are as historically accurate as they can be in regard to the locations in which the stories occur and the historical characters he meets.

I hope you enjoy reading of his travels, trials and tribulations.

Prepare yourself for the Seventh Century

People often only read the Foreword to a book when they have finished and enjoyed it. They then turn back to study this part which they should perhaps have read first. They do so because they are now hungry to devour every last morsel that has dropped from the writer's pen whereas at the start they were uncertain of how enjoyable their prospective literary journey would turn out to be.

In some ways I hope that you are doing that.

In other ways I hope you are not. I hope that you are reading this part first to prepare yourself for the story that will follow. To acclimatise your brain. To set the scene in your mind.

It is difficult for us, in this modern age, to conceive what our England was like in Botolph's time.

On the visual front you will need to drive from your mind the concept of roads; neatly ordered and bordered fields; lots of open spaces; rabbits; potatoes; tomatoes.

On the mental front you will need to eliminate the concept of peace and security and the certainty that your status quo will remain the same in the near and distant future. Many of your peers will be dying unexpectedly, sometimes for no apparent reason. Others of them will be snatched in raids to end up as slaves in faraway lands.

Even discounting the threat from human attack, your culture assures you that you are surrounded by elves and goblins and beasts and fiends who are as much of a danger to you as raiders or illness.

Your life is completely subject to the will of the gods. Superstition is the rote by which you live. Spells, charms, curses and witchcraft are the stuff of everyday life.

Apart from that, life in the seventh century A.D. for those who are rich, is probably better than you might have imagined: a plentiful supply of good food; strong warm clothes and soft leather shoes; good company and happy family life; but interspersed by tragedy and disaster which you must learn to take in your stride. Indeed things are rather better now than they were one hundred years ago when foreign raiders were a constant problem.

When you travel, you will usually do so on foot, or if you are lucky by mule or pony. Maybe you will hitch a lift on a wagon drawn by oxen or horses. You will generally not travel more than ten miles from your own family. If you travel further it will be because the family are migrating, ... often to get away from danger. The path you take will either be one of the remaining Roman Streets, or narrow tracks which criss-cross the countryside. The tracks will either have been made by travelling humans or by cattle or both. In open country the paths will only be wide enough for humans to travel in single file. Much of the countryside will not be "open" but covered by dense forests of oak and ash. The lack of light on the forest floor will have reduced the vegetation. Tracks cut hundreds of years before and used on a regular but perhaps infrequent basis, will have remained passable. Glimpses of the sun will be rare and the forest will be cold.

People you meet will be suspicious of you and you of them. Dwellings you come across will be inhabited by souls who have been attacked before and will suspect you of the same evil intent. Travellers you meet may seem friendly at first but, if they suspect you of having more than they do, may kill and rob you at the first opportunity in order to better their own lot.

In these early days, there has been little silting of the rivers and the countryside is indented by masses of watery inlets which either have to be forded or swum or crossed by ferry.   Bordering the rivers are marshy areas which can be fatal for unwary travellers, the wisest of whom keep to the high ground.

There are no signposts.   Planning for travel is difficult but your life may depend upon it.   People you meet on the journey will give you news of what lies ahead of you in return for news from you of the areas through which you have just passed.   Much of your direction of travel will be influenced by the position of the sun by day or, if you are rash enough to walk abroad at night, by the moon and the stars.   You have to persevere in honing your sense of direction and must consign to your memory the landmarks of your trail so that you will recognise them at another time.

Surprisingly, crossing the English Channel is neither out of the question nor unduly dangerous.   At least no more dangerous than it is going to be for the next thousand years.   Plenty of craft cross the water, some carrying cargo and others specifically carrying passengers. Such travel is expensive and, since the Romans left two hundred years ago, there is no coinage.   The only available currency is gold, salt or goods like clothes or spearheads or arrowheads. If you are a man of God like Botolph, and the boatman is a Christian he may choose to give you free passage in the hope that he will find his place in heaven.

Talking of God, your world is in a state of flux. Christianity is the new and up and coming religion. Paganism (the religion of peasants) is becoming unfashionable.   There is a strong movement to promote Christianity and consign the lesser gods to the bonfire. Nevertheless, Druidism and other pagan rituals are still being defended (sometimes violently) by their practitioners.

There is a clearly-defined class system in your new life.   It consists of Thanes, Churls and Thralls.   As a man of God you are pleased to avoid having the onus of a Thane to answer to, as you would if you were merely a Churl. You are certainly pleased to avoid the desperation and poverty of being a Thrall.

The Churls are farmers who rent land from their Thane and it is their fields that fill the open spaces between the forests. They grow cereal crops: wheat, barley and rye. They also grow vegetables in the form of parsnips, cabbages, carrots, celery and peas. Available fruit are apples, raspberries, blackberries and sloes. Livestock includes sheep, goats, cattle and pigs. Farmers have to work hard during the summer in order to produce enough food for their families to survive during the long hard winter. In the Autumn, the cattle are slaughtered and the meat is salted for later consumption.

In the twenty-first century, we tend to forget that slavery has been with us since prehistoric times. In the time-context of this story, slaves may also be known as Thralls or Serfs. They are often Britons who have been captured by the Saxons in battle. Many of them will have been sent abroad where there is a good market for white Britons. Others will be the property of farmers, kings or even monasteries where they will be expected, for example, to do the hard building work of digging deep pits in the chalk for the placement of the wooden poles that will support a new building.

There are artisans too. Potters now use a wheel for fabrication whereas, until recently, all pottery was made by hand. Blacksmiths, Bronzesmiths, Goldsmiths, Silversmiths, Jewellery-makers and Bone and Wood carvers can all be found if you know where to look.

The topography of the countryside is already changing continuously but subtly. It is only ten thousand years or so after the end of the last major ice age and the routine logical effects of, first the ice and then the water movement that attends such a melt is still in its infancy.

Many rivers are still wide and deep. The hills are higher and more pointed than today. The erosion that occurs with melting and drying has certainly started and the silt produced by this erosion is being carried by the rivers towards the sea. Much of it does not get that far however but falls onto the river beds and the process of progressive shoaling has just begun.

This is the different world in which you will live as Young Botolph.

So, noble Thane or Thaness ... read on!

Denis Pepper,
Folkestone.
November 2010.

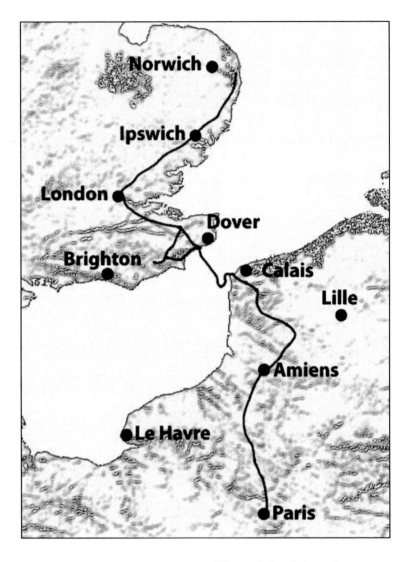

Fig. 1. The Extent of Botolph's Travels.

CHAPTER 1
Flight, 620 A.D.

The horses' hooves thundered past their heads as they lay rigid in the bracken. Leofric's arm was over the little girl in an attempt to keep her quiet and unseen. He felt his infant son squirm under his belly. His pregnant wife Kera was a few feet away and motionless.

They heard the hooves moving into the distance and then came the sound of shouting. Leofric wondered if now was the time to run and get further into the woods but he hesitated. Perhaps he hesitated too long? The shouting stopped and the hooves came back, searching, searching. He knew they would have orders to make sure there were no survivors. Leofric pressed harder on Matild's head, more as a warning than to physically stifle any incipient cry. He need not have worried. She was a good little girl and seemed to know what was expected of her. Even Adulph stopped his wriggling and Leofric kept his own face down in the bracken lest any stray beams from the setting sun should filter through the trees and signal his presence.

Again they passed close and Leofric tensed as he prayed repeatedly to Mithras that they would not be seen. The wound on his right arm throbbed and he wondered if the blood was dripping onto Matild's young body. There was nothing he could do now but lie still and hope and

1

pray that soon they would give up and go away. Like wild dogs they seemed to sense however that their quarry was close and as a nobleman's son Leofric's head would be a fine prize.

He wondered how many of them there were. From the noise, there could be as many as four. He heard them rein their horses to a standstill just a few yards away. Hooves stamped impatiently at first, as one of the riders barked out curse-ridden orders, but then there was a change of rhythm as one of the searchers set off down a path. It sounded to Leofric as if only one horse remained. It whinnied and Leofric visualised the horseman peering into the forest; smelling the air. Had the horse seen them? Was the whinny a communication between horse and rider?

The coppice edge creaked as the mount was urged gently off the path and twigs cracked as the horse picked its way across the forest scrub towards the prostrate bodies. The rider was a skilful tracker and he was using all his animal senses and intuition as he was drawn infallibly towards his prey.

Leofric heard the grate of steel as the searcher unsheathed his sword and the creak of leather and slight thump from his boots when they hit the ground as he slid from his horse.

The undergrowth rustled and then came the eeriness of the enemy's voice as he cooed, "I know you're there, Out you come my fine fellow, I shall get you, you don't have a chance so come out now; out you come!"

Leofric's heart was pounding so hard he felt sure his opponent would hear it. The noises came nearer and nearer and Leofric waited for the blow of the sword penetrating his back. The searcher's senses were accurate

2

even in the darkening forest but not quite accurate enough as, unbelievably, he crept right past Leofric's tense body. From the corner of his eye, Leofric glimpsed a passing leg and gambled his only chance. He grabbed the ankle with one hand whilst hauling himself up and punching the back of the knee with the other fist. Swift as an arrow from a bow, he cannoned into the falling body and grasped the now-roaring head wrenching it sideways and backwards. There was a satisfying crunch and the head's roars abruptly ceased.

A new sound came from behind. A second horse was crashing through the undergrowth towards his two-year-old son Adulph who was now standing confused and unsure what he should do next. The horseman's clear intention was, in one fluid movement, to ride Adulph down and kill Leofric with a single sword stroke.

Leofric only had time to shout a futile "Adulph ... look out!" before the horse's foreleg hit the child with a sickening thud and spun him round into the undergrowth. In a trice horse, sword and rider were then on top of Leofric who had no defence but to crouch to meet the inevitable blow. As his hands touched the ground, one landed on the sword dropped by his former adversary and he instinctively raised the weapon and clumsily parried the blow that was meant to remove his head.

The momentum of the horse's charge took it further into the woodland and the rider slid to the ground, sword in hand and came running back to finish the job he had started. Leofric was ready for him now though and, unfamiliar as the enemy sword felt in his hand, and painful as was his wounded arm, he felt nothing but a burning need to annihilate the man who had just killed his son.

The fight was fierce with the enemy swordsman initially confident of victory. He thought he had secured it too when Leofric seemed to trip and his opponent gave a triumphant shout as he lunged for the kill. Leofric's balance was still intact however and he deftly tilted sideways to avoid the blow while thrusting upwards with the sword onto which his opponent fell.

Leofric sank onto one knee, still alert and wondering if the noise might have attracted further unwelcome attention but all was quiet except for the tears of Kera and Matild who were sobbing over the inert bundle that they had retrieved from the bracken.

His fury unabated, Leofric rose and savagely stabbed the enemy sword into the ground as he returned to his family. He knelt and turned his head to place his left ear on Adulph's chest. He thought he could detect a sound; the body still felt warm. It was now too dark to investigate the extent of the injuries. With more confidence than he felt, he said "He lives! With Mithras' help he will recover. Come, we must get away from here. Wait while I get some material for a sling. Our enemies now have no need of their clothes."

A few minutes later Adulph was wrapped securely around Leofric's body and they made their way back to the pathway and headed westwards.

Leofric's first thought was to capture one or both of the horses so that they could quickly put in some leagues to the south. A Mercian horse would be remembered in every hamlet they passed through however and this would defeat his main aim of losing himself and his family to the forest. He decided to keep things simple.

Leofric took the lead with his left arm supporting the bundle that had once been Adulph, and in his right hand he held a snatched sapling before him, as he moved as quickly as he could into the blackness. A still-sobbing Kera followed, leading Matild by the hand. It was two hours before Matild started to falter. Kera swept her up and hurried on, straddling her little legs around her left hip but now there was a danger that if Kera fell she would land on top of Matild. Leofric knew that at most they could keep going for another couple of hours and then they would simply *have* to stop. That would put them ten or eleven miles from their hunters however and they might, with caution, be able to open the gap by a further twenty or so miles the next day.

He had originally chosen the path because it was one he had used before and knew it led south towards safety but he could recognise nothing about it now. Every so often they passed a clearing and then the path narrowed again. Occasionally sounds from the bordering trees made Leofric's heart leap into his mouth but he could do nothing but hope that the noises came from animals rather than men. He was tired from battle and from loss of blood as well as from walking. As fatigue and hunger overtook him, so did sadness.

Sadness for the loss of those who had been killed; despair at the slaughter of his dynasty; hate of battle and violence and a desire for a different life. He had nothing left to fight for now, except his immediate family. What was he going to do? How was he going to support them? There was nobody left to whom he could turn for help. He was on his own. He needed to find somewhere safe; somewhere where he could start again. Take on a new mantle. Now the virtue in being a noble lord had been lost. His fiefdom had gone. He yearned for the life of a simple working man and hoped he would never see battle again.   He was the last one left.   His spirit hit the bottom of its pit and bounced upwards a little as he managed to push despair to one side, knowing that it was a luxury he could ill afford.

They were approaching the top of a small rise and he slowed, making low warning sounds to Kera so that she did not bump into him.   He held her close with his free arm and, directly into her ear, whispered that they would leave the path at this point and go deep enough into the woods to be secure for the night.

Slowly they felt their way between the tree trunks, Leofric leading and probing with his sapling to try to find the kindest route.   Cruel branchlets slashed at their faces and surface roots conspired to trip them up.   They made a fearsome noise as they guessed and pushed and hazarded their way through the vegetation.   Leofric had just decided that they were far enough from danger when the density of the trees suddenly reduced.   Matild was still awake and Kera put her down and unwrapped the bundle of Adulph from Leofric so that his hands were free to push and pull and flatten the ground and prepare a rude shelter.   The place had but two virtues: it was dry and it seemed safe.

Again Leofric laid his ear on Adulph's chest and in spite of his tiredness a great feeling of joy surged through him as he heard the unmistakeable sounds of life.

"He lives!" he told Kera to renewed sobs of relief.

"Come, lie down here with Adulph between us. Keep him wrapped warmly and let us see what the Sun God will bring tomorrow."

They lay on the forest floor and clasped their arms around each other with the children between them and, in spite of their discomfort, were soon into the blessed sleep of the exhausted.

6

Leofric was first to wake. Dawn was just beginning to break. He lay still listening and wondering what had awoken him. He could hear the susurrations of the trees topped by the morning birdsong, but he guessed it must have been something else.

The noise came again. It was not from the trees but a rhythmic pulse from his side. Adulph was trying to vomit!

He quickly stripped the shrouding clothes from the little bundle and carried him away from the two remaining sleepers. He sat him on his knee and held his forehead while the little body contorted and retched. Suddenly a fountain of mush was forcibly ejected from the little mouth which in turn took in a great lungful of air.

This was balanced by an explosive yell of fear, pain, confusion and anguish!

Kera and Matild woke instantly and came rushing over to their two menfolk. Kera wiped Adulph's mouth clean with some grass and then took him to her swollen breast where he suckled hungrily.

Leofric sat on his haunches grinning stupidly and marvelling at the incongruous sight of his beautiful, grimy, tear-stained wife suckling the naked toddler with blood-encrusted, matted hair.

"We must find some food for Matild," said Kera. "I don't even have an apple for her."

The grin left Leofric's face as he greeted his next responsibility of the new day. They were lucky that it was mid-summer. There would be fruit, once it became light enough for them to see it, but five-year-old girls were ever impatient. Conflicting alternatives flashed through his mind. He could leave them here whilst he went and foraged but a hungry Matild might start to cry and make a fuss. He took Matild's hand.

"C'mon," he said. "Let's go and look for some berries while mother feeds Adulph," and, turning to Kera "We'll not be far away. We'll stay in sight."

She nodded and, mentally acknowledging their desperate situation, lovingly squeezed a cuddle into her cradled son. "What did it matter? They were alive weren't they? She had a good husband; they would survive!"

CHAPTER 2
Survival

It was not easy but they gradually fell into a pattern of finding food where they could. Often there were berries growing in the hedgerows. Once, they came across an apple orchard and Leofric picked a dozen apples. They had no bag in which to carry them but Kera stripped the leaves off some nettle stems and used them to quickly stitch an extra pocket into everyone's tunic so that they could carry the apples and yet keep their hands free. Leofric laughed fondly at her inventiveness and she also had to smile at his ungainly shape as the bundle of apples bounced on his hip.

They kept to narrow footpaths and hid from the few people travelling in the opposite direction. On the second day they saw a farm in the distance and they stopped and watched it for a while. They saw an elderly couple busily coming and going and attending to farm duties. It looked safe. They moved as close as they dared and then left the path. Leofric settled them in the cover of some low bushes and pressed on, stealthily nearing the farm.

The old man's back was towards him as he softly made his final approach but he was alarmed by the sudden gruff "What d'yer want?"

The man neither straightened nor turned to face him. Leofric stopped.

"I need food for my family," he said quietly.

"Bring 'em down from the wood," came the reply. "We won't harm ye."

"You know where they are?" said Leofric incredulously.

"Wife, toddler and child. Been watching you for some time. The rooks told us you were coming. Good watchers rooks are."

At last he turned and Leofric saw his grizzled face. He was still bent over however. It looked as if years of tending his crops in a hunched position had left him permanently angled and ready for work. He even seemed to be comfortable with it. There was a movement to Leofric's left and he turned to see the farmer's wife at the door of the hut.

"Go and fetch them," she said with a kindly smile, "and join us for a meal of newly-baked bread and goats' cheese."

Such an invitation was not to be left hovering in the air and Leofric wasted no time in bringing his little family into the warmth and protection of the farm. The old lady was shocked by the sight of Adulph and it was no time before some water had been boiled and the blood had been washed out of his hair and his wounds cleaned. She did not ask how the injuries had been caused and Kera guessed that she realised that it would be better if she did not know.

Once Adulph was looking more like a little boy again, the old lady turned her fussing in the direction of Matild to whom she gave a horn of warm cows' milk which was eagerly devoured. The old couple were generous with their offerings and Leofric felt an almost-forgotten warm glow from his stomach as mead soaked into his drying body.

"Where are ye bound?" asked the farmer.

"South," came the rather too obvious reply from the battle-hardened young father who did not want to leave clues for any pursuers.   Still, he reflected, although his answer might sound evasive to the farmer, it was in fact the truth.   Leofric had no idea where their ultimate destination would be.

"When are you due?" asked the wife, looking at Kera who was feeding Adulph yet again.

"Before the next moon," replied Kera.

"Stay with us if you like," said the woman looking questioningly at her husband who gave her an almost imperceptible nod.

Kera's eyes lit up at this kindness, but then it was her turn to look questioningly at her husband and saw that it was not to be.

"It's very good of you mistress," said Leofric "but we must press on south."

"Well at least stay for the night," said the farmer. "You will travel faster once you are refreshed."

They actually stayed for two nights and left well fed and much better shod with new boots made by the farmer as he burned his midnight oil.   More of the farm's leather store had been used to provide proper bags which were filled with produce to sustain them during the days ahead It had taken Leofric quite a while to lose his suspicions and jumpiness but he had eventually relaxed and enjoyed the company and help that the old couple so eagerly provided. Kera and Matild had meanwhile bonded with the farmer's wife who doted on young Adulph.

There were tears in her eyes as she stood in the doorway when the time came for them to leave.   Soon they were lost to view and both families forced themselves to adjust in the knowledge that they would probably never meet again.

Now they were rested and had food in their bellies, Leofric was able to think more clearly as they walked and his silence began to worry Kera. She eventually questioned him about it.

"I'm thinking about the future," he said. "I'm trying to work out a plan. You'll be having the baby soon and it will not be long after that before the winter comes. We've no access to any stores that will take us through to the spring. I need to find work and shelter.

We're heading south and within another eight days or so, I guess we'll be far enough away from our enemies for us to relax a little. If we keep going we shall eventually reach the sea and I really don't want to go that far or we'll end up living with the constant threat of marauding invaders.

"What sort of work would you do?" asked Kera.

"Any sort. I've no particular skills but, as you know, I can turn my hand to most things. I could work on a farm. I would've accepted the old couples' kind offer if they had lived further south. But there'll be others. We'll just have to hope that good fortune shines on us and shows us the way. All I ask is for a life of peace where I can work hard and support my family."

She squeezed his arm and they walked on and made good progress for the next few days, constantly driving towards the noonday sun. Leofric was more cheerful. It always helped him to get his thoughts in order when he shared them with Kera. Kera was also comforted and felt more confident that they were not just fleeing from a desperate situation but were travelling towards a new life of hope and ambition.

For the first few days Leofric continued to avoid other travellers. Although he would have liked to have received news of troubles that lay both in front and behind him, he was more concerned with cutting the ties with his past life and avoiding leaving a trail.

On the sixth day however, during one of his regular glances behind him, he saw an ox cart appearing on the brow of a distant hill. Kera and Matild followed his gaze and, as he had taught them, immediately left the path and were swallowed up by the forest. Leofric let them go but to their surprise he himself stayed in the roadway awaiting the cart's approach.

"Peace friend," he called when it finally arrived. The driver looked at him suspiciously and Leofric noticed that he had placed a longseaxe on the seat beside him. The lumbering cart did not slow or stop. Once it was past him, Leofric gave a quick wave into the woods and the watchers left their hiding place and followed at a safe distance. He quickened his pace and ventured "What news?"

"Not much. There was a big battle in the North a couple of weeks back but all seems to have gone quiet again now. I came up from the South two days ago and no travellers I've met have told me anything that might give cause for concern. Where are you bound?"

"South," said Leofric, striding quickly but carefully over the uneven tufts of grass. "I'm looking for work. Do you know of any?"

The driver looked across without answering and stared at him rudely as he weighed him up. Leofric's first appearance on the path had had all the warning signs of a ruffian intent on theft. On closer inspection however, he seemed an honest fellow.

"Might do," he said, mellowing, "Jump up and we'll talk about it."

"What about my family?" said Leofric.

"Family? What family?"

"They're behind us, but falling back all the time," said Leofric. "I can't leave them."

The carter reined his beasts to a stop. "Well, why didn't you say so before?" he said. "Go back and get them, I'll wait."

Leofric gave him a grateful grin, patted the side of the wain and ran back. He snatched Adulph from Kera's arms and the little group quickly gained the cart. The old boy seemed pleased with the company and they were soon settled on hessian bags in the back, while Leofric took his place next to the driver and the longseaxe was sent into temporary retirement under the seat.

"So what's your story?" enquired the driver, as the oxen resumed their original plodding pace, casually flicking at the buzzing flies with their tufted tails.

Leofric was ready for this. He knew it was an inevitable question and he had already made the decision to be honest with his new friend, but to tell him no more than he needed. "Our family were all killed in the last uprising and so we are heading south to start a new life."

"So, what sort of work are you looking for?"

"I don't mind. Anything will do. I'm young and my shoulders are broad. I'm not afraid of hard graft but I'm looking for peace. I'm sick of fighting. What I want is a place where I can defend my family if I have to, but not somewhere that is constantly visited by raiders."

The old man stayed silent. Leofric looked at him. His eyes were closed. "Well?" he asked.

"Well what?"

"Do you know of anywhere that could be suitable?"

"Reckon I might," and then further silence. Leofric studied him again. He was asleep. Leofric was sure of it. His head had fallen forwards and his breathing was slow and steady and there was an occasional rumble of a snore. Leofric raised his eyes and hands in despair and simultaneously turned to look into the back of the cart. Adulph was also asleep but Kera and Matild were both grinning at Leofric's frustration.

He was an impatient man and once he had made a decision, he wanted to get on and put it into effect. It seemed impolite to wake the fellow up however so he guessed he would just have to sit and wait. The oxen seemed to know where they were going so he forced himself to relax and enjoy the ride.

Half an hour later, without any change in his posture, and talking as if there had been no break in the conversation, the old man suddenly said: "Bloomery'll have ye."

Leofric returned to the fray. "What's a Bloomery?" he asked.

"S' where I work. T' Bloomery's nicely tucked into the Weald, well away from the coast so we don't see much in the way of raiders. Don't mean we won't never get none of course, and if they come we'll have to kill or be killed, but ain't seen none there meself."

"What do you do in your Bloomery then?"

"We're ironworkers. We extract iron ore from clay. Then we turn it into arrowheads and cooking pots and anything made of iron that'll sell. I've jest delivered a load a couple of leagues hence and now I'm on me way back to collect some more. Our boss Guberna is alwez lookin' for good workers.   Sounds t'me if it might suit youse just right."

"Sounds good to me," said Leofric.

The old man chuckled.   "I'll really be in favour with Guberna when I get back then, having safely delivered a cartload of stock *and* brought back a strapping young man and his family to swell the workers."

The rest of the journey seemed to pass very quickly. Leofric's mind was full of thoughts, plans and actions.   He had turned towards the back of the cart and told Kera of the man's offer and now her eyes were shining brightly too. The old man was alternately singing and whistling and it was a tired and happy group that rolled down the hill between the Bloomery huts as dusk likewise descended.

On arrival they were introduced to some of the villagers and Kera and the children went into the old man's hut to be looked after by his wife, as he and Leofric went off to find Guberna who had no hesitation in welcoming him to the workforce.

The smell of cooking pervaded the settlement as it was carried by the sweet woodsmoke that wafted through the thatch of the roofs.   As he walked back to his host's hut where he knew his family were safe, Leofric felt that the decisions he had made had been right.   He had led his family to security where they might find peace at last.

CHAPTER 3
A New Life.

During the next few days they were kept well occupied. First they were led around the dwellings and introduced to all the villagers. Kera and Leofric went off to try to find a site to build their hut. Once they had decided on a place, Guberna came and confirmed that it was suitable and said that he would arrange for a building-party within the next few days. In passing, he mentioned that there was an empty hut on a deserted farm just over the hill to the southwest. It was rather isolated, he said but it had the advantage of having a few chickens in residence which, in spite of everyone's best efforts, kept returning to the farm to roost.

"You would be welcome to use that until your own hut is ready," he said. "We could make it comfortable for you and there would be fresh hen's eggs every day!"

Later that afternoon, he took them to see the relic and Kera fell in love with it at once. She was impatient to have her own home again and so with no more ado they moved in with their few belongings.

That evening, just before the sun went down, Leofric was alarmed to hear the sound of an approaching mob. Motioning Kera to keep everyone quiet, he anxiously peered around the edge of the hut in preparation for a fight. To his relief, surprise and delight, it was a procession of villagers bringing gifts for their new home: a blanket from one family; a wooden stool from another; food and a mixing bowl; a shawl and some clothes and all manner of other things. Suddenly, from having nothing, they were, by the generosity of their new friends, equipped to start life again.

Mead and drinking horns had also been brought by the villagers who were determined that the arrival of the new family was a good excuse for a party. The fire was already alight inside the hut and burning embers were taken from this to light two more fires outside. Food was provided; music was played; dancing went on until the early hours of the morning. When the last revellers staggered away over the brow of the hill, Leofric pulled the door closed and a happy Kera snuggled up to him on the hay bedding of their wealden home. He did not need to ask how she felt. It was far from the comforts they had been used to but he knew they could find solace there.

A week later and it seemed as though they had been there for months. Leofric enjoyed learning his trade at the Bloomery and he returned tired and happy to the farm each night. They made the most of the balmy summer evenings by eating outside and relishing the beauty of the sun's crimson rays as the sky became ablaze with colour before settling down through a pale golden hue.

And then, in the early hours of one morning, a sudden cry burst through the night air.

The chickens roosting on a pole by the mud and wattle hut stirred. A few opened their eyes but the rest of the world took no interest.

There had been no time to summon help from the village. Kera had awoken as the contractions had begun. She had had little previous warning. Leofric rose and helped where he could but he had not been present at

18

either of her previous births. He had no idea of what he should do. Kera was having difficulty in thinking clearly but between gasps she managed to make requests that kept him occupied as she entered the first part of her labour. The final part of the process was over so quickly. Kera screamed and arched her back and suddenly the baby was there. Leofric was horrified at the sight of the blood but he picked up the slippery stranger who rewarded him with a lusty yell. The noise had woken Matild who appeared by Leofric's side and peered at the face of her newborn brother. She calmly and instinctively planted a kiss on his forehead. "Shall I go to the village and get someone?" she asked the white, shaking father.

"Do you think you can find your way?"

"Yes," she said "it is nearly light now."

"Right," said Leofric. "Off you go, carefully mind."

He looked at Kera and a feeling of panic wracked through him. She was lying still and looked pale. Was she dead? The birth cord was still attached to the child. Should he cut it? If so, then how? Use a knife? Bite it? Tie it or not tie it? A feeling of inadequacy surged through his soul. This was far worse than battle.

The child seemed fine. Arms and legs were waving about like trees in a storm. He grabbed one of the new blankets and wrapped it around the child, containing the little thrashing limbs. He decided he could not face cutting the cord. He laid the bundle next to his wife's inert body and grabbed a drinking horn into which he poured a small amount of mead. Returning to Kera, he wrapped a blanket loosely around her and then used his right arm to hoist her into a sitting position so that he could apply the drinking horn to her lips. She still showed no signs of life. He wetted her lips with the mead but it had no effect.

19

Suddenly the door burst open and three bossy women bustled inside. One of them took charge of Kera and another swept him out of the door which banged shut behind him.

He went forward and sat on a tuft of grass and sobbed and sobbed. His heart felt as if it was bursting. His soul seemed to be pouring out in the sobs. He did not know *why* he was crying. It was something he rarely did. Were his tears, tears of sorrow? Was his wife dead? He felt consumed by emotion and he was not sure where it began or ended.

He knew not how long he had sat there after the tears had all been spent. His head had dropped downwards and he was staring unseeingly at the foot of the tuft on which he sat. A small arm round his shoulder prompted him to raise his tear-stained face to look into Matild's. She was smiling. Hope surged through his body. He wondered where she had gone after raising the alarm in the village. He looked back towards the hut. The door was open and one of the women was standing at it. She was also smiling and gestured for him to come in. He stood shakily and entered the hut. There to his joy was his beautiful wife, half-sitting and half-lying with his newborn son suckling at her breast. She gave him a tired smile and raised her hand which he took in his as he bent and kissed her. And then the tears came again, flooding out of him as he collapsed on his knees. This time they were tears of relief and Kera's arm comforted and soothed him until the tears stopped. She never saw him cry again.

They named the baby Botolph.

CHAPTER 4
The Bloomery, 624 A.D.

When Botolph's big brother, Adulph, reached his sixth summer, Leofric decided it was time for him to sample the delights of the Bloomery since it was there that his future surely lay. Arrangements were made a week or so in advance, for a day when Leofric could arrive at work later than usual and bring Adulph along with him. He would then hand him into the care of some of the older workers who were used to introducing young lads to the rigours of Bloomery life.

When Botolph heard about this he would give Leofric no rest, insisting that he wanted to join Adulph on his visit. Both Kera and Leofric did their best to dissuade the eager potential ironworker but he was uncharacteristically stubborn.

"You are only four years old!" insisted Leofric, but Botolph would not be mollified and eventually Leofric and Kera acceded to his request.

The arrangements with the Bloomery were duly adapted to include the younger boy and the day came when the father and his two sons left Kera standing disconsolately at the doorway of their hut. She was sad that her baby son was growing up so quickly but amused by the insouciance of his joyful antics as Botolph jumped and bounced his way down the path ahead of the other two.

Although Botolph already knew many of the workers from his own village, he was looking forward to meeting other ironworkers who came from settlements on the other side of the hill. It was a pleasant spring morning and they made the most of their walk to the Bloomery since there was no reason for haste. With Botolph's little legs and his constant interest in all things rural, it took nearly an hour to reach the centre of the site. During their journey they had come across an ants' nest and Botolph had been entranced by the way the little creatures scurried after each other in a long line carrying their various parcels. He would happily have stayed watching this all day but Leofric urged him on.

When they arrived, Botolph was at first overawed by sight and smell of the sweaty muscular men who busily tended the furnaces but his shyness was short-lived. Other young lads were there too, learning the trade and doing menial tasks like collecting the grey lumps of iron ore "mud" from the quarry.

Leofric handed his two sons into the company of a boy who was somewhat older than they were. Atheran was a very mature 12-year-old with bright blue eyes and straw-coloured hair.

"What's yer name kid?"

Botolph looked up at his brother Adulph ... not sure whether he should answer.

"His name's Botolph" replied his big brother in his stead.

"C'mon then, you two can come with me and help me bring back a load of ore. I can bring back a larger quantity if you help me and then I'll get paid more!"

Atheran led them deeper into the forest and before long the noise of the Bloomery was far behind them.

"Where d' ye live?" asked Atheran.

"In the huts down by the hazel field," said Adulph.

"Don't know it," said Atheran "Which side of the Bloomery is that? Towards t' sun or t'other way?"

"Towards," replied Adulph "Haven't you been over that way?"

"I's bin everywhere," said Atheran "but I lives on t'other side of the forest and as far as I know, we ain't got no 'azel fields so I's not too sure what one of those is."

Soon they arrived at the quarry.

The quarry master had spread out dough-like lumps of clay to dry in the sun and under Atheran's guidance the boys collected the oldest, driest, most cracked balls, each of which felt unnaturally heavy due to the knobbly kernel of iron ore inside. They placed them in hessian bags ready to take back to the riverside by the Bloomery.

Atheran had squeezed as many lumps as possible into his sack which was now very heavy. He helped Botolph to lift a rather smaller sack onto his back; Adulph was already loaded and off they went, following a line of other lads whose sacks were bobbing away ahead of them.

As Botolph moved off he looked ahead and started to giggle.

"What's up wiv youse?" asked a puzzled Atheran.

"Ants!" giggled Botolph.

"What d'yer mean 'ants'?"

Adulph turned and laughed. "I know what he means. We were looking at an ants' nest on the way here and Botolph thinks we all look like those ants. Right?" he said, turning to Botolph.

The youngster felt a bit silly now and reddened as he looked down at the ground and nodded, avoiding the big boy's gaze.

Atheran sighed like he had heard his father do when little ones were being a nuisance and just said "C'mon you two," and headed off down the track again.

Botolph had to keep changing hands and moving his sack from one shoulder to the other. Going back seemed to be much slower than the outward journey.

When they arrived at the riverside they put down their bags and sat beside them. Atheran produced some bread and apples which he shared with them. After the brief rest he showed Botolph how to wet the lumps of ore and use a flint to break away the clay and expose the ore ready for roasting.

After half an hour of this Botolph was beginning to flag. Atheran had younger siblings so he was not at all surprised by the four-year-old's lack of stamina. The little one had, after all, been on his feet since early in the morning. Atheran let him sit back while he and Adulph finished cleaning and resizing the rest of the lumps. Soon they had finished and it was time to haul Botolph to his feet again and take the products of their labours to Montey the Measurer to be weighed so that Atheran could claim his fatter-than-usual fee.

Montey was sitting outside his hut by the Bloomery store when they arrived. He was a short stocky man with a mop of white hair. He had a kindly wrinkled face with twinkling eyes that flashed under the foliage of unruly eyebrows.

"Who's this then?" asked Montey.

"Leofric's youngest," answered Atheran "'is first day today".

"Good lad" said Montey, "Have a sweetmeat" and he dipped his grubby finger into a leather pouch and brought out an interesting nut-shaped pellet.

"Open," he instructed and then popped it into Botolph's eager mouth which promptly clamped shut and started devouring the honey ball.

"Good?" asked Montey.

"Mmmmm!" replied Botolph, relishing the sapid flavours.

"Oh dear" said Montey, looking at the other two "I suppose you both want one too ... but don't tell anyone else or I shall have none left for myself!"

They grinned and gleefully accepted the gifts, which looked a little like miniatures of the ore-buns they had been preparing.   The honey-balls were round and grey where they had been dusted with flour to prevent them sticking together.   Their surfaces were cracked where they had dried out.   Adulph put his inside his mouth in the pouch between his cheek and teeth and intended to leave it there to make it last for as long as possible.

It was no good.   After only a few moments he flicked it back between his teeth and crunched on it and savoured the explosion of aromatic herbs that burst from the honey as it sprayed into his mouth.

Montey watched his face with an amused expression.

"Pity my wife's not here," he said, "She reckons she gets more enjoyment from watching others eat her honey-balls than she does from eating them herself!"

"What do you do with all these lumps of stuff?" asked Botolph.

"Come along with me and I'll show you" replied Montey.

Adulph, also tired from his exertions, thought this would be a good way of avoiding another trip to the quarry for the moment. Atheran was torn between earning money from another sack of ore, and having a break.

It was a lovely day, he reasoned, and he would earn twice as much because of the brothers' help, so he decided to join them in a little leisure time.

Montey took them across to the shallow roasting pits where the fires had already been lit and were crackling away giving off pungent white smoke which made Botolph's eyes sting.

"Where are the ore-buns?" asked Botolph.

"There," grinned Montey, "under the wet hay! Look, I'll show you how it's done, over there is a new fire that's just been lit in that pit."

Over they went and Montey took some pieces of wood and placed them in a criss-cross fashion over the orange-white flashing embers ... which immediately became tamed. He then took some lumps of ore and began to lay them methodically over the sticks.

"C'mon," he said "I'm not going to do it all myself, this will be your job one day!"

The other three joined in and soon the sticks were covered. Montey then took some more sticks and put another layer over the ore.

"Right boys," he ordered after a while, "Get some of those turfs and start putting them on top".

"Gently!" he said "Don't throw it on like that Adulph or you will put the fire out!"

"What happens now?" asked Botolph.

"Not a lot," Montey responded, "It'll stay like that all night and" ... BANG!

One of the neighbouring piles of turf suddenly burst apart as a red hot projectile shot through it and then exploded in a thousand pieces.

"What was that?" asked Botolph as they all straightened up after instinctively ducking.

"'Appens sometimes" said Montey, "That's why this is not the place to come unaccompanied 'cos one of those blasters could kill you. What happens is that, if you don't do your job properly and put too large a piece of ore in the roaster, gases build up inside as the bun gets hot and then suddenly it explodes, so let that be a lesson to you. Make sure youse gets those buns to the right size! That's partly what the turfs are for. They slow down the bits when things get lively."

"What else are they for then?" asked Botolph.

"Why, bless me, you need to know everything in one day, don't you, young 'un. Well the other reason for the turf, is to keep the heat in so it does its job melting the ore. If none of these roasters had their turf-lids on you would hardly be able to get near them because of the heat coming out and that heat would all be wasted."

He looked down at Botolph who opened his mouth and then closed it again.

"Yes, I know" said Montey, "You want to know what happens next ... but you are trying not to push your luck. Come with me and I'll show you the next stage".

They went over to a corf full of rough red pebbles and Montey took up two and handed them to Botolph. They nestled interestingly in his hand but when he tried to separate them, they were reluctant to come apart.

"What do you think of that then?" asked Montey.

"Magic!" said Botolph. "Why do they do that? Are they brothers?"

Montey threw back his head and gave a great belly-laugh. "Bless you, no! We call 'em "Stickers". Alwez 'appens as the iron changes colour and cools down after being in the roaster."

"Look, here comes Guberna ... he is going to take these pieces of ore over to the furnaces to be smelted. They have already been re-hammered to break them down to size and sieved to get rid of the smaller pieces. C'mon, let's go with Guberna and look at the furnaces".

A wicked sulphur-pungent miasma exuded from the small violent ovens that were being pumped with bellows to bring them up to temperature.

"There ... d'y' see?" said Montey, "Guberna's topping up each furnace with a mixture of charcoal and ore-pebbles."

Two lads, stripped to the waist, were working at leather bellows and gave quick grins to the new arrivals.

"Those bellows" Montey said "add air to make the flames hot enough to melt the iron ore which then runs down and turns into solid "bloom". We send this off to the foundry where it's turned into cooking pots, hammers, arrow heads, swords, seaxes, javelins, pila, anjons and things like that".

"What a lot of strange names!" said Adulph. "I won't be able to remember all those!"

"You don't have to try," said Montey. "Like all things in life, those special words you use regularly will come as second nature to you and those you only hear once you will forget and they won't matter anyway." Botolph was to remember those words of Montey's for the rest of his life.

Botolph visited the Bloomery often during the next couple of years but did not start work there until he was six, and even then, it was more a way of life than an occupation.   There, he spent many happy hours in the company of the boys and girls alternating between play and work. When work was demanded, he applied himself diligently. Guberna was a good boss and supplied teaching and discipline in equal measure.

On summer days when there was no work due to one of the many festivals, the youngsters would go and bathe in the cool tidal waters of the river.

Five more summers passed and both the Bloomery and Leofric's family thrived and prospered and the boys began to turn into young men.   Both were tall for their age and, whereas Adulph had his mother's fair complexion, Botolph was developing the dark and swarthy appearance of his father.

CHAPTER 5
Ceolbert, 631 A.D.

In the spring, Botolph's life changed with the arrival of a visitor called Ceolbert.

Ceolbert was a monk who was travelling from the West to Cantwarebury.

He was walking alone, as Holy Men often do, and when he reached the ironworks he decided that it was time for a break.

He soon struck up a friendship with Leofric who invited him back to their hut where he stayed for four days.

During that time, he enthralled the whole family with stories about a child who was born in a stable in a far away country. He said that the child grew up to be the kindest, cleverest man who ever lived. He told them how he was so good that the king of the country thought the people might prefer *him* to be king so he ordered this man Jesus to be killed. Even death could not overcome his goodness however and three days later he came back to life.

"What happened then?" asked Botolph, while the rest of the family were still trying to absorb this new story.

"Well," said Ceolbert, "He went back to see his family and his twelve special friends. He had known how and when he was going to die and had tried to prepare his family and friends for the event. He even told his twelve special friends to be prepared for the fact that he would come back to life afterwards. They didn't believe him of course. He told them that his survival after death had a special importance. It was a sign to prove that sins and badness, like death, were not unchangeable. He did something that nobody else could do, he beat death and lived again.

He taught that just because someone had been very bad did not mean that they would always be beyond hope. If they said sorry to God and really meant it, their previous badness could be wiped clean and they could start a new life and when they eventually died, their souls would go to heaven and be with God and Jesus and live forever."

Botolph found this all very interesting but a bit hard to take in. He was fascinated by Ceolbert's lively face as he told the story. He noticed that his countenance had a certain radiance, happiness and peace. He brought this message of good news, hope and optimism and each family member noticed the feeling of joy which inexplicably settled on them. As the days wore on Ceolbert expanded the message further.

Botolph was not too happy when he reached the "turning the other cheek" bit. As a taller than average twelve-year-old he was just getting used to flexing his developing muscles. He rather enjoyed the odd sparring match with some of the other boys in the Bloomery. He was even getting quite protective of his older brother. But here was Ceolbert stressing the need for non-violence.

"What about *our* gods?" asked Botolph.

"What do you mean, *your* gods?" asked the monk.

"Well, our gods of the trees and the streams and the thunder and …"

"Oh Bless you boy" said the older man, "They are all under the control of our Almighty Father, we are all part of the one big family, d'y' see?"

Botolph nodded hesitantly although he was not totally sure that he did see.

Mealtimes changed whilst Ceolbert was there. They would all bow their heads before starting to eat and Ceolbert would say a prayer of thanks for the food that was before them.

On the night before his departure as Leofric, Kera and Matild were sitting round the glowing embers of the log fire and the two boys were sleeping peacefully in the hut, Ceolbert asked the parents how they saw the boys' future.

Leofric paused for a moment, and then confessed that he had assumed that they would just follow him into the Bloomery and become ironworkers, and what was wrong with that?

"They are bright boys," said Ceolbert.   "Yes, they would do well in the Bloomery and maybe, in time, become foundry-masters.   That would be good for their muscles and their physiques but would hardly stretch their brains.

Adulph is nearly fourteen and Botolph is twelve and yet they can neither read nor write and know nothing about anything other than the forest and the Bloomery. Send them to me at the monastery at Cantwarebury, and there I will ensure they have a good education and their brains are stretched and tested so instead of forging iron weapons, they may learn how to mould men's souls.

You remember the story I told you about Jesus' Parable of the Talents?" asked Ceolbert.

Leofric nodded.

"Well Adulph and Botolph are brimful of life and you must not allow their talents to be buried here in the Bloomery when they can be sent out into the world to help their brothers to turn it into a special place."

"They have no brothers, only one sister!" said Leofric with a puzzled expression.

"In our order," said Ceolbert, "all the monks are known to each other as 'brother' and nuns are 'sisters'. We are one ever-growing family moving forwards; an unstoppable tide bringing love and happiness and making a new world."

"So ..." said Matild slowly, "I could become a nun?"

"So you could" said Ceolbert "you would enter a nunnery and become the bride of Christ".

"What does that mean?" asked Matild.

"It means," replied Ceolbert, "that you would spend your time in worship and go and do good works in the community."

"What about having a husband and children?" asked Matild.

"Once you became a nun," said Ceolbert "you would not be allowed to associate with any man and you would live a life of pureness and chastity and bear no child".

"But I *want* children! I want a large family!" protested Matild.

"In that case" said Ceolbert nodding his head understandingly "the nun's life is not for you. Better for you to use your talents here at the Bloomery, looking after your parents and building a family of your own.

But, Leofric, what about your two sons. What do you think? I shall have to leave tomorrow but I would urge you to consider seriously what I have said. Think about whether there is any chance of the boys coming to Cantwarebury. I'll return in the autumn and if you wish, I'll take them back with me. If you make the alternative choice, I will accept it without question."

"We will think about it," said Leofric, seeing the concern on Kera's face at the thought of losing her children. "Kera and I will discuss it between ourselves and then with the boys. It is a big decision to have to take. Whatever we decide, the final decision will be with the boys and that depends upon how their thoughts and ambitions develop during the summer."

Ceolbert was up and about before first light the next day and broke his fast with a couple of handfuls of oats mixed in ewe's milk. As dawn broke, Leofric and Kera also rose and Kera gave Ceolbert some cheese and bread and four cooked hens' eggs and a couple of apples to take with him on his journey.

Ceolbert thanked her and packed them neatly in the leather bag in which he kept his meagre belongings. The bag he attached to one of the two sticks he carried. The first went over his shoulder. The other thumb stick was his walking staff, giving him support whilst also serving to test the marshy ground over which he must travel.

The children soon awoke with all the activity in the confined space of the hut. They had grown to love Ceolbert during the few days he had been with them and they were sad to see him go.

He strapped his sandals firmly to his feet; firmly enough to prevent movement and blisters but not so firmly as to restrict the blood flow. These feet, he told them, were his rights of passage. Once he started walking over the desolate countryside, there was no knowing when he would be able to rest and recover with people as kind as Leofric and his family had been.

He had to be as self-sufficient as he could until he reached the monastery at Cantwarebury. He tied the cord more tightly round his waist, snugging the brown habit against his body and then he was ready to go.

"Leofric, if you will permit me, I would like to say a few prayers with you and your family before I depart."

"Come children," said Kera "It's a beautiful morning. Let's go outside."

"It's still dark!" said Botolph.

"I always think this is the most magical part of the day" said Ceolbert. "When we go out you will hardly be able to tell grass from stinging nettle but whilst we are out there, the light will gradually come, the birds will sing more loudly, and soon the glory of another day will be with us".

The family knelt in the dewy well-trampled grass and faced to the East ... the direction in which Ceolbert would travel. The monk knelt facing them and repeated Jesus' words that whenever people were gathered together in his name, he would be there amongst them (Botolph opened one eye but could not see anyone else so he closed it again!). Ceolbert asked Jesus to forgive all of them for their sins. He thanked Jesus for their lives, their good health and the friendship and love that he had enjoyed. He asked Jesus to take care of him while he travelled and bring him safely to Cantwarebury, and also to take care of the little family until he returned again.

He then asked them all to join with him in the family prayer that he had taught them during his stay. "Our Father" he started, and they all joined in "who art in Heaven ...". At the end, Ceolbert stood and raised his right hand over the family and gave them God's blessing. He then swung round to the hut and blessed this too, and turned to the north and blessed the Bloomery and all its workers.

"Now," he said as they all rose to their feet, "I have a little gift for each of you" and digging deeply into the pocket of his brown habit he pulled out five little wooden crosses, each on a leather thong. He placed the first around Botolph's neck, placed his hands on his head and said "Bless you my child", and then did the same to Adulph and Matild.

He handed Kera's cross to her and placed his right hand on her left shoulder and said "Bless you, daughter". He similarly handed Leofric his cross saying "Bless you my son" and they hugged each other. Ceolbert picked up his shoulder bag and his thumbstick and strode away towards the rising sun, leaving Leofric with a problem to solve.

CHAPTER 6
632 A.D. Decision Time.

Botolph missed Ceolbert.   He had been fun and Botolph had enjoyed the stories he had told.

As a developing child of twelve summers with an ever-increasing thirst for knowledge, he had been impressed with the Christian tales.   He had always looked up to his father, Leofric, as the "top of the tree," the one who would protect the family and the one to whom they all turned for guidance.

The iron-working community had their gods whom they "worshipped" in a casual way, the Sun-god, and Rhiannon were the two main ones and there were plenty of others.   But this was not really serious stuff, more a way of talking and a way of the farmers invoking good harvests and the iron-workers calling for better weather.

Suddenly Botolph seemed to have acquired a new guiding star.   A star, not only for *him* to follow but a star even for Leofric, who normally followed nothing but his own instincts.   Even Leofric would be led and guided by this new god.

Somehow the stories Botolph had heard about that man Jesus who was able to perform miracles and yet died that horrible death, and then confounded everyone by coming back to life again   ...   suddenly that all had relevance for the young lad.

He looked up at the sky in his childish way and considered the prospect.

"I think I really *do* believe in this god", he said to himself "and I suppose if I believe in him then I will have to do something about it".

But he was not the only one. The other members of the family had been similarly affected and new routines were started from that day on. Before each meal, they would bow their heads and follow Ceolbert's pattern of thanking God for the food they were about to eat and asking for His blessing on it. When each day was over and before the children slept, they would all gather together in a circle in their hut and Leofric would lead prayers, giving thanks for the past day and asking for God's protection during the next one.

Botolph treasured his wooden cross, but he did not wear it round his neck all the time because of its tendency to become entangled in tree branches when he was playing or working.

The summer rolled on and the leaves began to change colour and fall from the trees and Leofric and Kera knew that a decision would soon have to be made about the boys' future.

One rest day, known as the Sun-god's day, after the whole family had enjoyed a meal of roast pig, a rare and extravagant delicacy, but, as Leofric reflected, "It has been a good year". They were all sitting outside the hut gazing into the cooking fire which was slowly losing its heat and Leofric took the plunge and said "Well boys what do you want to do?"

"Father?" said Adulph.

"Well," said Leofric, a little awkwardly "Are you going to stay here and be iron-workers for the rest of your lives, or are you going back with Ceolbert when he comes, and do your learning and join the monastery?"

Adulph spoke first and he and Leofric became embroiled in deep conversation. Botolph was only half-listening and busy with his own thoughts. He was excited. He was not sure why. Was it because of this new religion? He was a Christian now and proud of it! He wanted to tell the rest of the world about it. If he stayed in the Bloomery he could help all his friends to become Christians too and he could be an iron-worker at the same time.

He looked up towards the heavens and wondered what Jesus would have done. He knew that Jesus had kindness and consideration for others above all things. Even as a child of twelve, Botolph knew that his parents would be devastated to see them go. His mother would hate losing her boys and, on the practical side, they would also lose some of the income that the boys made at the Bloomery.

He silently prayed to Jesus and asked what he should do but even as he prayed he knew that his mind was made up. He was not destined to stay in the Bloomery all his life. He had been blessed with all those talents that Ceolbert had been talking about and now was the time he should go forward and, as Ceolbert had said, "love and serve the Lord".

The conversation had gone silent and the family were all looking at him. He knew the time had come for his definitive answer.

"Father," he said, in his young clear voice, "I love you all so much and I do not want to leave you. But I feel so excited. I feel like one of the iron-ore buns that is in the roaster and suddenly ... BANG! ... I am exploding. I have to travel. I have to reach out. I have those talents that Ceolbert mentioned. I have to use them."

"Mother" he said, turning to Kera and seeing the tears in her eyes "I *have* to go!"

She nodded. He went to her. She cradled him in her arms and hugged him tightly.

"Right then" said Leofric, wanting to put this torture to an end. "That is decided. Both you boys will be off to Cantwarebury when Ceolbert comes which I expect will be sometime within the next fortnight. We have a few days to prepare ourselves and for you both to do your duties and make your visits to people to say goodbye."

CHAPTER 7
Autumn 632

It was ten days later just as the sun was settling behind the oaks in the west when Ceolbert arrived.

"Hallo-o-o-o!" he called as he turned the corner by the side of the huts.

Leofric burst out through the doorway and the two big men clasped each other in their arms, grinning.

"Good to see you Ceolbert, how have you been? Did you have a good journey?"

"I am getting used to that trip now" said Ceolbert, I have made many friends along the way, both of the human kind and animals!"

"You must be hungry" said Kera, and Ceolbert was not going to disagree so he sat down and flipped off his sandals and waited while Kera prepared some food.

The two boys went over to him. "We are coming back with you!" announced Adulph.

"What, *both* of you?" asked Ceolbert, and Botolph nodded. "That is *wonderful* news" said Ceolbert. "I've made all the necessary arrangements with the Abbot and the other novitiates are really looking forward to your arrival. They are a good bunch, rather lively, and one or two can be a little naughty at times, but generally they are great fun."

"How many are there?" asked Adulph.

41

"We have nine at the moment, and you two will make it eleven, but of course they come and go. Sometimes we get lads who are really enthusiastic when they arrive but then they either get homesick or miss the working life they have left and so we have to send them back home again. We don't want to have anyone at the monastery who is not happy and dedicated to what they are doing."

While Ceolbert was saying these things, tired as he was from the journey, he was looking deeply and penetratingly into the eyes of, first Adulph and then Botolph, so that each of them knew that this was not just a conversation but part of their first tests. He was looking for a commitment.

Botolph was *still* excited.

He was excited about the journey to Cantwarebury. He was excited about meeting the other boys. He was excited about the prospect of a new life. He was excited about becoming a servant of God.

"Now boys" said Kera, placing a trencher with bread and cheese on the rough table, "Let Brother Ceolbert eat his supper. He's had a long journey and I am not sure he will be staying with us long enough to let his blisters heal before he is away again. How long will you be here brother?"

Ceolbert did not answer immediately but clasped his hands and closed his eyes and said a short Latin grace while Kera stood silently by his side. He opened his eyes and said "Thank you sister" and breaking the bread, continued "I shall stay with you tomorrow, but as long as the weather remains good, we shall leave the day after."

The weather did stay good and it was less than thirty hours later that the boys found themselves up and ready to go. Many from the neighbouring huts came over to wish them safe travel. Some brought the boys little mementoes as keepsakes and the boys tucked these into the leather bags their mother had prepared for them.

Dawn was beginning to break and time was fast running away so they had to take their leave without any more fuss. Each parent in turn clasped each of the boys in a fond embrace, as did Matild.

"I shall miss you" she told Botolph "but at least I won't have to put up with your smelly feet, and there will be more room in my bed!" She punched him playfully and a wave of love passed over them both as they hugged and then it was time to go!

"Please kneel" commanded Ceolbert and the gathered company duly obeyed. Ceolbert asked for God's blessing on their journey and for His blessing on those who remained. Just a short prayer by Ceolbert's standards; it was clear that he too was anxious to be away and to cut the farewells short.

"God be wi' ye" they called as the three travellers took up their staves and bags and started off up the path towards the ridge. "God be wi' ye" came back the answers.

They reached the top of the ridge and turned to wave at the small group of people standing outside the settlement, and then turned into the cover of the forest and they were on their way!

They travelled along a sheep path that led the length of the ridge and through the oak forest. Ceolbert strode away in front and the boys trotted behind, chatting happily. Both were wearing their leather-thonged crosses around their necks.

They saw few animals apart from some grazing sheep when they came across a clearing. They knew this part of the forest quite well so there were no surprises. Soon they came to the part they knew as Beorg Aesc where the ash trees grow in a startling clump on the side of a hill and then they were descending towards the water where the River Rother was flooding up towards the Bloomery.

"If we had had more time" said Ceolbert "I would have planned this journey better so that we could have forded the river at low tide, like I did on my journey here. No matter we will give Ecci a call" and he turned to face the huts by the waters edge on the other bank. "Ecci" he called through bugle-cupped hands "Ecciiiiii".

A figure appeared out of one of the huts, placed his hands behind his hips and stretched as if he had had a rough and uncomfortable night. He obviously recognised the caller and waved and then went round the back of the hut to push his boat into the water.

Soon he was rowing over to where the travellers waited.

"Well then, Brother Ceolbert" he said.

"Well then" replied the monk.

"I seed you got both of 'em" he said.

"Yes" said Ceolbert, "I and the monastery have been blessed by the gift of these boys and they will be company for each other too".

Ceolbert had obviously shared his hopes with Ecci on his various journeys to and from the Rother. In fact he and Ecci had been friends for many years, and Ceolbert had passed the night in Ecci's family hut on a multitude of occasions.

"Will you break your fast with us?" asked Ecci. "My wife has baked some bread and there is some new honey we collected yesterday."

That seemed too good to miss. "We must not stay long," said Ceolbert, "but thank you".

Mistress Ecci fussed around the boys placing two flagons of warm ewe's milk in front of them and they were about to gleefully tuck into the repast when a stern glare from Ceolbert had them demurely closing their eyes and awaiting his incantation before they "amen-ed" and did justice to the wonderful spread. An hour later after more "God be wi' ye's" to new-found friends, they were climbing the escarpment and heading north, away from the blossoming sun.

"Are you sure we are going the right way?" Botolph asked of Ceolbert. "I thought Cantwarebury was in the East".

"So it is" replied the monk "but if we go due East we shall have all sorts of rivers and wetlands to wade through and the water is getting colder as winter approaches. Never fear, I know this journey like the back of my hand and I have tried all the routes. Believe me, this one is best for what we want today. We shall head to the North to get onto higher ground and then turn East again and that way we shall stay dry all the way to Cantwarebury. That is," he said turning to look at the sky, "if the Good Lord keeps His rain to Himself and does not scatter it over us!"

Gradually more wildlife began to appear and the forest was not so dense. Botolph could see hawks wheeling overhead and suddenly diving towards some unsuspecting animal.

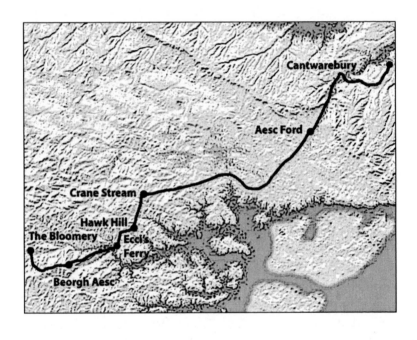

Fig. 2. Route taken by Adulph, Botolph and Ceolbert from the Bloomery to Cantwarebury.

Later they found a stream with an amazing number of cranes and herons. They had just rounded a clump of rocks when the first of the birds took off with a clatter and frightened the daylights out of Adulph.

"Did you think it was a Spectre of the Woods?" chided Botolph, and then ran off as Adulph, grinning, lunged at him. Adulph pursued closely and Ceolbert smiled as he heard their boyish cackle ahead of him on the path. They were boys yet and he looked forward to the joy of seeing them turn into men and hoped that he would be able to help mould them into strong servants of the Lord.

Soon after that, as Ceolbert had predicted, another track joined them from the left and their path turned eastwards. The heat had now gone out of the sun which was falling low in the west and would soon be behind the trees.

"Now" said Ceolbert "There is a small shelter just around the corner, where we may spread our blankets and rest up for the night".

* * *

The next day, the ground was flatter and they made good progress heading just north of east, walking through lush pastures and in and out of the many woods.

They met a surprising number of people on the way and exchanged friendly greetings. "Pax vobiscum friend" "Pax vobiscum brother".

They crossed one of the main routes from Lundwic to the coast. This was quite busy and wide with several ox-drawn carts laden with produce and plodding persistently towards the city. There were similar carts now empty and heading in the opposite direction.

The flat countryside continued for many miles. Every so often Ceolbert would urge the boys to stick to the path in certain areas.

"There," he would say, "See those tufts of grass that are a different colour from the rest? That is a bog and although you cannot see the water, you would be up to your knees in it and sinking fast before you realised what was happening. I know, I have done it" he said ruefully. "Take my advice, if it ever happens to you, don't follow your natural instincts to run forwards since you never know how wide these bogs are. Start running by all means, but turn back the way you have come, and if you get really stuck, lay flat and paddle your way back to terra firma. Not an easy decision to take when you feel that you are drowning in mud but remember: "Flat is better than Upright" in these circumstances!"

The holm oaks intermingled with ash trees, the sudden spectacular clumps of which often heralded their arrival at a larger settlement. They passed through such an area crossing another busy route and Ceolbert told them that down to their right to the south-east lay the towns of Folcanstane and Dofras but to reach them meant passing through a ford which was just to the other side of the trees.

Botolph wanted to go down and see this since he loved the water and was beginning to find walking on the flatlands rather boring. He was delighted when Ceolbert concurred and said that they were close to the end of another day and down at the ford would be a good place to rest up.

They settled into a disused barn on the edge of the wide shallow river and, after eating, Botolph went and sat on the river bank, watching the ox and mule carts trundle their way through the slow-moving shallow stream.

He thought of his parents and wondered how they were feeling. He wondered if Matild was lonely and missing him or if she was just enjoying having more space around her and more attention from her father and mother. Botolph guessed that she would be spending more time with her mother, giving her comfort and learning to run the household so that she would be prepared when her time came to take a husband and start her own family. It surely would not be long now.

The next day they arose early and regained the path following the river northwards through a col between the North Downs after which the river spread its banks into a wider stream. Several times, the path ran inland to avoid little inlets and after one such diversion they turned the corner and Botolph saw a larger settlement appearing ahead.

"Is that it?" he asked Ceolbert excitedly, "Is that Cantwarebury?"

"It is indeed" laughed Ceolbert. "The Romans used to call it Durovernum Cantiacorum of course but you will hear that name used but rarely now."

"What is the name of this river?" asked Adulph.

"Why, bless you, this is the River Stour which, if we were to follow it past Cantwarebury towards the sea, would bring us out to the Wantsum Channel, the other side of which is the island of Tanatus where they light beacons every night to help guide the shipping.

Anyway, it is time for you to make friends with the River Stour and dip your feet in it, for it is easier to cross here where it is narrow and shallower than when we get closer to Cantwarebury. So hitch up your tunics lads and take off your sandals and make sure you keep as dry as possible. We are going paddling!"

They easily made the other bank and dried themselves off.

"Now" said Ceolbert "This is the final part of our journey. You will soon be meeting the Abbot and the other monks and novitiates so we want to make a good impression, don't we? Let's smarten you up as best we can." He dipped his hand back into the River Stour and wiped first Botolph's face then Adulph's and ran his fingers through their hair to achieve some semblance of sartorial elegance!

Botolph began to get really excited as they neared journey's end. He could see the outer stockade and a large collection of buildings, some of which were made in stone. Ceolbert led them around the outside of the stockade however and then he pointed.

"There! That is your new home; the abbey dedicated to Saints Peter and Paul, built by our glorious founder, the saintly Augustine, whose body now lies interred in the portico. Come, let us go and meet the brothers."

CHAPTER 8
Cantwarebury

Augustine's brotherhood consisted of a wonderful group of fellows with different characters from all walks of life.

"Are we going to meet the Archbishop?" asked Botolph.

"Eventually" said Ceolbert "but Father Honorius is in East Anglia at the moment, visiting his old friend Father Fursey at Cnobersburg".

"Well, there are some funny names" said Botolph, always amused by words and their foundations. 'Fursey', he reflected, sounded like 'furry', and his overactive imagination started to run away with him as he pictured a furry animal dressed in a monk's habit but he was suddenly brought back to earth as he realised that Ceolbert was speaking again.

"Well," said Ceolbert obliviously, "Father Fursey! You will enjoy meeting him; he is a larger than life individual ... rather like Moses but with a thick Irish accent. He is great fun but unpredictable. He has a remarkable talent, they say, for performing miracles! Come now. It's time for you to meet Prior Peter."

Prior Peter was a tall and elegant man, dressed in a brown habit with his cross on the familiar leather thong, draped around his neck. He had white hair and bushy grey eyebrows beneath which there were a pair of very twinkly eyes.

"Adulph, Botolph, welcome to the monastery of Saints Peter and Paul. I hope you will be very happy here. How old are you Adulph?"

"Nearly fifteen sire, and Botolph is thirteen."

"Well it is kind of you to answer for Botolph," chided the Prior gently, "but I shall have to find another question to ask him now, won't I? I know, let us do it the other way round, have you any questions you would like to ask me, Botolph?"

"If you are the Prior sire, why are you dressed the same as all the other brothers?"

"A good question! Well one of the rules by which we live is a rule of ownership. We each individually own nothing. Any items we had when we joined the monastery, we gave away to the poor. We rely on God through the monastery to clothe and feed us and, as such we are all equal."

"But you cannot be equal if you are the Prior and therefore in charge," persisted Botolph.

Prior Peter threw back his head and laughed and turning to Ceolbert said "Oh my, the Good Lord has sent us a bright one here, he is obviously going to soak up our learning like a dry cloth and then polish us with it."

He turned back to Botolph "You are quite correct my child, there are some areas where total equality is just not practical. It is true that God has chosen me to lead our brethren here but it is a duty I gladly perform, rather than an honour that I flaunt. We consider a surfeit of pride to be a sin, so we rather try to keep that to a minimum. Does that answer your question?"

Botolph conceded.

"Right then, boys, Ceolbert will continue to introduce you to the rest of the brethren. We are like a family here, a happy but well-disciplined family. We all work hard and do our best to help each other. Anything that you do which makes more work and worry for the others will be frowned upon. You are here to learn. Shortly you will meet our nine novitiates who have decided that they would like to take up Holy Orders and are therefore training to be monks. Maybe you two will decide one day to become novitiates, but there again, maybe not. Look and learn, and ask your questions but not continually. You might have to save up some of your questions and pose them at the correct time."

He pointed to a board on the wall. "This was painted by our very first novitiate who never knew what time he was supposed to be anywhere, he thought it might help newcomers like you. The rule by which we live is "Ora et Labora" ... "Prayer and Work" and at certain times every day we meet in the Oratory where we pray together."

Prior Peter pointed at the board and read through it running his finger over the relevant letters as he did so. Because neither of the boys could read, this was not in fact a lot of help but Botolph vaguely recognised some of the shapes and looked forward to the day when he would be able to read this board for himself:-

"Our first service is at midnight and is called *Matins*.
The second is three hours later and is called *Lauds*.
Three hours later again when the sun is beginning to rise, comes *Prime*.
After this we gather in Chapter so that the brothers may receive their instructions for the day's work.
We then have *Terce* and High Mass.

At noon is the office of *Sext* and then lunch after which   there is a rest period."

Botolph stifled a sigh of relief.

"At 3 o'clock we have *Nones* after which the main work   of   the day is carried out.

As the sun goes down, we celebrate *Vespers* which is followed three hours later by *Compline*."

"I think I might find this board very useful" said Botolph ruefully.

The Prior smiled "Well, you will not have to attend all these offices, certainly not at first anyway.   Now off with you to the kitchens and get some sustenance and then you will be shown to the dormitory.   I will now wish you a good evening and may God be with you."

"And   with   you   Prior"   the   boys   chanted simultaneously.

CHAPTER 9
Spring 633

Adulph and Botolph spent the next few days meeting the rest of the monks and settling in.

Both boys started by being tired after their journey; then intrigued by their new surroundings; then excited about the future; and then homesick.

Botolph particularly and much to his surprise, missed Matild. Adulph missed his father with whom he had just started to build up a good 'manly' relationship.

The most severe pangs of homesickness did not last for long however; they were kept too busy for that.

Not only were they introduced to the full running of the monastery *including,* in spite of Prior Peter's words, *all* the offices of service, but they also had their regular instructions in reading and writing Latin.

They took their turns in helping in the kitchens and in the vegetable gardens and were settling into a nice routine when, suddenly, all was overturned with the return from Cnobersburg of Archbishop Honorius.

The boys were summoned to meet him. The kindly Prior Peter collected them from their cells and ushered them through the cloisters and into the presence of the great father Abbot.

He, too, was kindly though and bade them tell him all they had been doing since their arrival. This however, was more to put them at their ease and allow him to assess them, than it was to obtain any specific information.

When they had finished and the butterflies had stopped performing acrobatics in their stomachs, the archbishop told them that he had some exciting news. He had just returned from Cnobersburg where there was a new monastery that had just opened its doors to pupils. Four students had already been enrolled and they were looking for more.

"Much as we would all like you to stay with us here in Cantwarebury, it is further north on the East coast where I foresee a great need for missionaries to spread the word of Christ. For this reason therefore I am proposing to send you up to Father Fursey's new monastery school.

Abbot Fursey is a most remarkable man with a reputation for holiness which is magnified by miraculous events which seem to occur in his presence on an almost daily basis. He is certainly one of the most amazing people I have ever met and I believe you would benefit by his presence and tuition."

The boys' agreement to move into the wild and woolly north was clearly not part of the archbishop's agenda but he had no difficulty in persuading them that this was the way their lives would now be run. The prospect of a seventy-league walk was not particularly appealing however.

Ceolbert reassured them.

"Our journey here was necessarily on foot because few people follow that route. The journey to Cnobersburg however, at least for the first part, follows the ancient Roman Watling Street to Lundwic. Our monastery has many friends who trade in the city and they will be pleased to provide transport in one of their horse-drawn wains, so

56

you will be lucky my boys. I shall be coming with you and will enjoy the journey too. The journey back here I shall also enjoy because, although I will have to walk most of it, I shall be able to visit other monastic organisations along the way; besides which, I enjoy walking!"

There was no time to be wasted, the next daybreak saw the three of them perched on a wain carrying salted fish from Folcanstane to Lundwic.

The driver was a gap-toothed, long-haired young man called Hessa. He had left Folcanstane just after midnight and had changed horses at the monastery just before picking up his passengers. He was a jolly and carefree sort of fellow and Adulph and Botolph took turns to ride up the front with him while he clicked his teeth and flapped the leather reins to encourage the pair of horses in their westward route along the bumpy cobbles.

By mid-morning they had reached Hrofsceaster and once again Hessa drove into the cloisters of the monastery and changed the nags before the final stage of the first half of their journey.

"What's the bridge like now?" Hessa asked the ostler.

"Passable but not good" came the reply. "If you take it very slowly and carefully and watch where you are going you will be alright. Otherwise you will have to follow the river down to Cuckelstane and ford it there."

"Blow that for a game of Saxons" said Hessa, "We will use the bridge."

Sure enough, the original wooden roman bridge was still standing but had been repaired and repaired again and was not looking at all as serviceable as it had when under Roman imperial control. They passed over satisfactorily enough though and with the fresh horses

57

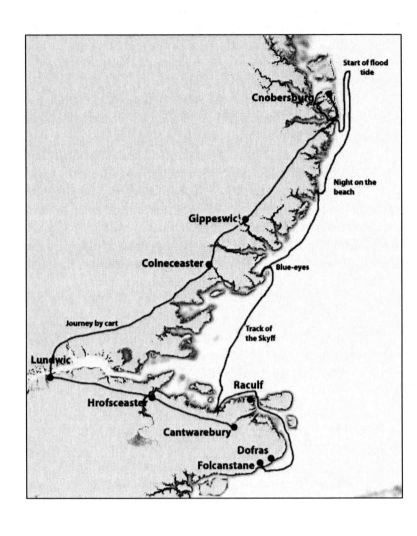

Fig. 3. To Cnobersburg by land and return journey by sea.

were soon heading across the rolling hills towards the busy capital. Hessa had already managed to sell two crates of salted fish to the monks at Hrofsceaster and that left more space in the cart for Ceolbert to stretch himself out and sleep.

By mid afternoon they could see the skyline changing and an hour later Botolph noticed the distinctly different smell that comes from a large city. Soon they came to a wide river and there were more houses than the boys had ever seen in their lives before.

"Well, this is it" said Hessa. "This is as far as I go. I am off to sell my fish before heading back to my wife and family. I will take you to the brothers at Beornmund's monastery and they will give you a bed for the night and make arrangements for your transport tomorrow."

True to his word, Hessa dropped them off on the south side of the river and they were welcomed by the brothers and fed and watered and allocated a sleeping area.

Botolph passed a fitful night, still bouncing up and down from the unusual cart ride but he felt rested well enough when he was roused in the darkness just after *Lauds* the following day.

After breaking their fast the three were hustled into an empty cart that took them up the street to Colneceaster where they arrived just after noon. Here a transfer into yet another wagon took them to Gippeswic and on to Cnobersburg.

CHAPTER 10
Cnobersburg

And then, there was Father Fursey!

As they arrived at the gates of the monastery his figure burst through crying "Welcome me boys, and a thousand welcomes to all three of ye!" And he shook brother Ceolbert's hand firmly and clasped him in a warm embrace.

With each of the two boys he peered intently into their faces and held their gaze with his green eyes while he clasped each hand gently and warmly between his two great paws. He stooped a little, so that his six and a half foot frame did not seem so overwhelming and said "It's good to have you here at Cnobersburg. We're going to have a great time. Now I will say right at the beginning, that I am a bit of a rebel. But that does not mean that you can be. I expect you to conform tightly to the rules and not cause me or anyone else any trouble! I have had many years to turn into a rebel and I am only one now because I find that that helps me serve God better.

So! Do what I say, do not do what I do. If you must copy anyone, then copy Prior Matthew," and his face burst into a delighted grin as a tubby little monk bumbled round the corner with his hands outstretched in greeting.

This Fursey giant with the white flowing locks then reached for his staff which he had placed in a corner and with a swirl of his brown habit turned for the doorway and said "Come, come, let's get you travellers something to eat and rest those weary sandals," and the troop of five with Fursey in the lead, swept through the cloisters and down into the refectory where they found the monks silently eating while one of their order read the Lesson in Latin.

But not, Botolph noticed, reading just in any old way with a constant drone, that, if you were tired would make your eyes close and, if you were not careful, your head fall into your bowl of broth. This monk was reading brightly but carefully. The tones in his voice went up and down. The tone raised when he was reading words that someone had actually spoken, then fell when the narrative was rejoined.

Botolph's knowledge of Latin had improved immensely during his few weeks at Saint Augustine's and he found that he could understand the gist of this reading, even though there were words he had not previously met.

He sat there mesmerised while others fussed around and placed some broth and bread before him. Father Fursey smiled and indulged him while the rest of them, after a short silent personal prayer of grace, tucked into the victuals.

Eventually, during a pause in the reading, Botolph's soul returned to earth and he came to the realisation that there were others in the room besides himself and the reader! He glanced round sheepishly at Father Fursey who smiled and nodded and pushed his bowl towards him. The reader had started again and Botolph grasped his spoon but Father Fursey raised his finger and frowned. Botolph looked quizzically at him but then, embarrassed, realised his error and clasped his hands together and silently thanked God for his food and asked for His blessing on it.

He opened his eyes and the Abbot's jovial face broke into a kindly smile and he nodded, and Botolph tucked in.

The following day Brother Ceolbert took leave of the boys and Father Fursey to start his long walk back to Cantwarebury. Both Botolph and Adulph were rather horrified on his behalf but Ceolbert assured both brothers that he was looking forward to the journey and those he would meet.

Fursey proved to be a "hands on" Abbot, in the nicest possible way. He was here and there and everywhere. He seemed to have an unbounded source of energy. He always seemed to have time for everyone. A kind word of encouragement, a concerned query about progress being made, a brief but strict admonition, all seemed to flow with ease from this joyous mobile mountain!

Needless to say, Botolph was totally overwhelmed and was in some danger of becoming a hero-worshipper.

One day he was sitting studying one of his books when Prior Matthew came and sat by him.

"How are you getting on?" he asked. "Are you making progress with your studies? Are you enjoying your time with us here?"

"Oh, yes," replied Botolph "It's all absolutely wonderful. I do so much enjoy everybody's company. They're all such *interesting* people, and Father Fursey is an amazing Abbot."

"Well" said Prior Matthew, "that is one of the things I want to speak to you about. You will remember that, when you arrived, Abbot Fursey told you that he was a rebel and that you were not to regard him as ... as ... let us say, as a 'role model'".

"Yes," said Botolph, "but I do not understand that, because he is everything that I think a good Christian should be, he is almost like God himself!"

"Aah, exactly!" triumphed the Prior. "Indeed he is, but we cannot have you worshipping our Abbot. He lives and works for the promotion of Christianity both within these walls and outside them. He has been blessed with special powers which you will hear about later. He has also been blessed with an amazing physique and an astonishing personality. He finds that, in *his* case, deviating from the dress and style that is normally accepted helps "his worldly congregation" to see God through him. Indeed to many he *does* seem like God personified, but he would be shocked to hear you say such a thing.

He wants you to see God *through* him, not to see *him* as the personification of God. Do you understand me?"

Botolph considered for a moment, his head slowly nodding. "Mmm ... yes, but I would really like to be like him when I grow up".

"Botolph, Botolph," cooed Matthew "You will be like *Botolph* when you grow up, and as *Botolph* you will love and serve the Lord. And, as I am sure our Abbot would agree, you will be able to follow your destiny every bit as successfully as him, even *without* all the special blessings God has heaped upon him.

Now I will leave you to your studies. I have had this same conversation with Adulph, as I do with all the novitiates once they have been with us for a few days. I like to let everyone settle in and then tackle such issues as these when they become apparent. Peace be with you my son."

"Peace be with you Father." Botolph stood respectfully as the tubby Prior arose from the bench and left the room.

The two boys settled in well at the monastery. Their studies started again but this time under the watchful eye of Markan, a young and quietly intelligent monk with a great passion for numbers.

Markan was slightly built and had a head of black, naturally curly, unruly hair which he kept under control as much as he could by chopping it with scissors every few days. He had taken his vows and was in the first year of his novitiacy although he was older than the average novitiate, being nearly ten years ahead of Botolph.

They got on well together though and Markan kept up a varied routine of reading, writing, learning and numbers.

The boys had just settled down and started to feel at home in the monastery when Prior Matthew approached them and announced that they were expecting a new intake of students within the next couple of days.

"I was wondering about that," said Botolph to Adulph. "Prior Peter told us at Cantwarebury that the new school was starting here, but up until now there certainly seems to have been a shortage of pupils."

Adulph agreed but said he had not really thought about it much as he was too busy recovering from the journey and getting used to the changes.

The next day the "rabble" arrived. There were seven of them. The great monastery doors swung open to admit the first three soon after the office of Terce. They were a motley crowd ranging in age from eight to sixteen.

The second bunch of four arrived after Nones. These four, Botolph discovered later, were all of similar ages to himself but they varied enormously in size from a tall gangly one who went by the name of 'Bean' to a tiny, stocky dwarf called Luka.

Botolph had never seen a dwarf before and he could not help but stare at the newcomer. Luka glared back stubbornly at him. Botolph remembered his manners "Hello" he said, "My name's Botolph".

"Hrrrrrr" growled Luka and turned to pick up his leather bag and follow the rest of his friends to be installed in the dormitory.

Lots of huffing and puffing was going on in here as Botolph and Adulph's beds were pushed across and the other seven palliasses installed. Suddenly what had seemed to them as a spacious luxurious billet was turned into a very crowded one.

For the next few days, Botolph decided it was better not to pursue a friendship with the bad-tempered Luka. His forbearance eventually paid off.

One day as they were breaking their fast in the refectory, Luka came over and muttered "Alright if I sit here?"

Botolph started with surprise and nearly choked on his bread but gave a smile and moved over to make space.

Luka sat backwards on the bench and then lithely flipped his strong legs across in the right direction.

"I've come to say sorry" muttered the dwarf.

"What for?"

"I was rude to you when we first met. I have no excuses. My rudeness has been weighing heavily on my mind. I don't normally apologise about such things but today, I do!"

"Forget it" grinned Botolph, punching him on the shoulder just as the reader started the lesson. The reader stopped and glared at the boys, who, sufficiently contrite, busied themselves with the process of eating. The reader recommenced.

The two lads were entirely different from each other but the bond of friendship was firmly fixed.

Botolph grew at the rate of about four inches a year for the next three years whereas Luka felt lucky if he increased by an annual inch!

Botolph was kind and bright, whereas Luka was often dour and depressed. Luka was also pugnacious and not averse to getting into a fight. In fact he seemed to rather look for confrontations and what is more he was rather good at fighting, particularly if a weapon of some sort was at hand. In such circumstances he would suddenly become a rather frightening ball of violence!

This of course did not go down well with the authorities at Cnobersburg where they did not want short-tempered students turning into short-tempered monks.

Botolph did his best to extinguish Luka's fiery passions before they developed. Luka's contribution was to provide somewhat over-zealous protection for Botolph.

They worked together, ate and prayed together and Botolph's cheery nature gradually infected Luka and the black cloud of depression which had hung over him in the early days slowly lifted.

Cheery and good as Botolph was, he was not averse to mischief and Luka took great joy in encouraging this.

Midnight parties were held in the dormitory. Tricks were played. Challenges were made, taken and resolved. The lads at the monastery were just the same as any like-minded crowd of lads always had been and always would be.

Although Botolph and Luka were very much part of the group, they also stuck together and had their own independent agenda of mischief. The first item on this agenda was the challenge of escaping from the monastery one night and doing a thorough reconnaissance of the local area.

Botolph had become very interested in making maps and Luka shared this interest. It was one of the few things they had in common, and so the plan was hatched. They would escape one night and head off into the wild yonder, memorising everything they could, then mark it all out on parchment on their return.

Where were they going to get the parchment from? Ah, that would be the next challenge!

CHAPTER 11
An Unexpected Development

The fact of Botolph and Luka's total lack of any common foundations became more apparent the longer they were together. Such is true friendship when the differences do not jeopardise the strength of the bond.

They were both monastic pupils.

Botolph had assumed, since Ceolbert had first revealed to him the existence of God, that he would end up serving God in some way, either as a monk or as a priest. He took it for granted that his presence at Cnobersburg was merely a step in that grand plan.

Luka however had no such aspirations. He came from a noble family. He had always had a rebellious streak. His father had sent him to Cnobersburg to be educated and in the hope that the monks might teach him some humility. He was prepared and seemed to be at ease with living amongst the principles of Christianity, but there were few or no signs that he actually believed in it.

His language, given the opportunity to express himself freely, was atrocious! He tried never to curse or swear in Botolph's presence, and certainly he managed to restrain himself in the presence of other 'holy' people.

But given his freedom and the task of tackling a tricky project in solitude and he would be cussing and swearing like the Devil himself!

Given his "earthly attitude", he had no problem then when Father Fursey called them together to announce a deviation in the timetable of their studies.

"King Anna founded this monastery" he said "and he also founded the school in which you study. Now ...". Clearly the Abbot was having some difficulty with getting his message across and the more he wrestled with it, the more anxious the gathered company became.

"... When he agreed to found and support the school, he placed a condition on the pupils who would study here. The condition was that, when he requested it, those pupils should be taught to bear arms on his behalf and to fight for him when needed."

He looked round at the expectant faces. Some were looking horrified, some were looking amazed, Luka was looking infinitely excited!

"I'm sorry to have to tell you," Fursey spat out (literally) in his rich Irish vernacular, "that Penda ... the pagan pestilence who is a constant pain in our posteriors," ... some of the novitiates started to giggle ... "has raised his horrible ugly head again. He has a vehement hate of Christianity in general and monasteries in particular and the talk is that he is now looking in our direction and that it will not be long before we can expect the unpleasant prospect of his company."

Luka was looking even more interested "Pagans I'll pagan 'em" he muttered under his breath.

"What was that Luka?" asked the Abbot.

"Er, sorry Father, nothing important."

"Hmm". Fursey glowered at him. "Anyway, the long and the short of it is that, starting today, all nine of you are expected to attend King Anna at Burgh where you will receive daily instruction in horse-riding, swordsmanship and archery!" he finished in a rush.

"Vorroof" said Luka, with the biggest grin that Botolph had ever seen him display. Several of the other pupils were looking similarly animated. A couple, including Botolph, were looking as worried as Father Fursey.

"Are there any questions?" asked the Abbot.

"Are we expected to actually *kill* people then?" asked Botolph.

"Well, dear boy, to be sure, the truth is that Penda and his party are going to be doing their best to kill you and me and anyone else in the vicinity, so they are. We can pray, we can refuse to fight, we can appeal to their better nature, but in truth, a show of strength and awareness is likely to appeal to Penda more than a state of submission. That young pup wants as many men as he can get, in order to swell the ranks of his army. He hates Christian attitudes and is more than happy to despatch what he regards as 'useless monks' to their maker. He even claims that he is doing Christians a favour by sending them to paradise more quickly!

I and the brothers here have taken our oaths and that binds us not to kill, so we have no option in the matter. We have to hide or run or stand firm and defy him. You boys have an option: you may join us and take your chance, or you are free to take up arms and yes Botolph there is no point in carrying arms unless you intend to use them and that means you have to be prepared to kill and believe me, my children, I am so sorry to have to tell you that.

I want you all to go to the Oratory and pray about this and ask the good Lord what He would have you do. Then I will expect you at the main entrance after Nones, when those of you who are going to the castle will leave and the others will join the brothers for a meeting in the refectory.

Let me make this clear. I want you to go to the Oratory and pray first, *then* talk about it amongst yourselves, NOT the other way around! Now off you go SILENTLY!

They did as they were told and Botolph spent a long while with his head bowed, discussing with Jesus the ins and outs of the problem and wondering what he should do about it. He wondered what Jesus would have done, faced with the same problem, but he knew the answer to that and it did not involve horse-riding, swordsmanship or archery!

But then, he reasoned with himself, he was not Jesus. But then, he reasoned again, as a Christian his main aim should be to be more *like* Jesus. He sighed and glanced round to see if Luka had heard him. Luka was not there, nor were the others. They had reached their decisions and left.

He sighed again and re-bowed his head, he was not ready yet.

He discussed the matter further with Jesus. He pointed out (in case the Lord had not already noticed) that it appeared that this 'arms business' had now become a condition of staying at Cnobersburg. Refusal to comply might mean being expelled. Botolph saw a glimmer of hope, perhaps he could become a monk and then he would not have to decide. No, he was too young. And in any case, that was abrogating his responsibility to come up with a decision. It was now his duty to decide one way or another.

He remembered the biblical passage "Give unto Caesar that which is Caesar's" and thought that perhaps his body was Caesar's now, in the shape of King Anna. Part of the duty of being a pupil at Cnobersburg was to learn to fight.

He let his imagination run and saw a crowd of brigands breaking down the monastery door and Father Fursey and the brothers just standing there and being hacked to death.

A small shard of emotion jagged at him deep inside and he felt the unfamiliar twinge of rage. He looked up at the cross and imagined the face of Jesus. He was smiling down at him with compassion. He sighed for the third time and said to himself "A pupil's got to do what a pupil's got to do!" And crossed himself, rose, bowed to the cross and left the Oratory.

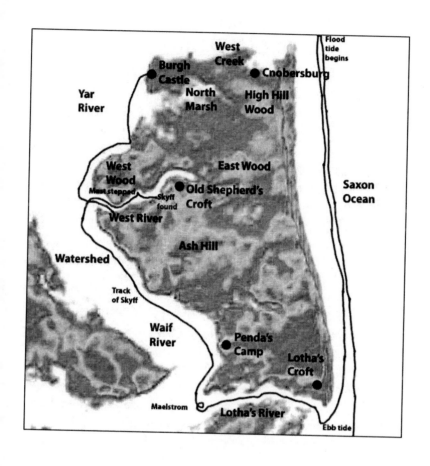

Fig. 4. Waif Island and
Skyff's later voyage to freedom.

CHAPTER 12
Military Training

The next day saw them up at cock-crow and assembled in the refectory.

"No breakfast here for you lot today!" grinned the duty monk, "You have to earn it! King Anna's master-at-arms will be arriving and he is going to give you a little exercise before you break your fast at the castle. You had better all make sure that your sandals are comfortable and that they are suitably adjusted for running."

A ripple of murmuring broke out from the boys, not one of whom had accepted Abbot Fursey's offer to skip the arms training, and they spread out and either knelt or rested their feet against one of the refectory benches as they relaced their sandals more appropriately and adjusted them for comfort.

The duty monk appeared with a tray of water horns which they just had time to drain before the refectory door burst open and a figure, bristling with weapons, clanked furiously into the room.

"Right you rabble, SIT DOWN!" he roared. Shocked ... they sat!

"My name is Caelin, I am King Anna's master-at-arms and today and every other day you will be MINE!" This last word was expressed at full volume and made all the boys jump. Botolph caught Luka's eye. Caelin paused for effect as the word continued to echo around the refectory.

"I expect *strict* obedience.   You will call me 'MASTER'.   You will *watch* me, *listen* for my voice and *hang* on to every word I say.   Whatever I tell you to do, you will do *instantly* and without question.   Is that clear?"

The boys muttered a mixture of "Mms" and "Yesses".

"I said 'IS THAT CLEAR?"   "Yes!" came the boys' louder reply.

"Yes WHAT?" "Yes MASTER!"

"RIGHT!   We will have one more try.   IS THAT CLEAR?"

"YES MASTER!" came the unambiguous and co-ordinated response and the thunder of it reverberated unusually around the refectory walls and the door re-opened sharply revealing Father Fursey in its frame.

"Good morning Caelin" came Fursey's soft Irish voice in complete contrast to the previous explosive speech.

"You will have our walls tumbling down so you will, they are used to quiet and peace and gentleness, not your rude and garrulous vulgarities.   No wonder King Anna has to build your castle so strongly, it's less to keep out our enemies than to resist all *your* violence!"   The boys grinned.

"Now away with you, take my sons off and treat them gently and bring them back in one piece!   God be with you all," and he stood aside as Caelin clanked through the door, closely followed by his new group of hobby-soldiers.

Once through the massive abbey door Caelin untied a squat muscular horse and swung himself easily into the saddle.   "Follow me" he roared and set off up the track with the boys stumbling in his wake.

Father Fursey sadly watched them go and once the last one had disappeared from sight he shook his head and heaved a sigh and turned and re-entered the haven of his vocation.

Burgh Castle was three miles away from Cnobersburg monastery and the boys had no option but to follow Caelin at a brisk trot.

The master soldier led the way for a while and then, when there was an open space and the castle could be seen in the distance he wheeled his horse round and the boys came to a grateful stop, heaving and puffing as they leaned against the nearest tree or collapsed on the ground.

Caelin came back to them.   "Well you lily-livered lot of layabouts!" he shouted.   "How do you expect to fight for your King when you are all as unfit as a rat in a rickyard?   What's your name boy?"

"Botolph Master".

"And yours?"

"Luka, Master".

"Hmmph.   Right, well up you get, this ain't no holiday, see the castle there, ... off you two go and don't look back and don't stop until you get there.   Take my advice, don't go shooting off like a rat down a drain, because all your little laddie friends here have got to try to keep up with you.   Try and get yourself into a pattern and maintain a steady beat.   Right GO!"

Botolph let the way with Luka hard on his heels. Botolph, always considerate about others, realised that Luka's legs were not made for running.   He had to take twice as many paces as the reasonably well built Botolph.

But Luka was a sturdy little chap who enjoyed a physical challenge and he was joining in enthusiastically. Adulph, further back in the line was struggling rather, as were several of the other boys, but Caelin kept his horse trotting alongside them shouting words of encouragement mixed with colourful epithets and they were soon at the castle walls.

"OPEN UP" yelled Caelin. The gates swung apart and they found themselves in the yard. Caelin dismounted and handed his horse to a groom. "C'mon boys, follow me ... let's get some breakfast into you."

They entered a wood-and-wattle construction that was built more for function than beauty and inside were benches and tables that had obviously just been vacated by the regular inmates.

"Cook!" yelled Caelin, "Come on, hop about! Let's get some vittles into these children so that we can begin to turn them into men. You have half an hour boys. Get tucked in but don't stuff yourselves so much that you can't move, 'cos 'leaping about' is what you are going to be doing!"

It hardly seemed five minutes before Caelin was back again and they hauled themselves off the benches and followed him out of the hut and round to the parade area.

There were in fact ten of them, because as well as the nine students, their hapless young teacher had been dragged along too. Markan, bright as he was with words, was not well-suited to physical exercise.

Caelin lined them all up with the tallest at each end of the line (Bean was at one end and the teacher at the other) and Botolph contrived to be with Luka in the middle.

Caelin was standing by a box, the lid of which he now threw open and leant in and picked out a curved knife. "What's this called?" he yelled.

"A Seaxe" grinned Luka joyfully.

"A Seaxe WHAT?" boomed Caelin.

Luka's grin vanished and he looked confused "A Seaxe *knife*?" he ventured.

"A Seaxe knife WHAT?" said Caelin venomously.

Luka looked even more confused. The light suddenly came to Botolph and out of the corner of his mouth he hissed "MASTER!".

Luka took his cue and managed the correct sequence of words to the partial satisfaction of their instructor who now walked up to Botolph and, standing rather closer than Botolph would have liked and holding the ominous Seaxe close to Botolph's nose, he said "Whereas on the field of battle, your timely assistance for any of your pals will be greatly appreciated, when you are on my parade ground YOU WILL NOT SPEAK UNLESS YOU ARE INVITED TO DO SO! IS THAT CLEAR?"

What was clear was that Caelin had eaten a good strong herb-flavoured meal the night before and Botolph received the full benefit of the remaining odours to the point that he thought he might fall over. He stood his ground however and said "Yes Master".

"Good" said the now-satisfied Caelin, "Now let's get down to work. Yes, this is the Seaxe knife from which our ancestors took their name. It is very sharp and pointed and well-suited to passing under the ribs, through the heart and up into the neck. You only have to do that once to each Mercian.

There is a lanyard to pass around your wrist to ensure that you do not lose the bloody thing, as 'bloody' it will be in a very short time if used properly. So one at a time please ... Step forward and pick a Seaxe and return to your places. You first Bean and SMARTLY!"

The first exercise completed, Caelin started on them again. "What is this called Adulph," he said, holding up a leather belt.

"A baldric Master" Adulph correctly replied.

"Yes, a baldric, which can be worn on the left shoulder or the right shoulder depending upon your best sword-hand. And here" ... he bent into the box and retrieved a wooden pole "is your sword".

Luka looked aghast. The arrival of a proper Seaxe had heralded lots of bloodthirsty fun to come, but a wooden sword? What sort of set-up *was* this? Luka had been kinsman with swords ever since he could stand. "I come from a noble family" he thought. "It's alright for these peasants to practice with wooden swords but that's kids' stuff."

Caelin seemed to be reading his thoughts. "Alright my little terrier" he said, "I have heard all about your history and your noble birth but you are part of a fighting group now and I am going to teach you to fight as a team and I don't want you cutting each others' heads off before we have even got properly started."

The wooden swords were duly issued and cuts and thrusts were taught and learnt and the standard sacks of hay were suspended from gibbets and duly set about by the boys. Soon they were all puffing and sweating again.

On went the training, until a halt was called for lunch. Caelin was ever-mindful that his troops needed regular feeding. In the afternoon there was more marching and more swordplay.

This same sort of process went on every other day for the next month. The boys were introduced to the joys of using spears and anjons and hurling axes. Archery was a regular event and, although they were not permitted to use them yet, Botolph had a sense of nostalgia when they were shown some arrows with sharp iron tips that looked just like the ones he had helped to make at the Bloomery.

For days after their first visit to Cnobersburg Castle, the boys arms and legs had ached with every movement they made. Gradually though, under Caelin's tutelage, their supple young bodies began to harden up and their brains sharpened and their reactions quickened.

Caelin was a good teacher and in spite of his rugged exterior and his colourful language, he was very fond of his charges and fought hard within himself not to show it. The more he favoured any one of them, the more stick he would give that boy and drive him until hate and fatigue began to show in the boy's face. Caelin then cleverly re-directed these emotions towards the hay-stuffed Mercian bags and let the boys wreak their vengeance and use up their energies in a productive mind-setting way.

Soon came the time when the wooden swords were replaced by real swords and the boys wrists began to ache with their attempts to wield the heavy steel as deftly as they had learned to use the wooden learning sticks. Gradually though, their forearms started to develop muscles they never knew they had.

And then came the horse-riding and attacking the hay-bags at a gallop. And that started stretching the muscles of the thighs and calves.

Four months had passed and thankfully there had been no attack. More recruits had arrived from other monasteries and from the neighbouring villages. It was not until they saw the antics of the new recruits that Botolph and his chums realised how far Caelin had brought them since their first ragged arrival.

They had learned a lot and grown a lot, both in stature and in martial wisdom and now, they reckoned, they were a pretty good fighting team.

Caelin now left them to jog on their own between the monastery and the castle and they took pride in doing so in an orderly military fashion.

One day, their routine was changed and, instead of their usual day of monastic study following their day of military training, there were two successive visits to the castle.

This time, *all* the recruits were present from the other schools and monasteries and local villages.

They were lined up on the parade ground with the full-time soldiers, and then an awe-inspiring vision of a man rode out and stood silently before them.

He maintained the pause from his position on a raised mound and scrutinised each face in the ranks.

"I am your king. I am Anna ... king of the East Angles. I expect your loyalty and your devotion and I expect you to fight for me, to the death if needs be.

But you are not just fighting for me, you are fighting for your towns, villages, wives, sweethearts and friends. You are also fighting for Christ. Penda and his Pagans are determined to exterminate Christianity in this country and I am even more determined that Christianity will prevail. God bless you all.

"Three cheers for King Anna" roared Caelin.

"Hurrah, hurrah, hurrah" echoed around the parade ground as the king turned his horse and left.

CHAPTER 13
Taking to the Water.

But King Anna was not only a pragmatist in terms of using all facilities that were available; he was also aware of the wider picture.

Having achieved his first aim of organising all available personnel who had the potential of fighting for the defence of his realm, he then set about blocking off bottlenecks of access to the peninsula.

Penda was fanatically anti-Christian and woe betide the monks at Cnobersburg should they ever have to submit to the Mercian king. It was important therefore that Anna lend his thoughts to the further protection of his people.

He had already done what he could by training the boys and had ensured that, should they ever be caught alone at the monastery by Penda's forces, they would at least be able to put up a reasonable fight to provide sufficient time for Anna and his troops to ride the three miles from Burgh Castle to give support.

This however, Anna reasoned, was not enough. He may well be away on another campaign when Penda struck so he really needed to make other provisions for the safety of the monks.

The monastery was in a thickly wooded area on a promontory with a muddy creek on each side and views to the Northeast across the sea.

The prevailing wind for the area was south-westerly so a sailing vessel moored in one of the creeks, should, if the tide was right and the ship was afloat when needed, be easily able to get away and take the monks to safety.

The problem was that none of the monks had any knowledge of sailing and most of them were unlikely to wish to learn, even supposing that Father Fursey had the unlikely inclination to grant them leave from their devotions.

Clearly it was back to the boys again. Caelin had told King Anna that he had been very impressed with the way they had all, even Markan, that long streak of a Mathematician, responded well to the call to arms. Perhaps Anna could make further use of them now.

The old Roman port of Venta Icanorum, the Trading Place of the Iceni tribe, was nearly twenty miles to the west of King Anna's stronghold which itself was three miles west of Cnobersburg monastery.

The Iceni had long since been wiped out but their port was still flourishing and was now becoming known as Northwic. Access was via the wide and fast-flowing River Yar. Fishing vessels regularly landed their catches there and these same vessels were persuaded to transport stores and materials between both the castle and the monastery.

King Anna had set in motion some enquiries of the fisherman and the merchants that he hoped would lead to his ability to make use of the vast amount of water that surrounded his castle. The result of these enquiries were that in a comparatively short while a rather beaten-up but still serviceable fishing smack arrived in the West Creek at Cnobersburg. On the decks were bundles and bundles of rushes. So many in fact that it was difficult to estimate what the normal carrying capacity of the vessel would be.

The strange package stayed there for several days until at an opportune time King Anna arrived with some henchmen and the vessel was unloaded and the rushes placed on the beach. Artisans then set to work, lashing the bundles together and setting a wooden pole just forward of centre, held in place by rope stays.

Thin wooden leeboards were lashed to each side and a steerboard with a long handle, lashed to the stern, for indeed, this was a boat. All it needed now was for a horizontal spar with material attached to act as a sail and it would be ready.

By this time the construction work had attracted quite a crowd. Prior Matthew had totally given up on trying to run an orderly monastery and, in any case, he also wanted to watch. Even Father Fursey was out there, sometimes scratching his head and sometimes rubbing his beard as he considered the efforts of the workmen. Indeed apart from the Cellarer and the Cooks who were preparing the evening meal, everybody was out there watching the activity.

Eventually the reed boat was ready for its trials, so a hapless lad from one of the fishing families was pushed out on the ungainly vessel and told to unfurl the sail. He hesitated for a while and let the wind blow him down the creek. Then, gaining confidence, he unfurled his cloth and away the craft went at quite a spanking pace. Not wishing to enter the estuary, he pushed a leeboard down and leant on the steerboard bringing the little craft up into the wind, of which, fortunately, there was not much. He successfully crossed the creek, changed over the leeboards and leant on the steerboard again, whereupon there was a sudden gust and disaster struck as the craft capsized.

This all caused much merriment from the land party but nothing daunted, the little lad soon had things up the right way again and the sail furled and he paddled his way back to the launch site.

It subsequently transpired that this had all been an experiment. King Anna had asked for a light, easily manoeuvrable and inexpensive craft which could be used to teach his people to sail. The fishermen had provided a traditional inland waterways boat that was normally sculled or poled around the reed beds. They had rather hoped that with minor modifications it could be made to sail. They were right to a limited extent ... a *very* limited extent.

The day's entertainment was over, leaving a surly king to enjoin his fishermen-friends to think again and produce for him, without delay, a craft that really *was* designed for sailing.

A few weeks later the new vessel arrived and she really was as sweet as a nut. She was very similar in many ways to the design of the reed-boat but she was made of light wooden planking fixed in place with wood nails. She had two leeboards and a steerboard just like her predecessor and a short mast and cross spar. She had two sets of thole pins so that two people could use the proper rowing oars rather than having to scull or paddle. She was a lot heavier than the reed boat but not unhandy.

She was also a lot more expensive.

Apparently King Anna's face went a nasty shade of purple when his exchequer presented him with the bill. He made all sorts of expostulatory noises but when he saw the boat herself, he was mollified and made a deprecatory wave towards the fishermen and said "Pay it!"

The next day was "Castle" day for the boys to maintain their skills of combat and to learn new skills so the rising sun saw the Cnobersburg troop jogging eastwards along the waters edge.

Botolph had by now become reconciled to his unexpected military vocation. He still did not relish the prospect of having to kill someone. However, he reasoned, it would be pagans that they were fighting and therefore as they were fighting for Christ it must be alright.

All the boys had benefited from the physical activity and they were full of admiration and respect for King Anna and proud to be members of his "Fyrd".

Whereas the run to the castle had been an ordeal in the early days, it had now become a pleasure and most of the former students of Latin were looking forward to testing their abilities against the wind and the waves.

Now that Caelin had done the harder graft and knocked the rough edges off his pupils, King Anna often came to watch them in mock combat. The number of available horses was limited but, somewhat reluctantly, some of Anna's huscaris (his professional household troops) were persuaded to allow their horses to be used for training.

Luka loved this. In spite of his small stature he was really at home on a horse and was really not too fussed whether it had a saddle or not. Luka was apt to rather overdo the weaponry bit and habitually hung throwing axes all around a horizontally-worn baldric. Another diagonal baldric held his sword, the pommel of which could just be seen over his right shoulder. He kept one seaxe at the top of each boot and rode triumphantly round holding his spear vertically like a Roman centurion.

All this caused a little amusement and some scoffing but once Luka spurred his horse into a gallop and lowered his spear on his approach to one of the long-suffering haybags, there was no doubt in the sincerity of his intentions. Caelin had remarked more than once that the "little demon would be a frightening opponent in battle."

Luka's oft-quoted watchwords were "Pagans? I'll pagan 'em!" In fact he was frequently referred to as Luka Paganem!

Botolph had also become quite adept at horse control, although he admitted that he did like to use a saddle. Horses were not something that he had had the luxury of before, at least not horses like these. There had been the work horses at the Bloomery and the younger children were often placed on their backs and given rides whilst they were hauling, but the Huscari horses were something different.

They were not exactly graceful but they *were* no-nonsense-practical and the riding he did, Botolph rather enjoyed.

Before they left for the jog back to Cnobersburg, King Anna gathered the boys together and told them that the day after next would be the first of their sailing tuition and instead of coming to the castle they should gather at the head of West Creek.

This prospect caused great excitement and the studies in the scriptorium the following day seemed to drag uncomfortably.

The group convened as instructed and were met by Torrel the sail-master.

He was a stocky, somewhat bandy but athletic man with a grey sharp-pointed beard and a rather high-pitched voice.

"Now" he said, "You cannot have a boat without a name so I have named this little craft the *Skyff* whereas the larger vessel over there was already called the *Manigfual*".

He had already pulled the *Skyff* up onto the beach and the boys gathered around while he showed them how to raise and lower the spar to set and reef the sail; how to work the leeboards and the steerboard and to unlock and prepare the oars.

He went on to explain how important it was to balance the boat by moving position and how to trim and work the sail.

"Everything you learn on this little vessel" he said, "will be exactly the same on the larger one, except, being heavier, you can do a lot more damage. So learn what you can and make your mistakes on *Skyff*, if you are in danger of hitting something, you can easily put a leg out to fend yourself off, or if you run aground, she is light enough to get your feet wet and heave her back into deeper water again. Apart from that you can't really go too far wrong. If all else fails, get out the pads and row yourself back here. Don't expect me to come and get you.

There are a few new words to remember. The front of the boat is called the 'prow', the back of the boat is the 'stern' and the middle part is 'midships'. The further you go towards the prow is known as 'forward' and the further back you go is 'aft'. Got that?" They nodded.

"One other thing. When you are standing in the stern and looking forward, the right hand side of the boat is called the "steerboard" side, quite logically 'cos that's the side the steerboard's on, and the left side is called 'larboard". When you are in the prow looking aft, then of course the sides reverse and the *right* side then becomes larboard!"

Luka shook his head in a dazed sort of way and glanced across at Botolph who permitted a curl of amusement to pass his lips.

"Right, there are ten of you.   You!" he pointed at Botolph "and the little fella and lanky-boots (he pointed at a tall thin boy called Richbert), take *Skyff*, and the rest of us will take *Manigfual* out for a jolly.   C'mon all of you, let's get her launched now."   They gathered round the little craft and ran her bodily down the beach and into the water where the others held her steady while our little band of maritime hopefuls clambered aboard and then they were off!

Botolph found himself in charge of the steerboard as they drifted down the creek with the light breeze behind them.   Luka could stand quite easily, whereas Richbert's height made him rather a liability.

Nevertheless, the two boys up forward soon had the spar hauled up to the top of the stubby mast and the boat was picking up speed.

Botolph marvelled at the acceleration and the silence as he steered through the rush-bordered waterway. He was enchanted by the ripply-tinkling sound as the prow cut through the water.   They disturbed a heron, nesting in a reed bed;   it took off with a frightened cry.   Those great wings flapped frantically and then stilled as the heron settled again out of their sight.

Skyff rounded another bend and then they were out into the open estuary where the waves gradually became larger.

"Where shall we go?" called Botolph.

"Let's go across towards that town on the other side of the estuary," suggested Luka and Botolph set off for the opposite shore.   "Can you remember what it's called?" asked Botolph.

"Haven't a clue," said Luka. "Richbert, what's the name of that town over there?"

"That's Caistor on Flegg Island," said Richbert knowledgably. Luka was very impressed and immediately marked Richbert down as the local geographer.

Botolph kept the prow pointing faithfully at the land in the distance and was rather enjoying himself as the wind began to pick up and blow on the back of his neck.

By the time they were in the middle of the estuary he noticed that the wind seemed to have changed a bit and was blowing more on his right cheek.   The sail started to flap.

"What's causing that?" asked Luka.

"Don't know" said Botolph looking puzzled.

"Try pulling on that rope to tighten the sail up a bit" offered Richbert.

Luka did as he was bid and the flapping stopped and *Skyff* leapt forwards.

The wind was firmly on Botolph's right cheek now and out of the corner of his eye he noticed a movement on the horizon.   He glanced across and there was *Manigfual* coming out of the creek.

But she was not right behind him where she should be, she was well to the right.

Confused, Botolph stood up and peered past the sail to check that it really was Flegg Island that was growing gradually but oh-so-slowly larger in front of the prow, and that it was not some sort of mirage.   No doubt about it, that lump was the same.   He was still pointing the boat nicely at it but....actually it was not getting closer, it was getting smaller.

Suddenly Botolph realised his mistake.   The tide! Of course, the tide was flooding in from the open sea and they were being swept up the estuary, there was absolutely no chance that they were going to reach Caistor now.

"We're going to have to turn" he called to his crew. "I think you will have to release the ropes on your side Luka."

The ever-obliging Luka immediately did so and the sail started to flap and beat and make a terrible noise and *Skyff* stopped.   Botolph pushed hard on the steerboard but it made no difference.   The noise of the beating sail invaded Botolph's brain and made it difficult for him to think straight.   Both crew members were looking at him with worried and confused faces, hoping that he was going to find a solution.   "Shall we pray?" suggested Richbert.

"No, not yet" replied Botolph, "Try pulling in the rope on your side Richbert".   He did so with very little effect except that that side of the sail stopped flapping but the other side continued to make a terrible noise as it streamed away from Botolph who suddenly realised that Luka's rope was in danger of breaking free.

"Luka ... grab your rope" he called.   Luka did so and the sail started to calm.   *Skyff* was moving forwards again now and Botolph leant on the steerboard to turn her towards Northwic to which she bounded joyfully with the benefit of the tide beneath her and the fresh breeze now firm on Botolph's left cheek.

CHAPTER 14
Consolidation.

The learning experience was not over yet however. *Skyff* still had another lesson to teach them as Botolph found out when he tried to turn a little further to the south to get away from the rapidly-approaching northern coast. She turned alright when he pushed on the steerboard. That is to say ... her aspect turned, but she still slithered sideways to the west.

Suddenly a dark shape loomed across them and there was *Manigfual* with Adulph grinning happily as he pushed on the steering oar and Torrel standing by his side quietly giving instructions. The other six boys were precisely-positioned at different points to give balance and all but two were looking very happy. The other two presented rather green visages.

Manigfual crossed astern of *Skyff,* came up on her steerboard side, her taller sail unblanketed by the smaller vessel's.

"Lower your leeboard" came Torrel's cry.

"What?" came the impolite answer.

"Lower your leeboard. No, not that one Luka, you daft midget, you always have to lower the leeward one."
Luka did his bidding and Botolph felt the boat benefit as the board bit into the water and curbed her determination to skid sideways in spite of his previous best efforts.

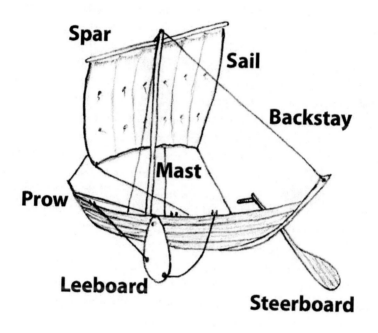

Spar

Sail

Backstay

Mast

Prow

Leeboard

Steerboard

Fig. 5. Skyff

"Now tighten up that leeward sheet as much as you can" called Torrel and Richbert duly hauled on the hemp rope that pulled the corner of the sail.

"Botolph! Bring her up into the wind gradually now. Watch that sail and as soon as it starts to flap, ease her off a little. That's good. See that little puff ball of a white cloud over there? Now keep her pointing towards that for the moment."

Soon Botolph felt that *he* was controlling the boat rather than vice versa and *Manigfual* continued to reach close to them as Torrel shouted further words of comfort and instruction. When the western bank began to get uncomfortably close there was another lesson which this time involved tacking onto another course to come up into the wind from the other side, and Luka achieved his ambition of being able to lower the larboard leeboard.

The sun was going down by the time both boats approached West Creek and the boys were wet, partly from spray, partly from perspiration and partly from paddling in the water as *Skyff* was hauled onto the beach.

Torrel's jolly wife Betta was there to meet them and had brought some mead and a batch of newly-baked buns. They made themselves comfortable in the lee of the forest and reminisced about the day's adventures.

Like Caelin before him, Torrel kept them hard at their seamanship training for the next few weeks. This all had to be fitted around studies with Markan in the scriptorium and further visits to the castle to ensure that their weaponry skills were kept in a finely-honed condition!

Torrel was a great believer in shuffling the boys round. "Can't have you sticking together like soggy mud" he said. "You need to be fluid, like this, and he picked up some dry soil and let it flow through his fingers.

"I want you all to be able to work together, no point in separating out into helmsmen and crew at this stage. Like in life, you each need to be able to do *all* the jobs so that if you find you mysteriously develop into a captain why then, you will know from first-hand experience the problems your crew has to endure."

Botolph instinctively recognised this as a key philosophy that might serve him well in the future and he mentally tucked the idea under his belt. He would often muse in the future that it was perverse that it should have been a grisly old sailing-master who unwittingly put his finger on something that became a prime principle of Botolph's life, that he should always try to understand the other person's point of view.

So he split them up, did Torrel. Botolph often found himself on *Manigfual* watching Luka's antics sailing *Skyff* on the other side of Yar Bay. But then they would be back together again and testing their developing skills between each other.

Ultimately, like the water in which they sailed, the likes and abilities of the nine boys found their own levels. None seemed to enjoy the watery-life as much as Botolph and Luka who really were developing into a well-coordinated unit. Indeed, on the days that sailing was mandatory, most of the other boys preferred to go out with Torrel on the larger boat. In these circumstances, Adulph had developed into a useful coxswain and Torrel was able to take his place amidships and teach the boys a bit of rope work while Adulph did his best to control their destiny between the mud banks. Torrel said that he reckoned the two brothers had saltwater mixed in with their blood!

With the other boys being occupied on *Manigfual*, *Skyff* became free for the other two to use, which they did at every conceivable opportunity. There was nothing they liked better than to get out on their own skimming up and down between the reed beds. They would sail as close as they dared to the opposite bank and then, putting in a board at the last minute, tack away out of danger.

They had their failures, it is true. One time Botolph misjudged and the boat struck the bottom so hard that they felt sure she had been holed. Luka was promptly projected over the prow into a bank of reeds, while Botolph landed in a heap on the boat sole. He sat up just in time to see a wet and bedraggled Luka appear grinning out of the bank. Mistakes are good teachers however and no harm had been done. These dunkings and their ever-increasing knowledge of tides, currents, eddies and marsh life were all useful experiences.

Some of the days on which they sailed were part of the new curriculum. Other times were periods designated as free and they simply gained permission and then took *Skyff* off for one of their outings. They were learning the lay, not only of the rivers but also of the land, since they would often sail deep into a creek, haul the craft up onto the beach and set off to explore the locality.

The most accessible inlet was West River on their own Waif Island. Botolph had been intrigued by the island's name and one day had asked Torrel if he knew its origin. Torrel was equal to that question, as he was to most, and he instantly replied that it was because there had been many shipwrecks in the area and the castaways (or waifs as they were called) nearly always ended up on the island.

Botolph was never sure about the veracity of Torrel's answers. He certainly never hesitated, but he *did* seem to have an answer for everything, almost as if he followed a creed that a boy *needed* an answer and "Don't know" was not good enough. Botolph was beginning to feel sure that he made half of them up as he went along! But this didn't seem to matter, he still loved Torrel dearly.

It seemed a good idea then, to go 'Waif Hunting' when they went up West River. They clambered ashore and listened. Nothing. A reed warbler cried. Nothing. A green woodpecker laughed at them from the edge of the forest. Botolph shivered. Nothing.

"C'mon then" said Luka and Botolph shook himself out of his trance and they headed up the hill through the scrub. The southern half of the island was all bracken and marsh whereas the northern part where Cnobersburg was, was heavily forested.

Suddenly there was a movement from the scrub on their right and Botolph grabbed Luka's arm; it was only a sheep however. Then they found lots more sheep, and then an old and apparently deserted shepherd's hut.

In the absence of trees they could see down the length of the island towards the place that Torrel had named as "Lotha's Croft" where Lotha's River spilt out into the sea and completed the encirclement of Waif.

No waifs were found that day, or any other come to that. But the idea that they *might* be there gave the boys a good reason for caution as they explored the region. Once they had lost sight of West River, there were few landmarks, apart from the Shepherd's Hut. Most of the marshy areas were fairly obvious because the grass changed its colour and texture. But every so often one or other of the boys would give a yell as he sank up to his knees in ground that otherwise looked quite firm.

After that first visit they were to come back quite frequently, often bringing some food and making a proper day of it. Although in fact the days were really just afternoons, since their routine had now changed and they were expected to rise just after Lauds at about 4 a.m. and, after breaking their fasts, work at their books in the scriptorium until mid morning when they would have their lunch. After this their duties fell between war games at the castle, sailing instruction with Torrel, or free time, depending upon the day.

The early starts to each day had not been popular at first since the boys were now so active that they needed a good night's sleep but Prior Matthew had reasoned that a change of routine was the only way that their studies would avoid being neglected.

When pressed, Prior Matthew would also admit that several of the boys were now so talented with their writing skills that their work in the scriptorium had become a valuable asset. The beautifully illustrated manuscripts that were produced there were already being bound into holy books that not only were a tribute to God but also would, from the right person, fetch a good price to provide support for the foundation.

And so the days passed and the boys grew in strength, size and knowledge and the monastery prospered. It was, as Torrel said, the "Pax Pendarum".

Travellers would frequently come to the castle and the monastery. In such circumstances, since they were usually travelling north, they often asked if there was a chance of them being transported across the Yar to the mainland.

If there was only one such traveller, Botolph and Luka, now being the recognised sailing experts, would be asked to take them across in *Skyff*. Sometimes *Manigfual* would even be commissioned for such an expedition, particularly if there were horses or goods to be carried. Normally it was not too much hardship for those with horses to ride back south and pick the mainland up again at Lotha's Croft but exceptions occurred from time to time.

Two hobbled horses were the most that *Manigfual* could carry with safety. Torrel had made some timber "stalls" that he could rig for such an event. This structure supported the horses and provided a means of controlling them in difficult conditions.

The travellers always brought news of happenings in the areas through which they had passed and one day came the intelligence that Mercian forces were moving eastwards and approaching the coast. This was not good news. In fact it was what all the "Waifneys" had been dreading.

Orders were issued that the security of the castle should be reinforced. New trenches were dug. A good supply of fresh sharp stakes were prepared. Patrols were increased.

At Cnobersburg there were similar preparations. Everyone was drilled in the actions they were to take if war came to them. Each monk had a leather bundle in which he could put a few items of food and any personal possessions of which they had a minimal amount anyway. These bundles were ready to be grabbed at a moment's notice.

The precious books that were small enough to be transported were wrapped and sealed against water incursion and placed in a chest that could easily be carried to *Manigfual*. Those books that were too large or too numerous were similarly wrapped but placed in as many secret chambers as the monks could devise. Some were taken to the castle for safer keeping.

Everyone prayed.   Life at Cnobersburg had been idyllic for so long.   All had appreciated it and nobody wanted it to end.   The threat from the south could not be ignored however.

Or *was* the threat from the south?   Might a raiding force come in boats from the west?

Anna's forces were strong in that direction and it was felt that, in such an event, the Waifneys would have the upper hand.   A two, or even three-pronged attack was a distinct possibility though.   Penda might deploy some forces from the west to keep the castle busy, while other "boat forces" landed further south in the region of West River. This would threaten the castle on all its river-fronts, leaving Penda's main force to cross Lotha's River and come up from the south.

Anna posted guards at strategic parts of the island with instructions to ride like the wind to the Castle with any news of an incursion.   Beacon pyres were prepared with the intention that lighting the appropriate one of these would alert Anna to the main direction of attack.   More barricades were erected with sharp evil-looking stakes, daring foreigners to intrude.

Within the castle, everything was a frenzy of activity.   The fletchers and bowyers were busily producing the wooden weapons.   The anvils were ringing in the forges.   King Anna was thinking, thinking, thinking.   Was there anything he had missed?   Could he provide any better for the protection of his people?   There was nothing else he could think of.   All was as ready as it could ever be and anyway perhaps they would never come.

CHAPTER 15
June 637 ... Attack!

But come they did!

It was a lovely midsummer's day at noon when the smoke from the South Beacon was sighted and then another beacon fired off to the west.

Anna divided his forces between the castle and the narrow strip of land south of Cnobersburg between the marsh and the coast, where the trees finished and the scrub started. He had already prepared various traps and defences in this region and these were all activated.

He wondered if now was the time to load the monks into *Manigfual* and send them away but, bearing in mind that nobody had any idea where they were going to go, he decided that it was best to delay until there was no alternative. Besides which, he needed the boys to make up the numbers of his fighting troops and he hoped that some of the sturdier monks might also join battle if the situation became desperate.

He had already taken the opportunity to visit the monastery and prepare the monks for the event. They all knew of Penda's hate of Christianity. Anna had seized the chance of stoking the fire further and described Penda as the devil incarnate, in the hope that this would focus the attention of the monks more positively.

The boy-students were all prepared. Luka was clanking about clad in his weaponry; his two seaxes were honed to perfection. The problem was that he did not have a horse! None of them did! All the horses were back with the regular soldiers who were each going to be well-tested that day.

The boys' job was to defend the monastery and the monks and, if the decision was made to abandon Cnobersburg, the boys would delay the attacking forces as much as they could while Torrel led the monks in their escape.

A stockade of stakes and pits had already been prepared around the area and the boys had chosen their favoured positions. The wooden, mud and wattle huts of the monastery looked rather vulnerable now and Botolph wondered if the monks would not have been better within the stone walls of the castle. Too late for that now though, the attack might come at any moment. They waited. Dusk came. They waited. Night fell.

"They will attack at dawn" said Torrel authoritatively.

Dawn found King Anna and his men ensconced in the woods at the bottleneck between marsh and sea just south of Cnobersburg. Caelin had been left with a similarly strong force to defend the castle three miles to their east. Botolph and Luka had found themselves a comfortable position from whence they had good views down the coast. Everyone was silent. Nothing stirred except the birds which performed their usual chorus in salute to a new day.

Breakfast had been taken before the first glimmer of twilight in the expectation that battle would soon be joined. But the sun rose further into the sky and there was neither sight nor sign of the presence of an attacking army. The men began to get bored and Anna knew they were falling off their mettle. He was getting bored too. He was also worried that perhaps the first assault would be on the castle and he wanted to be at the site of the battle's first ignition.

In mid-morning his patrol took him past the boys' position and he gazed silently beyond them, trying to detect the slightest movement or cloud of dust that might suggest an influx. "Perhaps they're not coming?" he thought to himself, but then swiftly threw in "But that would be what Penda wants me to think. I need to know! I could send scouts out but I need every single man here". He continued to ruminate on these possibilities and was just aware of a small sound to his right.

"Sire" it said. He looked down and saw Botolph, who had, apparently, been reading his thoughts. "Sire, with your leave, we could take *Skyff* down to Lotha's River. We would then be able to get good views of the mainland both to the south and the west.

Anna considered but was not convinced. He could foresee an easy capture if *Skyff* lost her wind or hit a sandbank. Besides which, they would stand out like the proverbial "sword thumb" and would just as easily be cut off!

"Thank you Botolph" he said, "I appreciate your suggestion but I think that would be too risky. If they do not make their move today however I may take you up on your offer later this evening so get as much rest as you can. I will return before nightfall."

The boys were too excited by King Anna's words to consider any possibility of rest. They had a fair idea of what he had in mind. Botolph calculated the time of high tide. There was little wind but they could take the flood from Cnobersburg and drift down to the watershed south of West River. If they arrived there at slack water they could then row down to the south of the island as far as Lotha's Croft. This was bound to give them a good view of the lie of the land. Wherever the pagans were, they would be encamped for the night and expecting neither attack nor espionage.

"How would we return though?" Botolph asked Luka, "unless the wind rises". By the time we reached Lotha's, the Waif ebb would have started and we would be in danger of being swept straight out to sea through Lotha's River, right under the nose of the enemy! It would be a hard pull back to the watershed to catch the Yar ebb to sweep us back to Cnobersburg. Alternatively though," he reasoned, his brain still racing, "we could take the Yar flood down as far as West River and pull *Skyff* up there and carry on by foot towards the south of the island. With the lack of trees there we should easily be able to see the camp fires from a distance without having to get too close. We could then get back to Cnobersburg using the Yar ebb!"

"That's it!" exclaimed Luka triumphantly, as if he had devised the whole plan himself. "We could take *Skyff's* mast down and stow the sail furled round the spar in the bottom of the boat. That would make us less obvious. The moon is in its first quarter so there should be enough light for us to see but hopefully not enough for our enemies to see us. But will we be able to find our way in such darkness?"

"I think we should be able to make West River safely" said Botolph. "We have been there so many times before and the sweep of the tide should guide us there. All we have to do is to recognise the entrance and choose the right moment to rig the oars and pull into it. What worries me more is how we are going to find our way across the land once we leave the boat. A right pair of chumps we would look if dawn rose and Penda found us stuck in a bog close by his camp!"

"Well" said Luka. "What do we have? Old Shepherd's Croft will give us a point to aim for. Then there is the clump of trees over to the right that marks the edge of South Bog and the Ash Grove over to the left that marks the edge of North Bog. If we pass between those two, we cannot go too far east because we will be on the beach! We can then follow the beach down to Lotha's Croft. Easy!"

Botolph stared at him in disbelief. "Easy?" he said. "Easy? It might be easy in your mind now my little fire-eater, but in the middle of the night when you can't see a thing and every twig that snaps as you walk makes your heart jump; easy it is not going to be!"

Luka looked glum. "We're not going to do it then?" Botolph stared at him unsmilingly. "Do it?" there was a long pause as Botolph gazed vacantly ahead, considering the possibilities and visualising his hero Jesus on the cross. A silent prayer of request fluttered across his consciousness and just as briefly there fluttered back a realisation that approval was given. "Of course we're going to do it!" and he slapped Luka on the shoulder and they clasped each other's arms to the astonishment of a couple of burly foot-soldiers who had been observing them and wondering how they could get so animated in the face of almost-certain death!

The day wore on and all remained quiet; neither any signs of beacons nor of camp fires. King Anna was minded to take a small force and head down to the south of the island himself but he worried that, as soon as he left, Penda would make a surprise attack from the west or the north. After wrestling with his conscience at sending two such young lads into so dangerous a situation, he determined to accept Botolph's offer.

In the late afternoon he returned to the front line in the woods, where, on his approach, everyone sprang into activity from their relaxed positions of boredom. He found Botolph and Luka and he could not help but let a smile curl his lip as he saw their excited and hopeful expressions.

"Alright" he grunted laconically, "I have made the arrangements with Torrel. Make your way to West Creek an hour after sunset and either Torrel or I will be there to give you instructions. Take off all your weaponry Luka, or Penda will hear your clanking a mile away. Besides which, if you fall in, you will sink like a stone!" Luka grimaced slightly but accepted the order on the basis that, although he loved his fighting gear, it *did* have its drawbacks.

"Go back to the monastery now and get some food inside you and try to get some rest. I am hoping that you will be back before sunrise, but in my experience these things never go to plan. Be prepared to be away for longer;" "(if you ever come back at all!)" he thought to himself.

The boys followed his instructions. After eating, the cook gave them a small bundle of provisions to take with them. Resting was still out of the question however. Botolph kept going over the plan in his own mind to make sure they had not overlooked anything. In his imagination he threw in a few 'what if?' scenarios. These filled him with horror and he realised the dangers that he and Luka were getting into. But he forced himself to calm his mind and managed to foresee a solution to each one.

They were in the dormitory, jettisoning unwanted items and dressing appropriately when the door opened and in came Father Fursey.

"Well me lads" he gazed. "So you are off on a brave mission. Have you finished in here, because I would like you to come with me to the Oratorium".

Off the three of them went and Father Fursey led them in supplicative prayer for the success of their dangerous task. He asked the Lord to keep them quick-witted, and to grant them wisdom above their years and grace and guidance to make the right decisions. Lastly he asked that they should be brought back safe and sound into the bosom of the monastery family. He added the usual caveat of: "but whatever happens Lord, thy will be done."

Luka thought that this was a bit of a cop-out, but then even he reasoned that, whenever fate took a hand, it usually turned out best in the end. He let his mind drift further, thinking that if fate had not taken a hand in events five years previously he would never have found himself at Cnobersburg now; but that was another story.

The prescribed hour arrived with a rush and the boys found themselves at West Creek, where Torrel was pushing *Skyff* into the water. The mast had already been lowered and was neatly stowed and lashed, together with the furled sail, to one side of the thwarts. The oars had rags bound around them where they passed between the thole pins so that they did not squeak under pressure.

To Luka's joy, Torrel insisted on applying mud to their faces and hands, in order to darken their skin and provide some camouflage. There was noise of an approaching horse and King Anna himself arrived and swung easily down beside them.

"Ready boys?"

"Yes Sire" they chorused.

"Right, well this is what I want you to do ."

Half an hour later saw them sliding down West Creek with Botolph at the oars and Luka manning the steerboard and straining his eyes into the cave-like blackness. They were just past low water, so the creek was shallow and the young flood was beginning to push against them. They passed down the steerboard side of the massive shape of *Manigfual* which was well-aground. As Botolph saw her disappear back into the murk he fervently hoped that Penda's attack would not come at dead low water or it was 'dead' the monks themselves would be. There was a lurch as *Skyff* touched the edge of a mudbank and his thoughts were forcibly returned to the matter in hand. They glided over it but Botolph was struggling as his larboard oar kept hitting the bottom and was not in deep enough water to propel the craft forwards. He unshipped the oar and used it as a pole to push the boat into deeper water and the flood caught the larboard bow and started to swing her across the creek. Quickly he shipped the oar again and pulled both hard together. Luka skilfully straightened her course and suddenly the sounds changed as they entered the rippling waters of the flood crossing the creek as it came in from the sea.

Rowing was easier for Botolph now as he turned into the deeper water and they headed west along the northern edge of the island. He kept up the slow but regular pulsations that pushed them along and he could feel his heart pulsing in sympathy, partly from exertion and partly with excitement. Was it fear? No, certainly not, they were competent soldiers of Christ, (he hoped!).

Neither boy talked but both listened intently. The water's noise was so close and distant sounds were so far that they were in danger of the former masking the latter. Botolph had the additional disadvantage that he was facing away from their direction of travel. He thought that Luka had the better position. Luka on the other hand, rather envied Botolph. At least he could see where they had been whereas all Luka could see were shadowy bulrushes on the larboard side and pitch blackness ahead. Already they were lost! He decided to communicate that fact to Botolph.

"Where do you think we are?" he whispered.

Botolph stopped rowing and turned around. He could just make out the land to his right and he strained his eyes looking for a sight of the castle walls as they rounded the headland.

"Well, wherever we are we are not there yet!" he hissed. "I am going to move further away from the land and stand out more into the stream so that it sweeps us along faster, or else at this rate it will be daybreak before we arrive."

He pulled hard on the larboard oar and then both together as they moved out of the slack water eddying gently around the rushes. After only a few pulls, they felt *Skyff's* bow shudder as she hit the faster-flowing stream which spun her stern parallel to the bank again. Botolph's rowing was now more a matter of keeping the boat's aspect steady than actually propelling them forwards, the Yar had already taken over northerly control.

A thin sliver of moon appeared over the land to Botolph's right and he used this as a marker in his endeavour to keep the boat orientated. Suddenly though something felt wrong, they had spun sideways across the current...... and then the moon vanished causing Botolph's mouth to go dry. Something loomed over them, and then it was gone.   Botolph worked at straightening the boat's travel.

The sky was still clear but the moon had vanished. He glimpsed something over his shoulder and turned his head to have a better look, and there was the glimmering crescent.   "Aah.   There she is, but *behind* me now?"

Realisation came.   The shape that had loomed over them had been Burgh castle.   They had been swept around the headland and were now heading south towards West River entrance.

They had sailed this route many times before, but in peaceful times and always in daylight.   They knew however that the two great currents that flooded in from the sea, one through the Yar entrance and the other past Lotha's Croft, both surged around Waifney in a pincer movement that culminated at mid-tide in a mass of bubbling water close to the West River Estuary.

It was, as yet, early in the flood but already Botolph could sense the change in the water's movement.   He ceased rowing and turned and looked ahead again.   A dark mass was beginning to obscure what little of the skyline was revealed by the inadequate moon.   That dark mass was West Wood and they were being swept towards it in a back eddy.   The last thing they wanted was to be pushed onto the beach on the northern side of the headland and be pinned there until the flooding current abated.

"Keep us away from West Wood" he urged Luka, indicating the dark mass with a nod of his head, simultaneously realising the uselessness of such an action as he knew Luka would be unable to see his head in the darkness.   A grunt came from the stern and the boat swung to the west as Botolph pulled hard again fighting his way further out into the stream.

The bubbling and the bucking became more pronounced, together with ripples and splashes against the hull. It seemed only a short while before they were past the wood and an unspoken command of mutual assent had Botolph reversing his efforts as the boat swung back to the east and Luka aimed the prow at the point where the high dark mass ended.

Suddenly Botolph's larboard oar hit an obstruction and then the prow turned as they hit the bank and a muffled curse came from the stern. Botolph took the offending oar out of its thole pins and undignified it further by poling it between the border rushes and down into the swirling water to push the boat further out into the stream again. Quickly the oar found its home again and the rower continued up the now-quieter waters of the inlet. From time to time the tip of the larboard blade, like a beetle's antenna, found the river's edge and a harder pull on that side steered them back into mid-stream.

Soon it was clear that the trees on the northern bank were receding from them again and the boys knew that they were well within the haven.

"Now!" said Botolph. There was an acknowledging grunt and Luka heaved on the steerboard as Botolph pulled harder on that side and then both together and the little craft cleaved the rushes and the prow raised in salute as it found the bank. Luka left his position and nimbly stepped past Botolph and swung himself off the prow and into ankle-deep water. He held the boat and waited while Botolph tidied the oars and then joined him.

Together they took the thick hemp painter and scrambled onto the higher, drier part of the bank and pulled the craft up over the high water line. Botolph untied the painter, coiled it and placed it diagonally over his shoulder. Luka took two willow staves from the bottom of the boat and gave the longer one to Botolph.

They collected both their leather food bags and their wits and prepared themselves for their next move.

All was quiet. There was no wind. A faint smell of burning wood was in the air. The thin lunar crescent was higher in the sky but still shedding very little light.

They had agreed on the need for silence. The last thing they wanted was to be jumped by a Penda patrol. Botolph took the lead and, using their staves as feelers, they followed the river bank to the east until they reached a clump of trees which they continued past until a smudge of grey appeared on their right. This they turned towards and found the Old Shepherd's Croft nestling just where it ought to have been.

By now it was approaching midnight and the crescent was high in the sky. The night air felt colder. "Let's eat" whispered Botolph and they settled down against the side of the croft and opened one of the leather bags. Soon they were tucking into chunks of Cnobersburg bread alternating with bites of goat's cheese. The site of the croft had obviously been chosen with the presence of the nearby spring in mind. The boys took full advantage of the cool water to wash down the food and slake their thirst. Soon they were ready for the next phase and Luka tucked the empty bag under a wooden paling and they stood and gazed southwards towards the moon.

They knew that the woods on Ash Hill were their next landmark and that so long as they did not stray too far to the west, they would remain on hard ground. The black trees rose silently in front of them confirming that they were nicely on track and they altered their course aiming to keep the monstrous shapes to their right.

The ground was soft and their movements were stealthy. The blessed absence of twigs allowed them to glide like black ghosts across a black terrain.

Botolph was, as usual, in the lead but Luka was not just a follower. He was constantly looking and sniffing and checking and turning, and making sure that they had not been spotted and tracked. Luka was a "thinker" and the 'follower-tactics' he adopted that night, he would use frequently in the years ahead. More than once such tactics would save both their lives; but not tonight. Tonight there was nobody who might attack from the rear. They were on their own.

When they reached the corner of Ash Hill they stopped and listened but could only just hear what they wanted, the sound of waves crashing onto the beach. This was the tricky part of the journey. There was a clump of trees ahead and leaving those on their right would take them clear of the southerly marsh but after that there were no more landmarks until they reached the sea.

During daylight hours, navigating this stretch was easy because the safe passage meandered between the bogs that were rendered visible by the colour changes in the different types of grass. At night-time however it was an entirely different matter. The danger was increased both by the tortuous nature of the route and also by the presence of a narrow bottle-neck at the final egress.

Once they had reached the final clump of trees, Botolph took the length of hemp that he had liberated from its position as *Skyff's* painter and knotted one end around his waist and passed the other end to Luka who did likewise.

They stood side by side and sniffed the night air. Botolph cupped his hands around his ears and finely adjusted his aspect to the smell and the sound of the sea ahead. They then boldly stepped forward in line abreast into pitch blackness, wondering who was going to be the first to fall off the edge.

It was Luka!

He gave a muffled squawk. There was a slight splash, and the line tightened around Botolph's waist. Botolph braced himself and then started to haul on the line.

"No, wait" came a hoarse whisper and there was more splashing about.

"What's the matter?"

"I've lost my staff!"

"Leave it, we'll get another."

"No, just a moment," and the splashing continued and then suddenly stopped. The line tightened in waves and soon a panting Luka was by Botolph's side.

"Did you find it?"

"No".

"Let's go then."

Poor Luka was not only wet. smelly and uncomfortable but he also felt quite vulnerable without his staff. He had been using it constantly to prod the ground before him and to steady himself. Not only that but he had secretly been hoping that he would get the chance to use it to break some pagan's head! He checked his belt and found with relief that both seaxes were still in position. Botolph had veered across to the right in order to keep clear of Luka's bog and they put both the bog and their thoughts behind them as they strode forwards.

Botolph suddenly stopped.

"Down!" he hissed and they threw themselves to the ground. It was only then that Luka heard the sound of movements to their left, together with the murmur of human conversation. Both lads remained prostrate and hoped that they would neither be seen by the riders, nor stepped on by the horses. The voices gradually increased in volume as the hooves approached. Botolph wondered if they were directly in front of the horses' path. He resisted the urge to move; they were too close for that. He wondered what he would do if he were trodden on. Would he be able to take the pain silently? He strained his ears to try to make out what the riders were saying but it was impossible. Suddenly they were on him and one horse whinnied as its horny hoof thudded onto the turf near his head. Then they were gone.

The boys rose from their cramped positions and after pausing for a while to make sure there were no others following, they edged their way forwards again and found themselves on the beach.

Botolph untied the rope, re-coiled it and placed it back over his shoulders and they turned to the south towards the now-setting lunar crescent.

The smell of burning wood was stronger and soon they could see the glimmers of camp fires.

"What do we do now?" asked Luka.

"Not sure. There is no point in us going closer and risking being seen by the sentries. We are far enough away here to get a good view of what is going on and we can get some cover from those trees over there. Let's settle down and watch. We can take it in turns to get some sleep and then when things start to happen we will have time to get a rough count of their numbers and types and then run back the way we have come."

"What do you mean 'types'" said Luka.

"Well, I suppose it will be useful for King Anna to know how many horses there are and what the proportion of spearmen to archers might be, and so on."

"Hmph" grunted Luka.

They settled down in the cover of the copse. Luka was still a little wet, so he suggested Botolph took the first sleep while he took off his clothing and rung it as dry as possible before replacing it. It seemed only a short while before Botolph found his shoulder being shaken and woke to find that the first glimmer of dawn was visible.

"My turn now, soldier" said a grinning Luka, already settling down by his side. "See you at sun-up" and promptly shut his eyes, curled into a ball and went out like a light.

Botolph stared into the distance but could neither hear nor see any change in the camp's aspect. He sat up and hugged his knees and began to think and then began to pray. He said all the usual prayers that he would normally do at this time of day. He followed these by specific prayers appropriate to their present situation.

He asked God to keep both Luka and himself safe and to grant his protection to the monks of Cnobersburg and the soldiers of King Anna. He asked that he was not put in the position of having to kill someone, because he really did not want to do that! He asked for God's guidance on what they should do today and His blessing on whatever they did. He finished with his usual pattern of the Lord's Prayer and then a grace which included a request that God granted his blessings to his mother and father and Matild and to the now softly-snoring Luka!

His devotions completed, he sat and watched and hoped for divine inspiration regarding their next move. It did not come. Irreverently he wondered if his message had got through or whether the canopy of leaves above them was keeping them and any messages cocooned in solitude. But he knew that God was always listening and would answer in His own good time, so he stood and stretched and moved a little within the protection of the neighbouring trunks.

A bird began to sing in the tree above him. It was then joined by another sparrow-like voice and then another and another and soon the whole chorus were enjoined in their usual salute to the continuing pattern of God's order.

The light was slowly brightening promising a sunny summer's day. The air was damp though. Botolph shivered and stared towards Lotha's Croft. Everything was in monochromatic silhouette except for the stab of camp fires that penetrated the backdrop. Botolph again marvelled at the wonder of the dawn. Only a short while earlier and he had hardly been able to see his hand in front of his face, but now he was beginning to be able to make out the shape of the grass beneath his feet. The bushes and trees and the rest of the landscape was slowly, oh so *very* slowly, changing from a dusky grey canvas to three-dimensional reality. He thanked God for another dawn.

The noise from the camp began to increase and he could see some movement. The fires were fading but he was not sure if this was because they were being extinguished or if it was in deference to competition from the rising sun.

The blackbird sang again but this time it was different to his initial salute. This was a song of sheer happiness and joy in living. A wood pigeon took off from the trees and then folded its wings and fell towards the ground, then spread them again and swooped back up to

117

the sky, only to refold them and fall back down and repeat the pattern, taking pleasure in flying.

Botolph was surrounded by a mixture of danger and beauty. There was every chance that he was going to die today. And yet here he was, at peace with God and Nature. Alone in his thoughts but in company with his dear friend Luka, sleeping like a baby; at one with God and the world. He felt a warm glow of pleasure pass through his body and he knew that whatever happened today, he was ready for it. Live or die, it would be a success. On a day like today, there would be no failure.

CHAPTER 16
Subversion.

He gently shook Luka awake. The camp was on the move. Tents were being struck, the horses were being mounted, a column was forming and in no time at all they were heading ... not towards the boys but across their view to the beach.

"They're going to march up the beach," said Luka. "That way they are sure of solid ground and will keep out of the bogs."

"Unlike you!" teased Botolph and received a playful fist for his pains.

"It's a pity we can't move the bogs into their path," said Luka, "That'd slow 'em down a bit!"

"Yes, well stop dreaming Luka, there is no chance of that, I reckon that was what our friends of the night patrol were doing, they had ridden up the beach to check the route. C'mon, there's nothing more we can do here. We must get back and light the beacon to warn King Anna that they are on their way."

It was still twilight, light enough for them to see what they were doing and to keep the enemy in view but dark enough (they hoped) for them not to be spotted as long as they were careful. They kept on the edge of the tree-line but stayed within the bounds of the copse and worked their way quickly back towards the north.

They reached the edge of the wood and turned to the west where they could now see the boggy marsh that in their night-blindness had threatened to claim Luka as its victim. They ran along the edge towards Ash Hill that they could now identify as it loomed out of the grass like a black spectre. Not wishing to take any chances, they didn't turn until they reached the corner of the hill but when the ground started to rise they turned again northwards and soon arrived, panting at the tall beacon by Old Shepherd's Croft.

They entered the shelter and Luka retrieved an oiled cloth from the leather bag at his belt. He unwrapped this, feeling for its contents in the dark and laid the strike-a-light steel and flint on the floor. From another oiled cloth he took some charcoal linen and tinder which he prepared for use. Botolph meanwhile felt around at the back of the croft where he knew was the lighting stick that had been used for the beacon many times before. As he turned back into the hut he could hear Luka striking the flint against the iron and cursing softly at it as if he hoped that would help. Soon enough a spark dropped onto the char and Botolph saw the glow reflecting on Luka's face as he blew onto the embers. As soon as the tinder caught, Botolph held the lighting stick above it and the brand quickly ignited. Wasting no time, he ran outside and held it under the hay-peat mix in its iron framework. For a moment nothing happened and then suddenly there was a whoosh and a crackle and an orange glow burst upwards.

"That'll upset 'em" said Luka. They were straining their eyes through the now-smoky air and waiting to see the first riders of the column appear around the edge of the copse where they had spent the night. Botolph was still thinking about Luka's previous comments and wished that he could lure them through the gap into the West River bogs but he could see no way of doing that. He even considered the prospect of standing on one side of the bog and shouting insults in the hope that an unwary soldier might drown himself in an attempt to capture him. He came to the conclusion that this would be undignified and probably also fruitless since a well-aimed arrow would solve the problem instantly.

"We'd best head back to the boat," said Luka "in case they decide to come and see who's cooking their breakfast on top of a pole!"

"Yes, we had better be off" agreed Botolph "but we will never reach Cnobersburg before they do. Let's just move away from these flames and smoke and get back to Ash Hill. They won't expect us to be there and maybe our watching will turn out to be useful. We will need to be quick though!"

Back they ran southwards and a few minutes later saw them approaching the rise just as the first of the foot soldiers appeared around the edge of the copse. They didn't appear to have been seen however since all the soldiers' attention was on keeping their feet dry as they marched the narrow path between the ocean on one side and bogs on the other.

Botolph shivered suddenly. He was not sure why but realised that a breeze had picked up from seawards and the air had become colder. He blinked! The soldiers had vanished and had been replaced by a white wall of sea-fog! The muffled sound of an army on the march had been replaced by cries and curses and splashes. Bugles sounded and orders rang out but the sounds of chaos were unmistakeable. Botolph had an inspiration. "Quick!

C'mon!" he pulled Luka and they ran towards the sound of the mayhem.

Luka wondered what the Hell was happening. Had the strain been too much? Was his now-crazy friend going to rescue the enemy?

When they reached the next set of trees, Botolph stopped and listened. The cries were louder now but still distant. He moved forwards again and Luka was horrified to see some blurred shapes appear.

"This way" called Botolph to the shapes, and then turned and pushed Luka back the way he had come. He waved a silent finger at his friend, pointing towards Ash Hill. Luka nodded and moved off in that direction. Botolph ran parallel to the invading army. "Over here!" he called. He could see ghostly shapes stumbling towards him. There was still a cacophony of noise but through it he could discern Luka's voice urging his followers on. The enemy were clearly totally disoriented but Botolph and Luka still had their bearings or had they?

Luka still had his because he had identified the trees of Ash Hill which had still been just visible over the foggy border. But Botolph began to wonder if he was going in the right direction and if there was a chance that he might perversely end up drowning in the very spot that Luka had fallen in earlier. No sooner had the thought passed through his mind than before him appeared a familiarly-shaped staff stuck carelessly in the soft grass. It was the one that Luka had lost the night before, and it marked the edge of the bog. Botolph skidded to a halt and retrieved the welcome guide.

He redoubled his shouting "This way! C'mon men! Over here." He was amused to hear Luka's voice sounding quite authoritative mimicking the tone and the voice they had previously heard directing the pagan troops. Their ruse was certainly working. Like dogs herding sheep, but pulling rather than pushing, they were gradually luring them through the gap and into the trap. At its narrowest point the solid path was twenty paces wide and the soldiers were even happier to find that beneath their feet rather than the less-than-solid beach they had just left.

They were happily following what they thought were the commands of their leader taking them northwards into battle whereas in fact the sound was coming from a miniscule but fearsome dwarf who was really having a good day, leading them westwards to their doom.

Luka was doing such a good job that Botolph gave up shouting and concentrated on working his way around the bog, back to where he could still, above the fog, see smoke rising from the beacon. There was plenty of noise, including some splashing as soldiers fell in the mire and their colleagues tried to pull them out. Botolph had the feeling that lives were being lost and a pang of guilt passed over him. Luka's voice had now also gone quiet and Botolph wondered if he had been caught. He reached the beacon and stopped, wondering if Luka was more likely to make his way to the boat or the beacon. They should have arranged a place. He waited a few minutes but there was still no sign of his friend. However, there *was* a narrow path that they had used previously which led from the beacon into East Woods and from here it was about three miles to Anna's barricades.

The sounds of a confused army were everywhere, with men stumbling, falling, drowning, and forever cursing, cursing,cursing as they ran about like the lost dogs they were. He could now hear a few words of command as the officers tried to bring some order out of the chaos.

Sounds of shouting were coming from the direction in which the boat lay and these sounds were getting closer. He could wait no longer a quick prayer "Please keep Luka safe Lord" and he was on his way, carefully picking his way between the tufts of sedge interspersed with glinting water that marked the edge of the track.

The fog was thick and the trees of East Wood found him before he expected to find them, when suddenly something hit him behind the knees and he fell to the ground to find himself in an arm-lock. His rest was short-lived as he was hauled to his feet to face two stocky pagans.

"What have we here then? You're no Penda's man."

Botolph was standing just within the wood facing the path along which (in happier times!) he had just come. His arms were painfully pinned behind him by the one who had knocked him down. The other was standing by a bush facing him but with his back to the path. He was squat and solid and looked rough and unhappy! His steel helmet looked menacing enough but it was the long seaxe he held that looked more frightening.

Botolph's mind was racing. He was lithe and young, these men were old but strong. They were also ruthless and experienced and he was not sure if they had yet realised that it was their victim who had been responsible for their recent discomfort. Once they did so, their wrath might turn to a desire for vengeance. Botolph considered a swift kick to his captor's shins but his soft leather shoes would probably just bounce off the man's brawny legs and he might end up with the other man's seaxe in his gullet as a reward.

He had no time to think further about his imminent death though, because the bush inexplicably erupted knocking his captor to the ground.   Botolph kicked at his opponent's shins with as much force as he could muster. By good fortune, his heel found an old wound and there was a howl of agony as the man collapsed sideways. Botolph took off through the woods as if the devil was after him. He could hear sounds behind him as if at least one of the animals was intent on recapturing its prey but he was a fast runner and he felt he was getting away.   He was just reaching the edge of the wood when disaster struck for a second time as the ground beneath him collapsed and he fell straight into an animal pit.   He lay still for a few seconds, momentarily stunned and aware that he should be doing something but he was not sure what!

He had half risen when his thoughts and actions were interrupted by the arrival of a heavy flying object. Once again he was knocked to the floor and turned, his right fist raised, anticipating that he would be planting it into the evil features of his previous tormentor.

Luka!   His fist stopped in mid-air, assisted by Luka's parry.   The relief flooded over Botolph and the two friends clasped each other in greeting.   Botolph cut the greeting short, "C'mon, Quickly!" and he pushed the surprised Luka up and over the side of the pit and, with Luka's reciprocal help, climbed out too.

They left the wood but used it for guidance as they ran alongside it until it petered out completely as they neared their own lines.

"High Wood's over there somewhere", said Botolph. "We are going to have to hope that we don't end up getting shot in mistake for the enemy."

"Why don't we just call?" asked Luka.

"Good idea" ... Botolph cupped his hands to direct the sounds and called through the fog. "In the name of King Annaaaaah." The sound echoed eerily .

"Who calls?" came the similarly eerie reply.

"Botolph and Lukaaaaah!"

"Advance and be recogniiiiiiiised."

"Here we come ... where are you?"

"Over heeeeeere," and suddenly the two heroes found the positions reversed as they were guided by shouts which they hoped would not have them stumbling into the same sort of danger they had already thrust upon their opponents.

Two Annasmen appeared through the mist, seaxes drawn. They relaxed when they saw Botolph and Luka. "What news?" they asked.

"We have a report for King Anna" said Botolph, not wanting to precipitate an unauthorised evacuation of the barricades which might subsequently prove disastrous.

"It's urgent!" he added.

"Right, King Anna's at the castle ... come with me," and they ran through the defensive positions into the wood where the horses were tied. The soldier was about to detail two riders to take them to the castle but Luka's pride stepped in. "We'll just take the horses" he said "They'll go faster with just one rider and we will be quickly back."

Botolph would have liked a saddle but there was no time for that and Luka was happier without one so within seconds they were urging the nags through the familiar territory of the wood and then along the foggy path to Burgh.

They were let through the gates and taken to Anna who greeted them hastily, relieved that his protégés had been able to handle themselves so well and avoid capture. He listened to their report which he considered.

"I have received other intelligence that Penda has brought a massive army with him this time," he said. "If this turns out to be true, I think we are bound to be overrun but we will give them a good hiding first. Come!", and they ran back to their horses and followed Anna and his group of mounted henchmen at a gallop back to High Hill Wood.

Here he quickly selected a group of his best archers and, leaving the others to defend the barricades, they made their way down the beach as silently as they could until they heard through the fog the sound of the bog-stricken army on their right. They turned inland and advanced until they reached the edge of the marsh when they knocked their arrows to their bowstrings and, relying on sounds alone to aim, they fired their darts into the whiteness. The noise turned satisfyingly into howls of anguish and they fired again and again. They heard volleys of arrows fired in return but most of these went over their heads and none of them were struck.

The fog began to lift and dim shadows appeared on the other side of the marsh. Anna had gained an advantage and he was not about to squander it so, as silently as they had come, they made an orderly withdrawal back to the beach and thence at a steady jog back to High Hill Wood. They were halfway there when the fog dissolved in the noonday sun. Anna looked back and to his horror saw a cloud of dust followed by a huge second wave of Pendasmen charging up the beach a couple of miles behind them.

They sprinted the last few hundred yards and hurled themselves over the barricades and regained their defensive stances.

"Go to the monastery" Anna told the boys. "Get *Manigfual* launched and away with the monks. They know what to do, the boat is all prepared but there is no time to lose. We will not be able to hold the barricades for long. Both of you go with them too. I have already given Torrel his orders to sail for France. God be with you all. Now quickly GO!"

The boys turned and sprinted up the path towards Cnobersburg, hearing behind them the disturbing sound of war cries as the two forces clashed. When they broke through the edge of the wood, they found a grim-faced Torrel standing by one of the long mooring lines that tethered *Manigfual*.

"Now?" he said.

"Yes" Botolph gasped.

The monks were already coming out of the huts, led by Father Fursey and Prior Matthew and in no time at all they had made it across the wooden plank that linked *Manigfual* to the grassy shore. Betta was standing by the plank looking hopeful and Torrel told her to get aboard but she was unsure and looked at Father Fursey. He smiled at her and nodded and then came to the gunwale end of the plank and extended his hand and, like a flower in a herb-garden, she joined the monks as did Botolph and Luka. Torrel let go the two stern lines and then ran up the plank which the boys helped him to pull aboard.

The monks were manning the oars in a well-planned routine. The boat was now well-immersed in her laden state. There was no wind. They were too close to the bank to get a purchase with the steerboard oars. The two forward warps were long lines attached to strong poles at the end of the creek however. Torrel had prepared them like this, ready for just such an eventuality.

He let go the steerboard warp and he and two burly monks heaved on the larboard warp and *Manigfual* slowly moved away from the bank and into deeper water where the oars could bite and maintain her forward motion.

The noise of the fighting was getting closer though and Botolph kept glancing nervously aft expecting to see a hoard of Pendasmen at any moment. The attention of the rest of the crew was similarly distracted. The creek was narrow, the ship was low in the water and unwieldy and suddenly the larboard oars were finding the shallow water on the other side and within seconds they were aground and ... the tide was falling!

The steerboard warp having, it was thought, done its duty, had gone over the side. Botolph looked at Torrel and saw the terror of despair in his eyes. The larboard oars had been shipped and the vessel was close to the reedy bank. Botolph leaped over the side into the reeds and started to struggle through to harder ground. There was another splash and he turned to find Luka right behind him.

"Get back in the boat" he ordered.

"Where you go, I go" came the reply.

The tide was falling, there was no time to argue. They raced back up the creek, around the top end and back again on the eastward side to the pole to which the landward end of the steerboard warp was still attached. Botolph untied it and they hauled the rest of the rope out of the water and ran back up the creek until they were level with *Manigfual*. Botolph gave Luka the rope end and then hurled the rest of the stork's nest in the direction of eager hands that were stretched out to catch it.

Inevitably the knotted bundle seemed to knot itself further as it flew through the air and fell well short of the boat. The noise of the fighting had changed and was *definitely* getting closer. Botolph hauled the soggy hemp line in again and this time, in spite of the ever-increasing cacophony of urgency over his shoulder, carefully coiled it. He told Luka to stand on the loose end of the rope and then he divided the heavy coils into two, giving one to Luka telling him to let it go as soon as he threw his.

"Please help me God" he cried in his heart as he put body and soul into heaving the sodden mass into the air. Success was sweet and Torrel gave a grimacing smile as he grasped the warp. The boys ran back to the shore post, made the end fast and the line tightened as the monks pulled but *Manigfual* didn't budge.

It was Torrel's turn for inspiration now though, and he had the monks leave their positions at the larboard oars and join their friends on the steerboard side. The craft suddenly heeled over at a crazy angle which almost made the line-haulers lose their balance but they heaved again as she bounced back on the water and then she was free and the ebbing stream, stronger in the delay, was taking her down towards the estuary. This time Torrel made sure that both lines remained attached until they had passed the shore posts. As they drew level with Botolph and Luka, Torrel called, "Come on, JUMP! We will pick you up!"

Botolph shook his head, knowing that any further shenanigans (as Father Fursey would call it) might have them aground again. "No," he called "We'll take our chance. GO and God Speed!"

In truth if Botolph had taken Torrel's offer there was a good chance that they both would have drowned there and then since *Manigfual* was now in the grips of the stream and hurtling towards the estuary from whence she would be thrown into the arms of the waiting ocean. There was not time for them to watch this however, and he and Luka ran back up the creek towards the sound of chaos. He considered. They had no weapons except Luka's two seaxes. It sounded as if Anna's forces, as he had predicted, were being overcome. Anna would, as a last resort, withdraw his men to the safety of Burgh in the hope that once Penda saw that his intended victims had escaped, he might leave Anna in peace. Their duty as Botolph saw it was to save themselves and get to Burgh as quickly as possible. He had no time to convey the intricacies of his thoughts to Luka but relied on the blind trust of friendship as he called "C'mon!" and they sprinted through the woods and out onto the open ground that led to the castle beyond.

They arrived at the castle at the same time as the vanguard of Anna's horsemen cantered up behind them, closely followed by the running foot soldiers and behind them came Anna on horseback. His already blackened face turned even blacker when he saw the two boys.

"What happened? Why are you two still here?" he asked irritably. Botolph briefly explained that they *had* obeyed his orders but circumstances set them ashore again. Anna had no time to enquire further so merely grunted. He turned away from them and set about getting his men into their defensive positions at the castle walls.

CHAPTER 17
Battle

All through that afternoon came the noises and evidence of Penda's army in and around High Hill Woods. From the castle they could see part of the encampment in front of the wood. A good lookout was kept on the river side of the castle in case of a waterborne attack but that was generally thought to be unlikely.

Penda seemed to be in no hurry. He was resting and feeding his army and preparing for the next stage of his assault, whatever that may be.

Luka and Botolph were unsure of their positions now that the monks had left and they asked to see King Anna. It was the following day before their request was granted and when they were ushered into his presence he was slewed in one of the refectory's wooden armchairs looking tired, gaunt and worried. During their ensuing interview there were constant interruptions with people coming and going and asking for directions as to what to do about this or that. King Anna's replies were curt and measured.

He told the boys that he was expecting the castle to be overrun shortly. The enemy would attack at different places with rams to batter the doors and climbing ropes to throw over the walls. He had no doubt that at present Penda was taking full advantage of the shelter and comfort that Cnobersburg had to offer to treat their wounded and prepare themselves for the next assault.   Once the monastery buildings ceased to be useful, they would be razed to the ground.

Botolph said "What would you have *us* do sire?"

Anna raised his tired eyes and looked first into the honest face of the monk-like youth and then down at his sturdy but eager companion.   He looked again at Botolph.

"You may take your choices," he said.   "You are the next generation and, if spared by God, will lead good Christians to a better way of life.   You are both able fighters and Ceolin would value your aid."   He closed his eyes and was silent.   Luka thought he had fallen asleep but perhaps he was conversing with God in silent prayer.   They both started back as his eyes suddenly flashed open again and he jumped to his feet.

"No!" he said "You shall not fight, you ARE the next generation.   You ARE tomorrow's leaders!"

He pointed a powerful finger straight between Botolph's eyes.   "YOU are destined to be a strong, good, wise and moral man and will lead all you meet in the ways of Christ."   It sounded more like an order than a prediction.

He turned to Luka and pointed the same finger.   A startled Luka was not sure if he was about to get a blessing, a pronouncement or an accusation but in the event it was similar to that issued to Botolph.   "YOU will protect and aid Botolph and, *in your own right,* also become a leader of men".

"I am not sure how we can get you to safety though" said Anna.   "Even under the cover of darkness, Penda is too close for you to hope to get through the enemy lines.   We could try disguising you."

"Sire" said Botolph.   "If they have not found and destroyed *Skyff* she might still be in West River where we

133

hid her in the reeds. If we could get to her, we would be able to use her to cross Waif River and then travel on foot. Maybe," he continued, his imagination moving apace and his heart warming to the idea " we could travel *right* up Waif River and get to Beodricsworth or Ely Island."

"Maybe ... maybe! Maybe God will guide you but I really feel that south is the only way for you to go; perhaps back to Cantwarebury. Anywhere in East Anglia or Mercia is a dangerous place for Christians. Cantium or Gallia would be favourite. I really wish you had sailed safely away on *Manigfual* but clearly it was not God's will". He had started to descend back into thoughtfulness but once again he forced himself out of it.

"NOW! How do you propose to get back to *Skyff*?"

Botolph considered the prospect but did not need to consider for long. "Sire, we could be lowered over the Yar Wall after dark at low water. We would then be protected from sight by both the castle and darkness and could then make our way on foot to West River."

Luka looked at him in amazement. "We'd drown!" he said. "The Yar banks are oozy enough at the best times, and then we have to cross the marshes and won't find a firm patch to stand on until we gain West Wood!"

"Hmm. You are right" conceded Botolph, reconsidering his plan.

The King interrupted his thoughts. "Well, you two are the 'Experts of the Deep' and I have no time to hear your deliberations. Just get yourself out of my castle and to safety; that is all I ask. I shall give instructions for you to be given every assistance and any equipment you need. Do not forget to take plenty of food and some dry clothing and God be with you."

He rose and, uncharacteristically and to Botolph's surprise, clasped him to his chest, then turned and looked fondly down at Luka before patting him on the shoulder and striding away to perform kingly duties.

It was late in the afternoon but darkness was still a couple of hours away. For the next half an hour, the boys sat on a refectory bench and planned their movements. They then hurried to the west wall of the castle and looked firstly out over the River Yar and then down at where the mud was exposed around the castle walls. They watched some debris and tree-parts washing down towards the estuary. The tide was still ebbing and would not start to flood for another two hours. It would be a further eight hours before high water when the river would be lapping around the castle walls. They made their way to the south wall and looked across the marshes towards West Wood where they hoped they would find *Skyff* still nestling safely amongst the reeds.

They squatted down on the stone paving within the protection of the battlements. "How are we going to do this?" asked Luka.

"Not sure," replied Botolph.

"Getting down there is easy," offered Luka "but it is going to be no fun at all struggling about in smelly oozy mud in the dark. We have never even *tested* that mud before. It could be firm enough to walk on or soft enough to drown in!"

"Now there's a happy thought!" said Botolph. "If we are not going to walk, we will have to float."

"How are we going to do that?" said Luka. "Are you proposing a giant inflated pig's bladder, or perhaps hope that a few tree-branches might support us?"

"They're both good ideas but neither of them will work" said Botolph.   Luka sniffed and became silent as they both thought further.

"A raft!" Botolph suddenly said.   "There's plenty of wood and rope in the castle and we have time enough before the tide rises.   We will make up a raft and lower it over the western wall before the tide rises.   Then as soon as it starts to float, we will get ourselves lowered onto it.   The tide will still be rising and we will have a couple more hours of flood to take us upstream."

"How are you proposing to propel and steer this unwieldy invention?" asked Luka.

"Well, we can find some flat pieces of wood to use as paddles and take a couple of poles with us to push on the bottom" came back Botolph.

"Right then" said the still-slightly-sceptical Luka, rising from the paving stones.   "Let's do it!"

Botolph found the carpenter and commandeered some wooden beams which he left him cutting to a man's height.   Luka searched out the quartermaster and persuaded him to part with some rope and some twine which he took up to the parapet.   Botolph went into the kitchens and the cook waved vaguely at food in the pantry and told him to help himself which he did gladly.   He stowed the fodder in three leather pouches and headed back to the parapet passing Luka who was on the way back down to get some flagons of water.

Botolph eyed up an area of the parapet where they could construct their raft and then went off to the workshop to get the rigger to fix up a pulley-block so that they could lower the finished item down the wall without wearing the rope out on the rough stones.

The carpenter had finished his sawing and provided workers to carry the beams up to the parapet where the boys lashed them together. It took three attempts before Botolph was satisfied and each time the twine had to be completely unlaid and a fresh start made. Eventually it all looked relatively seamanlike and, as an afterthought, Botolph added some cross-bracing to stop the whole structure twisting and tied the thickest and longest length of rope securely round a cross-beam.

The rope was then fed through the wooden block which the rigger fixed high in the middle of the west parapet and some soldiers helped to carry the raft to the base of it and placed it on top of the wall. All was now ready except for a couple of poles and two pieces of wood to use as paddles. These were easily acquired from the wood store and the boys returned to the refectory to fill their stomachs before it was dark enough to start the night's adventure.

By that time, the whole castle knew what they were about and the cook ensured that they were duly stuffed and watered and gave them a few sweetmeats to help them on their way. They grabbed their bags and ran quickly up the stone stairs to the parapet, eager now to get started. Willing hands helped them haul the raft off the wall and up to the wooden block and then swing it out clear of the west wall and gently down into the blackness until the rope went slack as it met the two feet or so of water that they could hear lapping at the base.

The rope was taken out of the block and a new one reeved and tied by Botolph around his waist using a knot that Torrel had taught them would not pull tight and strangle him. He spared a quick thought for Torrel and

Betta and hoped that he and the monks were now safely ensconced in some southern monastery.

A quick prayer (he never left God out of anything these days) and he was over the side and twisting crazily round as he descended. As he approached the water, he saw the raft bouncing against the wall ten feet away from him but there was no way that he was going to keep his feet dry, so he accepted the inevitable and found himself up to his knees in the muddy swirl. He untied the rope and gave it a tug as a signal to those above to haul it up again and he moved over to the raft and pulled it back to where he had landed, arriving just in time to enable Luka to get aboard keeping his feet dry.

"I can see now why you let me go first" he said wryly. Luka grinned and untied the rope and sent it up again for the provisions. After four or five more lowerings they had everything stowed and with Luka's help Botolph was able to leave the cold water and scramble aboard the raft. One quick slash of Luka's seaxe and a combined push on the wall and they were away. They took a long pole each and, from each end of the raft they pushed her out sideways towards the stream which was easing as the tide approached high water.

"Good Luck. God be with you!" came the cries from above. "Thanks, and with you" they called back to the unseen faces.

Botolph tried to pole the vessel along but the gelatinous bottom was not helping at all. Luka positioned himself at what had become the bow and tried to use one of the improvised paddles to pull them forwards but really not much was happening. Botolph gave up with the pole and moved the stores to the middle of the raft. He knelt down on the larboard side and used the other paddle to make strong powerful strokes.   Luka gave a shout as the raft spun round but he could see the wisdom of Botolph's actions and came aft to mirror them and counteract the spin.   Soon they were making progress ... but oh so slowly!   There was still some current which at least was travelling in the right direction but they did not have enough power to get the lumbering beast out into mid-stream where they could have obtained most advantage.

The silhouette of the castle was smaller now and they were approaching the reed beds off North Marsh.   It was pitch black and they were aware how sounds carry across the water and so were trying to minimise the chance of advertising their presence by talking in whispers and paddling strongly but noiselessly.

They in their turn could hear the noises of camp life coming both from the castle and from Penda's men but there was no sign of aggression for the moment.   Botolph wondered if Penda would attack the castle, or try to starve Anna out, or just accept this campaign as a lost cause now that he knew the monks had escaped.   Botolph hoped it would be the latter.   He pushed the thoughts to the back of his mind and searched the starry sky ahead for a sign that they were approaching West Wood.   Every so often they would plough through a nest of bull rushes but Botolph never touched the bottom with his paddle until suddenly the stars vanished and they hit the bank.   West Wood had arrived!

They could not disembark here because they would then still have to cross West River.   In any case, Botolph was becoming less and less confident about being able to find *Skyff* in the dark, even supposing that she was still there and that some Penda vandal had not burned her for the fun of it!

CHAPTER 18
Blindfold in Enemy Territory

Botolph laid down his paddle and felt for the pole. Still kneeling in order to keep the raft stable and reduce the danger of his falling over the side, he extended it towards the bank until it found its mark and then he put all his weight behind it and forced the heavy bundle of tree trunks back out into the swirling water.

They were getting close to the watershed where the floods from the two estuaries meet and although it was now close to high water when the currents would normally have slowed, Botolph could hear the water still swooshing and gurgling in the dark. His imagination started to run away with him as he wondered if he had miscalculated the tides. Or maybe the noises were from a host of Pendasmen, marching up the river in the darkness or maybe it was a sea monster that only roamed at night so that nobody had ever heard about it before and they were going to be the first ones to meet it!

He shook his head and pulled himself together, telling himself that the noises in the dark were the same as the noises would have been in daylight. It was just that, without the benefit of his eyes, the sounds became all-pervading.

By seemingly random but apparently judicious use of the pole, Botolph was surprised to find that he had persuaded the raft back into deeper water and the boys

140

reapplied themselves to their efforts with the paddles. The black blanket of the wood slid silently by but as soon as it threatened to vanish in favour of a clear sky riddled with glimmering pin-pricks, they turned the craft in order to keep company with the black edge of trees.

Rushes again brushed against the outer trunks of the raft and Botolph had to ignore their intrusion on his paddling space for fear of losing the rhythmical momentum of movement. A rush end went up his left nostril and for a moment he thought he was going to sneeze but managed to overcome it. He persuaded himself that the rushes were his friends. They were telling him how close they were to the banks and that they were still in West River and not still hurtling down the Yar.

He was reckoning on the fact that they had found the corner of the inlet and now they were gradually making their way up into it but he could not be sure how far around the corner they had come. He dare not leave the guidance of the rushes and cross to the other side until he was certain that they were well out of the main stream.

They were getting into enemy territory now. This was where they had carried out their blind ambush in the foggy marshes. A sudden shiver of guilt passed through Botolph's mind as he thought of the poor men being assailed by deadly speeding arrows whizzing in from unseen bows. He had been part of this and guilt and sorrow mixed confusingly in his mind. The fact that they were enemies and pagans was of little comfort. "May their souls rest in peace," he muttered.

Luka neither heard him nor gave one thought to his part in the slaughter. He was still battling on with his paddle but had his head turned towards the place he guessed the opposite bank to be and was sniffing the air in the hope of gaining confirmation. He too was aware of the fact that they were approaching what was now a holy site, but in contrast to Botolph, his only thought was that if one of the bastards was to raise his head over the edge of the raft he would slit his throat with his seaxe without a second's hesitation.

They paddled on, now having good views of the stars all around the boat. The bull-rushes on the larboard side were the only indication that they were still moving forwards. Botolph was gazing thoughtfully at the 'W' of Cassiopeia when it was suddenly eaten by another black blotch. This must be the trees at Old Shepherd's Croft, he reasoned. He hissed "Cross now?" at Luka and applied renewed power to his paddle to bring the raft athwart the stream.

Once the blotch was firmly brought round to larboard, Luka did his part by re-applying power and their cumbersome craft was slowly navigated to the south bank where it ploughed through the rushes and then struck a vertical edge with a jolt. It then bounced back and slewed round with the steerboard corner close to the bank but the rushes helpfully held it captive.

Botolph felt around for the remains of the painter. He was not sure if Luka had had the foresight not to cut it too short or whether it was just a lucky circumstance. Never mind. Now was not the time to ask. Either way the piece of rope, though short, was long enough to be useful "a bit like Luka" he thought with a smile.

And 'smile' he might. The first part of their voyage had been successfully completed. Five miles gone, how many more hundred to go?

All these thoughts flashed through his mind in a second whilst at the same time he was accepting that 'muddy and wet' was the only way forwards at this point, so grasping the remains of the painter in his left hand he made his way to the corner of the raft that was nearest to the bank and tried to locate a tuft of grass with which to haul himself ashore.

The reangulation of his body increased the force on his feet which encouraged the raft away from the edge and he suddenly found that he was inadvertently disembarking! The painter escaped his grip but he regained it and then managed to roll himself over onto the bank. He stopped and listened. All was quiet except for the usual noises of the water lapping and the occasional hoot from an owl.

He could see nothing to which he could successfully tie the painter, but then he could see nothing anyway, so he hauled the rope in as tightly as he could and knelt on it, while Luka soundlessly passed their cargo up for him to lay on the bank.

Once the raft was fully stripped, including poles and paddles, he gave Luka his hand and the double clasp they had used so many times before quickly brought a dry Luka onto terra firma.

It was now close to midnight and the tide would soon start to ebb. If they were lucky and found *Skyff* quickly, they could be off and away within the hour and could pass the enemy-occupied southern part of the island under a cloak of darkness.

If *Skyff* proved to be elusive (or even worse, was not there at all) then by the time they finished searching it would be getting dangerously close to daylight. They were both crouching on the river bank with their heads down. Botolph whispered his thoughts to Luka who grunted his acknowledgement.

"We'll leave our stuff here," whispered Botolph. "I am sure we left *Skyff* westwards of this point. We'll follow the riverbank for two hundred paces. You lead the way counting and using your pole to guide you along the bank and I will hang on to your belt and use my pole to probe the reeds. If we have not found her by then we will have a rethink."

Luka grunted his assent and off they went.

CHAPTER 19
Skyff Reclaimed

They made their way slowly along the bank. At first Luka stumbled in and out of the water several times as he lost and then re-located his way in the dark. He was hard put to stifle his curses but eventually found his bearings and made good progress. Botolph kept a good grasp on his belt as he relied on his friend to guide him forwards whilst he pushed the pole sideways into the reed-beds.

Botolph could hear Luka counting under his breath and subconsciously Botolph was doing his own count. They stopped several times when the pole hit something hard, but it proved only to be a stone or something similar because further probing revealed nothing.

They had reached eighty-four paces when there was a satisfying wooden 'thunk' and further gentle probing revealed the outline of the boat. Botolph quickly laid down his pole and felt around for the prow which he soon found. He turned and set his shoulder under it and pushed with all his might. Nothing happened. She seemed to be stuck fast. Luka tried to help but, due to his lack of height, could not get a good purchase. The tide was still rising but Botolph was aware that this happy state would not last for much longer and if they did not get her afloat within the next few minutes, they would be set back another twelve or even twenty-four hours.   He tried unsuccessfully once again.   She just seemed to be too heavy but it was now or perhaps never!

He offered a quick silent prayer for strength and inspiration as he applied his shoulder to the prow once again.   Then he stopped.

"Luka" he said, "Do you think you can get into the boat?"

"How's that going to help?" growled Luka "She'll be even heavier!"

"Not if you go right up into the stern, as far back as you can and then jump about and sway her as I push and she might just give up her affection for the mud."

Another effort and in spite of Luka's antics nothing happened, although Botolph thought that he could detect a little movement.   Thus encouraged they repeated the process and with a superhuman effort on Botolph's part, the prow suddenly rose a little and then down she slid into the water.

Botolph had her painter in his hand and he was letting it slide through his fingers as the boat slid out into open water before he checked it once he was certain she was free.   On his call, Luka swarmed back onto the shore and stood ankle-deep in the muddy water holding the painter while Botolph found his pole again and made his way back to where they had beached the raft, counting the paces as he went.

He struggled to pick up all the goods and then found it difficult to carry them and at the same time use the pole to guide him back.   As a result the return journey was rather slower.   Eventually, with relief, he saw Luka's shape in front of him.   There was not a moment to lose.

No words were necessary.   Luka handed the painter to Botolph and nimbly jumped into the boat and took and stowed the items as Botolph passed them to him. As soon as everything was on board Botolph pushed the prow away and simultaneously leapt over the side to end up in an untidy heap on the sole.   For once Luka did not make one of his quips but ignored him and concentrated on shipping the aftermost oars.   He began to row but she was not ready yet.   Botolph regained his equilibrium and his dignity and grabbed a pole and plunged it into the water near the bow.   He found the bottom and pushed at an angle with all his might while feeling the reciprocal pressure of his feet against a thwart.

She obeyed his will and Luka's efforts now bore fruit as the blades bit into the water and the boat slid backwards into the stream.

They were up and away now and both sets of oars were in use as, with the help of the ebb tide, they felt their way back towards the confluence of the three rivers.

"We need to step the mast," hissed Luka.

"Steer her over to the north bank under the trees," whispered Botolph in reply.

When Botolph felt the branches brush his head he made a successful grab at one and bade Luka find the painter with which they secured the boat temporarily. Once they were settled, by judicious feeling around, they located the mast in its customary position on the sole and unlashed it.   They then had to push it skywards through a gap in the branches and Botolph gingerly stood and held it in place while Luka lashed the stays tightly to the sides of the boat.

In seamanlike fashion they stowed all other loose objects, tying them to the sides and thwarts so that they would not be unseen hazards as they made their night passage.

"Best we press on then and make the most of the darkness," said Botolph.

"I'm starving," said Luka.

"Me too," replied Botolph. "Let's get some sustenance into us now while we can." Luka had been anticipating this and had only lightly lashed the leather food bag to the thwart. This he now liberated and they ravaged some drying bread and cheese and washed it down with a cool draught of water. This only took a few minutes and thus satisfied, Luka returned the bag to captivity.

Their main challenge would be getting past Penda's base camp without being seen, particularly since the mast and furled sail stuck out like Ceolin's proverbial sword thumb. Botolph wondered if they should have left the mast unstepped but he had reasoned that, if the wind rose, they would be ready to take advantage of it. There was no doubt that, had they been travelling in daylight, the mast would have been better in the bottom of the boat. He reflected that they might well find their voyage to be one where the mast becomes stepped and unstepped with the frequency of a rebecker's elbow according to the measure of light available for prying eyes.

The plan was to make their way as far up Waif River as they could. By the time they reached the shallows and had to abandon *Skyff* they would, hopefully, be well away from Penda's force. They could then make their way overland towards the noonday sun until they crossed the river that marked the separation between Mercia and Wessex. After that they should be safe.

"Right, you ready now?" asked Botolph.

"Certainly am. I'll grab the oars while you get us out of the clutches of this tree."

Once again, Botolph balanced precariously on the thwart while he extricated the mast from the clutching fingers of the overhanging branches. As he untied the painter, Botolph had time to reflect sadly that he was loosening the last bonds that were securing them to the Cnobersburg that had been and that they were now slipping quietly away towards the world that was.

He hauled his thoughts back to the practicalities of this mission. If his original calculations had been correct and they had not lost too much time finding the boat, it should now be fairly slack water as it came up to high tide.

If they were too much later, the ebb would have already started and, instead of being able to make their way down to the watershed, the current would sweep them back towards Burgh. No time to think about that now though, they were committed and had to make the best of whatever the Good Lord provided. He made his way to the steerboard. "As quietly as you can then Luka."

In spite of Luka's best efforts, the creaking of the oars against the thole pins, seemed to penetrate the night but the water and the trees were anything but silent and Botolph hoped that the oars were not as noisy to others as they seemed to him.

Although it was very black, his eyes still managed to pierce the gloom sufficiently for him to make out the tree-lined border of the river and he steered snugly close to the left bank and was relieved to find that the current did not appear to have turned against them yet. An owl hooted and there was a shimmer of wind through the trees, something that had been absent for the past few days.

CHAPTER 20
Back into the Yar.

Soon they felt the boat start to rock as she passed across the watershed and the Waif ebb started to pick them up and throw them towards the southeast.

The first sign they noticed of the enemy army was the smell; a mixture of fire, cooking and sweaty bodies. Luka quietly stowed the oars and they let the current wash them down the stream. As they closed they heard the sounds of horses and the occasional ring of metal on metal. Then came a low sound of human voices alarmingly close at hand and a sudden movement above the rushes. A guffaw of single laughter shot out and was followed by a combined group sound of hilarity and then oaths, as those who were trying to sleep roundly cursed those who were not.

The boys crouched down in the boat and both held their breath as they passed the last curtain of rushes and were suddenly exposed to an unrestricted view of Penda's base-camp. It was threateningly black and massive with the occasional pin-prick of light where some of the supper fires were still burning. Botolph could see a group sitting round one such fire, close to the river bank. They were drawing level and Luka was just wondering how they could possibly not see them, when there was a sudden shout of "Hey!" and the boys flattened themselves in the boat and froze, fearing the worst. Slowly, oh so slowly, *Skyff* continued to drift downstream and the boys were kept in suspense until the sounds were well behind them and they realised the shout could not have been directed at them. The enemy's eyes must have been night-blinded by the blazing fire as the boat slithered silently past them into the protection of the next curtain of bull-rushes.

Once the voices and smells had disappeared into the black distance, the boys again shipped the oars to counteract the effects of wind and current, both of which seemed to be conspiring to take them to the east. They pulled ever more strongly for the western bank hoping to gain a lee from both tide and wind. Then things started to go wrong. *Skyff* began to buck and toss as the ebb from the west met the ebb from Waif Island and both streams fought in their eagerness to get to the open sea.

The opposite shore sported no trees which could shelter them from the wind or to which they could tie. In any case, *Skyff* could make no headway either towards the shore or across to the river that would take them south. Botolph realised with horror that the tide had already turned and the currents were much stronger than he had expected. Suddenly they were gripped by a maelstrom and the boat spun in a black circle, disorientating them both. The oars came alive as if some sea-monster was tugging at the outer ends and they stowed them before they became lost over the side. There was nothing they could do; they were at the mercy of the currents.

The boat rocked alarmingly as they spun in another black circle, and then again twice more. Luka was in the stern and had taken charge of the steerboard but nothing he did seemed to alleviate their situation. A few stars became visible but the clouds were building up, as was the wind and they were hurtling in a spiral motion towards somewhere!

Botolph suddenly realised where that 'somewhere' was. His worst fears were being realised. They had been swept into Lotha's River from whence the sea monsters of the Saxon Ocean were beckoning them. He shivered.

Skyff skidded sideways through the gap and then stopped her gyrations as Luka won his battle with the steerboard and managed at last to point her in the same direction as that in which she was travelling. A glimmer of light was beginning to show in the east as dawn approached and Botolph found he could just make out some tents on the northern bank. Exhorting Luka to keep *Skyff* steady, he stood and moved forwards to release the brown square canvas sail.

For a moment it flapped noisily but then it filled and began to draw. The boat surged forwards and Luka felt control satisfyingly restored. They had yet to pass the headland at Lotha's Croft. Luka steered to the south as much as he dared. At least he could now see the outline of the banks but the last thing he wanted was to risk getting too close as running aground at this point would spell certain disaster.

Inch by inch, it seemed, they moved closer to the headland. They willed their four eyes to pierce the lightening gloom and focus on the point that marked, they thought, their last hazard before freedom.

They were getting close now. There was a shout followed by some arrows hissing over the boat. The boys threw themselves flat and tucked themselves under the larboard runners for protection. The next volley came and some found their marks, but on the boat rather than on the boys. *Skyff* had maintained her direction for a while but was now turning up into the wind and towards the enemy bank as if she were ready to surrender!

"I'll get it" said Luka, preparing to move over to grab the pole and bring *Skyff* back on course.

"No!" said Botolph, but then had an inspiration and took a short piece of rope and made a loop in it and handed it to Luka. "Well, if you must do something, try looping this over it."

Luka chose his moment and immediately after the next volley of arrows, he leapt across to the other side of the boat and secured the rope to the steerboard pole. He had just finished when he gave an "Oomph" as an errant dart whistled in and pinned him to the side.

"Luka!" shouted Botolph as his little friend lay still with his eyes closed. One eye opened and he grinned. "Still alive" he said, as he wrenched his sleeve away from where the arrow had pinned it to the boat. He handed Botolph the line and as Botolph tugged on it, the steerboard bit again and *Skyff* remembered who her masters were and obediently turned, giving them better protection as well as a faster passage.

They sensed a change in motion as the boat gained the sea. The arrows had stopped falling and they cautiously poked their heads over the runners. They had passed the headland and were still heading out to sea. Directly in front of them, the sun was peeping over the horizon in his struggle to start another day. "A good day for a sail!" said Botolph slapping Luka on the back. Luka responded by taking the steerboard pole and turning the craft to the south so that they ran parallel with the shore. Botolph joined him on the steerboard side and they savoured the moment, watching contentedly as the sun gloriously succeeded in his struggle for supremacy over the night sky.

All seemed to be wonderful for the first few minutes. The wind was off the land and the sea was calm. They were on a comfortable reach and carving nicely through the easily-manageable wavelets. Luka was at the helm with his back to the shore and Botolph was lying amidships, his weight nicely balancing the boat. They were both dozing intermittently in their attempts to catch up on lost sleep and from time to time Botolph would open his eyes and gaze sternwards.

After one such casual glance astern and then at the shore he sat up quickly and focussed his eyes again.

"What's up?" asked Luka.

"Isn't that Lotha's Croft that we're passing again?"

Luka swung round in disbelief and they both tried to puzzle out what was happening. They were pointing forwards, but actually going backwards. Luka looked over the side, expecting to see a rope fixing them to the bottom or a sea monster with them on its back, but nothing! They really seemed to be sailing in the right direction in fine style but there was no mistaking it, Lotha's Croft was passing them by and, after all their efforts, they had not escaped at all but were being inexorably drawn backwards towards Cnobersburg!

"It must be the tide" said Botolph. They were well-familiar with the phenomenon in the inland waters of the Waif and the Yar, but they had never sailed out at sea before and were not expecting such a setback. Having had a night without sleep their befuddled brains were having difficulty in reasoning the problem out.

"What shall we do?" said Luka. "We want to go south but there is no way that we can fight this. It would make more sense to turn northwards if that is the way the current runs hereabouts. At least then the tide will help rather than hinder."

"Yes," agreed Botolph "but what then? We will be back in pagan territory and have even further to walk when we do eventually make land than if we had continued down the Waif River. Perhaps God is calling us back to Cnobersburg for some reason?"

"Well, He certainly seems disinclined to let us go," said Luka " but surely He would not have let us escape through Lotha's River if our actions were not part of His grand plan! We seemed to be doing rather well up to that point."

They looked back to Lotha's Croft again and, depressingly, it had moved considerably further to the south.

"Alright," conceded Botolph, "let's not fight the inevitable, turn her round and we will see what the north has to offer."

Luka complied and with both wind and tide in their favour, they shot up the coast at a great speed. They kept well offshore to avoid lurking sea monsters and sandbanks and some three leagues and two hours later they were adjacent to a plume of smoke which seemed to be coming from a tree-lined part of the shore.

"Cnobersburg!" they both said at once. Botolph felt a mixture of anger and sadness as he realised that Penda had not finished with their friends yet. The exhilaration of the last two hours of sailing evaporated as they sat miserably watching the plume rising from the homes they loved. Botolph felt concerned at the anger welling up inside him. Father Fursey had told him that anger was a sin and, although he felt sure that that was right, there were

155

times he could not control the demon. He silently asked for God's forgiveness but his lips set more firmly as he gazed at the smoke and began to hate the men that were causing the destruction. He thought of his Saviour on the cross and he visualised the Pendasmen as he said bitterly "Father, forgive them, for they know not what they do."

"What was that?" said Luka and it was only then that Botolph realised he had spoken out loud.

He repeated it.

"Hmmph" said Luka, his face flushing red, "I really cannot go along with that. I would really like the chance of getting ashore and giving that lot a really good thrashing. I'd Pagan'em! What about it? Do you think that's why we are stuck in this wretched current? Is your God telling us to get back and sort them out?"

"MY God?" Botolph shouted, his fatigued emotions having taken another jolt. "MY God? He's your God as well, Luka."

"Well, I don't know" said an equally tired Luka. "My faith never has been as strong as yours, and He's not doing much to help us now. King Anna and his soldiers, all our friends have been slaughtered; the castle has probably been sacked and Cnobersburg has been razed to the ground. Here we are, having sneaked away by the skin of our teeth, out in the ocean sailing in totally the wrong direction, instead of being nicely tucked up at the end of Waif River getting ready to start a pleasant walk back to Cantium!"

"Oh, come on" said Botolph, "good things have happened. For one thing we are still alive, and for another we managed to get Torrel and the monks away didn't we?"

"Well, yes" agreed Luka, and then not willing to be mollified "but we don't know if they are safe. This rotten northerly current has probably swept them up to the Land of Ice and frozen them all to death!"

Botolph stayed silent, knowing that Luka was not susceptible to rational argument at the moment so he let his friend win the bout. Luka also let it drop, grateful that he did not have to dig deep for further anti-Christian evidence. In truth, he *did* believe but not as deeply as Botolph. He greatly admired his friend's ever-developing confidence in his faith and he usually found Botolph's conviction gave strength to his own poor offerings.

They stared morosely at the smoke as *Skyff* continued on her way. Luka realised that his instinct to go ashore was totally impracticable and nothing would be gained by it anyway. They continued to stare at the smoke in silence, each with their own thoughts. The smoke persisted. They had been watching it for rather a long time now. On the basis of their previous rapid progress, Luka had expected them to be well past Caistor island by now. He groaned.

Botolph was still worrying about Luka's lack of faith and his eyes had become unfocussed. "What's the matter?" he said.

"We're going backwards again!"

"WHAT?"

It was true, the plume of smoke was definitely further to the north than it had been previously. The sun was high in the sky and approaching its zenith.

"NOW what are we going to do?" bleated Luka as despair started to set in.

Botolph considered. "I suppose that the currents that go backwards and forwards in our rivers at home do the same thing out here. We came out of Lotha's River with the ebb and I guess that the ebb has sent us all the way up here. If I am right, then the flood should start again now and take us back to the south."

"Are you saying we have to turn around and go all that way back again?" said Luka.

"I reckon so" said Botolph "but that is better than getting swept up to your Land of Ice and freezing to death, isn't it?"

"Are we going to be swept back up Lotha's River then and end up at West Wood again?" asked Luka glumly.

"No, I think as long as we stay far enough away from the land, we should be able to pass the river safely. We will just have to see how long the current will run in this direction and as soon as we see signs of it turning we will have to run in to the land and beach *Skyff* while we wait for it to turn back in our favour."

Turn they did, with Luka grumbling all the time and retraced their passage back towards Lotha's Croft. This time they seemed to reach it quickly and they were pleased to see it rapidly disappear into the distance again. At last they began to see new and unfamiliar features and this restored Luka's normally-cheerful nature. They made good progress for several hours but then the lower edge of the sun began to kiss the top of the tree-lined shore and it was Luka's turn to shiver.

"Are we going to sail all night long until the current turns then?" he asked.

"Well at Cnobersburg we used to have two high waters every day, which means six hours each of ebb and flood. If it is the same out here in the ocean, we turned at noon and the sun is now going down. I have been watching the sun for some time as it comes down over those trees. An hour or so ago the sun was travelling with us and the trees were moving backwards. Watch it now.

158

Do you see? The sun has started to go backwards and the trees are moving forwards."

"What?" Luka stared at the crimson ball that looked as if it were going to set fire to the woods. It was dropping quickly now, but Botolph was right. As the top of the sun disappeared it fell into trees further to his right that it had (presumably) passed earlier. "What does that mean then?" he said.

"That means" said Botolph triumphantly "that current out here lasts a quarter of the day, just like it did at Cnobersburg and that it has now turned and it's time to get the boat ashore while we still have enough daylight to see what we're doing."

They tightened the square sail and Botolph took the steerboard and pointed *Skyff* as close to the shore as he could, but she would, of course, not go directly into the wind as he would have liked. The boat still pointed to the south-west but made no headway in the increasing tide. She obligingly crabbed sideways until gently finding the bottom. They clambered out and hauled her as far up the beach as they could although it still left them a long way from the protective tree line.

Botolph took the painter and extended it by joining on another couple of ropes. He tied the end to a broken branch which he dragged as high up the beach as he could. They retrieved their leather bags and took them to a sheltered spot under the edge of the trees where they still had a good view of the boat. They gathered together some soft bracken that would make a reasonably comfortable bed.

The place seemed remote and deserted and they eagerly plundered their scrips for some scraps of food which they devoured and washed them down with a draught of water; and then they slept!

CHAPTER 21
The Voyage South.

Botolph awoke as usual with the sun. Luka was already sitting up. "Where are we?" he asked.

"I haven't the faintest idea" said Botolph. "Somewhere south of Lotha's Croft, but well clear of the Land of Ice! I see *Skyff* has moved up the beach to join us. The tide's ebbing now. We will need to keep her afloat as the tide goes down, although, as I see it, the current won't start running in the direction we want to go until dead low water and that must be three or four hours away!"

They stood, stretched and scratched, yawned a few times and tested their aching limbs and then, leaving their few belongings by the trees, they ambled down the beach to the position where *Skyff* lay beached on the shingle.

Luka had untied the painter from the broken branch on the way past and he threw the rope over the bows. The water had only recently left her but it took more than a little effort to lift the prow and wobble and wriggle her back into the water. Soon she was swimming again and Botolph held her while Luka collected their belongings from the trees.

They reloaded her and Luka clambered aboard while Botolph took one of the spars, together with the coil of painter, back onto the beach. He plunged the spar as deeply as he could into the shingle, looped the painter over it and returned to the boat.

"I've been keeping my eyes open for a small rock or heavy stone to use as an anchor" he said to Luka, " but there's nothing except those little pebbles which are no use at all!"

"Why not " said the never-to-be-beaten-Luka "empty one of our leather bags and fill it with pebbles and use that?"

"Brilliant!" said Botolph. "Where did *that* idea come from?"

"Aah" said Luka with mock hauteur "just because I'm beautiful, it doesn't mean I'm not bright!"

Botolph retraced his steps with the empty bag which he then filled with pebbles and retrieved the spar from the depths of the beach. The spar was duly replaced by the bag as being the working end of the painter and Botolph joined Luka in the boat.

They spent the next few hours nibbling at their meagre rations and dozing and occasionally poling *Skyff* off as she grounded. The leather bag did its job well and gradually slid down the beach as the boat followed the tide's recession. The sun slowly rose in the sky and the rate of their sternwards travel reduced as the King of the Seas decided whether or not it was time to push the water back from whence it came. The wind was still blowing off the land, but very gently. The sailor in Botolph decided it was time to go.

They hoisted the square sail and the boat drifted lazily sideways into deeper water. They hauled on the painter and the dripping leather sac was eventually heaved over the side. Luka pushed down the leeboards and

162

suddenly *Skyff* ceased to be a dead fish on the beach and was alive again and ready for service.

Botolph reasoned that if his hunch had been correct and the tide *was* with them, it would be stronger the further they went out to sea and so for the first hour they concentrated their steering on getting as far away from the beach as possible.

They did not have the setting sun to use as a transit to check the rate of their southerly (or was it northerly?) progress, but small puffballs of white cloud were hovering over their recent resting place and Botolph noted with satisfaction that they definitely gave the appearance of going *with* them whereas the trees were travelling backwards!

They were making good progress but the land seemed to be slipping away into the distance and Botolph started to worry.

"What's the problem?" asked a happy Luka.

"Well, if we are too far away from the shore when the current turns, we are going to end up back on our shingly beach by the trees," said Botolph.

"Aha!" said Luka, waggling a confident finger, "That's where my magic bag of stones comes in, we'll just drop 'em over the side again and wherever we are the painter will hold us until the tide changes when we can haul 'em back in.   See, I've thought it all out, just ask me if there's anything you want to know."

"Alright then clever-clottle, how deep is the water here?"

"Err, I don't know."

"Well, guess!"

"Err, twenty men's height?"

"Right then, how long's the painter?"

"Err, five men's hei--ght!   Aah!   Best we head in for shore then sailor?"

"Right?"

"Right!"

Heading for shore was not that easy. The wind had picked up and seemed to pick up further as they battled their way as closely to the west as they could. The current was strong though and before long the land was noticeably closer and soon after noon they saw that a hook of land curled out ahead of them towards the larboard side. This was almost as alarming as no land at all but they reasoned that, as long as the wind persisted, they could, if necessary, free the sail and run eastwards.

Botolph remembered his journey to Cnobersburg on the wagon and his stay in the monastery at Lundwic. He recalled that, until they had reached Lundwic, the noonday sun had been on their left, but after Lundwic it had been behind them. That surely meant that the world was the shape of the roman L sign for 'fifty" and that the land they could see ahead of them now, might be close to where Cantwarebury lay.

They pressed on and the land slowly took shape. They could see some huts on the beach and some movements near the huts.

"Let's hope they're not Pendasmen" thought Botolph, only to have his mind read by Luka who verbally expressed the same sentiment.

Soon they saw that the huts were few and the movement was that of children. Suddenly the action changed and mothers came running from the huts and gathered the children up and disappeared into the vegetation.

The boys expertly guided their vessel onto the river bank, raised the leeboard at the last moment and stowed the sail. They made her fast and went ashore, calling as they did so.

They went to each of the five straw-thatched huts but the place was now deserted. There was, however, the smell of fish cooking on an open fire.

"What do we do now?" asked Botolph.

"Well," said Luka, "That fish is going to burn if we leave it there, and it will be no good to anyone! I think a friendly thing to do would be to test it to see if it is in danger of overcooking." He took out his seaxe and prodded the unfortunate fish. A piece of white flesh fell away and he balanced it on the point of his seaxe and delicately transferred it to his mouth. "Mmmm!"

"I take it you approve" said Botolph.

"Certainly do" came the reply as Luka prepared to make a second sortie.

"I will just have another go at trying to find the cooks; back shortly," said Botolph, and headed off in the direction of the woods, calling as he went. After a thorough and fruitless search, he returned to the fireside and found Luka getting ever more enthusiastic about the prospects of his meal. Eventually they threw caution to the wind and found some bread and wooden platters and a little wine and settled down to enjoy the best meal they had had for weeks.

By now it was mid afternoon and they had been up early. They stretched out in the long grass and soon were fast asleep.

It seemed they had been asleep for only a few minutes when Botolph woke to find a foot on his chest and a longseaxe at his throat.

CHAPTER 22
Capture!

He tried to get up. The pressure increased. He accepted the inevitability of staying where he was. He kept the rest of his body very still as the tip of the longseaxe dug into his neck. The only movement he permitted himself was that of his eyes as they followed the outline of the limb that was attached to the foot which was now restricting his breathing.

The short but very muscular (he noticed) limb disappeared beneath a rough hessian garment which continued upwards into the sky. Somewhere in the blue yonder it was joined by the arm which held the longseaxe which persisted in digging further into Botolph's neck. His assailant did not appear to have a head since the afternoon sun was sitting on his left shoulder and its brilliance was burning into Botolph's eyes. The head moved and cast its shadow so that at last he could see a rough full beard surmounted by eyes the colour of the sky.

The beard parted. "You ate my dinner!" it accused.

Botolph stayed silent, not out of choice but due to the inconvenience of the longseaxe. He kept his head still but swivelled his eyes and saw that he was surrounded by a village of people, all of whom were staring at him. There was a movement to his left as the crowd parted and an increase of noise as a wriggling, swearing, roped-up-Luka was hauled in front of Blue-Eyes who scowled him into silence.

Blue-Eyes looked from one to the other and back again. "Well" he said in perfectly-understandable English. "What have you got to say for yourselves before I cut both your heads off and eat *them* instead of my fish?"

Luka opened his mouth but then closed it again as Blue-Eyes was boring his gaze into Botolph and clearly expected an answer from *him*.

Botolph was beginning to feel dizzy from his inability to breathe properly but he attempted an answer which came out as a pitiful "Earghhhhh!" This at least had the effect of the longseaxe being withdrawn by a fraction but the foot remained crushing his ribs. At last he could think straight however and he closed his eyes just long enough to issue a quick prayer to the Almighty asking Him (if it was His will of course) to kindly get him out of this mess.

He flashed his brown eyes back open again and returned the bore directly into Blue-Eyes face. "Sorry?" he said, allowing himself the luxury of a half-smile.

"Sorry? Sorry?" Is that all you have to say after eating one of the best fish we've caught this year? Sorry?" He removed his foot in disgust.

"It would have burnt!" persisted Botolph, raising his head a little. "We looked for everyone but they had all gone."

"Well what did you expect? Turning up here in a strange boat like a couple of savages. Where are you from?"

Botolph decided that 'respect' was the only weapon he had that might be of some use. "From Cnobersburg Monastery on Waif Island sire!"

"Waif Island! ... Cnobersburg! ... Never heard of them. Get up!"

Four strong arms hoisted him off the grass and held him as he faced Blue-Eyes who now had the point of his longseaxe resting on his navel.

"Monastery eh? And what were you doing there and, more to the point, why have we now been cursed with your presence here?

"Oh dear", thought Botolph "I wonder whose side this man's on. If he is a Pendasman our heads will soon be on his dinner platter." He took a deep breath, wondering if it might be one of his last and closed his eyes in prayer and hope while he said "We are kinsmen of King Anna!"

There was silence and Botolph mentally braced himself for the longseaxe to penetrate his abdomen. Suddenly there was a loud guffaw, followed by the loss of pressure on his stomach and before he knew what had happened, the hairy monster was clasping him in his arms and the crowd were bursting into happy chatter.

Once again he felt his ribs crushed. It had not been a good day from the breathing point of view. The pressure came off and Blue-Eyes grasped him by both shoulders and said "Sigeberht of East Anglia!"

"Sorry?" said Botolph.

"Sigeberht, he was King Anna's predecessor and we fought together for many years. I was the captain of his guard and loved him like a brother, and he loved me too. But then he loved all his men and they him. We fought and conquered and conquered and fought. He was the best general there ever was! My, they were good days, and then he gave up the crown and became a monk."

It all became clear. Botolph remembered Abbot Fursey telling them about the revered man. He remembered how he had ruled with Ecberht, Anna's nephew, who some had said was the rightful king. He recalled how Sigeberht had founded the monastery at Beodricsworth whilst he was regent and then handed the crown to Ecberht and retired to the monastic way of life. When Penda started his reign of terror and vowed to extinguish the Christian flame, Ecberht, recognising his own inadequacy as a fighter, asked Sigeberht to put on his armour and lead them to victory once again.

Sigeberht had declined, saying that he was now a monk and so could never bear arms again. Ecberht was furious and desperate and had him hauled out of his monastery and sent onto the battlefield armed with nothing but his staff. Predictably the old soldier was killed and Ecberht's death followed the same day. It was King Anna who, in the aftermath of the disaster, accepted the crown and brought the East Anglians together again.

Botolph fired off a quick prayer of thanks both for his and Luka's apparent salvation and for the life and times of Sigeberht of East Anglia.

"Come!" Botolph's traumatised mind came back to earth again as the brawny hands first left his shoulders and then returned with a painful thump. "Let's eat. Bring out the tables, bring out the wine, let that little fellow go. We have a Feast of Celebration to prepare for the Monks of King Anna!"

Botolph wanted to point out that they were not monks, although he found to his surprise that he was rather proud to have been called one, but there was no time. They were feasted and entertained and washed and given new vestments and generally had a wonderful time with their new-found friends.

When he finally had a chance, he said to Blue-Eyes "How is it that we have eaten so well? I thought you said that was the best fish you had caught this year?"

Whether it was the effect of the wine or genuine embarrassment, Blue-Eyes' face flushed as he laughed and said "Best fish? We are *fishermen*, we have *loads* of fish! I just wanted a good excuse to kill you!" and he slapped him hard on the back to Botolph's further respiratory consternation.

The feast lasted well into the night and good friendships were made and many stories exchanged.

The next morning they found that *Skyff* had been pushed out into deeper water where she was tied between two fishing vessels. The vessels had obviously arrived the previous afternoon whilst the boys had been enjoying their sleep in the long grass. They broke their fast gloriously and prepared for departure. Botolph asked if they could beg some water to take with them but their friends just smiled and said that it had all been taken care of.

Blue-Eyes had said that two of his boats would accompany them for a while to ensure that they kept clear of the sandbanks which they had been lucky to miss the previous afternoon. He also told them that they would have to follow a course which would take them out of sight of land for a while. The next land they would see would be the north coast of Cantium. All they would need to do would be to study the aspect of his two vessels in relation to the waves and the sun and, once he was happy that they were steady on their course, he would veer away and bid them farewell.

The whole village came down to the shore to watch them go. After much smiling and shouting and waving and hugging, they were put into a small rowing boat which took them out to the raft of vessels. On regaining the deck of *Skyff* they found her stowed with food and water and spare dry clothes wrapped in waterproof skins. Botolph felt his eyes well up and a lump in his throat, "just close to where the longseaxe nearly penetrated it" he thought wryly.

They soon had the leeboard down and the steerboard set and as they let go the mooring line they hoisted the big brown sail and followed Blue-Eyes' boat up towards the northeast and then round the point until they lost sight of the watchers on the shore. The ships all wore round to first a south-easterly then a southerly heading as they settled on course.

The two fishing vessels were faster than *Skyff* and the one that Blue-Eyes commanded was soon on the horizon, whilst the other reduced sail and remained contentedly behind them. After an hour or so, they noticed Blue-Eyes' sail had changed its aspect and the aftermost vessel spread more sail and came up on their leeward side.

"See where she is now?" said the young fellow at the helm, indicating Blue-Eyes' boat. "Keep going in that direction but stay a touch to the west. Don't follow her any more because she'll be taking the tide to the east. I'll stay with you for another hour or so to make sure your course is constant and then you'll be on your own. Farewell!" They reduced sail and fell back in behind *Skyff* again.

An hour later, true to their word, they passed down *Skyff's* leeward side under full sail and then, once clear, sliced across *Skyff's* bows towards the east and followed Blue-Eyes to the fishing grounds.

CHAPTER 23
Landfall Cantium!

The wind blew steadily from the west and well after the sun had begun its downward passage they spotted low-lying land ahead of them.

Blue-Eyes had told them that their landfall would place them close to Cantwarebury but had also warned them that the shores were marshy and they would be lucky if they landed on one of the few solid spots.

And so it proved to be. *Skyff's* hull found the muddy bottom an hour or so before sunset and, after stowing the sail, Botolph stood on the side of the boat clutching the mast to see if he could see any sign of a path through the watery reed beds. Nothing was immediately obvious and the last thing they wanted was to get stranded in such a desolate place. Already the ooze was clutching at the planking and Botolph hastily changed positions with Luka so that his extra weight in the stern could lift the prow a little and enable Luka to pole them back into the draining creek.

Luka plunged their quant spar into the soft mud and it went down and down before he could get a purchase on it and push with his muscular but tiny legs on the wooden thwart. The boat moved a few inches and Botolph swung from side to side to help to free the hull from the glutinous mud, and she obligingly slid back a little further.

Luka pulled on the pole but the mud was disinclined to loosen its grasp. Luka pulled again; *Skyff* slid back a little more and with a shout he found himself more attached to the pole than the boat. Botolph quickly left his position at the stern but his movement pushed the vessel back further. He ran to the bows and grabbed Luka's legs just before they went over the side into a muddy grave. Luka was still clutching the pole as if his life depended on it, which maybe it did and there came a point where it looked as if both the boys were going to end up 'ashore' whether they wanted to or not. Slowly, with Botolph pulling Luka and Luka pulling the pole, *Skyff's* prow came round and Luka's aspect changed from being nearly horizontal to a much more workable 'vertical'!

"Let it go!" said Botolph.

"No, I can get it!" pulling again but slipping in the process.

"Let it go!" Luka conceded defeat and they both returned to the stern and half wobbled and half rowed the boat back into the wider channel.

Luka was grumbling. "That was a very good pole. We might live to regret losing that!"

"I'd have regretted it even more if I had've lost you! Anyway, the tide has started to fall and from the look of those clouds, the weather is worsening. We'd have looked a right pair of idiots stuck out on those marshes in half a gale!"

Luka joined Botolph in looking up at the sky and sure enough, the clouds were building up. There was still light enough to see what they were doing but it looked as if they had a very dark and moonless night ahead of them.

They were pushing on the oars as they rowed *Skyff* backwards towards the open sea from whence they had come and Botolph noticed the grey murk of an island moving away to his left.

"The current's *with* us!" he cried. "I'm sure that Cantwarebury is somewhere over there. All we have to do is keep offshore and the current will sweep us round until we find the corner and the river that will take us right into the city!"

In spite of the clouds the ever-helpful westerly wind was still of a useful strength and they soon hoisted sail and stowed the oars, taking it in turns to steer towards a smudge on the horizon. From time to time one of the leeboards would clonk as they touched the ground and, depending upon which leeboard it was, the steersman would quickly push his oar over to spin the boat into deeper water. With the wind directly behind them, they did not need the boards to stop them skidding sideways so they had both been raised in order to create less drag. They still dangled six inches or so beneath the lowest point of the hull however and were proving very helpful sounding boards in the flat, dark conditions.

The dark smudge ahead soon became the outline of a distant church on the steerboard side. The name of 'Raculf' came inexplicably to Botolph's mind. He had heard it somewhere before in relation to Father Augustine's Monastery but he could not recall where or when.

Suddenly the note of the water changed and, with what little light was left to them, they could see that they had entered some sort of whirlpool which pushed the prow round to larboard and threatened to spin the boat in a circle. Luka was at the helm and he quickly corrected this but they seemed to be going sideways over a waterfall. There was a roaring sound which was increasing and seemed to be coming from the larboard side. Botolph quickly lowered the leeboard and grasped the control ropes for the sail. He shouted to Luka.

"What?" came the reply.

"Go with the current!" shouted Botolph. "Don't fight it, turn a bit more to the steerboard side!"

Luka and *Skyff* concurred and the lads held on tightly as they were swept through the rapids into blackness. Spray was coming over the stern and every so often a larger wave would hit the aft quarter and splash into the boat. The prospect of bailing the water out occurred to Botolph but the noise was so great and the ride so vicious that he could do nothing but maintain his grip on the side and wish that the butterflies which had invaded his stomach would sit quietly and allow him a chance to think. He floated a quick prayer off in the direction of the Lord but truly the rude incursion of the sea into his senses hardly gave scope for even that.

Luka was manfully heaving on the steerboard, trying to keep the vessel straight in its plunge down this apparent ravine. He was acting instinctively rather than rationally since he could see nothing. He was sitting on the larboard side and could feel the wind on the side of his face as he kept his head turned in the direction of their crazy skelter. His arms, though short, were powerful and he was at first pushing and then pulling his steering spar as he struggled to maintain some sort of order in their passage. He longed to he able to see ahead and prayed that the sun might arise early, like 'now!' to help him see where he was going. This prayer remained unanswered but his secondary wish that they might not hit a sandbank, seemed, for the moment, to have been granted.

Gradually the worst of the noise ceased and they returned to some sort of stability. They still seemed to be travelling fast but the craft was steady and Botolph took one of the leather bags and released its occupants from captivity. He used the empty bag to bail out some of the water that was sloshing around in the boat. Once that was done to his satisfaction, he returned to the foodstuffs that he had just liberated and shared them with Luka. He then took his turn at the helm.

They were not sure what they had passed through but as all seemed to now be quiet, they reverted to their easterly course and watched as a low island passed down their larboard side. Soon after this, the water gave voice again but less violently. The wind veered and eased and they found they were being swept down a narrow channel with low shadows on each side. The low shadow on the steerboard side, grew and grew until it towered above them. Awestruck, they eased away to keep this monster in sight, but at a distance.

The wind was still quiet but the waves had increased and they felt themselves tossing and rolling. Occasionally there was a whoosh and a roar and God would deposit some of his sea back in the floor of their boat. Botolph was still at the helm so Luka busied himself with bailing when he could. He also tried to tidy the sail ropes that were sloshing about in the bottom of the boat.

At last Botolph saw what he had been praying for; the first signs of a new dawn. The very slight lightening of the sky; the crests of the waves showing a lighter shade of grey; the contrast developing between the sky and the high shadow in the distance. The high shadow slowly developed into white cliffs and Botolph realised that they must be passing Dofras and he remembered that there was a haven there. He tried to turn *Skyff* towards the land but the current was strong and the wind was weak and, although he was still closing the land, he saw the tallest of the cliffs disappearing into the distance.

The sail fluttered and the spar rattled. Botolph turned his gaze away from the cliffs and across to the other side of the boat. His attention was captured by a roll of clouds away to the south. He watched them for a while as they tumbled towards him. They looked like the moustache of a Pendasman, he mused.

Suddenly they arrived! Just in time, Botolph noticed the spume blowing off the wave tops a mile away on the larboard side and he shouted at Luka to get the sail down as the gust hit them. The sail was blowing out towards the land and cracking and banging with almighty force as the newborn waves pounded the side of the boat. The ropes from the sails whipped and flogged and threatened to take the eyes from anyone who came too close. Luka and Botolph struggled together to tame the tangled mass as the second generation of waves combined their onslaught on the larboard side. Botolph just had time to see the fearsome moustache of the sky immediately overhead when he felt *Skyff* rise up below him and turn at a crazy angle to dump him headfirst into the thrashing ocean. He inadvertently gulped in a mouthful of salty water and then spat it out as he felt his clothes filling and beginning to cling to him. *Skyff* was on her side and the sail and the mast were lying flat on the water. He was hanging onto the side of the boat which every so often was being lifted up by a wave and then smashing down into the sea again. He was too close, the next wave might bring the boat down onto him directly. He was conscious of the need to move away. He shouted Luka's name. He could not see him and a feeling of terror and foreboding passed over him.

"Luka!" he shouted again.   Nothing, perhaps he was on the other side of the hull.   Perhaps he could work his way round and find him.   He started to move towards the stern but then suddenly realised with his horror that he was trapped.   Something was wrapped around his left ankle. He brought his right foot round and tried to push it off.   It felt like a rope.   He pushed again.   Nothing happened except for the fact that the rope tightened.   At that moment another wave came and rolled *Skyff* right over so that her mast pointed vertically downwards.   This had the effect of Botolph being dragged downwards by the rope around his ankle.   His head was pulled under the water. He managed to pull himself back and get his mouth clear enough to get one last breath before, like a sea monster claiming its prey, the rope pulled him once more into the depths.

He had no choice. He had to get that rope off or die. A 'help-me-God' prayer was all he had time for before he doubled up and wrenched at his ankle.   He could still feel himself hurtling upwards and then crashing down again as each roller took him and the boat towards the even more cruel breakers that were waiting on the shore.

His lungs felt as if they would burst. He was losing consciousness.   He could hold his breath no longer.   He must. He tried. He failed. He surrendered and opened his mouth. He had to. There was no fight left. "Into Thy hands O Lord, I commend my spirit."   His lungs expanded and he breathed in the salty water.   There was a flash in front of his still-open eyes and a sudden movement as a sharp seaxe sliced through the seething mass that had tethered his now almost-lifeless body to the upside-down mast-top.

Strong little hands pushed him upwards and ran under his armpits to the boat's stern and supported him as he vomited and coughed and choked and heaved and vomited again. He was surprised to find that he was still alive. He had no energy to try to talk or even move but he was his own man again for the moment. He just had the chance to look into Luka's eyes and nod his thanks when the submerged mast struck the underwater rocks and *Skyff* pole-vaulted into the air and came down with a sickening awesome crash on top of Luka.

The boat's flight through the air was her final undoing as the wooden nails separated from the planks they secured and in an instant the craft became a mass of firewood. Some pieces were larger than others and the larger pieces were threatening to finish the job that the rope had started.

Botolph looked to where he had seen Luka only a few moments previously. He was not there. He gave a sob of despair and panic and thrashed in the water looking for his hero. Another prayer, what it was he did not know but he knew he needed God's help now as never before. In his thrashings his right hand found a bundle of rags a foot below the surface. He grasped and pulled and there was Luka.

Even in the poor morning light, he could see the great gash on his forehead and the blood pouring out of it. He grabbed a piece of wreckage which he recognised as *Skyff's* mast step and used it to support them as he endeavoured to propel their bodies towards the shore. His efforts were meagre compared with those of the sea however and he soon felt his feet touch firm sand. Twice he fell with the force of the waves, but the beach was gradual and at last, dragging Luka behind him, his feet obtained a purchase on firm ground.

He looked at Luka whose eyes were shut.   He listened to see if he could hear him breathing but the roar and crashing of the waves made that impossible.   He placed his ear to his chest in the hope of hearing a heartbeat, but could hear nothing.   There was no escaping it.

Luka was dead.

Botolph sobbed and cried and sobbed and sobbed again.   He felt absolutely drained, - of life, - of energy, - of hope itself.   He had reached the absolute depth of despair.

"Why, Lord?" he cried.   "Why? He was such a good man.   He would have served You well.   Why? Why? Oh why?"

Later, he would remember to his surprise that, even at this time, he did not lose his faith in God.   The prospect of his love for his Maker turning into hate did indeed cross his mind but only for a fleeting instant and then it was gone.   Even then he knew that Luka's death must have a purpose.   Thy will, O Lord, be done.

There was a cough.   He turned, expecting to see a fisherman.   Luka's head was facing the other way.   He was still alive!   Botolph put his hand on Luka's chest and felt slight movement beneath.   From somewhere and somehow, he stood and gathered his friend in his arms and struggled up the sandy beach.

To his left he could see a fortress on the hillside, but a river flowed between it and where he stood.   He followed the river up the hill onto a grassy bank, having to stop regularly for breath but conscious of his need to keep going in order to get help for Luka.

He kept looking hopefully at the river bank, wondering if it were shallow enough to cross, or if he might see a boat that he could use. He could see a cluster of huts on the other bank. He shouted "Hello!"

A face appeared at one of the doorways and then some bodies appeared. "I need help!" shouted Botolph. The bodies started to run and for a moment Botolph thought that they were running away in fear in case he was a raider. But no, they were running up the bank of the river on their side and urging him to do the same.

It was another mile before he reached the ford and both sides crossed to meet in the middle. Strong arms took Luka and other strong arms supported Botolph as they were guided back to the huts and then Botolph's thoughts faded into oblivion.

CHAPTER 24
Folcanstane.

He had no idea of how long he slept. Vague dreams of being tossed in the ocean kept coming back to him. And then drowning, going down, down, down, unable to breathe. And then the flash of the seaxe and Luka's face; and then Luka's gentle, familiar smiling face was replaced with an ugly scarlet gash on his forehead and the face came nearer and nearer and nearer and Botolph shouted "NO! NO!" and leapt up in his bed into strong arms which held him as he sobbed.

A cool damp cloth was rubbed over his temples and when the height of his sobbing ceased, he was laid gently back on the straw where he drifted into more peaceful rest.

Several hours later, the morning sun found its way through the door opening and played on his face. It flickered as people passed and eventually Botolph opened his eyes. He moved his head so that it returned to shadow and lifted it so that he could see around the hut.

In the centre was a clay hearth with log smouldering on it; the sweet smell of the wood-smoke was comforting. Suspended above the fire was an iron pot and an elderly woman was dunking a ladle into it. To his right, between him and the hearth lay Luka.

Was he dead or asleep? A feeling of panic gripped Botolph's abdomen and he moved as if to shake and waken his wounded friend.   A strong fist came out of the dark corner behind him and gripped his arm.   He turned and looked into the frightening face of a Cantium fisherman.   A finger went to his lips and the grip on his eager limb was relaxed.

Botolph surrendered and looked again at Luka.   His wound had been dressed with something glutinous.   He was lying still and breathing regularly.   He was alive.   One step at a time.   That was all Botolph could ask for at the moment.   He had no doubt that his power of prayer would restore his friend to health.   God could not want him to die or it would already have happened.   He would pray every hour of every day and devote himself to God, if Luka would only be restored to him.   He looked back at the fisherman, who gestured to the open doorway and rose from his haunches.

Botolph went to move also but every limb was aching.   Each movement created agony in his body somewhere.   His head was throbbing with pain.   He felt sick.   The fisherman's strong hands clasped his and hauled him to his feet and propelled him out of the door.   The bright morning light flashed straight into the centre of his brain and he winced and stumbled.   More hands guided him to a wooden bench by another smouldering fire and he sat and leaned forwards, his head in his hands, and then, inexplicably, sobbed again.

A kindly arm was placed around his shoulder and hugged him until the paroxysm passed.   He shook his head.   That was it!   It was over!   He had cried enough. Self-pity was never going to get anyone anywhere.   What could he do to make Luka better?

He put down his hands and turned to his left, expecting to see the rough old fisherman again, but he gazed into the tender and smiling face of a woman who instantly reminded him of his mother. His dear sweet mother. He had not missed her until now. When he left, she had seemed to accept that that was what boys did when they turned into men. He had thought of her occasionally and prayed regularly for her and his father and Matild. But now? But now, he had an overwhelming urge to see her again. All in good time. For the moment he had a surrogate in this kind Cantium stranger. First they must get Luka well. Then they would make the journey back to the bloomeries and, God willing, see his family.

The woman's name was Martha and the old fisherman was Eric. He was her father-in-law. Her husband was away fishing. She had three young children, two boys and a girl and they were out somewhere playing with other children from the hamlet.

The settlement consisted of about twenty huts. They seemed randomly placed between the cliff to the west and the river to the east. All the houses were thatched and most were the same sort of size and design but scattered amongst them were four larger 'halls'. Across the river and to his right, the waves crashed onto the shore. An involuntary shiver ran through him. A warm soup bowl was placed in his hands. It brought comfort as well as sustenance. He held the pot up and looked across it back at the seething water. "Drink" said the small voice softly on his left. He did its bidding and felt the warm broth trickle through his body. He supped again, and again.
The strength-giving arm was removed from his shoulders as the soup restored his independence. He began to feel alive again. He put the bowl down on the rough table and picked up a chunk of newly-baked warm bread that had been placed in front of him. As the bread reached his

mouth, its aroma pervaded his nostrils and he wondered if it was wrong to eat it. Perhaps he should just smell it and then it would last forever. The thought was soon past however and he gratefully sank his teeth into the crusty bake.

His attention was distracted as a blackbird landed in a tree sprouting from the cliff just above their heads. The bird started to sing. Botolph turned and looked back at it. The black chest was thrust outwards, the yellow beak held high in the air, the black eyes bright and sparkling as he thrilled his song into the morning light. Botolph felt a surge of optimism. The song was his gift. If the little black creature could be so happy and positive at the beginning of this new day, then surely so could he. He looked back at the sea. This time he saw, not crashing, threatening waves, but beautiful powerful rollers lifting to the sun which glittered through them exposing a blue transparency at their tops before the brilliant white spume cascaded down their faces to crash on the golden shore.

Truly life was beautiful and the greatest beauty lay in the fact that Luka was still alive. This gave hope for the future.

He returned to the hut and sat watching his friend who seemed to be sleeping peacefully. He placed his hand on his left shoulder and shook gently. "Luka! Luka, can you hear me?" He shook again. He looked up as the old fisherman came through the doorway and stopped and looked at him and then grunted.

"You'd better get used to the idea son. He's going to die! I've seen it before. He has had a heavy blow to his head and people don't get over that. Take my word for it, he'll go on like this for a few days and then he will just stop breathing and that will be that. We can't feed him anyway. He can't eat or drink. He is just going to fade away. Get used to it and prepare to put his soul to rest."

Botolph was looking at the old man in wide-eyed horror. His stomach lurched terribly. It couldn't be. He couldn't lose Luka, not after everything they had been through. Luka had saved his life. If it wasn't for Luka that wretched rope would still be tethering him by the ankle somewhere down in the bottom of the bay.   He knew in his heart though that Eric was right; he should just accept the inevitable and prepare Luka for his future. He knelt by the side of him and then, on impulse, traced the sign of a cross on his forehead. It did not satisfy his needs. He stood up again and went to a shelf. He poured water from a flagon into a cup and returned and placed it by the side of his fallen comrade. He dipped his finger into it and remade the sign on Luka's forehead. The excess water ran down the side of Luka's nose and onto his lips. They moved in response.   Botolph looked up, expecting to see Eric hovering above him and watching. He wanted to be able to say "There! Did you see that?" but he and Luka were on their own in the hut. He dipped his fingers in the water again but this time applied them directly to Luka's lips. There was no reaction for a moment but then, once again, the lips moved and a few drops of water made it into Luka's body.

"Luka" he called, shaking the body again, "Luka ... can you hear me? Luka wake up!" but the success with the water was the only success he was going to achieve today and he would have to be satisfied with it.

He closed his eyes and started to pray. He prayed aloud, following the liturgy he had learnt at Cantwarebury and Cnobersburg. At the end of each prayer, he opened

Fig. 5. Botolph's Folcanstane.

his eyes and applied more water to Luka's lips. He started with the Adoration and went on to Confession, moved further to Thanksgiving and then to Supplication, primarily for Luka but also for the community in which he found himself. Many of the prayers he recited in Latin as he had been taught. His confession and supplication were in plain English.

The supplication went on and on. He kept his eyes firmly closed and his face tilted upwards. He prayed deeply for Luka's life. He prayed for his soul. He prayed that God might see fit to heal his friend and restore him to his company. But if this was not God's will, then please take his soul and grant him peace in the company of Jesus for ever more. He followed with the Family Prayer and finished by asking for God's grace on them all. He lowered his head, tired from the praying. His eyes remained closed as his mind returned from intense ethereal concentration back to the rigours of the Earthly world. He had neglected Luka, he would need more water.

He opened his eyes, located the cup and dipped his fingers in once again and transferred them to Luka's lips. Something caught his attention and he looked up and across Luka's body. In front of him was a vision and his immediate thought was that this was a sign. God had heard his prayers and they were going to be answered.

The vision was of a perfectly-dressed nun, kneeling on the opposite side of Luka's body, mirroring Botolph's position as it had been a few moments previously. The vision's eyes were closed and her tiny perfect white hands were held together in prayer. Her lips were still. Botolph stared, open-mouthed. He had heard of people seeing visions before, but he had no idea what he should do next. Should he prostrate himself on the floor in recognition of

188

the fact that he was in the presence of Christ's messenger? He was still contemplating his next move when the vision's eyes opened and leant across and dipped her fingers into the cup and made her own sign of the cross on Luka's skin.

She then floated to her feet and silently made the sign of the cross in blessing on them both and with a swirl of her white habit, slid through the doorway. Botolph would have followed but Luka suddenly gave a moan and turned his head to one side. Botolph repeated his entreaty "Luka, Luka, wake up!", but he was still again.

Botolph rose and went to the doorway as Martha approached from one of the other huts. He was not sure what to say. Perhaps he should stay silent in case Martha thought that *his* head had been damaged too. But he couldn't. His mind was bursting. He had to tell someone.

"I've just seen a vision!", he blurted out.

"A vision?" said Martha.

"A beautiful nun in a white habit, came and prayed with me and then Luka moved!"

"Well, she is quite a vision!" admitted Martha.

Botolph was confused. "Did you see her too then?" he asked.

"Certainly did!"

Botolph was a little crestfallen, thinking that the vision had been sent especially for him.

"You can still see her and her retinue at the top of the hill." Martha pointed.

Botolph raised his eyes and, sure enough, there was the white habit and flowing headpiece riding on a sturdy horse and about to enter the gates of the fort.

"Who is she?"

"She's the king's daughter, Eanswythe. She is the Abbess of the nunnery inside the fort. As pure a little lady as you are ever likely to meet. She often comes to visit us. She brings gifts. She asks about our troubles. She finds out the names of any of us who are injured or unwell and she and her nuns pray for us. We had no sweet water but she performed a miracle for us and built a culvert and a pond. Do you know why that's a miracle?"

Botolph shook his head.

"Because the water in the culvert runs *uphill* to get to the pond, that's why!"

It had already been a day filled with emotions and Botolph's mind was beginning to whirl: death, reprieve, despair, hope, God's gifts, a vision, a miracle.

He could take no more.

"I'll go and look after Luka".

CHAPTER 25
Eanswythe.

Luka did not seem to change. He just remained asleep. Botolph frequently tried to rouse him when he sensed his sleep was not so deep, but all to no avail. He sat with him for hours, talking and tending. He moistened his lips regularly and dribbled larger quantities of water into his mouth which he seemed to swallow easily most times, although it sometimes made him cough. He talked constantly about this and that, their travels, their excitements, people they had met. He hoped that his efforts were not being wasted and that Luka was hearing him and assimilating his words, even if he was unable to answer.

Martha helped. She regularly changed his dressing, his bedding, and his clothes. He was now just dressed in a hessian shift which would have been short for a normal man but was long for Luka. The days wore on and the routine did not alter but the red scar on his forehead started to look more angry and his breathing became quicker and beads of perspiration formed on his pale upper lip.

"Won't be long now!" grunted gloomy Eric.

Martha was becoming more concerned that Eric might be right. Botolph was becoming frantic with worry. Martha sent a message to the nunnery, asking for their prayers. Botolph prayed and prayed.

The result of Martha's message was the arrival of a wain to transport Luka to the infirmary in the fort. The result of Botolph's prayers was an irrepressible feeling that God wanted him to build a chapel on the eastern hills above the bay where they had landed. The two events coincided nicely, since with Luka's translocation, Botolph was unable to spend time with him, and yet he needed to keep his mind occupied and in the service of God since he felt his efforts in this direction would lead to Luka's recovery.

Once his friend was in Eanswythe's infirmary and under the care of the nuns, Botolph was deprived of any contact. Martha tried to give him some comfort and extolled the virtues of Eanswythe's healing powers. She asked him if he had heard the story of "The Beam". On finding that he had not, she proceeded to relate it to him:

It seems that Eanswythe's father had in mind that she should marry a prince from Northumbria where her Aunt Ethelburga was married to a King. Eanswythe was only thirteen years of age at the time and regarded all men except her father as being hairy, smelly and uncouth. In this she was probably quite perceptive. No matter what her father said, she was totally resistant. Eventually, in an unguarded moment, she agreed to allow the potential suitor to visit. The lad made an appearance and was gawky and spotty, just as she had expected. By good fortune he turned up just as the cross beams were being placed on the building that was to become her nunnery. The carpenter had cut one of the beams shorter than its partner and the work had suddenly come to a standstill.

Eanswythe was called out of her father's house to greet the Northumbrian prince and his entourage and, on her way, was informed of the latest building problem

After greeting the prince, the group walked over to the site where the foreshortened beam was just being lowered back onto the ground.

"Can Northumbrian magic extend that beam so that it is the right length for my nunnery?" she asked.

The young spotty prince stumbled and stuttered.

"Well, speak up sire, can it or can't it?"

"I regret to say my Lady, that it can't".

"Well in that case, your magic will not succeed in wooing this lady either. Kindly go home and leave me to serve Christ in peace!"

The prince, somewhat affronted by so swift a rebuttal after his long journey, managed to find some vestige of spirit and said: "I shall, my lady indeed go straight home, if you can show me Cantium magic that will extend the beam as you wish."

"Huh!" said Eanswythe, reaffixing her gaze on the master-builder. "Turn the beam round and replace it with the opposite end on the uprights." This they did. To everyone's amazement it fitted and the defeated prince immediately turned and left the fort, secretly quite pleased that he did not have to marry such a formidable woman. Eanswythe's father gave up his efforts to get her married and accepted that she should instead be a bride of Christ.

Martha finished her story with a flourish and Botolph remained deep in thought for several moments. "That's *two* miracles", he said. "Perhaps she can manage a third one and bring my dear Luka back to life again."

Martha placed a hand on his shoulder. "Trust her", she said. "If anyone can do it, then Lady Eanswythe can. Just leave her and the sisters to do their work".

"I want to build a chapel on the east cliff", said Botolph. "A memorial to Luka. If he dies, I shall bury him there; if he lives, it will be a memorial of our deliverance from the sea and his deliverance from death. It will also be a shelter for others to use, should they find themselves overcome by the same fate. It will be like Old Shepherd's Croft."

"I beg your pardon" said Martha.

Botolph blushed, suddenly remembering that this woman who he seemed to have known all his life, was in fact just an acquaintance of a few whirlwind days.

"Just somewhere at home".

"Oh! Right."

Botolph set to with mixed enthusiasms.

His heart was heavy because of Luka's condition and yet he felt that building the chapel was the only positive thing that he could do for his friend that would occupy both his mind and body. He tried to push behind him the terrible thoughts of what life might be like if Luka died.

He concentrated all his energies on the daily ritual of fording the river, climbing the hill and collecting the stones from a nearby old roman villa. The transportations he did in the morning when it was still cool. In the afternoons he would concentrate on building work. When night fell he crossed back over the ford, feasted wordlessly but thankfully on the evening meal provided by Martha and then collapsed onto his pallet of straw until dawn woke him to begin the next rite.

The ruins of the Roman villa had been pointed out by Eric and it was *his* suggestion that it would be a waste not to use them. The villa was made of blocks of the local rag stone which the Telemaci troops had cut from the shoreline four hundred years previously. It was not difficult to disconnect the stones and he only had to transport them a short distance to the site he had chosen overlooking the river. He was grateful that he did not have to add quarrying and transport from the shore to his labours. He might otherwise have had to settle for a wooden building but he knew that a stone building would last longer and he wanted Luka's chapel to be durable.

Gradually, little-by-little the building progressed. He was no stone mason and had to use a wooden framework to give the structure shape and stability. He made mistakes and often had to repeat areas that collapsed. But he was patient and learned from his errors. The roof trusses were of course of wood and Eric helped him thatch them. It was only a tiny chapel, pointing towards the East, but with a doorway to the south, giving onto the bay. He placed a tiny cross on the wooden altar and then stood in the doorway and looked out to sea with a faraway gaze reliving the disaster that had brought them there.

He hoped that others who might be similarly shipwrecked in the future, maybe at night-time, maybe in the winter ... would have the strength to crawl up the hill and find shelter in Luka's chapel. He thought of his friend and wondered if his condition was changing. Was it worsening or improving or just staying the same. When would his friend be restored to him? His gaze came back into focus and fixed on the waves rolling into the shore. He looked at them for a few more minutes and then turned back into the newly-finished chapel. The work was done but the hollow feeling had returned to the pit of his stomach. He dropped to his knees in front of the little wooden cross and gave the chapel its first use in the purpose for which it was intended.

His eyes fixed on the cross, but then he closed them and imagined the *real* heavy cross being transported up the hill towards Golgotha. He imagined Jesus being forced to carry the bulky mass, somewhat like the stones that Botolph too had carried. He felt the weight of the cross that had been so much greater, - felt Jesus' exhaustion, -felt Jesus' gratitude when Simon took over the task. And then the pain of the nails, the despair, the heat of the day, the knowledge that this was one man suffering for a purpose. This was the watershed like the one between the Yar and Waif rivers; the watershed where from now onwards a man's sins would be forgiven by God, if he were truly penitent.

The emotion bubbled up through his body and the tears burst under his closed eyelids as, with his vision securely fixed on the face of Jesus on the cross, he implored that his sins be forgiven and Luka made well.

The tears poured down his cheeks and dripped off his chin wetting the rough cloth around his neck. He dabbed at it with his hand to cure the itching that had started. He reverted to his prayers and again finished with the Pater Noster and the Grace. He had done all he could. He had no idea what he could do next. He slumped back on his heels, his head on his chest in depressed submission to whatever the future brought. How long he had stayed like that, he never knew. Perhaps it was minutes or maybe hours. The slightest of sounds made him open his eyes and turn to the right. The sun was low and some of its rays were streaming through the door. Other rays were blocked by the slim upright body of a nun, standing perfectly still, her hands together as if in prayer.

Botolph could only see the silhouette but he guessed and hoped that it was Eanswythe. He stood and turned and faced her and bowed his head and waited. It was several minutes before the cool, clear voice said "Peace be with you. I bring you news."

There was no suggestion in the tone of her voice as to whether the news was good or bad. Botolph raised his head and opened his eyes and looked deeply into hers. "Your friend Luka."

"Yes?"

"He is restored!"

Botolph promptly fainted!

He awoke only a few moments later and struggled to regain his composure whilst mumbling his apologies. The trace of a smile played at the corners of her mouth.

"Sister, ... my Lady, please tell me again! Is he completely restored? When can I see him?"

She nodded and unable to contain her own joy any longer a radiant smile burst forth and dazzled Botolph even more than the sun's rays had previously done around her body. "Now!" she said, collecting the bridle of her horse which was grazing nearby. She hoisted herself effortlessly onto its back and said "Come, walk beside me and we will return to the fort and you can become reacquainted with your amusing little friend."

CHAPTER 26
Salvation.

Botolph wanted to run. With her horse's cooperation Eanswythe would have had no trouble keeping up with him. But he felt this would be both undignified and a poor reward for her efforts so he contented himself with ambling by her side and trying to make intelligent conversation. In truth, all he could think about was Luka and all that would come to his mind's eye was the picture of his friend with the ugly poultice on his head, lying lifeless on his palliasse.

He tried to imagine Luka as he would be now. Would he be weak? Would his speech be slurred? Would he be able to stand? How long would it be before they could put his illness behind them and walk and run and hunt and fight like they had in the past?

"I'm sorry!" She was asking him a question but he had not heard.

"How long have you and Luka been friends?"
"About four years now. We hated each other at first, but we just seem to get along really well together. It doesn't matter what he does; I can accept anything in Luka that others might find tiresome. He saved my life!"

"Really? He does not seem big enough to save a strong lad like you. When was that then?"

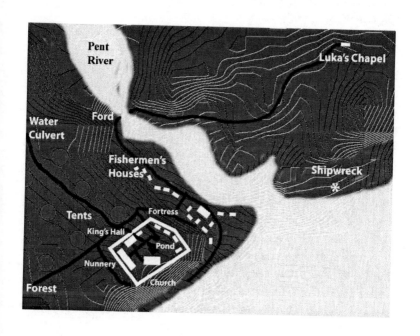

Fig. 6. Map of Botolph's Folcanstane.

"When we were shipwrecked. I suppose it must be a month ago now, although it seems like a lifetime."

They had reached the ford and were wading through it. They both stayed silent for a while as they picked their passage carefully through the quickly-flowing water and then turned back along the river bank towards the south.

"What happened?"

"We had sailed hundreds of miles safely but then there was a storm with enormous waves. Our boat capsized and I was underneath and trapped by a rope. I was convinced that all was lost and I was just in the process of commending my spirit into the Lord's hands when Luka appeared like magic, cut the rope and hauled me to the surface."

Eanswythe laughed but with a serious look on her face. She could just imagine the sturdy little dwarf having total disregard for his own life but being absolutely certain that he was not going to allow Botolph to die.

"You see" she said, with great prescience, "God will decide when we are going to die and when He is ready for our company. Clearly He has great things in mind for you to do here on earth and I have no doubt that He wanted you to start at Folcanstane!"

They had climbed the hill and were about to enter the grounds of the fortress. They waited while a cart rumbled out through the gates which they then passed through and the guards slammed shut behind them. They continued up the slope to the flatter ground where Eanswythe slid down from her mount which was taken to the stableyard by a young lackey.

"Come!" said Eanswythe as she strode purposefully past the little church to their left. "My heavenly Father's house is to your left and is dedicated to the glorious Saints Peter and Paul." She smiled impishly. "My earthly father's house is to your right! In the normal way I would have been bound to have taken you first into my father's presence but he is out hunting and whenever he is away the fortress becomes mine! The infirmary is over there next to my nunnery, so let's reunite you with Luka."

They passed through the doorway of the low building and found Luka propped comfortably on a low bed. Botolph knelt down by the side of him. He was shocked at his friend's appearance but Luka offered a weak smile and said quietly "Oh, you've found time to come and see me then! They tell me you've turned into a builder in my absence!"

Botolph laughed with the relief of finding that Luka's caustic humour was still in good health. He felt sure that it would not be too long before the rest of his body followed suit. Eanswythe was standing and watching the interchange; she had a benign smile on her face and now said "Well, I will leave you two gentlemen to catch up on the latest news. I have work to do!" She turned to go but stopped as Luka said "Sister!"

"Yes?"

"Thank you."

"Just you concentrate on getting well, Luka."

Botolph and Luka were alone in the infirmary and spent the next hour exchanging stories of recent events, although, by necessity since he had been unconscious for so long, Luka's stories were rather less numerous than Botolph's. The invalid soon began to tire and Botolph helped him to drink a little water ... but then his head suddenly dropped. Panic engulfed Botolph who thought that his friend had died at last! He shook him back to wakefulness and then regretted disturbing him as he realised his mistake. Once confident that it was merely Luka's weak state that made him sleep so much, he made him comfortable and let him slumber on.

For nearly an hour he sat there, watching his measured steady breathing. Memories of their times together came flooding back and fondness seemed to first envelope his stomach and then move upwards to pervade his heart. One of the nuns came in and busied herself around the room so that Botolph felt he was intruding and that he should seek the fresh air again.

He stood in the doorway contemplating the fort. He supposed he was at liberty just to wander around, no doubt he would be told if he overstepped a threshold. He walked past the nunnery towards the church and entered through the western doorway and gazed down the nave.

It was a simple but graceful building. The slits that served for windows were glazed with a primitive glass and the shafts of light they admitted were to Botolph like the shafts of hope that were re-entering his life now that Luka was recovering. He walked up to the altar rail where he crossed himself and then knelt and closed his eyes in prayer.

He asked for God's guidance as to what he should do next. He had already bargained with God in his prayers for Luka's life that, if spared he was, Botolph would devote his own life to the service of God. It looked as if the time was coming when God would call in this debt.

What *should* he do next? Where was his life leading to? He was nearly eighteen and by that age he could elect to become a novice monk. Should he do that? Was that his life's destiny? And yet a monk was expected to stay within his monastery's walls whereas in Botolph's soul there had developed a great joy for travelling and meeting people. There *were* monks who travelled though. The Abbots Augustine and Justus had travelled all the way from Italy for the express purpose of founding the religious life in England. Father Fursey had spent many years in Ireland before travelling to Cnobersburg and since his escape from Penda he was probably still travelling somewhere.

Botolph allowed his thoughts to drift off as he knelt at the altar rail of Saint Peter and Saint Paul's church within the confines of the Folcanstane fortress. Father Fursey was a kind and lively man. He exuded the presence of God and yet he was also of the world. He understood the problems that faced the common man and he could communicate with all without giving the appearance of being too pious. Yet he was also very holy. There were many stories of his having performed quite amazing miracles, so surely God must look down upon him with favour, in spite of his travelling and worldliness?

Botolph admired Father Fursey and enjoyed his company but even at the age of seventeen, he wanted to be his own man, not a second Father Fursey. His thoughts stopped rambling and came back into God's presence. "So what *should* I do, Father?" he repeated.

No answer came, so he finished with his usual Pater Noster and Grace and then stood and made his obeisance to Jesus represented by the cross and turned to take his leave.

The aisle in front of the western doorway was blocked by the burly frame of an impressive personage. "Well young man, and who might you be?" it said.

"If it please your lordship, my name is Botolph and I am a guest of Sister Eanswythe" he ventured.

"Oh, are you now? Botolph eh? So you are the young man who has been building chapels on my land without my permission?" The church echoed its support as the fearsome voice issued the accusation and the glowering eyes looked down at him.

Botolph's eyes opened wide. So this was King Eadbald, Eanswythe's father, the fount from whom all authority flowed. Botolph gulped. "I'm sorry sir, I thought it was common land."

There was a prolonged silence as the monarch studied him and Botolph offered just one short prayer which said "Help!"

Wrinkles suddenly developed at the corners of the king's eyes and he said softly "Common land? So it is, so it is... *but it's MY common land!*" This final blast of fury made Botolph jump back in alarm but the king moved forwards and said more kindly: "A nice little chapel. You did well, it should stand for quite a few years before our south-west gales blow it down. Until then it will serve to welcome any more waifs and strays who get washed onto our coasts in the middle of the night!"

Botolph was still not sure where he stood in the opinion of this king who blew hot one minute and icy cold the next.

"Your sick friend's name is Luka, I recall. How's he doing?"

"Well, thank you sire. His mind is restored and I believe that it is just a matter of time before his body will be restored also. He is small, but he has also always been very strong. He saved my life!"

"Did he now? Well that says a lot for him. Let's hope he continues to make good progress. And what are you proposing to do then? I could do with two strong young heroes for my army!"

Botolph's spirits dropped again. How was he going to get out of this? Is this the payment that he would have to guarantee to the king for his assistance in restoring Luka's life? He had never felt the calling to become a soldier, although he guessed that the idea might quite appeal to Luka. As the king watched his consternation a smile played at the corner of his lips and he moved forwards again and placed his hands on Botolph's shoulder.

"Never fear, young man." he said. "I perceive you are built for service in the army of a higher king than I. I am honoured to have you and your little friend here. Pray for me now and when you become a monk of renown!" God's answer to Botolph's question had come through most unlikely lips!

"Stay as long as you like, you are most welcome!" and the king turned and strode out of the open door. Botolph was about to follow but remembered that, even with God, good manners are important and he turned back to the altar and gave his thanks.

CHAPTER 27
The King's Family.

Luka made steady progress and was soon able to join Botolph living with Eric and Martha. Eric was particularly pleased to welcome a lad who had cheated death in a way that he had not thought possible. Both boys had free access to the fort and during Luka's recuperation they often spent time there, meeting soldiers with whom they had made friends; occasionally meeting King Eadbald and Queen Ymme, and often spending time with their daughter Eanswythe.

She was a bride of Christ and yet she and Botolph became like brother and sister. They spent hours together discussing holy scriptures. Botolph told her that he intended to become a monk and she hoped that he might become chaplain to her nunnery. They discussed their hopes and fears and their families and friends.

Eanswythe started to tell him how her father had wanted her to marry the Northumbrian prince but Botolph interrupted her and told her that he had already heard the story. She giggled and said that she was sure that it was God's will that she should become a nun rather than marry a foreigner. Botolph asked her about the beam. She replied that the miracle that God kindly worked on her behalf settled the matter of marriage once and for all. Botolph pointed out that he had never actually worked a miracle himself. How did she do it and what did it feel like?

Eanswythe replied that it was easy. She was absolutely convinced that it was going to work and she was not in the slightest bit surprised when it did. She felt no sense of a triumphant victory over the poor spotty Northumbrian prince, just a mild satisfaction in receiving the confirmation that she was doing God's will. Botolph considered her replies and could tell by the sincerity in her demeanour that all she said was true. He wondered if he would ever work any miracles, but he was beginning to see that if he did, it would really be God working the miracles through him.

Eanswythe told him that her Aunt Ethelburga had married a Northumbrian king called Edwin and that was how the introduction to "Spotty Face" occurred. Uncle Edwin had died in battle some years earlier. In fact, to Botolph's surprise, he found that Edwin was one of Penda's first victims.

"You will probably meet Aunt Ethelburga and her daughter, my cousin Eanfled" said Eanswythe. "After Uncle Edwin was killed they managed to escape to Cantium, much like you have done. My father gave them sanctuary here. I had just founded my nunnery, I was only fifteen then. Aunt Ethelburga was impressed with it and happened to say that she herself would really like to do the same thing. Father overheard this and agreed to give her some land in a village called Liminge, a few miles to the west of us here. Auntie decided that, rather than a nunnery, she would found a mixed monastery housing both monks and nuns and we believe this is the first in the country. Everything starts here in Cantium. We were the first to receive Christianity and now we are leading the way with religious institutions.

Granddad Ethelbert was a staunch Christian but Daddy was not too keen on it to start with. In fact when Granddad died, Daddy at first steadfastly refused to become Christian. Once he converted however there was no stopping him and Aunt Ethelburga was only allowed to marry Uncle Edwin on the understanding that he would allow her to continue to practise her faith and that he would convert to Christianity too. He was as good as his word, so you can see that we have been doing our share in spreading the word of God from Cantium!"

Botolph was very heartened by all this which made the prospect of his becoming a monk even more exciting. He was beginning to formulate a plan for his future. Once Luka was strong enough, he would like to take him to visit his parents back at the Bloomery. After that, he felt that his next move should be to go back to Abbot Augustine's monastery at Cantwarebury and recommence his studies there. These ideas had been going around in his head for some days now. He would also like to travel further and meet more people, gather different ideas, see more monasteries and even, he was now beginning to think, maybe start a monastery of his own one day.

He asked Eanswythe if she thought her Aunt Ethelburga might allow him to visit her monastery at Liminge.

"She would be delighted, I know she would," said Eanswythe "but I am sure you will be able to ask her yourself. She often comes to visit. Leave it to me and I will see if I can arrange something."

Luka continued to make good progress and Botolph realised that he would have to run these ideas past him to see if they fitted in with any plans that he might have. Botolph broached the subject one day when they were sitting on the banks of the Pent River, dangling their feet in the cool water. Botolph knew that Luka came from noble stock and he wondered if he too had plans of revisiting his parents.

"To tell you the truth" Luka said, "I was never really happy at home. Because of my smallness I was always picked on which made me cross so I became aggressive which made me unpopular both with my parents and my brothers and sisters. I was really rather glad to get away and although I hated Cnobersburg when I first arrived, I came to love it and found the greatest peace and fun that I have ever had. And you!" he blushed and faltered a little "I am a bit embarrassed to say this, but you have become the best friend I have ever had! There, I've said it now! You mean more to me than all my brothers or family. We have been through some exciting and breathtaking times. I really enjoy your company and I admire immensely your book-learning and your wisdom and your holiness!"

"Holiness?" Botolph exclaimed.

"Yes, holiness" Luka repeated. "That is the only word for it. I find that you always see the best in people, even when there is a lot of bad to see, you always make the most of things even when they are not going our way. Your trust in God seems infinite, you have great faith that everything that happens is God's will and you do your best to help in that cause. You are always happy, never miserable, you never want to upset or harm anyone or anything be it man or creature! You are more like Jesus than Christ himself! You amaze me and I admire you immensely, but I must admit I have no desire to copy you!"

"How do you mean?" said Botolph, a little dumbfounded at this outburst from the usually-reticent Luka.

"Well, now this is where I have learnt from you. You have somehow shown me how to analyse myself honestly and see the bad and the good in me, the things that I can change and those things that there is no hope of my changing. I am basically a fairly evil sort but I do my best to overcome it. I am intolerant. I neither like to be fussed over nor to have to fuss about other people. I like things plain and simple. I enjoy a good scrap and I am only sorry that we didn't get to grips with more Pendasmen before we left Waif Island. It would have given me the greatest satisfaction in the world to send them off to their Maker. So you see I am not holy like you. I believe in God and I do what I can to serve him. I try to be like Christ, but I fail miserably ... both in my heart, because there are many less-than-holy things I would like to do, and in my actions, because there are many good things which I fail to do. So there we have it. That's me!"

"So who is the best Christian?" asked Botolph. "The person who possesses the sort of character which makes him find it easy to do, what you would call, holy things, or the person whose inner nature has a tendency towards evil and who spends his life constantly fighting his natural instincts?"

"Well the former of course" replied Luka.

"I am not so sure you are right" said Botolph. "If it is easy, I doubt that there is much virtue in it but still, I am sure this discussion is for philosophers greater than us!"

The final outcome of this talk by the Pent River, was that Luka had no desire to revisit his family home. Botolph wondered if Luka was making the right decision, but felt that he could not question it.   Like Botolph, Luka wanted to travel and to see and experience different peoples and places.   He wanted to travel alongside the friend whose company he enjoyed.   He felt some responsibility for him, knowing that Botolph would never choose to fight but would always take the peaceful way out and Luka wanted to protect him in situations where the peaceful way out might end up with a dead Botolph.

So as far as he could see into the future, Luka said, he was happy with Botolph making the decisions as to which path they travelled and he would fall in with Botolph's plans and give him all the support he could.   If there came a point in the future when he became unhappy about the way things were going, Botolph could be assured that he would voice his opinions immediately, and he offered his hands on it.

Botolph took his hands gladly and they clasped each other, glad that the air had been cleared and that they could see their future stretching ahead of them.   And an exciting future it was going to be.

The effect of Eanswythe's "seeing what she could arrange" resulted in a banquet being organised for the two boys in anticipation of their departure for the Bloomery.

Eanswythe had told her parents of the discussion with Botolph and appraised them further of his character and aspirations.   From their first meeting King Eadbald had taken a liking to the lad and he was pleased about the friendship he had formed with his daughter.

The banquet was held in the king's hall within the fortress and Botolph was given the opportunity to invite those friends he wished to be there.   Botolph chose Eric and Martha and well-pleased they were to dine with royalty.   All the king's family were there including Auntie

Ethelburga and Cousin Eanfled, together with Ethelburga's brothers Eormenred and Eorcenberht.

Eanfled was a sweet dark-haired little girl aged about eight and Botolph had the opportunity to ask her mother about the monastery at Liminge. Ethelburga was a soft and attractive lady in her late twenties and she was only too pleased to talk about her project which had clearly become the focus of her life since the death of her husband.

Botolph remarked upon the monastery's name. Ethelburga said that the hamlet's name came from the fact that the tribe that lived there had come originally from the region of the Limen River which itself ran past the Roman fortress at Portus Limanis to which it also gave its name. The monastery itself, she said, was on the side of a hill overlooking the hamlet but protected by the slope from the worst of the southwest winds. In a valley at its bottom was a sweet-water spring which was the source of the Naylebourn River which ran up towards Cantwarebury. She invited the boys to come and visit for a few days and Botolph replied that they would like to do so and would include it on their route from the Bloomery to Cantwarebury.

All too soon, the evening was over. Botolph felt that they had made some good new friends and they took their leave of the family knowing that it would probably be many months before they met again. As Botolph and Luka took the path that descended towards the fort's gate, the stars were shining brightly and Botolph continued to study them as they made their way down the hill towards the cluster of huts. This was a sad night for Eric and Martha because they knew their young friends would be leaving the following morning on their journey to the west

Martha in particular had enjoyed the liveliness of Botolph's company and she was quite tearful on retiring.

* * *

The following morning, in spite of the late night and the quantity of food they had consumed, they were up before dawn and on their way at first light. They gladly took the parcels of food that Martha had prepared for them and Botolph thanked his hosts profusely for the hospitality they had shown him. Not wishing to prolong the sadness of departure, they took the first opportunity of a gap in the conversation and struck out along the Pent River, turning to wave as they climbed up towards the fort and waving again just before they were lost to sight behind the fortress stockade.

They walked up between the soldiers' tents and then followed the path that led through the oak trees and which, they knew, led to Portus Limanis about which they had been speaking the previous evening.

It was three hours later before they found the stone castle that the Romans had abandoned more than two hundred years previously. Much of it was still standing and there were a few habitations nearby but nothing compared to the bustling port it was reputed to have been in its heyday. The harbour, which could have held a dozen ships, was still wide but they could see it had silted up and at low water was just a mass of mud washed down from the hills.

The river too was a bit of a disappointment, only being a narrow tidal creek filled twice daily by the sea. A narrow fresh-water tributary flowed along the base of the Downes Hills and filtered into the salty creek right by the fort itself. They had broken their fast with Martha and Eric but the boys were hungry after their march and so sat on the river bank and explored and sampled the delights that Martha had packed for them.

A young boy of seven or eight years, wielding a long staff, came up to them as they ate. "Got some fer me?" he said.

"No!" said Luka. "Yes!" said Botolph and shared some bread and cheese with him. Luka caught Botolph's eye and scowled. Botolph could not resist a smirk, which immediately made Luka's scowl disappear and then they both burst into hysterical laughter to the consternation of the youngster. When they had finally wiped the tears from their eyes, the boy asked "What was that all about?"

"You wouldn't understand," said Luka.

"Try me" said the boy.

"Well, put it this way" said Luka "He's a holy man and I am always unsuccessfully trying to make him see sense and live practically. We hardly have enough food for ourselves. We have a long way to go, and here he is giving it away!"

"Well" said the boy, "One good turn deserves another. My dad's the ferryman here and if you want to cross I'll take you over for free. How's that?"

"Wonderful!" said Botolph, "That would be very kind and gratefully accepted. What's your name young 'un?"

"Hansa. What's yours?"

"Botolph ... and Luka!"

The boy was as good as his word and took them one by one in his fragile boat which he poled across the wide, fast-flowing, shallow, muddy stream. They reached the other side both grateful and dry and prepared to set off along the river bank.

"Where are you bound?" asked Hansa.

"To the iron bloomeries of the South Saxons."

"Never heard of them!"

"No, they are a long way hence. We just need to cross the marsh and then get up onto some high ground and I will know my way as soon as I cross a track I have taken before."

"Well, there's only one way to go anyway, so you can't get lost unless you leave the path and I certainly wouldn't recommend that. Just follow the Lower Wall, that's this path here, and keep straight on turning neither left nor right. It'll only take you four or five hours to get to Apuldre. Unless the ferryman's there, you're going to get your feet wet but its shallow to cross. If he *is* there though, you can take your choice whether to go across to Ox Island or back over the Liman again to the path that leads up to Tenetwaraden. Anyone'll give you further directions."

An hour later they were well out into the Marshes of Rumniae with several miles behind them and many more in front. Hansa had been right, -there was no way that they could take any short cuts and had to hold directly to the path or the boggy mess to left and right would swallow them up for sure.

CHAPTER 28
The Marsh

The Marsh was certainly a desolate place. Since they crossed the Liman there were no villages, just flat, flat land and dykes and bulrushes. The land had clearly been cultivated once upon a time and the rectangular remains of saltpans were occasionally visible. Every so often they came across areas that were still under cultivation but they saw no signs of farmers actually working the land. At one point however they saw a wain coming towards them, pulled by a shaggy pony. When it drew level the driver reined the animal to a stop and decided he was going to pass the time of day with them.

"Where are you two from then?" he asked cordially. He was a rosy-faced individual, his skin gnarled from many years of facing the wind and the sun.

"We've come from the fort at Folcanstane and are heading west." said Botolph. "How about you?"

"Well, there's a funny thing. I'm heading to the fort at Folcanstane myself. I've some produce here in my cart for the king's cook."

"Would that be Uffa?" asked Luka.

"Well God bless you now, so it would. Do you know him then?"

"He's a great friend of mine. I was very ill for several weeks and Sister Eanswythe and her nuns looked after me and brought me back to life again. It was Uffa whose broths and remedies served to give me back the strength I needed, so I owe a lot to him!"

"Well, see here now. I have all sorts of vegetables for Uffa's kitchen, and some meat too. There's some mutton and some beef and a couple of sacks of freshly ground flour for his baking. I also have some fruit. Here, have an apple!" He tossed a couple of apples to the boys and then clamped the wedge on the cart wheel to stop it turning and jumped down to join them. "Come, it's lunchtime. My wife has packed enough to feed half a dozen. Look, there's a flagon of mead too that we can share. Find yourselves a comfortable dry patch by that dyke and we'll have a banquet!"

While they ate they discovered that he was known by the name of Farmer Mosel and that he and his wife and family lived in Apuldre which was about another ten miles further to the west.

"It's going to be late afternoon before you get there. Why don't you stay the night with us? It's a pity I didn't meet you on the way back or I could have saved your feet, but it won't take me long to make my deliveries. I shall be home well before nightfall and you can bide your time in Apuldre and move on when you are ready. The clouds are building up and I think we are in for a spot of bad weather, so you certainly don't want to be heading to the west in driving rain, particularly if your friend here has only just returned from being at death's door. No! It's decided! You're staying with us, I won't hear a word said against it!"

Botolph and Luka could not help but laugh at the farmer's single-mindedness and they surrendered to his decision. Having reorganised their lives, he brought his "banquet" to an abrupt end and said that, in view of the

217

changed circumstances, he would need to be on his way. He swept everything up into the rough blanket on which they had been sitting and dumped it in the back of the cart.

"Now," he said, pointing in the direction from which he had come. "Now, you can't miss our farm. You just keep walking straight along this track. At one point it curves around to your right and there is a crossing but you just keep on going straight over. Soon after that you'll find yourselves climbing up onto the Rhee Wall and an hour or so later you'll find yourselves on a causeway which dips down into a shallow ford. You just go through that and bear around towards your left and you'll find the little habitation of Apuldre right in front of you. There are only a few dwellings there but Mosel Farm is the first that you will come across and it's on the right hand side of the road. You just sing out for Mistress Mosel and out she'll pop and you'll be able to tell her your story about meeting me and the fact that you will be staying the night and perhaps a few days afterwards."

Botolph opened his mouth to protest, because he really felt that they should be getting on their way, but Farmer Mosel waved his potential protest to one side, saying "Yes, yes, I know, you youngsters are always in so much hurry. We'll see, take it easy, one step at a time. See you later, God be wi'ye!" and in one fluid movement he swung himself up into the driving seat, knocked out the wedge and shook the reigns so that the willing little pony was off to Folcanstane in a trice.

"How's he going to get that cart to the other side of the river?" asked Luka.

"I've no idea! There must be a bridge or a ford. We can ask him later tonight. C'mon, those clouds are darkening and getting lower.   We will be lucky if we get to Mosel Farm in the dry."

They pressed on, although one of Botolph's feet was getting rather sore where it was rubbing on his leather sandal.   He stopped and picked some grass and stuffed it down inside to give some protection.   They found the Rhee Wall and turned to the right.   The wind was picking up and the clouds were scudding across the sky but at least the rain was holding off.

In due course they found Mosel Farm and called as the farmer had bidden them.   Sure enough, out popped a buxom happy woman with red cheeks that matched her husband's.

"Come in, come in," she said.   "It started off such a lovely day, but we are going to have a downpour soon." No sooner were the words out of her mouth than great gobs of water started hitting the thatch of the roof and Botolph gave one of his instinctive shivers at the thought of how narrowly they had missed getting a dowsing.

Mistress Mosel bade them take off their outer garments and settle themselves down and make themselves comfortable.   Two rosy-cheeked children, one girl aged about seven and a boy, a year or so older, were playing in one corner of the barn-sized dwelling.   Their mother asked the name of her two guests and then brought the children across to be introduced properly.   They were rather shy and after the introductions were very happy to return to their game.

"It will soon be time for them to go to bed, but I will keep them up until Farmer Mosel gets home.   He will then be able to say goodnight to them properly.   In fact I am surprised he is not back by now.   If you reckon you were about halfway across the marsh when you met him, that would have given him plenty of time to get to Folcanstane and back. You would have crossed the Liman at half ebb but he always times his journey so that he crosses an hour or so before low water and then he is able to return an hour or so after the tide has begun to rise."

"How does he cross?" asked Luka. "We didn't see a boat big enough to take a horse and cart!"

"Lor' bless you no! The horse is used to fording that river at low water. The bottom is quite hard if you know where to go and Farmer Mosel could do it with his eyes shut! I am still beginning to get worried though. He should really have got back soon after you arrived but a couple of hours have passed now and it will not be long before it starts to get dark. The Marsh is not the place to be out on in the dark, particularly on a night like this."

"We will go and look for him!" Botolph suddenly said.

"What?" said Luka."In this? Are you mad?"

"Yes, he's right" said Mistress Mosel. "I am worried about my husband but you don't know the Marsh and even if you did, it's not safe for anyone to be out there on a night like this. Anyway, if he has had an accident or something, it could have happened anywhere between Folcanstane and Apuldre, you wouldn't know where to start looking. I am afraid that we are just going to have to wait and hope that he arrives home soon. Otherwise we shall have to gather our neighbours together to make a search in the morning.

"The tide is rising, you said so yourself." said Botolph who had a strange sense of urgency hovering round in his brain. "Tomorrow morning may be too late. I have a feeling that he is not far away and that we need to go now and that we shall find him.   Come on Luka, let's get going."

"You don't know the Marsh," wailed their hostess.

"I know the part we walked over today" said Botolph "and that is good enough for me.   God will guide us, you will see."

He sounded so convincing that she gave up her protests and instead turned and gave them two blankets to wrap around them to keep out the worst of the rain.   She then found two stout poles and urged them to walk with those testing the ground in front of every step once they left the Rhee Wall.

The boys set off and as soon as they rounded the corner of the dwelling they were hit by the full force of the wind that nearly tore Mistress Mosel's blankets from their backs.   Botolph led the way and Luka followed, clutching his blanket together under his chin and keeping his head down.

The gale was from the south west and as they crossed the ford the wind was pushing across them from right to left; the water was noticeably deeper, colder and more choppy than a few hours previously.   As they scrambled out of the water, they climbed up the causeway onto the Rhee Wall which left them totally exposed to the gale.   Fortunately there was a full moon but most of the time it was obscured by the clouds.   They were racing across the sky so quickly however that every so often the moon would appear and cast its welcome light and then vanish again.

As he marched forwards Botolph was having his own private conversation with God, asking for guidance towards what he knew for certain was the stricken farmer. He felt something he had never experienced in his life before, the absolute certainty that he was on a God-ordained rescue mission. It was weird. It was illogical. He could not discuss it with Luka who already thought him mad, but fortunately, whatever his feelings were, he knew that Luka would follow him into the jaws of death if necessary. And without God's help, he thought ruefully, the jaws of death might well be where they would end up. He glanced behind. Luka was still there and gave him a grim nod. He looked forwards again. They were just coming to where the path across the marsh peeled off from the Rhee Wall.

Down they went, slithering along the pathway. Botolph skidded and nearly went over but collected himself. He checked to make sure that Luka was still alright. Luka, with his low centre of gravity was having less trouble. Soon they were on flat ground again and they slowed their pace, prodding ahead with their poles. The moon flashed and Botolph saw the path ahead and consigned the picture to his memory. He increased his speed again.

Luka was following Botolph's black shadow. He wanted to shout to Botolph and tell him that this was a really stupid idea and how about giving up and going back to the farm. But he knew that his words would be in vain and would simply waste time. The outcome would be the same, they would press on, so he might as well save his breath and keep up this plodding march after his friend. One thing was certain and that was that he was glad he was not out here on the marsh on his own!

They had been in the driving rain for nearly an hour. Fortunately the pathway was comparatively straight and every time the moon came from behind a cloud Botolph made a mental note of the terrain ahead and was able to press on quickly without too much fear of falling into a dyke. Knowing his friend so well, he was acutely aware of how he would be feeling and he half turned and shouted "Not far now ..." but his words seemed to be blown away in the wind and he doubted that Luka had heard him.

The problem was that all their senses were under assault from the storm. The noise was phenomenal and the howling of the wind rose to a crescendo and then fell and rose again and again. Botolph's sight was riveted on the glimpses of the pathway ahead and Luka's sight was riveted on Botolph. They were both aware of the firmness or otherwise of the ground upon which they walked; all of it was slushy but they were intensely alert to any change that might indicate they were heading into danger. Luka would rather that they walked more slowly but Botolph was striding along at, what seemed to Luka, a reckless pace.

What Luka did not realise was that a 'sixth sense' was driving Botolph along in a state of urgency. He knew that there was not a moment to lose and that time was running out, but what he did not know was 'why'!

Suddenly he stopped and Luka promptly walked into him and they both nearly fell. "What was that?" said Botolph.

"What?"

"A noise, I heard a noise."

"Noise? I can hear nothing *but* noise" grumbled Luka.

"Over there, I'm sure I saw something. Oh please God, give us some moonlight!"

God did better than that, there was suddenly a simultaneous flash of fork lightning and an almighty clap of thunder. Luka let forth an expletive that he saved for

223

special occasions.   Fortunately Botolph did not hear it because by then he was already running towards two shapes, one of which was moving and one which was not.

By the time the next flash of lightning came, they had reached their quarry and saw that both objects were in the dyke, the one that was moving was a pony up to its stomach in water.   Behind it was the non-moving object, and that proved to be an upside-down cart.   The pony was trapped partly by mud and partly by virtue of its still being hitched to its cargo.   The boys worked quickly and as a team, in the way that Caelin had taught them at Burgh Castle.   Botolph held the pony's bridle while Luka's razor-sharp seaxe sliced through the leather traces.   The horse needed little encouragement; one tug from Botolph and, with violent movements of mud and water, the animal was on the bank.

Botolph had at first wondered if it was Mosel's cart they had found or if by some coincidence they had chanced across another unfortunate traveller.   By now however, he had recognised both the cart and the horse and so his concern was for Mosel.   Was he in the water?   Was he under the cart?   Had he been thrown out further back along the track.

They called his name but no reply reached their ears.

A third flash of lightning.   Its thunder was less dramatic than previously and Botolph hoped this meant that the storm had passed its worst.   During the flash he noticed that the upturned wagon had only one wheel.   He signalled to Luka to look round the far side of the cart while he used his staff to prod into the mud on the side nearest him, all the time calling Mosel's name.   They were both working halfway down the dyke bank and Botolph was acutely aware that if one of them slid in, the situation would be even more grim.

Luka's strangulated voice came from the far side of the cart and Botolph's immediate instinct was that his worst fears had been realised and Luka was in dire trouble. Quickly but carefully, with the aid of his staff, he climbed back up the bank a little way and across the shafts to the other side.

"Luka! Where are you?"

"Over here."

"Where? I can't see you."

"Down by the edge of the cart at water level. I've got Mosel. He's still alive but his body is trapped under the cart. We will have to lift the cart off him."

"Is he conscious? Can he talk?"

"Yes, he's alright but he says that either he and the cart are sinking or the water is rising because his head is now only just above the water. In fact I am having to hold his head up all the time now. I think the rains must be making the water rise quite quickly, so it's all up to you old son. Just get this cart off him would you?"

Botolph realised that this conversation had passed quite easily. The wind was dropping and he could see that the lightning was now flashing well over to the east and he guessed that Eanswythe would be suffering it now. The benefit of the lightning had now been lost but the clouds were thinning and the glorious moon was back as a welcome ally.

Botolph still could not see Luka as he was in shadow. He put his shoulder under the left shaft and heaved but all that happened was that his feet sank deeper into the mud. The cart was really heavy.

"Hurry up" came Luka's voice.

Fig. 7. Crossing the Marsh
and the journey to Ox Island.

Botolph looked around wildly. He wondered if he should climb onto the cart but reckoned his weight would make the situation worse. He saw the rope lashings that Mosel had used to keep his produce from bouncing out as he travelled. He went back to Luka's side. "Give me your seaxe."

"What?"

"Your seaxe! Pass it up to me."

A hand bearing the sharp blade rose from the murk and Botolph gingerly retrieved it. The horse was grazing on the bank. Botolph went and examined what there was left of the leather traces. He tied some together and then returned to the cart and salvaged what items of cordage he could from that. None of them looked very strong but there was nothing else available. He tied them all together and attached one end round the axle where the one good wheel of the cart remained.

He coaxed the horse as close as possible to the back and then, using a sailor's knot, attached the other end of his lash-up to the severed traces.

"Are you ready?" he called to Luka.

"Yes, yes yes, hurry up for God's sake!"

Botolph returned to the horse's head and pulled at the harness making encouraging noises. The animal responded willingly enough but the cart did not move one inch. Botolph realised that desperate problems need desperate measures and Mosel was only going to be given one chance. He left the horses head and returned to its rear where he gave it as hard a slap on its hind quarters as he could manage whilst emitting a blood-curdling war cry.

The startled horse's nerves were already somewhat frayed and at this further sudden indignity it leapt forwards and the side of the cart rose into the air, only for the lashings to break and for the heavy machinery to come crashing back down again.

"Oh God no!" thought Botolph "I've killed them both! ... Luka! ... Luka!" He splashed down into the muddy water.

"It's alright, it's alright" said Luka, "it worked, we are both clear and the cart slid away from us. Just help me get poor old Farmer Mosel to the bank!"

CHAPTER 29
Apuldre

After much pulling and skidding and struggling, the three of them found themselves on the firm pathway again. All of them were soaking wet and covered with mud. Farmer Mosel was conscious and able to communicate but, not unsurprisingly, seemed disinclined to do so. Botolph and Luka were in reasonably good condition although Luka seemed to be the better of the two.

"What's next O Holy Man?" he quipped.

The humour was lost on Botolph who was thinking as practically as his fatigued brain would let him.

"Our first need is to get Mosel home as soon as we can. Thank the Lord the wind and the rain have stopped and we have good moonlight but from the height of the moon the time is halfway between midnight and dawn."

"Where's the horse?" said Luka.

They spun round looking at where the horse had last been seen but there was no sign of it.

"Wonderful!" said Luka "It's had enough and has gone home. Blessed animals; just when we need him too."

"To be fair" said Botolph "*he* has had a bad night too and if he had not given us that burst of energy our efforts would have been totally wasted. There's nothing for it, we are going to have to carry Mosel. We will either have to find something to make a stretcher or else it will have to be me giving him a piggy back."

"What?" said Luka. "We must be at least six miles away from the farm, you are never going to manage to carry him all that way!"

"Well I have to try!" said Botolph and turned towards the farmer who was sitting, huddled on the bank. The farmer managed to make one last contribution to his rescue and he suddenly tilted his head back and emitted a piercing whistle.

"Christ Almighty, what was that for?" said Luka. "My nerves are shattered enough as it is. I could do without any more noises."

"Well how would the noise of galloping hooves suit you?" said Botolph as the horse appeared out of the gloom.

Botolph could now see his way clear and his mind swung into leadership mode again as, with Luka's help, he hauled Mosel up onto the horse's back. He then retrieved what bits of lashing he could find and used them to tie the farmer's uncooperative body onto the steed.

"Right, up you go!" he said once he was finished.

"What? Why me?"

"Well, for one thing you are a better horseman than me and for another, you are lighter than me. You will be able to get this nag back to the farm in the quickest possible time and I will be able to walk back at my own pace without feeling that if I slow down I will be putting Mosel's life in more jeopardy."

Luka saw the sense of this and allowed Botolph to help him onto the horse in front of the flagging Mosel. Botolph tied more lashings around the two of them.

"There we are! Now both of you will fall off or neither of you will, so I trust you to make sure it's not the latter my friend.   It's all down to you now, so God's speed - GO!"

Botolph gave the horse's rump its second slap of the night as Luka dug his heels in and off they went into the darkness at a brisk trot, the beast seeming to realise the urgency of the situation and doing its best in spite of the heavy load.

Botolph stared into the darkness until the sound of the hooves had disappeared and then looked around him. The moonlight illuminated the upturned cart but little of it was showing above the dyke water now.   The sides of the dyke were scarred by ruts and skidmarks made by the limbs of both man and beast.   He looked across the marsh towards Denge Ness where the horizon was full of shadows.   He looked up into the now cloudless sky with a myriad of stars twinkling their blessings down on him.

"Yes." he thought, "their *blessings!*" and he felt the soggy earth once again as he knelt and gave thanks.

He did not rush his prayers; he was in no state to rush anything at that moment.   He prayed with his eyes open for a change, and he could see and feel the beauty of the marsh as it enfolded him.   The marsh was not his enemy, it was his friend.   It was not the marsh's fault that the wheel had come off the cart.   It was not the marsh's fault that old Mosel had been catapulted out into the gums of the dyke's mouth.   Botolph felt not only the beauty of the marsh as it enfolded him, but he also thought that perhaps the marsh might be grateful for the removal of its involuntary assailant.

Later, Botolph often said that he felt that it was at that point, on his knees in the middle of the night, soaked to the skin and covered in mud like the marsh itself, that he suddenly became at one with the setting.   He felt welcomed into its territory. He no longer saw the desolate place that he initially perceived, but relished his presence in a very special part of mother earth which would nurture him with her life-milk and protect him for as long as he needed her.

He finished his prayers in the usual way and then crossed himself and stood. He found his staff and turned to follow his long-gone friends. He was tired. He was perhaps even exhausted. But he was also filled with a kind of strange euphoria as he concentrated on placing one foot in front of the other at the start of his long painful trek back.

An hour passed, and then another. Botolph had no perception of whether he was awake or asleep. All he knew was that he had to keep going as he kept up the automatic rhythm. He sensed a noise but he did not hear it, and then another noise, but again it did not register in his brain. He must keep going. One foot. Next foot. One foot. Next foot. Something roughly shook his shoulder and the noise was repeated. He looked up through glazed eyes and at the other side of the foggy haze sensed the face of Luka looking down at him. He knew no more until two days later when the same glazed eyes revealed the rosy-cheeked face of Mistress Mosel tenderly gazing at him.

"Hello!" she said. "Thank you for saving my husband's life!"

CHAPTER 30
Ox Island

Botolph was developing into a strong young man and his feats of endurance on that particular night were probably beneficial to him in the long run. After an extended rest he soon returned to normal and received the thanks and accolades of Mosel, his family and all the villagers. He in his turn owed a debt of gratitude to Luka who, as soon as he had given Mosel into his wife's tender care, had, without thought for his own tiredness, turned back and found his friend still two miles away from the homesteads. Somehow he had managed to get Botolph onto the back of the long-suffering pony and run the last two miles, half leading the horse and half endeavouring to stop the semi-conscious rider from falling off.

Once they were all fully recovered the farmer organised a feast to which the whole village was invited and Botolph and Luka were told time and time again that their heroic efforts had made them members of the village family and they would always be sure of welcome and help there as long as they and the village survived.

The time had come though, when the boys had to move on. New clothes and spare clothes had been provided by the village and arrangements had been made with the ferryman for them to be taken across the Liman River to the eastern end of Ox Island, where a cart would be waiting to take them to the south-westernmost point of the island. From there, another boat would take them up the Rother River to Niwendenne from whence Botolph was convinced that he could easily find his way home.

Thus revitalised and encouraged, they set off. The whole village accompanied them to Apuldre Jetty. The boys were hugged by all the members of the Mosel family and they then clambered into the ferry. Everyone was waving and crying as the ferryman pulled away from the land.

"That was more painful than the Black Night itself!" said Luka. Thereafter, whenever they talked about that particular adventure, it was always referred to as "The Black Night".

The ferry called first at Ebon's Island to drop off a small package and then soon arrived at Ox Island. Luka was amused to find that, true to the island's name, the cart that was to take them across to the other side, was indeed drawn by two oxen.

"Well this is going to be a less lively ride than Mosel's horse would have given us" said Luka.

"Well, at least the wheel is not so likely to fall off" replied Botolph. "It worries me a little that he might have been rushing back to entertain us and that it was as a result of his driving more recklessly than usual, that the accident happened."

"Well don't lose any sleep over it. There were no bones broken. He managed to retrieve and mend the cart. And we all learned a lot that night!"

Botolph looked at his friend and wondered if he realised how significant his comment was. Luka looked steadily back at him. Their eyes locked for longer than was necessary. Luka knew. Such was friendship!

The ox cart took them up the hill away from the jetty and onto the ridge where Botolph asked the driver to stop. The boys descended and walked to the edge of the track, looking across the woods to the northeast. "What a wonderful place" he said. "Luka, doesn't this remind you of Cnobersburg? The island is much smaller, but it has the same atmosphere with the extra benefit of the glorious marsh, beyond which of course are our first-found-friends at Folcanstane and our newer ones at Apuldre!"

"Glorious Marsh?" said Luka. "Glorious Marsh, indeed! I can see that it has somehow got under your skin but count me out! I have had more than enough of it for the moment thank you. Let's have a change of scenery and see what your Bloomery is like, and I hope you don't have any more nasty surprises for me on the way."

Botolph opened his mouth to reply but closed it again, realising that, as usual, Luka was overstressing the point and that, once his thoughts on the subject had had time to mature, his feelings would probably be more or less in line with Botolph's.

They returned to the ox cart and continued their journey to the other side of the island, at last descending the hill to another jetty where an open boat similar to the old *Manigfual* was patiently waiting. The ox cart driver discharged his precious passengers into the care of a bad-tempered boatman who told them that they almost need not have bothered to come since if they had left it another ten minutes, the boat would already have lifted off the mud and been halfway to Niwendenne. This was less than a heroes welcome and they came back to reality with a bump and meekly stepped aboard the vessel and made their way between the other passengers, which were mainly sheep and goats, and sat themselves down on a thwart.

Only a few minutes later the boat spoke as she lifted to the tide and it was not long before the warps were let go and the sail hoisted and they were on their way up river. Two other sturdy lads had joined the boatman and they manned the oars when necessary and followed the expletives spat out by the sullen skipper.

As he predicted Niwendenne jetty hove into sight in a short time and they stepped ashore giving their thanks to boatman and crew. They were privileged to receive a grunt from the boatman in reply and frightened looks from his two crewmen.

"I shall pray for him tonight" said Botolph, as they climbed the hill away from the port.

"I shouldn't bother" said Luka. "It'll take a hundred talents of prayers before you'll get as much as a smile from him."

Once again, Botolph opened his mouth, considered, and then closed it again.

CHAPTER 31
Walking Westwards.

They followed a track that led at first to the east where they passed what looked like a long-abandoned Roman earthworks.

Here their route looped round to the northwest and they continued their journey in relative silence, enjoying the privacy of their own thoughts and the beauty of their surroundings.

They came to the crossing of another track and were about to continue but Botolph suddenly stopped. "Hah!" he said triumphantly. "What do you see up there Luka?" he asked, pointing skywards.

"Clouds!"

"What else?"

"More clouds. Oh no, it's not going to rain is it? What delights await us now?"

"No, you oaf, it's a bright sunny day. The birds; what sort of birds are those?"

Luka squinted at the sky. "Hawks?" he said, hopefully.

"Yes, exactly, they are hawks and that means I know exactly where we are and we need to turn left here and head towards the sun again."

"Oh, come on Holy Man, hawks move about you know and there must be thousands of them in the country.

237

You can't base your tracking skills on a few hawks flying around."

"Nevertheless" said Botolph "Hawks there are and here we be and we have to head down that way."

Luka enjoyed teasing his friend but Botolph had proved himself right so often in the past that Luka's gentle chiding was merely a token gesture to keep his guide on his toes.

They headed south and then a little more to the southwest. Botolph was getting excited now that he saw so many things that reminded him of his childhood home. He virtually ran down the hill towards the hamlet on the banks of the Rother. Ecci was standing outside his hut watching the travellers coming down the hill and his face broke into a wide grizzled smile as, at the last moment, he recognised Botolph.

"Well then!" he said "How you've grown up! Mistress! Mistress! Come out here; 'Tis Leofric's lad that's come to see us. And who's your friend, Botolph?"

"Sorry Ecci, it's so good to see you I was forgetting my manners. Mistress Ecci, how wonderful to see you too. This is my great friend Luka who has protected and guided me in good times and in bad. I commend him to you."

Botolph of course, was keen to continue on to the bloomeries but Ecci and his family were so welcoming and indeed so interested to hear what had been going on in the outside world that they felt bound to stay and eat and then pass the night there.

Botolph had not really realised until the point of telling his tale, just how much he had done and seen and achieved since their last meeting. They talked far into the night and both boys could see how the apparently banal existence of running the ferry brought its own benefits as

Ecci and his wife were able to experience samples of the lives that their passengers had enjoyed.

Although Ecci and his family were very sociable and friendly, the boys eventually twigged that they were going to be prisoners until the ferryman had drained them of every last detail. They gradually became less forthcoming and more taciturn and were finally allowed to sleep.

The next morning Ecci rowed them across the river to start the last stage of their journey to the bloomeries. They took their leave with a mixture of gratitude and relief and Botolph resolved that he would endeavour not to get tangled up with them again.

The track to Beorg Aesc took them up a hill and through the forest of ash trees that brought back memories to Botolph of his journey with Ceolbert five years previously. He wondered what had happened to the friendly monk and also what had happened to his brother Adulph. He had intended to ask King Eadbald if he had any news of the passage of the *Manigfual*. He still had no idea whether the vessel had survived or foundered and, if the former, where they had made their landfall. He wondered if Adulph was still alive. Would he also have, sometime previously, made this pilgrimage back to his birthplace? Botolph's joy and excitement at the possibility of seeing his family again, turned to apprehension.

Would they all be alive? Had the whole village been exterminated by Saxon raiders?

Luka noticed Botolph's mood and correctly guessed the reason. He left his friend with his thoughts as they pressed on through the forest. The answers to Botolph's unspoken questions would come soon enough.

The path curved round to the north and the trees thinned out to reveal the huts beneath them. Botolph moved to the edge of the path and leaned against a tree.

"Well, there they are! What shall we discover?"

"Only one way to find out" said Luka, not wanting to prolong the agony any further. "Come on!" He stepped in front of Botolph and half jumping and half running started to slither down the scree bank. Botolph had no option but to follow in like manner. Their arrival had been noticed by some of the villagers who paused in the middle of their various duties and gazed enquiringly as the lads reached the flatter ground and raced nearer.

Botolph had identified his family's group of huts, although they looked strangely different to how he remembered them. Two women were outside one of the huts. One woman was sitting and a baby was suckling her breast. The other had been tending the fire beneath the outside cauldron but now she turned and watched, wondering if it could be, hoping that it was, but not daring to believe until she was sure of a happy day.

CHAPTER 32
Home!

The reunion was massive! There was sudden uproar as neighbours came running from all parts of the village. Kera clasped Botolph in her arms as if she would never let him go and she sobbed and sobbed. The woman suckling the babe turned out to be Matild and, once Kera had released Botolph so that he could breathe properly again, he was introduced to his four month-old niece and her two-year-old brother.

Poor Luka was quite left out in the cold and he sheepishly kicked his toes in the dirt for a while, secretly feeling rather envious at the reception Botolph was receiving and knowing that he would never be received by his family in the same joyful way.

Botolph was acutely aware of his friend's feelings however and did not leave him alone for long before he called him over and placing his arm around his shoulders introduced him to his mother and sister and the rest of the neighbours.

The men were all at work and there was obviously a new man who had been added to the family. Botolph wondered who had fathered Matild's children. He wondered if it was one of the villagers who he would remember, or whether it was a newcomer. The community had certainly increased in size for he could see that extra houses and halls had been built.

He did not have long to wait before the second wave of greetings fell upon him as the sun went down and the men returned from the Bloomery site. His father, Leofric, had grown older and fatter and was limping slightly but his greeting of Botolph was no less emotional than Kera's.

It was Atheran, the lanky lad that Botolph had first met as a twelve-year-old, who came home to claim Matild as his wife. He now had grown into a fine man of twenty-three summers and was obviously a great asset to the family.

That night was one of the most memorable in Botolph's life when he sat down with his whole family to eat and exchange stories of events that had occurred during the previous five years. An official feast to celebrate his return had been planned for two days' hence. The whole village would be involved in that. People from other villages who knew Botolph from his Bloomery days would also be invited and the whole community was buzzing with the excitement of his return.

His close family of course wanted to know how long he was staying and they were sad but unsurprised when told it would only be for a week or so. "Don't expect a welcome like this every time you come home!" grinned his father.

Matild had been a mixture of shyness and enthusiasm when she greeted him. She was very proud of her two children and she and Atheran made a nice couple. Botolph was careful to ensure that Luka was not left out of the celebrations but he seemed to be very happy with his status as an honoured guest.

The official feast was held in the main hall and each of the families attending had contributed items of food. They were all placed on the long table at the end of the hall and every nook and cranny of the building was occupied by somebody who was intent on enjoying themselves and celebrating Botolph and Luka's visit.

The meal started in the late afternoon. Mead was drunk from horn cups. A little home-brewed ale was available, courtesy of Montey the measurer, who had a brother who grew hops further to the east. Before everybody became too sleepy, Botolph and Luka were asked to tell their stories about their lives during the previous five years. They stood in the centre of the hall and took it in turns to speak, one taking over from where the other left off. They made a good team. Each of them was holding a horn-cup of mead from which they supped to keep their voices fluid. Luka seemed to be drinking his rather faster than Botolph and as time went on, Luka's part of the story became more flamboyant and dramatised. Botolph was beginning to worry that his friend would really become roaring drunk and cause either embarrassment or offence. As it turned out, the more inebriated Luka became the more amusing he was and he had the whole hall rocking with laughter. Sides were being slapped, stomachs were being held, tears were streaming down peoples faces as the little man mimicked people they had met and told of things that had happened and, as far as Botolph could recall, several things that had not actually happened.

There was no way that Botolph could compete with him, even if he had wanted to, so when his turn came he just concentrated on telling his part of the story as he remembered it. As soon as he could, he handed back to

Luka, and could not help but join with the rest of the crowd in laughing at Luka's antics.

Great was the applause and cheering when their tale was told, finishing with their thoughts as they saw again the village at the bottom of the hill with Kera and Matild outside the family home. As they finished Kera ran to Botolph again and fresh tears of love and joy flowed down her cheeks.

Then came the food followed by dancing. Then there were traditional songs and recitations of lyric verse. It was the early hours of the morning before the last stragglers left and the whole village slept peacefully feeling that life was good.

CHAPTER 33
September 637.

The next few days passed too quickly and the time came for the boys to take their leave. They had visited the Bloomery and some of the nearby villages in order to pay their respects to people who remembered Botolph but now it was time to start the next stage of their lives.

They had both become much attached to Matild and Atheran's two children and Botolph wondered how old they would be before he saw them again. Presents were exchanged together with good wishes and loving hugs and before long they were both climbing up the hill towards the path to Beorg Aesc. Just before they passed the tree line, they both turned and waved back at the village. They could see tens of hands and one or two coloured cloths being waved in return... and then they were on their way back to Cantwarebury.

The journey passed uneventfully and they were welcomed by the brothers at the Abbey. Archbishop Honorius took a special interest in the boys. He of course remembered Botolph from the time he had sent him with Ceolbert to Cnobersburg. He too was interested to hear their story but cast a sceptical eye over Luka when he tried a repeat performance of the entertainment he had provided for the Bloomery village.

The Archbishop pointed out that the boys were approaching the age of eighteen summers and therefore could, if they wished, apply to become novitiates with a view to becoming monks or priests. He was interested to know whether or not God was calling them towards some sort of vocation. To the Archbishop's consternation, Botolph replied that he felt that he was being called to serve the Lord in some way but that he believed 'travel' would be an important feature of his life.

Honorius replied that 'travel' was not a feature of the Benedictine movement to which the abbey was allied. Benedictine monks were expected to live static lives and to remain within the close confines of their communities.

"But what about Father Fursey?" Botolph found himself almost shouting.

"Ah, yes, Fursey. Well, he is rather an exception but you must remember that, for one thing, he is an Abbot and for another, he is Irish so if we do not expect him to conform to anything at all, we will not be disappointed." He steered the conversation in an alternative direction". And what about you Brother Luka?"

"Dunno" was about all he could get out of Luka who had not been impressed by the Archbishop's lack of enthusiasm for his attempt at artistic rendition. Luka followed his concept that whatever Botolph wanted to do was fine, and Luka's role was to help him. Such was their relationship.

One piece of news they did manage to dig out of the archbishop, was that *Manigfual* had survived her voyage together with Botolph's brother Adulph and all the other Cnobersburg monks and people. They had finally made landfall at the old Roman port of Gesoriacum in Gallia and had been accepted by a monastery somewhere over there.

Botolph resolved that that was the next on his list of places to visit. For the moment however, the archbishop decreed that it was back to the books at Saint Augustine's monastery so that both boys' brains could be re-stabilised and improved.

As they gained in knowledge and skills they jealously preserved the freedom they had tasted. Clearly it was hoped that they would both one day become monks. This seemed likely in Botolph's case but much less so in Luka's who was still very resistant to Christian teaching.

They were both well liked within the monastery and were keen to join in all the activities including work in the gardens and in the kitchens. Luka became quite an expert at making bread and, contrary to the monastery's precepts that life and food should be kept simple, he would often surreptitiously add a variety of herbs to the dough. This caused joy to the inmates but approbation from the Prior who threatened to keep him out of the kitchen if he insisted on producing such tasty items. Luka's defence was that the Lord surely gave us food and herbs and that combining them deliciously was all to the glory of God. Prior Peter refused to join battle with him on the subject but offered him two choices: plain bread or no cooking. Luka had little alternative but to accept the former.

The days at St Augustine's Abbey passed quickly. There was always plenty to do. They were up early in the mornings. They attended many of the offices but were excused some. They made great progress with their learning and Botolph in particular was rapidly becoming very proficient in Latin. They had a fair amount of free time when they were able to go out on visits, both in the immediate locality to the homes of local people they had befriended and further afield to other monasteries.

Wherever Botolph went, Luka went. He was just happy to be with his friend. He had always had a problem with his rebellious personality. Perhaps it was his size. Perhaps his stunted growth had caused an inner resentment of the rest of the world. There was nothing sinister in his relationship with Botolph. They were just really good mates. There was nothing over-subservient either. Luka was not like a dog which just followed Botolph around and did his bidding. He had his own plans and his own mind and ideas. Unsurprisingly, because of the link between their minds, the two sets of plans and ideas as often as not turned out to be the same.

It was true that Luka was a little lost in the academic side of life at the Abbey. His happiness lay outside in the fields, sailing on the Stour River, travelling a dusty road, riding when horses were available, fighting, swordplay, climbing and wrestling. These were all the things that Luka enjoyed. He knew however that he had to conform to monastic life and so when these frustrations threatened to overcome him, he had acquired the habit of halting his spinning mind; taking a deep breath, finding out what Botolph was doing and meekly following his lead.

In such circumstances, he would often find Botolph in the library. As befits the name of such a room, he would either be reading or writing. If writing, he would be under the instruction of Brother Ivan who would be watching carefully that he did not ruin the parchment or skin that was receiving the attentions of his swan's quill. In contrast to Luka, Botolph was a talented and neat scriptographer. Brother Ivan groaned inwardly when Luka appeared, but he knew where his duties lay and he motioned him to a desk and then searched out the worst of the skins, knowing that by the time Luka had finished with it, it would, like as not, have to be thrown away. He found a quill and was tempted to give it to Luka to sharpen but decided to give his pupil further instruction in how it should be done.

"Now look Luka," he said, "you take the quill and the knife and you place the knife just a hair's breadth up the quill, slice diagonally downwards and there you have a fine point. Luka looked at him and paltered "I know how to sharpen a quill, you must have shown me at least ten times before!"

"Yes I know you know *how* to do it Luka" said Brother Ivan, visibly trying to retain his patience "it is not so much *how* you do it as *where* you do it. I only have a limited number of swan's quills and unless you go hunting them for me I am going to run out of them before you have been here for another month. Your hair's breadth ends with your knife halfway up the quill and you make a great ugly gash at the nib so that you end up not with just one line of writing but with one central line and another furry line on each side!"

The other pupils, including Botolph, had stopped their work and were grinning at this confrontation which had become a regular event and always offered good entertainment. The two participants did not see anything funny about it however; their eyes were locked as if in mortal combat. The brother handed Luka the newly sharpened pen whereupon Luka took out his knife and was about to demonstrate how he would have performed the operation. His knife was poised halfway up the quill's shaft when Brother Ivan shrieked "No!" and snatched it back.

"It's sharp. Use it as it is!"

"But I just wanted to show you how well I can do it," said Luka, deliberately prolonging the agony.

The brother awoke to the fact that he had been an unwitting part of the morning's cabaret act and bent his head down to Luka's ear.

"Luka!"

"Yes Brother Ivan?"

"Just get on."

"I can't!"

"Why?"

"You have my quill!"

Ivan with great aplomb, held the offending item out to Luka, who took it with a nod and, catching Botolph's eye a silent grin passed between them as Luka settled down to slaughter another sheet of parchment.

CHAPTER 34
Early November 637

It was the week after Samhain, when the harvest had all been gathered in and the first frosts had come. Botolph was day-dreaming about his young life in the Bloomery. Samhain was the time for celebrating. The farmers knew by then how good or bad the harvest had been and how their cattle had done and they were able to make a reasonably accurate guess as to how much in the way of provisions their community was going to need from them for the winter. They could decide which cattle they would have to slaughter and which needed to be kept. They made sure to slaughter the condemned animals in time for the Samhain festival and the bones were kept for use on the bonefires. At sunset on the last day of October the festivities started. But this day was also traditionally the day on which the division between the world of the dead and the world of the living was at its thinnest and some of the favoured spirits were able to pass through.

For that reason, as in each of the huts in the Bloomery, Botolph's mother Kera would put a burning candle in an open west window to guide the spirits home. A place would be set at table for the recent-dead and their favourite meal prepared. Once the two bonefires were well ablaze, the domestic fires in the huts would all be extinguished. They were then re-ignited using flame from the bonefires and this common flame would serve symbolically to bind the whole village together. There was a procession during which all the people and animals from the village, passed between the two fires so that their souls could be purified. Then came a fantastic feast to celebrate the end of the old year and the beginning of the new one.

Botolph closed his eyes and let the characters and noise and flames and sounds and smells pervade his senses. He could see all his friends and family. He could even see himself at ten years of age, a small figure wide-eyed with excitement. He smiled and opened his eyes again, coming back to the present, which really was not so bad.

There was no feast of Samhain in the Monastery but in a few days they *would* be celebrating Martinmas with one of the biggest and best feasts the monks would enjoy. That was the good news. The bad news was that following that came the Forty Days of Saint Martin when they were expected to fast ready for the next major festival of Christmas, or "Christ-Mass" as Prior Peter still insisted on pronouncing it.

"Very appropriate," thought Botolph, "Six hundred years or so ago, we had the miraculous birth of the Son of God; a new beginning for the world. We put the old gods and Druidism behind us and were able to start the new year with proper worship of a God of love."

Botolph had not really known much of religion in his younger life, and he was only seventeen now. There were still Druids wandering the country and other "Holy Men" of all callings but he had never until now had any reason to think about them. They were a spectacle. They were to be taken seriously and revered, mainly because they were usually old and the culture was such that youngsters were taught to respect their elders.

Occasionally one of the wanderers would come into the Bloomery. He would be given shelter and food and before passing on his way would wander the site casting spells and incantations and shaking his staff and praying for whatever was the concern of the moment, be it protection from Saxon raids, a good harvest or deliverance from pestilence of some sort. He would visit the sick and issue a variety of chants and herbal medicines, for which he was well paid, before taking his leave. Sometimes the sufferer recovered and sometimes they died, Botolph had never been sure whether those who recovered did so because of the sorcerer's charms or whether they would have recovered anyway. He also had a suspicion that the reason that such Healers never stayed more than a few days was in case their "treatment" failed and the patient died and the family asked for their money back!

Botolph's young life had been quite protected really. He had heard stories of the Saxon raids that used to occur and the horrors that went with them, but he had never witnessed such events. Accidents occurred at the Bloomery, people were injured and sometimes killed. Mothers and children died in childbirth and people died of diseases and old age. All this had seemed very normal to Botolph.

It was only since he had left the Bloomery that the realities of life had hit him. He had made many friends at Cnobersburg and he remembered the veil of fear that preceded Penda's army as they advanced on the monastery with the purpose of hacking everyone to death. He remembered the shiver that went up his spine when they were within spitting distance of enemy soldiers during their escape in *Skyff*. He remembered the storm and their shipwreck off Folcanstane and his anguish when he thought Luka might die.

Life was certainly getting more complicated now. In some ways perhaps he might have been better to have stayed in the Bloomery, but this was the real life he was experiencing now. It was exciting. He had freedom to travel and meet more people and see more wonders, and he had something to pray for. He *needed* religion now, like he never did when living at home. He *wanted* Luka to live and to be happy, he *wanted* him to be as committed to Christ as he himself was. He felt pretty well the same about everyone else in the world too!

"Without God", he thought "*You* are the person sitting right at the top of the tree. There is nobody or anything above you. If the woodman comes and cuts down the tree with you on top of it, it is quite likely that you are going to die. It is all a matter of fate.

But *with* God, there is at least someone above you when things are going wrong; someone you can call on, someone you can appeal to. Prior Peter tells us that anything we ask in Christ's name will be granted to us. In Folcanstane I asked that Luka's life be spared and I built a chapel to show my faith in God, and my prayers were answered, Luka *was* spared. I suppose if you were sitting at the top of the tree when the woodman came along, you might pray for deliverance and if God thought you were a worthy cause and you had prayed hard enough, he might provide a soft lump of earth for you to land in and your life may be spared. Anyway, the point is, that *with* God, you at least have someone to pray to and are therefore richer than the poor man who has no God but himself."

"Ahem. Ahem?"

Botolph himself came down to earth with a bump. It was not a woodman who had chopped his tree down, but Brother Ivan who had brought him out of his trance.

"Might one be so bold as to ask whether or not you intend to sit gazing at that spider in the thatch all day, or whether we might perhaps expect you to finish this parchment by Vespers?"

"Ah, yes, sorry Brother Ivan, I was just thinking about Christmas."

"Christmas, yes we are all thinking about Christmas but that is a festival and after the celebrations we have a holiday and do not have to work. For that reason we have to work all the harder now, so perhaps you might see your way to pressing on a little faster?"

Botolph pressed on.

CHAPTER 35
February 638.

Christmas came and went.   It was a jolly time. Small presents were exchanged but it is not easy to give presents in a monastery where nobody is supposed to have any possessions.   The gifts tended therefore to be either of the variety that can be eaten, or of aid in one's work.   As a special concession Luka was allowed to bake a batch of his herbal loaves and he received many very discrete congratulatory and appreciative thanks from the novitiates and brothers, including Prior Peter himself: "Ahem, thank you for the bread Luka, it really was ... , Ahem most enjoyable, perhaps just for special occasions eh? I am sure we appreciate it even more if it is not a daily occurrence!"

The autumn had been very wet and in January there was a heavy fall of snow which curbed all extra-mural activities.   There were no visitors for a month and the boys and the brothers were more interested in keeping warm and alive than risking their lives going travelling.

The snow did, as Cantium snow does, eventually thaw and it was a delight to see the familiar landmarks reappear to give colour and form as the white blanket lifted.   A hint of spring was in the air.   Snowdrops appeared.   The birds seemed to be singing with new gusto. Life was reappearing from dormancy.   Botolph and Luka were itching to get out.

"We would like to go to visit King Eadbald in Folcanstane," announced Botolph to Prior Peter when he and Luka eventually managed to track him down.

"And how do you propose getting there pray?"

"Well, we thought we would walk. It is only five or six leagues."

"Well, I think that is what you are going to have to do because there are no wagons due to go that way during the next week. Perhaps you will be able to find a friendly cart driver who might help you on your way. I need to write to King Eadbald. Perhaps you will be kind enough to convey the parchment to him and give our greetings to himself and Queen Ymme and of course their daughter Eanswythe."

He said this last name with a hint of a smile as if knowing that Botolph and Eanswythe shared some special relationship. Maybe, just maybe, it was not just an urge to get out of the winter confines of the monastery into the open air. Maybe the hint of spring was turning a young man's mind and it was towards Eanswythe that this particular young man's mind was turning?

Prior Peter started to muse about times long ago when he also had such an affinity. His mind went back to the depths of a spring wood with primroses and bluebells and a pretty young girl in a loose woven shift ...

"Prior Peter?" He was shaken out of his thoughts to find Botolph's eyes piercing his.

"Prior Peter. Are you alright?"

"Ah, yes my boy, I am fine thank you. I was just thinking about a young man of a similar age to yourself. Long ago, long ago."

They waited for him to continue.

"Well then?" said Luka "What young man?   You can't stop there!"

"Well I did!" said the Prior, which stumped Luka entirely because it was not the answer that he was expecting and now he found he had lost track of the conversation he thought he was having.

Prior Peter gave him no chance to pick the track back up again as he brusquely interrupted Luka's confusion and said "Right boys, away you go, I have a letter to write.   You can leave first thing tomorrow morning.   Get yourselves to the kitchener and ask him to provide some sustenance for your travels and I will see you after Vespers tonight," and with that he turned and with a swirl of his habit headed towards the church.

Luka was still in confusion.   He shook his head rather violently as if that might unjumble his thoughts. "What was that all about?"

Botolph smiled.   "I think " he said slowly "That means that there is rather more to Prior Peter than meets the eye.   It means he has a history.   It means he was not always the holy man that we see now.   It means he was once like us.   It means " and now it was Botolph's turn to drift into a dream as he imagined what Prior Peter might have done as a young man, and what Botolph might also do.

"Botolph, Botolph!   Talk to me!   What's the matter with everyone this morning?   Is this trance only being shared by the privileged few or is there a chance that it might be my turn next?"

"No" laughed Botolph "It is just that suddenly the picture of life is becoming clearer.   Perhaps it is because the snow has gone.   Like the new spring soil, life is becoming revealed for the way it really is.

Look at it Luka. Life is not just there. It did not just happen. It developed slowly. Everyone's life develops slowly, from the same beginnings, following the same pathways at first. Then suddenly decisions have to be made. Do you see?"

"Nope!" said Luka, shaking his head slowly from side to side whilst staring intently up at Botolph. "Nope! Although I have heard that this time of year drives everyone a little mad and I think it has got to you and Prior Peter too."

"No, listen. You follow pathways and that is good. It is God's wish that you follow pathways and find the joys in life. But in the same way that the monks deny themselves your delicious bread, the time comes when you have to make a decision and stop yourself ever going down a particular pathway again. We are at the stage in life were we can go and experience its joys. It is right that we sample and enjoy as many of the delights of life as is possible in our youth, because soon, perhaps very soon, we shall have to give back to life by denying ourselves many of the joys we are about to find. Do you understand?"

"I understand."

Botolph heaved a sigh of relief.

"I understand that your mind has turned and I am going to have to put up with a mad thing accompanying me to Folcanstane."

Botolph looked down at Luka's big soft eyes gazing up at him and saw the serious straight line of his lips begin to twitch at each end and he realised that he was being teased. Suddenly they both burst out laughing and Botolph's intense introspection and Luka's dumb incomprehension evaporated and they placed their arms around each other and headed off to see the kitcheners.

CHAPTER 36
20th February 638

The following day the boys were up at first light ... not because the journey was that long but because they were excited to be sampling the freedom of the countryside again.

The kitchener provided them with cheese, bread and fruit which they placed in their leather bags. He also gave Botolph the letter that Prior Peter had asked him to take to King Eadbald. Botolph tucked it into a pocket and they made their way out of the monastery and on to the wide track that led to the southwest away from the direction the sun would rise within the next half an hour or so.

Luka was never too good in the mornings and he was trudging along by Botolph's side keeping his own counsel. Botolph on the other hand was looking up into the trees and relishing the dawn chorus which exemplified the pleasure and joy that he felt for life.

"D'y'hear that blackbird?" he asked Luka, and received only a grunt for his pains. Past him there was another blackbird and then a thrush, all singing their little hearts out together with the robins and sparrows twittering in the background. The observation stimulated Botolph's fertile brain. The sparrows and robins were putting in just as much effort as the thrushes and blackbirds but they were not being heard.   They were merely background accompaniment.

"People are like that in life too", thought Botolph. "There must be many folk who have important things to say, and yet their voices are never heard.   Prior Peter is a wise man but his voice is only heard within the confines of his Abbey."

He joined Luka's silence and they made their way up the cart track away from the monastery and the town that was developing by its side and headed for the high ground where they knew they would find Stone Street, the Roman road that would lead them south.   As they walked, Botolph continued to think about the discrepancy between the sparrows and the thrushes.

Botolph had no doubts about Christianity. He knew it was the one true religion and was convinced that his duty lay in spreading the message of Christ and doing his part to create a world in which there was love and gentility.   He calculated that he was fortunate in living in relatively peaceful times.   He had heard the stories of coastal raids and the terrors that they involved.   He knew that the raiders came from all over; the Picts sailed down the coast from the North, the Jutes sailed across the sea from the East.   The worst aggressors had been those of his own kin, the Saxons, who had followed a similar passage to the Jutes.

Some of the raiders had vandalised the dwellings and the population and then moved on.   Others, like his own ancestors several hundred years earlier, had stayed and integrated with the locals and made the land their own. They had brought with them their own religions, and a fine number there were to choose from!   Britain already had more than enough when they arrived. The Druids were an important force to reckon with but there were also those who prayed to the Sun God, to Isis, to Mithras, and so many others.

And then came the news of Christ and a God of love. Most of the other religions of which Botolph had heard, were violent and involved a lot of blood and sacrifice and hate and curses to one's enemies. But this new religion said that we should love our enemies and if they smote us on one cheek, to turn the other one and let them have a try at that! Christianity, Botolph knew, was not really a new religion. It had been going on for hundreds of years, since the Romans were in control of the country. But when they left two centuries ago, Britain had fallen back in so many ways, mainly because there was now no Roman protection from the Saxon invaders.

The old skills were abandoned. What point was there in making some beautiful piece of work when all that would happen was that it would be stolen during the raiders' next expedition of pillage and rape. In any case, on the East coast of England, there was hardly any time for the artisans to work. They constantly had to defend their families or flee inland to escape the terrors of the marauders. Skills were passed down from father to son. People were being killed so wantonly that the young father had hardly the time to perfect his family skill before he was struck down and the skill was therefore never passed to his son. The same applied to religion. The Christians who inhabited the country in Roman times were soon overwhelmed by the invaders who brought their own religions with them so that Britain had rapidly reverted to a pagan country, a country where the religion of the peasants held sway. The peasants by definition, were simple people; they lived from hand to mouth; they loved and they hated. If they hated they fought, if they loved they made children ... many of whom died. So their religion was simple too. They prayed to their god and if they had a good day, that meant it had worked so they prayed to the same god the next day too. The world in which they lived was a desperate and violent one.

But over those two hundred years the situation eased. When the Saxon invaders reached the British shores they found they were fighting their own kind, so gradually a type of peace began to settle on the land and, like water finding its own level, the pressures from the continent decreased and Britain became more peaceful.

The time for Saint Augustine to be sent to Britain was well-chosen. He arrived bringing the message of Christ, at a time when people were not too pre-occupied to listen. And people had had enough of war and fighting and fleeing and fighting and fleeing again. The idea of a loving religion where everybody helped each other; where "giving" was the creed, rather than "taking"; such a religion had its attractions.

Botolph supposed that deep down in the forest Bloomery, his family and forefathers had been spared the worst of the terrors of the raiding parties but, even so, the culture of fear and having to be ready to fight for one's family and possessions must always have been prevalent.

"Well?" said Luka, finally ready to give his voice a try.

"Well what?"

"Which way do we go now?"

"Ah, well we are just where we want to be, this is Stone Street. We don't want to go right because that is the other road that would take us back to Cantwarebury.

Down there to the left lies Folcanstane and Saint Eanswythe's Nunnery."

Luka's brain had woken up by now and he was in one of his talkative moods.

Luka chatted on ... about everything in general and nothing in particular, until he espied an ox cart coming over the brow of the hill ahead of them.

"Heyup!" said he. "We have company, it's a pity it's not going in our direction."

The ox cart pulled level and the driver reined his beasts to a standstill. He was a typical peasant figure dressed in dirty brown hessian clothing and he greeted them with a toothy grin.

"And where might you two young lads be a-going?" he asked.

"To Folcanstane" replied Botolph. "Do you have any news from thereabouts?"

"Nope!" said the peasant. "Nothing special. There is a lot of disease at the moment, but that's everywhere. People dropping dead all over the place, weakened by the winter I reckon that's what it is."

"Where are you off to?" asked Luka.

"I'm heading for Cantwarebury in the hope that I can sell this cattle feed. We lost quite a few head this winter and yet had a good harvest of feed last summer, so I have more than I can use and I am hoping to get a good price for it in town. Where are you two from."

"We're from the monastery" said Luka.

"Oh, you're trainee monks at Saint Augustine's are you? Tell you what, it's about half morning now, let's make ourselves comfortable and you can share your news with me and I can share my lunch with you. I am in no great hurry and my wife always packs me more than I can ever manage."

Luka was all in favour of that and their new friend chocked the wheels on the cart and retrieved a parcel from under the seat and they settled down on a grassy knoll. The peasant took a coarse-woven cloth from his parcel and spread it on the ground. Luka's eyes opened wide as from the same (apparently bottomless) package, he produced a loaf (which was newly-baked by the smell of it), and various pots ... which shortly afterwards they discovered contained butter and two different types of fruit jam, one was red and the other purple. There was cheese and there were some slices of meat and a dozen hard-boiled eggs.

"We have some food too" said Luka, reaching for his bag.

"Why, bless you, that's a kind thought" said the peasant, "but don't you think there is enough here for all of us?"

Botolph had to admit that, even with Luka's appetite, there was more than enough.

"Milk, water or mead?" asked the peasant, going over to the cart.

Predictably, Luka settled for mead while Botolph had some milk.

"It's warm!" he said.

"Of course it is" came the reply "That was in the cow an hour ago. Always better for you when it's still warm I reckon."

Luka was busily divesting one of the eggs from its shell. "Why so many eggs?" he asked.

"Well" said the peasant, "My wife knows I like a chat and to tell you the truth she always packs enough to feed a small army, so that I can share the food out and then tell her all the stories I have heard when I get home. We don't go short of food. Our small-holding is very compact and there are only the four of us at home, me, my wife and our two sons, so we have food to spare. Now this meat here is swine. You won't find much about as good as this. We take the beast and kill it and then we hang the meat in the smoke of our fires. This preserves it and makes it last for ages, you try that" he said, taking a slice on the back of his knife and handing it to Luka whom he recognised as a man of taste!

"Mmm ... Vorroof!" said Luka.

"That's a very strange expression!" said the peasant, somewhat taken aback.

"Don't worry" explained Botolph "It's one he saves up for things that really impress him. Somehow it always seems to astound those people he uses it on. We call it his "Magic Word"."

Gradually they grew more at ease in each other's company and as they ate the peasant told them about the farmers in Cantwarebury.

"You know" he said, "years ago there was nothing there but broken Roman ruins. Nobody wanted to live there. Nobody even wanted to go there. Somehow there was a bad flavour about the place. Perhaps it was resentment because when the Romans left, the town lost its protection. There are certainly lots of stories about raiding bands coming and killing the townspeople and setting fire to anything that would burn. When the Romans left, the town still looked prosperous you see, but it wasn't. It was also too close to the coast and that made it too easy for the raiders to plunder."

"So what happened? Didn't they fight back?" asked Luka incredulously.

"Well, I suppose they did a bit, but there were few decent leaders. The first Bretwalda, "

"What's a Bretwalda?" asked Luka.

"Bretwalda? That's our name for king, chieftain, whatever. Except that it means not just any old king of any old area like Cantium but king of all Britannia."

"Oh, I see" said Luka, hugging his knees and looking more interested than Botolph had ever seen him look in his lessons at the monasteries. "Go on then, did he have another name?"

"Bless you yes, his name was Vortigern and he wasn't from Britannia but was originally from far across the sea. My word he was savage, and savage in more ways than one. He ended up marrying his own daughter, but we won't dwell on that, such talk is not for the tender ears of young lads like trainee monks."

This was exactly the sort of talk that Luka wanted to hear about, but the peasant hurried on.

"Before Vortigern died, he brought in another couple of his countrymen, brothers they were, called Hengist and Horsa, and they were pretty evil too."

"Were they Bretwaldas too?" asked Luka.

"Well for one thing you can't have two Bretwaldas, and for another, No ... there were other strong men developing armies in other parts of the country and Hengist and Horsa only ruled this southern part of Britain. They did their best to fight off the Saxons and to bring some order to the country but it was still a very violent time. Now, to bring me back to what I was saying, the result, to put it in an nutshell, was that all the good citizens of Cantwarebury were either killed or ran away! The place was deserted!

It was only when your friend Augustine came along that things started to improve.

"*My* friend Augustine!" said Luka, finishing his third egg. "That's rich! He was a very holy man and a great saint but it has been pointed out to me many times that I am not worthy so much as to be able to kiss the hem of his outer garment, so I don't think you can really call him my 'friend'".

"Well" said the peasant "You come from the same stable and I reckon an 'orse is an 'orse however important 'e may be and all 'orses in the same stable have gotta be friends! Now look at me, I have seen fifty-five summers and I was born and bred here in this part of Cantium and I was just a few years younger than youse two when your friend Augustine and his cronies turned up.

We heard rumours out here in the villages that some people had arrived and begun to settle in the ruins of Cantwarebury but we didn't pay much attention to it. People had come and gone in the past. The old town was finished and done as far as we were concerned.

Then we heard that amidst their dwelling huts they had built a little stone church. I was about sixteen by then and me and some others went down to see it.

We were amazed, there were so many of them. They hadn't built their huts within the old town but just outside. We were given a very friendly welcome and taken in and fed and introduced to the whole community. You of course will be familiar with the tonsure haircut, but it was the first time we had seen anything like that and we were intrigued".

"You didn't actually meet Saint Augustine did you?" asked Botolph.

"Certainly I did" replied the peasant. "He took my hands and asked me if I wanted to become a monk. I said 'No thank you very much, I'd much rather be a farmer' and he laughed and made the sign of the cross on my forehead and said 'That's a very necessary occupation. May God and our Lord Jesus Christ bless you in your work. You go and be a farmer of beasts and the earth and we will be farmers of men'.

Now I've always put my success as a farmer down to that blessing he gave me. I can still feel the sensation of that cross being drawn by his finger on my forehead. At the time I was too astonished to speak but afterwards I came to realise that it was one of the turning points in my life."

"But did you become a Christian?" asked Botolph, laughing.

"Ah, err well, yes sort of!" came the stammered reply. "We ain't Druids and we don't worship idols but you must remember that we work the land. The sun, the rain, the snow and the weather affect our lives deeply so I must confess, there are times when we pray to the Sun God, and others when we pray to Thor and ask his blessing on our crops."

"Well" said Botolph "I am sure that the control of the sun and the weather come under the control of the one Almighty God, so I suppose in effect you are praying to him."

"Am I?" said the peasant. "Oh well then, I suppose the Holy Saint would say that that is alright? Anyway, we met lots of people that day we were at the monastery. One of them I remember was a man called Justus who was preparing to go off to Hrofsceaster to set up a similar monastery there.

"I've been there!" said Botolph.

"Have you?" said Luka, turning and looking at him in amazement as some of the red jam fell off the large chunk of bread he was devouring and dribbled down his chin.

"Yes. My brother Adulph and I stopped off there on our way to Cnobersburg, just before I met you. It was an interesting place, built near the banks of a river, the same as Cantwarebury I suppose, but the river at Hrofsceaster is much wider. Anyway, go on with your story..."

"Well, there's not much more to tell really. The monastery at Cantwarebury went from strength to strength. This gave previous inhabitants of the town confidence and some of them came back and resumed living there. Then the monastery started getting regular visitors from other parts of the country and abroad so merchants started to congregate there to sell their wares. Over the past twenty years or so the place has been getting bigger and bigger. I don't suppose it will get much bigger now though. Lundwic seems to be the place. But of course anyone coming from Gallia has to pass through Cantwarebury and Hrofsceaster to get to Lundwic so that cannot do trade anything but good."

"Well" said Botolph, "It's all very nice to sit chatting to you here and sharing your breakfast but we had better get on if we are to reach Folcanstane by nightfall. We wish you luck with your trade in Cantwarebury. Thank you so much for the food and God bless you and your family."

"Righty-oh" said the peasant, rising from the ground and wrapping the remains of the food in a hessian cloth. "My wife will be pleased to hear that two such upright young men have enjoyed her food. Maybe we

270

shall meet on this road again, if not some other. Peace be with you," and he hooked the chocks out from under the cart wheels and heaved himself up onto the seat as the oxen resumed their slow plod towards Cantwarebury.

Botolph and Luka shouldered their sticks with the leather bags swinging across their shoulders and continued up the hill.

The road was straight and it was a glorious day. In truth Botolph had become a little cold whilst sitting on the knoll and he was pleased to feel himself warm up again with the exercise of walking. It being late winter the sun was low in the sky and they were walking south with dense woodland on either side of them. Gradually the sun came over the trees on their left and offered them a little of its heat.

After a couple of hours they came to crossroads and there they stopped. This was partly because Luka was hungry again and partly because Botolph was undecided as to whether to turn off to the left or go straight on. Nobody was about and so they sat once again and opened their leather bags to make the most of what the kitchener had provided. They did not have long to wait before a horse-drawn dray came up the road from the left and Botolph jumped up and greeted the surly driver who surveyed him suspiciously.

He reined his horse to a standstill and glared at Botolph.

"Peace be with you brother" Botolph ventured, "We are travelling to Folcanstane and are wondering if it would be quicker to go straight on here or take this turning to the East. Could you tell us where this leads?"

"Go down to the end of this track and then turn south again and that will take you to the monastery of

Ethelburga at Liminge. Keep gradually turning to the east then and you will break through the hills and see Folcanstane in front of you. Watch out for the bears!"

Botolph opened his mouth to ask what he meant but the traveller flicked the reins and was gone.

Luka had stopped in half-mouthful and looked wide-eyed at Botolph who returned a similar gaze. "Bears?" they said simultaneously. Luka's comment was more of a splutter really and pieces of bread and cheese spattered over Botolph's habit.

"Sorry!"

"Don't mention it!   I think he was joking.   I think he was just trying to frighten us …"

"I think he succeeded!"

"No, I'm sure there won't be any bears."

"Oh, that's alright then!"

"Wolves and wild boars maybe!"

"Oh, great!   Let's get on," concluded Luka.

"There is one good thing I hadn't thought of," said Botolph.

"What's that?"

"The monastery at Liminge.   We don't need to go all the way to Folcanstone tonight.   I am sure Ethelburga will give us shelter.   She is Eanswythe's Aunt after all."

They walked on through the woods, eyes keen and ears pricked, listening for any rustling of the undergrowth that might presage a bear attack.   Nothing untoward occurred though and they gradually relaxed as the sun sank lower in the sky and they found themselves dropping down a slight incline to a new bourn trickling through the trees.

The path turned right to follow the bourn and they walked against the flow of water towards its source.   Soon it opened to a small lake and the density of the trees cleared to reveal a group of thatched dwellings nestling at the foot of another low hill. Figures flitted in and out of the trees and the closer they came the more apparent became the activity. Eventually they were able to distinguish between the mix of different dresses. Basically there were monks in brown habits who looked similar to Botolph and Luka and others, who were presumably slaves, wearing the loose-sleeved Gallic coats.

They crossed a narrow ditch and Botolph approached a monk who was tipping some doubtful-looking material from a wheelbarrow into the lake.

"Peace be with you, brother" said Luka as the pair stepped boldly down to the water's edge.

"Peace be with you" came the reply. "And how can I help two strapping young monks who come to visit us from the big outside world?"

Botolph grinned "Well, we're not proper monks, we are students," he said, "And we are journeying from the Great Abbey of St Peter and Paul at Cantwarebury to our lady Eanswythe's Nunnery in Folcanstane."

"Why so late then? The sun will soon be setting and you could have been from Cantwarebury to Folcanstane and back in a journey."

"Ah, well you see, we've met some interesting people on the way and have sat and talked and eaten with them, and, to be honest, we are in no hurry. As our Prior would say, 'we are learning about life'. We are enjoying the signs that winter is passing and spring is on its way; we are learning about the woodlands and the country in this area; we are familiarising ourselves with the birds and other animals and plants that live hereabouts."

"And especially bears!" broke in Luka.

"Bears?" said their new friend with surprise.

"Yes, bears!" enthused Luka. "Great black hairy things; big enough to ride on!"

"Where've you seen bears?"

"Well we haven't actually *seen* any, but we have *heard* about them." Luka was forced to admit.

"Perhaps you have also seen some of our famous pink mushrooms on your way?"

Luka was shaking his head innocently, "No, I can't say we noticed any of those."

"Oh, I wondered if you had perhaps made a meal of those too, because that is about the only way you are going to see bears in this part unless you know something I don't?"

Botolph was inclined to reply and explain about the traveller in the dray but decided that the explanation could wait for another day, so instead he said, "Look brother, the sun has now dropped behind yonder hill and our feet are tired. We are acquainted with Abbess Ethelburga and I suspect she will give us shelter for the night, so perhaps you would be kind enough to guide us to her?"

It was now the monk's turn to grin.

"Follow me" he said.

He led them along a pathway which bordered the narrow stream they had crossed earlier, and rose slowly up through the trees and past some small thatched huts. They came to a clearing defined by a v-shaped dry ditch and walked between the dwellings, nodding left and right to acknowledge all the people that caught their eyes. The monk left his barrow by one of the huts and then said "I expect our Abbess will be in the Great Hall which is a little further up the hill."

They followed him and duly came to a substantially-built wooden building with a heavily-thatched roof. The two sturdy slaves who stood at the entrance moved aside and the boys found themselves squinting into the smoky dark interior. Some logs were burning on a stone slab in the centre of the hall and most of the smoke was obligingly spiralling up towards the roof vent. Stray wisps were however circulating around the room and trying to make friends with the eyes and throats of all with whom they could come into contact.

The Abbess was tending a pot which was suspended over the burning logs. She had her back to them at first. Even in the gloom, Botolph could see that she was dressed in a vibrant purple dress. Her long brown hair was clipped into a bronze clasp and as she turned towards him, Botolph was transfixed by her beautiful hazel-green eyes. To his pleasure she recognised him instantly.

"Ah, Botolph the Chapel-builder, and his good friend Back-from-the-dead-Luka I believe!"

They bowed their greetings and she stood regally before them with a quizzical smile on her face and asked:

"So, young warriors, what brings you to my humble monastery?"

Botolph made to answer but she interrupted,

"No, the answer to that question can wait until later, the sun is already setting so we are clearly going to have the pleasure of your company for the night. Our modest evening meal is nearly ready, we shall eat together and you will tell me all your news and future plans as we eat."

And thus it was. The Abbess was hungry for news of the outside world, whether it concerned the rumour of bears in the forest (which to Luka's confusion made her laugh heartily) or details of the workings of the monastery at Cantwarebury. She was eager to learn and interested in the smallest detail. Botolph felt enveloped by the warmth of her personality and intelligence.

Before the meal there had been prayers and after the meal the whole community came together to give thanks at Compline. The boys enjoyed the worship in spite of the fact that the singing was well below the standards to which they were used. The enthusiasm and devotion of the communicants outweighed any lack of skill. The devotion, Botolph noted, was not only to God but also to the great Abbess herself.

They were led to one of the comfortable dry huts where each was allocated a straw palliasse. They were soon asleep in spite of the snores from the other occupants.

At first light, they were awoken by the noise of bodies stirring and they followed the sounds and shapes and joined in the service of Prime after which they joined Abbess Ethelburga to break their fast together.

"Well brothers" she said afterwards, "Are you staying another night or heading off towards my niece's nunnery at Folcanstane? What is your decision?"

"Much as we would love to tarry here longer and learn more of the workings of Liminge, I feel my lord Abbot would want us to be single-minded and fulfil the task we set out with, so Folcanstane it has to be my lady."

"Away with you then", she replied and each grasped her hands and bowed their leave. "Come and visit us again soon, you will always be welcome here. Give my love to Eanswythe and to my brother King Eadbald and his wife Ymme. God's blessing on you both and give you safe journey."

They walked back down the hillside and through the trees, marvelling again at the number and busy-ness of the monks and slaves working on the site. Soon they had regained the track which ran alongside the stream which led them to the lake. Here they turned to the southwest and followed the bank until the width of the stream had reduced to one which they could easily cross and head up the hill in a more easterly direction.

It was a beautiful spring morning and at the top of the Downs they had a lovely view over the rest of that part of Cantium. The birds were singing, the grass was green, the trees were budding and life seemed to be blossoming.

Botolph plucked a straw from the grass and thoughtfully chewed the end as he watched Luka striding ahead of him, using a willow pole to steady himself where the ground was uneven. Luka's "seaxe-knife", his constant companion, was dangling from his waist. Botolph mused on the incongruity of the peaceable monk's habit with the wicked-looking knife attached and wondered if the time was coming when the Abbot would also notice the incongruity and demand the knife's removal.

Botolph's memory flicked back through visions of Luka using the seaxe to peel an apple during their picnic on Stone Street; cutting down the willow branch which he was now using as a stick; cleaning out his horse's hooves with it during their time at Cnobersburg; cutting Botolph free from his underwater prison on *Skyff* during their catastrophic shipwreck at Folcanstane; and Botolph's latest use of it during the rescue of Farmer Mosel. To separate Luka from his seaxe was unthinkable, perhaps he would just have to hide it under his habit in order to give him more of a semblance of holiness and less of the appearance of a bandit!

"There we are!" Luka's shout brought Botolph back to the present as he climbed the last hill and joined his companion who was now pointing to the sea, of which it was their first sight for several weeks.   The hamlet of Folcanstane was still a league or so away but the journey would all be downhill from there onwards.

"You can see the nunnery sitting there on the cliff top," said Luka.

Botolph squinted into the early morning sun which was reflecting on the sea and followed the coastline round to the inlet where the fishing boats were pulled up on the beach.   His eye traced the river as it ran inland to the point where it narrowed at the ford and then became a stream lost in the trees.   He could see the escarpment rising from the river bank and the line of tree trunk half-pipes that were Eanswythe's clever solution to the nunnery's fresh water problems.   Even from where he stood, Botolph thought it still looked as if the pipes ran *uphill* from their source and was unsurprised that the local people had credited Eanswythe with a miracle!

"I see the king is in residence!" said Luka, pointing at the camp outside the nunnery walls.   They used their hands to shield their eyes against the sun and for several minutes they studied the activity going on between the tents.   Botolph's eyes were suddenly attracted by a movement towards the periphery of his vision.

"What's that, out in the bay?"

Luka swung round..   "Christ's blood, it's a raiding fleet!"

"Ahem," said Botolph.

"Ahem?   Is that all you can say?   Come on, we have to get to the camp to warn them, there is no way they can see that fleet from where they are, because their view will be obscured by the trees, Come *on*!"

"Not before you get on your knees and confess your sins to Almighty God and apologise to Him for blaspheming His Son's name!"

"There's no time. We must go!"

"There *is* time! I am not having you go into battle wielding that infernal seaxe of yours, with every possibility of being killed and ending up going to Hell because you have not confessed your sins, now *on your knees*!"

Startled by Botolph's sudden commanding attitude, Luka took one last glance at the approaching fleet and sank to his knees, clasped his hands, closed his eyes and tilted his head skyward towards the East. He knew that Botolph would brook no gabbling so he prayed dutifully and sincerely and then at the end opened one eye and added "and please guide us and guard us during this forthcoming battle and help us to slaughter the bas..."... "*Amen*" interjected Botolph!

"Amen" said Luka, rising with a grin. "Now can we go?"

"Yes, last one at the camp's an idiot" said Botolph and they hitched up their habits, tucking them under their rope belts and ran for all they were worth down the steep hillside and across the flatter ground, through the Pent Stream and up the escarpment. At this point, Botolph, with his longer legs was in the lead but he tripped and fell at the last moment and it was Luka who burst through the nunnery gates and rushed into the guardhouse in the nunnery grounds.

CHAPTER 37
Raiders!

"Mount the guard" he puffed, "There's a battle fleet coming from the west."

As he turned to leave the guardhouse, he saw that Botolph had passed him and was running up the hill towards the king's residence. He ran after him.

Botolph pushed past the bodyguards who turned and rushed after him as he thrust open the door just as King Eadbald was coming out. He stopped and bowed quickly and said "Raiders sire, coming from the West".

Eadbald grunted his acknowledgement and started shouting orders. Botolph ran back, almost knocking over the two bodyguards again and headed for the nunnery where Luka had already alerted Eanswythe and her nuns who had started the chore of hiding all the church valuables. Botolph just had the chance to greet her and tell her that her Aunt Ethelburga sent her love when he heard his name shouted. He turned to find King Eadbald striding towards him, accompanied by soldiers carrying different items of his war clothing. They began to dress the king as he talked.

"How many boats did you see?

"About five, but there may have been more hidden under the cliffs."

Behind the king Botolph could see women and children from the fishing community who normally lived down on the beach. They had climbed up to the fortress and were coming through the nunnery gates and heading for the slim protection of the nunnery walls. The whole area was becoming a frenzy of activity and from outside the walls came the sounds of men shouting, horses snorting and trumpets blowing.

"Hmm," said Eadbald, "if it turns out that we are severely outnumbered I may need to summon more men from Dofras or Portus Limanis or both. I would value your friend Luka's company here but, Botolph, if we need reinforcements, would you be able to ride to Dofras to summon them?"

"Of course" replied Botolph, "Do you want me to go now?"

"Not yet. My general and his aides have ridden to the end of the trees where they overlook the cliff. He will work out how big a problem we are facing and report back to me shortly. It sounds like just a small Saxon raiding party intent on snatching some slaves to sell over the water. On the other hand, it could be the advance party of a larger invasion force and that would be far more serious. We shall soon know."

He turned and ordered the trumpet calls and shouting to be quieted and Botolph realised that the king was hoping to turn the events to his own advantage. Another disturbance at the gate and Eadbald's general arrived on horseback in a cloud of dust, slid out of his saddle and confronted the king.

"Four boats, sire, each with about twenty people, fourteen oarsmen each and a few passengers, some of whom are bound and look as if they are the products of a previous raid, perhaps down on the marshes because that is the direction from whence the boats come."

"How close are they? Can they see the stade yet?"

"No sire, not yet, they are tucked away around the corner ... but not for long."

"Good, right, get the fishermen to dress in their wives' clothes but bring all their wives into the nunnery for protection. Take a troop of soldiers down to the beach in normal dress, without their horses and with their weapons concealed. Tell them they have to act as if they are fishermen so that the raiders are not alerted. Send a small group of horsemen across the ford and get them to conceal themselves behind the trees on the East Cliff in case any of the raiders try to escape by crossing the river or beach their boats on that side. Get one of your best men to lead that party. I do not want the raiders scared off by the sight and noise of horses.

You lead the group down on the beach. I am going to take the rest of our horsemen to the west and down into Sandgap and along the beach to cut off their retreat to the boats. Any spare men without horses will go with Luka here. Luka, I want you to take them quietly to the top of the cliff to the west of the nunnery and then as quietly as possible and remaining unseen, slide down through the undergrowth to the water's edge but keeping under cover of the trees until the last minute. Do you understand?"

Luka looked upset at the thought that there was any chance that he might *not* have understood. He had already taken his seaxe out of its sheath and was fingering its blade lovingly.

"Yeah, course, and then as soon as they step onto the beach we slit their throats, right?"

The king sighed. "No, Luka, you bloodthirsty little monk, that is *not* right. I want you to wait until all those boats are drawn up on the beach and *all* the warriors are ashore. They will probably leave one in each boat to guard the slaves. Even then I do not want you to do anything until you hear the first sounds of fighting on the stade. Then out you come from your hiding place. You will have already detailed which men you want to take which boat. Your job is to despatch the guards and free the slaves and get them ashore. This should give me and my horsemen just about enough time to get back to the stade from Sandgap so keep an eye open for us!"

Turning back to his general, he said:

"Now, I want everyone to understand that the point of this battle is not just our defence but is to turn the tables and take as many as possible of the enemy as slaves. If any cause trouble however, do not hesitate to kill them, I reckon that with any luck we will only have to kill about half, so that should leave us with thirty or forty new slaves if everything goes to plan. Any questions? ... No? ... Right! ... General, you take Luka and give him some weapons and men. Off you go Luka, as quickly and silently as possible.

Botolph, you keep close to the gatehouse. I shall leave three horses here. The gates will be closed but if things go wrong then I shall send you a messenger with this ring (he briefly waved his hand) and you will ride as swiftly as possible to the garrison at Dofras and use this ring as my authority to bring a squad of troops to our aid.

If things go *very* wrong, neither I nor the messenger will come back and you must use these horses to help my wife Ymme and Eanswythe to escape."

283

Botolph watched Luka running behind the general's horse as they made their way out of the nunnery gate on their way to the encampment. He reflected on the fact that they were about to enter battle and he had not had time to wish his friend God's speed and protection. He cast a short prayer behind Luka's fleeing feet.

Eadbald was by now fully battle-dressed and he clapped his hand on Botolph's shoulder and said "Go now and look after the ladies. Prepare everything as if you would expect the raiders to overcome us and storm the fort but hopefully it will not come to that. God be with you."

"And with you sire," replied Botolph as the king mounted his sturdy horse and followed his general's trail.

Botolph did not wait to watch his departure but swung round and headed for the chapel where he found Eanswythe with her nuns.

"Is this a serious attack?" she asked.

"Serious enough for your father to ask that I am ready to help you and your mother escape to Liminge should your father's forces be overcome. With God's help it will not happen. Send some of your nuns to bring your mother and all the other ladies here to the chapel where we shall pray for your father's success and the safekeeping of our men and for guidance regarding our actions. We can then plan and discuss our escape should that be necessary."

Eanswythe did as she was bid and before long the chapel was packed with nervous ladies and noisy children. Some of the pandemonium was eased once Botolph had them kneeling for prayer and he was gratified by the way calm seemed to come out of chaos. They prayed fervently under Botolph's ministry and took the holy sacraments of bread and wine as further fortification.

Once the devotions were over, and to prevent the ladies' cacophony starting again, Botolph immediately launched into details of his plans for escape which he had been furiously turning over in his mind ever since Eadbald had announced them as being his responsibility. He pointed out that the safety of Eanswythe and Queen Ymme were of ultimate importance and that it was up to everybody to help protect them. Four soldiers had been left in the garrison and Botolph would join them in guarding the gate and watching the progress of the fighting down on the beach. The royal party would return to their hall and the nuns would remain with Eanswythe in the nunnery. Two of the three horses would be taken and tethered outside the palisade, close to the west wall and the third would remain inside the gate in case Botolph was called upon to get reinforcements from Dofras.

"There is a problem in that there is no back entrance to this fortress," he said. "I would prefer that if the raiders were to come and attack the gate, we could escape via another route but the strength of the walls is also our downfall and I cannot see a way around this at the moment. However -". He carried on talking to the throng about other finer details of his plan. His concentration was constantly interrupted by the effect of repetitive tugs on the hem of his habit by an annoying little urchin, sitting on the ground sucking his thumb and looking up at him with wide blue eyes.

Eventually he could stand it no longer and he crouched down and said "Now look, little man ... "

The thumb was removed from the mouth and the urchin said "You can get out by the water pipe!"

Botolph only half heard and the half which he *did* hear, he did not understand. "What did you say?"

Suddenly a lady was at his side, clearly his mother. Botolph wished she had been there earlier to stop the little horror's annoying intrusion into his flow of thought.

"He says you can get out by the water pipes."

"Well what does *that* mean?" said Botolph.

"I think it means that he knows a way out of the fort that we could use instead of the front gate. He's always vanishing for long periods and I search and search but can never find him. I think this may be an answer to that mystery. He must have been going through the gap by the water pipe and out into the encampment."

Botolph's initial irritation suddenly turned to loving gratitude as he scooped the boy up and with his mother in hot pursuit, ran through the crowd, out of the chapel and across to the north wall.

"Come on now son, show us how you do it." urged the mother. The child ran across to the pipe and pulled aside some rubble and wood and in a trice was gone! The mother screamed but Botolph at once leapt down and followed and found him laughing his head off on the other side of the wall. Botolph laughed too and opened his arms. The child came to him in a rush whereupon Botolph fell over backwards and they clasped their arms around one another as they laughed and rolled on the ground. The mother's anxious face appeared through the hole by the pipe and Botolph came back to reality and ushered his little hero back through the hole and reverted to the process of preparing for disaster.

Luka meanwhile had acquired a shield and a spear and six soldiers, none of whom were initially very keen on the idea of being led by a midget monk but they were under the general's orders to do so, and he had long since taken the rest of his troops down to the beach in their role of fishermen.

Luka's personality had hardened into its warrior form and he soon had his men's attention as he outlined the plans for their part of the deception, stressing the need for speed and silence. Wasting no time, with Luka in the lead, they ran round the back of the fort's west wall and started to descend the escarpment under the cover of the shrubland. Luka could hear sounds coming from the sea but he could not be sure if it was the waves lapping the beach or oars beating the water.

Quickly and silently, with the exception of a few snapping twigs and an occasional oath from a soldier as he slipped on a near-vertical part of the embankment, they slithered down to the seaward edge of the undergrowth. Luka peered out and then hastily pulled back again as the nearest of the four enemy boats loomed up in front of him as it crashed onto the beach. Neither Luka nor Eadbald had expected them to land quite so far to the west of the Pent River, but the raiders obviously knew the area and were planning to creep around the headland and take the fishermen by surprise.

They were so close that Luka dared not look out but he heard the other three boats ground and low voices and grunts and splashes as the occupants stowed their oars and tumbled into the water and splashed up onto the shore. He could hear orders being given in a low voice but could not make out what was being said and then came the sounds of movement heading towards the stade. Luka cautiously moved forwards and peered again through the leaves. He could see the main party now creeping eastwards under cover of the cliffs. The four boats were pulled up high on the beach and three guards were standing talking in front of them.   A fourth guard was doing something in the westernmost boat.   Luka was itching to move forward and get on with the job but the raiding party was still in view and he remembered Eadbald's specific instructions not to attack before he was sure the fighting had started on the stade. He turned to his soldiers and tapped them one by one on the arm, and indicated to which boat they were assigned ready for when the time came to free the slave-hostages.   In a low whisper he told them that their first Priority was to make a combined attack to kill or capture the guards. He looked again in the direction that the raiding party had gone but there was now no sign. He saw one of the guards' heads jerk up as the first sound of fighting came from further along the beach. He raised his arms and looked back at his soldiers, they each nodded their readiness and then he was out on the beach and running with his eyes focussed on the nearest guard.

He did not have far to run before he was on his chosen victim. He had discarded the borrowed spear in favour of his short and trusted seaxe but the borrowed shield he used to good effect, brushing away the raider's shield as he thrust upwards with the knife.   The Saxon twisted sideways and the blade made a harmless scratch on his arm but his sword came slicing out of a seemingly empty space. Luka leapt aside and just had enough time to think that this fighting business was not as easy as he had assumed.   He felt quite indignant that his opponent seemed intent on *killing* him. The realisation fuelled his resolve however and his mindset changed to take this into account.   His eyes locked with the raider's for a brief second and then with a roar he re-attacked, feinted to the right in order to get the raider to twist again, which he obligingly did and Luka then thrust the seaxe upwards under the guard's ribcage, twisted it, pulled it away and then spun sideways as his opponent fell to the ground. Job done!

One of the other guards was lying wounded, perhaps dying and the other two had surrendered. One was having his hands tied with a piece of rope mooring line and the other, who had been on the boat was in the process of clambering over the side and into the water from whence he too was taken and roughly tied. Luka went across to the boats and used his knife to cut away other mooring lines which he coiled and placed obliquely over his shoulder thinking they might be useful later.

Apart from his ferocious roar, which apparently had startled everybody, the whole event had taken place quite quietly. None of Luka's squad had been injured and they were busily boarding their allocated boats when the muffled sound of hooves broke above the noise of the shoreward waves and a line of horseman with Eadbald in the lead thundered past them in the direction of the stade.

Luka had remained on the beach ready to direct operations once his men had released the slaves and brought them ashore. He looked expectantly at Eadbald as he passed but was spared hardly a glance as with determined looks on their faces the horsemen rode to close the trap.

Luka's mental stature had grown since that first parry of the fight and he had reached a new realisation that a battle is never over until it is won, so he swung back to his men and urged them into further rapid action. There were about twelve hostages: men, women and children and they, together with the captured soldiers, were hurried out of the water back into the cover of the foliage at the bottom of the cliffs.

Luka wondered what to do next. His instinct was to go and join the fighting that he could hear going on by the river but he knew that Eadbald had placed his faith in his intelligence to lead the six fairly stupid but brawny soldiers. He decided that he had better stay with his party. He then began to wonder what to do with the boats. He did not want to destroy them as they would make a useful addition to Folcanstane's fleet. On the other hand, the last thing he wanted to see was the survivors from the melee rushing back along the beach, taking to a boat and escaping. The answer suddenly came to him, the oars! He selected two of the burliest slaves and two of his soldiers to go back aboard the boats again, to disconnect the oars and throw them over the side. The rest of the group were then to drag the heavy blades from the water and bring them up the beach to hide them in the foliage. "Quick ... Go!" he said.

Luka stayed by the tree-line adjacent to the boats, and realised that he felt quite proud to be in charge and directing events without having to do the hard work himself. He still had his seaxe in his hand and was waving it and pointing it to good effect as he emphasized his directives.

Even the slave children set to with a will and it was not long before they had hidden all the oars away as best they could. Once this was done Luka, still being very aware of the need for speed and cover, led his party westwards along the beach for a few minutes, away from the fighting and away from the boats, before they then once again ducked into the scrubland at the foot of the cliffs.

Luka looked hopefully for a way to ascend and gain the high ground behind the fort but there was no way that could be done due to the sandy nature and steepness of the soil.   He satisfied himself therefore with sitting everyone down and encouraging silence.   The two captured soldiers he sat back to back and tied them together with the rope he had salvaged and then gagged them for good measure. They had dragged the injured raider with them but he was now unconscious.   The rest of his charges sat quietly chatting to each other as Luka stood at the entrance to the hideout, looking eastwards and wondering if there was anything else he could or should be doing.   They were too far away to hear if the fighting was still continuing.   An hour or so passed and then four horsemen came around the headland and cantered in their direction.   The ever-cautious Luka dropped back as he watched them stop and examine the boats.   He was still not absolutely sure whether they were Eadbald's men or perhaps raiders on stolen horses.   They made no attempt to dismount however but looked up and down the beach in puzzlement. Suddenly one cupped his hands round his mouth and "Luuuuka!" came echoing along the beach.

Relieved, Luka stepped out of his hiding place and waved his arms and the searchers cantered across.   He recognised Eadbald's general with three other soldiers whose faces were familiar to him.

"Well done Oh Bloodthirsty Monk!" said the general with a grin, echoing Eadbald's words.   "What have you here for us then?"   Luka flushed his people out of their hiding place for inspection.

"How did the fighting go?" he asked.

"Pretty well.   We lost six men with another three injured but they lost a lot more.   We have about thirty captives so that will make a bit of money for the king at the next slave market. They are digging a burial chamber for twenty-six but it looks as if they will need to make space for a couple more."

"That one *was* still breathing" said Luka "but the one we left on the beach is dead".

"Yes, the one on the beach was *very* dead" said the general. "Your work I presume?"

"Err, yes" said Luka "and it looks as if this one has now passed over as well, so I am afraid I can only add two slaves to the tally."

"Right" said the general. "Rope those two together so that they can walk. We will leave the two bodies here and send a cart for them later. Bring the rest of your party along to the stade and we will sort them out there." He dug his heels into his horse's flank and they cantered off.

CHAPTER 38
Victory Celebrations.

That night there was much feasting and celebration in the fortress at Folcanstane. The two boys were entertained in the King's Hall and Eadbald stood and praised them and gave them credit for their vigilance which had turned potential disaster into a triumph.

Botolph suddenly remembered the letter he had brought from Prior Peter and handed that to the king. Luka had become the hero of the day with the soldiers and, after the formal meal with the king, he was whisked off to the camp outside the nunnery walls where he was feted by the general and his other new-found friends. Meanwhile Eanswythe and Botolph were locked in conversation in the King's Hall, catching up on the events of the months that had passed since they had last met. Eanswythe had only visited Aunt Ethelburga's monastery once when it was founded and she was keen for news of the progress that had been made. Botolph told her all he could but her questions still came thick and fast.

"Why don't we arrange a visit later on in the year and then you can see for yourself?" was the solution that suddenly came to him.

"What a good idea!" she said. "I could take my nuns with me. It would be quite an outing for them and something to look forward to. We could stay for a few days and worship with the brothers and sisters there. Oh that is really exciting. I think early May would be best, when the weather is warmer and more settled."

Their conversation drifted on towards the future and Eanswythe asked Botolph if he felt God was guiding him in any particular direction. He looked into her green eyes and noted the soft lines of her features. Her voice was mellow with just a trace of the attractive lilting drawl that is characteristic in that part of Cantium. Something passed between them that Botolph did not quite understand and he felt it lodge in the pit of his stomach. He opened his mouth to reply but no sound came out. Their gaze was locked and neither spoke for what seemed a long time although it must have only been a few seconds.

They both dropped their eyes and turned away at the same time.

"I ..." said Botolph in some confusion. "I ..."

Eanswythe was now facing away from him. She was gazing at her hands, her palms upturned as she fought to get her thoughts back on to a straight line. She coughed to clear her throat and this helped regain her self-control. "Come," she said, "Let's go and take the night air," and she swept out of the hall with strong firm strides which she hoped would serve to quell the trembling she felt in her limbs.

Botolph rose and turned to the king who caught his eye and raised his goblet in salutation. Botolph bowed in response and Eadbald gave a brief smile as the young monk turned and followed Eanswythe through the doorway.

He found her outside gazing northwards into the sky. She was breathing deeply. He could see her breath condensing in the cold night air. He held back and watched her from the edge of the thatched hall. She saw him and turned and began to walk back towards him. Likewise he moved towards her and when they met they both turned and followed the well-worn path which followed the perimeter of the nunnery grounds.

Neither said anything for a long time. They just walked and wrestled with their thoughts. They had already completed one slow circuit before, at last, Eanswythe spoke.

"I am a bride of Christ," she said falteringly. "My love must be for Him alone. I must love Him and follow Him and have no room in my heart for earthly things."

They continued to walk. Botolph said nothing, granting her the courtesy of allowing her to get her thoughts in order. She too was silent and she considered the implication of the words she had just spoken. She had spoken them many times before, but never previously had she realised how important they were; just what their implications were; how drastically and finally they affected her life. She was twenty years old now, two years older than Botolph. When she had founded her nunnery she had been barely twelve. She had been excited at the romantic prospect of having charge of six sisters of similar age with whom she could share her spiritual development. She had enjoyed the challenge of building the nunnery and organising the worship. Some months ago there had been a sister who had fallen in love with a young fisherman from the stade and Eanswythe had been forthright in her actions to get her to renounce the romance. She had eventually been successful in regaining the nun's soul for her foundation. But now?

Now, suddenly she understood so much more. She understood that sister, far more than she had at the time.

Today she understood her own duties and obligations, far more than she had yesterday.

One reason that she had founded the nunnery was in order to avoid marrying a wholly-undesirable Northumbrian prince. At the time, she had assumed that all men were undesirable and best kept at arms' length. But now?

Now, she had a problem. She was a resourceful young lady, as she had proved by her feats of engineering within the nunnery. She was strong in character and purpose. Tonight, suddenly and unexpectedly, she had seen the glimmer of an alternative path that she would really like to pursue. She looked up, they were passing the chapel. She had absolutely no idea how many circuits of the nunnery grounds they had completed. She glanced across at Botolph. Strong, intelligent, kind, handsome, tall Botolph, striding alongside her. *Alongside her.* Alongside. He might always be alongside. How much more good they could do in the world if they were both together. She found with alarm that she was looking *fondly* at him and she quickly averted her gaze again and concentrated on the path in front of her.

She was committed to God. She had chosen her path. She could not change it. She *must* not change it. Botolph would have to go.

Kindred spirits as they were, Botolph was thinking similar thoughts. He too had been alarmed by the burst of fire which had passed between them in the king's hall. He still did not understand it, nor would he for many more months. He knew however that it was good, and bad. He knew too that his life was committed to God, and, worse than that, he knew that Eanswythe's life was also committed to God.   He was honour-bound to do nothing that would cause her to consider any other pathway.

Suddenly he knew what he must do.   "You asked," he said, "if I felt that God was guiding me in any particular direction."

She felt her heart thumping in her chest as she realised the enormity of what she might be about to hear and an involuntary "Oh!" escaped from her lips, but it was more of a miniature scream for help than anything else. She waited and looked straight ahead as their feet continued to crunch in the gravel.   She dreaded what he was going to say and yet longed for it at the same time. She wondered how she would answer, she saw her life in turmoil, she prayed for help.

"I am going to become a monk.   I am going abroad to Gallia to complete my training at the Abbey of Evoriacum."

She felt shock, disappointment, relief and sadness, but also a frisson of joy.   She was confirmed in her vocation as an Abbess.   Her future was now secure.   She and her soulmate Botolph had passed together through that archway of experience that leads to maturity.   They had rejected diversion.

"It is God's will," she said.

Thereafter, the cloud that had briefly settled over their heads lifted again.   They never spoke of the warmth that had engulfed them and each recognised it as an ever-present danger.   Nevertheless, they were able to enjoy an enriched friendship as they held each other's personalities at bay.

Luka instinctively knew that something significant had occurred.   "What's with you two?" he asked, looking from Eanswythe to Botolph and back again.

"Nothing" shrugged Eanswythe.

"We're fine," said Botolph.

"Hrmmph!" said Luka, disbelievingly but then dropped the subject.

They spent five pleasant days at Folcanstane. Luka spent most of his time with the soldiers whereas Botolph became a sort of honorary chaplain to the nunnery. He led the nuns in Bible Study and in their prayers and devotions and added his own brand of Christianity to that which Eanswythe had already installed. Together the Abbess and the Student made a whole and it was not long before the warmth of their worship spread and the rest of the community, royalty, soldiers and fisherfolk alike, were coming to the chapel to join in the devotions.

Secretly both Eanswythe and Botolph prayed for forgiveness for enjoying so much the satisfaction and pleasure that working together brought them. They each felt that it must be a sin and the anguish gnawed constantly at their souls.

CHAPTER 39
26th February 638.

The five days passed quickly and soon it was time for them to be on their way back to Cantwarebury. This time they travelled with Eric, Martha the fishwife's father-in-law who had helped to tend Luka when he was in a coma.

"You're still alive then?" said Eric gloomily as Luka bounced up onto Eric's cart.

"Certainly am!" said Luka.

"Won't last." said Eric.

"*What* won't last?" said Botolph climbing up beside Luka on the smelly fish-wagon.

"All this energy and leaping around, he should have died six months ago, t'aint natural, it'll catch up with him eventually and he'll just drop down dead, you mark my words!"

Luka looked at him in wild-eyed alarm. "Well I feel alright, I don't *feel* as if I'm going to die!"

"Worst way to feel," said Eric clicking the pony to a trot as they rumbled their way along the bank of the Pent River.

"Lovely day!" said Botolph, trying to create a diversion.

"Won't last!" said Eric for the second time.

"*What* won't last now?" said Luka, irritated.

299

"The weather! It's always like this when I take the fish to Cantwarebury market but you can wager that by the time you get over the Downs and on to Stone Street, the rain will come and the wind will start to blow. Terrible day!"

"Do you have the letter from King Eadbald for Prior Peter?" Botolph asked Luka.

"Yes," said Luka handing it over "You had better have it in case I suddenly keel over and die!"

Botolph glanced at Gloomy Eric who obviously had not heard this exchange and was hunched up and morosely watching his horse as it picked its way through the stones on the rough track.

Botolph leant over toward Luka and whispered "He's probably waiting for the horse to die too!"

Eric remained silent all the way to Six Mile and the boys surmised that he had perhaps fallen asleep with his eyes open. They chatted happily together and Botolph easily lifted Luka out of the instant depression that Eric's comments had caused.

After Six Mile the road was straight and flat and they saw the first houses of Cantwarebury well before noon.

Luka, revitalised, could not resist getting his own back on Eric. "Well we didn't get the wind and the rain then? It's still a lovely day!"

"Terrible," said Eric predictably.

"What's terrible *now*?" said Luka, falling off his peak and tumbling back towards a crestfallen state.

"The market! With this weather there will be loads of people there, all jostling and fighting and trying to beat my price down."

"Well, surely that's good," said Luka, "With all those people you will be able to sell your fish easily."

"No, it's *not* good," said Eric.   "If I sell all my fish and get a good price for it, I shall have all that money to take back through the woods to Folcanstane.   *Someone* will have noted it and I am more likely to get robbed before I get home; it's not good at all!"

"Leave it," whispered Botolph as Luka opened his mouth for another sally "You are not going to win."

Luka closed his mouth and looked at Botolph in wide-eyed astonishment.

Botolph grinned.

The spell broke and Luka shrugged and grinned back as Eric, having issued his last tirade, fell back into sadly watching his beast's haunches as it drew them the last half league to the monastery walls.

Everything was much as they had left it.   Botolph found Prior Peter and gave him Eadbald's letter.   He had already heard about the raid but had not realised that his boys had played such an integral part and he wanted to know every last detail.   Botolph discreetly avoided telling him about Luka's victim.   The Prior also wanted to know all the news about the Monastery at Liminge and the Nunnery at Folcanstane.

When all had been imparted, Botolph tried to say "I have reached a decision" but the inevitable frog became caught in his throat and, whereas he had previously been talking quite freely, this important statement to which he had been mentally building up, simply came out as a prolonged squeak.

"I beg your pardon," said Prior Peter somehow realising that something of note was approaching.

"I have reached a decision..." ventured Botolph successfully.

"And what, pray, is that my son?"

"I have decided that I want to take the tonsure and devote my life to God, but ... "

A warm glow came over Prior Peter's face and he smiled a broad smile as he rose and grasped Botolph by the shoulders. "I am so pleased that God has called you to join us."

"There is more," said Botolph.

"Tell me," said the Prior, patiently resuming his seat.

"I would like to go abroad for my novitiateship."

"But why?" said Peter. "We need you here. You have been such a great asset already. Everybody likes you, why not become a novice here?"

"It is difficult to explain," said Botolph pausing while he searched his mind for the solution to a major problem that had presented itself. He did not want to go into all the complex details of explaining just why he could not stay in this part of Cantium, and yet he knew he must neither lie nor make up some part-true excuse. He shot skywards a quick prayer for deliverance.

Prior Peter was watching him intently and was aware of Botolph's inner turmoil. He let him suffer for a few more moments and then said softly "Evoriacum".

"Evoriacum?" said Botolph in surprise.

"That is where you should go," said Prior Peter. "I would send you to Lugdunum but that is too far away. Evoriacum is relatively close and so," he said with a rueful smile, "there is a good chance we shall see you in England again one day."

"We have a good relationship with Abbess Burgundo-Fara and we have exchanged students many times over the past fifteen years. I will start making the necessary arrangements."

Two weeks came and went and Prior Peter gave Botolph no indication of how the "necessary arrangements" were progressing.

Botolph had tried to break the news gently to Luka about his decision to "go foreign" as Luka now called it, but he need not have bothered. His friend did not turn a hair about the disruption in their lives; in fact he looked rather pleased about the prospect of further adventures and discomfort. He would not even begin to consider whether or not he should stay behind at Cantwarebury or whether indeed, Botolph may not actually *want* his company at Evoriacum. Where Botolph went, Luka went ... and that was all there was to it.

Botolph prayed hard about it. He needed God to convince him that he really was doing the right thing. Inside, he had little doubt, but he did sometimes wish that God would set the odd bush on fire or something similarly dramatic so that his innermost thoughts could be confirmed. Another week passed. More prayers. God still refused arson. Botolph sighed.

"What's up?" said Luka.

Botolph looked at him but did not speak.

"Well?"

"I haven't heard from Prior Peter yet. Nothing seems to be happening. I wonder if he has changed his mind about letting us go."

"Us?" said Luka.

"Well, yes, *us*. You are still coming aren't you?"

"Oh yes, I'm coming alright," said Luka "but does Prior Peter know about that.   I haven't asked him, Have *you*?"

"No!   You are right, we don't have permission for the two of us to leave."

"Mind you," said Luka, "I should think there are a lot of brothers who would be glad to see the back of me."

"Oh surely not," grinned Botolph, "although Brother Ivan's stock of parchment and quills will certainly go down much more slowly in your absence."

"Hmm. I shall be glad to see the back of him too," muttered Luka.

"Anyway, that's good," said Botolph. "I wanted an excuse to go to see Prior Peter, and asking for permission for you to join me, will do very nicely."

Prior Peter seemed to be making himself scarce however and it was another couple of days before both Luka and Botolph were called to his office.   The Prior was not alone and Botolph recognised his companion as Archbishop Honorius. He knelt and kissed the ring on the Archbishop's extended hand and, to his surprise, Luka meekly followed suit.

Prior Peter shrunk into the shadows and Honorius' quiet but resonant voice engulfed the boys.   He looked sternly at Luka and then transferred his gaze to Botolph when his features visibly softened.

"I have heard great things of you Brother Botolph," he said.

Botolph was shocked and lost for words.   He searched mentally for a reply but the Archbishop rumbled on.

"Two weeks ago I heard that you believed that God was calling you to take the tonsure and that Prior Peter recommended the Holy Abbey of Evoriacum."

"Yes Archbishop."

"Have you continued to pray about this since you made your decision?"

"Yes Archbishop."

"And do you still believe that God is calling you in this way?"

"Yes Archbishop."

"Hmm. I too have been praying for you, as has Prior Peter and the rest of the monastery." Botolph reeled slightly in surprise.

"You are surprised? You shouldn't be. Your decision affects all of us here. You have the gift of a personality which both reaches out to people and enfolds them. Even I, who have met kings and popes can feel the warmth of your presence. You have been blessed with kindness and consideration for others. You *are* a special person and your departure will be a sadness for many in the community."

Botolph moved as if to speak but the Archbishop raised his hand.

"You are a child of this monastery and you go from us carrying our name and the blessings of the Holy Saint Benedict and all his teachings. We are expecting great things of you Botolph. We charge you to love and serve the Lord in all you do and to use those gifts which God has given you to become a notable force in this world for the furtherance of His word."

He turned to Luka.

"You!" he thundered.

Luka returned his stare fearlessly and a silent second of energy passed between them. To his surprise Luka saw the eyes change from two dagger blades to a soft twinkle and at the same time the straight grim lips changed to a wavy line.

"You, my brave impetuous soldier, do not need me to tell you to look after Brother Botolph, nor do I need to tell you that we would all like to see you applying your gifts of soldiership more for the service of God than in your more usual warlike way."

His eyes continued to twinkle ... "You *are* undoubtedly an asset," he said, seeming to pause in his search for suitable words, "but I think we are still looking to see exactly what your assets are!"

Luka looked uncomfortable and shifted his weight onto the other foot, and the Archbishop decided that he had said enough.

"You both leave at first light tomorrow. Abbess Fara is looking forward to your arrival and you will be her responsibility then. God bless you both and grant you success in all you do and bring us safely back together again one day."

CHAPTER 40
16th March 638

Sure enough, first light saw them atop a wagon that was to take them and their minimal luggage to Folcanstane whence a boat would be arranged for their journey to Gallia. Botolph had a wad of parchments which would serve as introduction to monasteries along their way and a further, more detailed epistle for Abbess Burgundo-Fara.

They arrived at Folcanstane before noon and left their luggage with Martha and Eric before going down to the stade. Two boats had been pulled up on the beach but the tide was nearly full and there was great activity all round as they began to float.

"How are we getting across?" Luka asked Botolph.

"Hmm ... not too sure. The Archbishop just told me that a boat would be arranged. I did not think to question him further. On reflection I am not sure if he meant that someone would be here to organise one for us or whether he was referring to Divine Providence. Looking around at the general lack of interest that anyone is showing us, I now have a nasty feeling that it was the latter. Apart from God, Luka, I think we are on our own!"

"Oh, great! Well let's ask around and see if God might be going to provide us with any clues to this mystery!" he said sardonically, and was rewarded with a warning shot from Botolph's eyes.

"Where are you bound?" called Botolph to a man in the prow of one of the boats.

"Gippeswic," came the answer.

"How about the other boat?"

"Same! Where do you want to go?"

"Gallia."

"That'll be Gesoriacum then. You are out of luck. The tides are all wrong for Gesoriacum at the moment. You should have been here earlier. All the Gallia boats left at first light. There will be more coming in from Gesoriacum on the afternoon tide though and they will leave early tomorrow morning so book a passage with one of those."

The boys nodded their thanks, wished their informant a good passage and turned back towards the village.

"What are we going to do now?" asked Luka. "And what was all that about the next tide?"

"Well," said Botolph "the next high water will be about midnight so I guess the next boats will be arriving sometime between now and then. Let's go and ask Eric."

"Oh no, Gloomy Eric, must we? There will be more quips of amazement that I am still alive and he will give me that penetrating look of his in the hope that I will expire there and then for his entertainment."

Botolph grinned.

Sure enough, Eric fulfilled Luka's expectations and Botolph did his best to keep a straight face as his friend endured it all with only a rolling of the eyes. Eric told them that the flood tide ran to the north-east for about two hours before high water to four hours after, when the south-going ebb started. The boats coming from Gesoriacum and Amblethuys would have already left and would arrive at Folcanstane between half tide and low water. They would then be unloaded and reloaded as necessary, depending upon whether they were due to sail elsewhere in England or simply returning to Gallia.

"When would we go aboard then?" asked Luka.

"Well," said Eric "best you go down to the stade and then once the boats have grounded and the water left them, you can go right up to the boats and bargain for your passage. Don't make a nuisance of yourselves mind, as the skippers will have a busy job making sure nothing is stolen from their cargo and yet ensuring that it is all unloaded before nightfall. The way the tides fall at the moment, I doubt if they will reload tonight. They will probably wait until daylight and then leave as soon as they can after that. Once they are fully laden you will get your chance to nip aboard."

Suddenly it appeared that time was short. Botolph had, for some time, wanted to revisit the chapel he had built: first in hope and then in thanksgiving for Luka's life being saved. He winced slightly when he realised that he would really like to make the visit on his own but tried to push the thoughts from his mind as he realised the contradictions.

The chapel came into view as they made their way up the hill. It was much as Botolph had last seen it. Nothing had been disturbed although it was clear that it had been used regularly for private worship ... "but by whom?" Botolph wondered. They knelt and prayed silently and then, in case Luka was using the silence as an opportunity to let his thoughts run away with him or to snooze, Botolph led into a series of monastic prayers followed by supplications for safe passage. Luka showed goodwill by sealing each prayer with an enthusiastic "Amen".

When they left the chapel and looked towards Gallia, they could make out the shapes of several vessels coming in on the flood tide. It would be a couple of hours before their arrival so they headed back down the hill and through the ford before climbing again and seeking entrance at the fortress gates.

They were instantly recognised and welcomed by the soldiers on guard duty and they made their way towards the Great Hall where Botolph begged an audience with the king. Once again, after a pause, they were ushered into the smoky chamber where Eadbald and Ymme were gazing thoughtfully at the logs burning on the central fire. The king rose and greeted the boys like long lost sons. They explained that the purpose of their presence was to take their leave for an extended period. Eadbald sent a slave to fetch Eanswythe from the Nunnery and Botolph felt something clutch his throat as she swept tall and serenelyelegant into the hall. He saw a flush pass over her face as he once more related their plans. She would be as sorry to lose him as he was to leave her. Their eyes locked for a few seconds and a jumble of indefinable messages passed between them, the result of which was that their resolves were further strengthened; they had silently affirmed before God and before each other their commitments that Eanswythe was a nun and Botolph was destined to be a monk.

Eadbald offered them a place to sleep for the night but the boys declined, having already accepted the same offer from Martha and Eric and wanting to be close to the Stade. Having taken their leave and not wishing to prolong it, they headed back down to the beach where they found three craft in various stages of taking the ground. One, clearly the first to arrive, was high and nearly dry and an ox cart was already standing axle deep at its side while it was unloaded.

"Where are you bound?" called Botolph to the skipper.

"I ain't bound anywhere, I'm unloading me bleedin' boat," came the irritable reply.

"Good start" muttered Luka. Botolph pretended he had not heard. He tried again.

"We want to get to Gallia, any chance of a passage tomorrow?" The verbal silence was filled by grunts, puffs, groans, thumps and squeals as the cargo continued to make its way from ship to cart. Botolph kept his patience and eventually the scruffy hairy owner of the skipper's voice made his way to the prow. He squatted down, laid his arms on the rail and rested his chin on his arms and glowered at a spot somewhere between Botolph's eyes. "What?" he said.

"Gallia, tomorrow?" replied Botolph unabashed.

"Daybreak! Just the two of you? How much you going to pay me? You're not a couple of bleedin' monks are you? I s'pose you expect free passage? Well think again, I'm certainly not going to ... Hello Eric!" he said looking at Luka.

"My name's not Eric," said Luka in astonishment.

"Not *you*, you idiot!" said the skipper as the voice of Martha's father-in-law crackled over Luka's head.

"These boys," said Eric placing a hand on Luka's shoulder, " are good friends of mine and of King Eadbald, so, you smelly, flea-bitten, half-dead, hairy old ragbag, you will give them free and safe passage to Gallia and no more of your nonsense. Right!"

"Well since you ask so nicely, Eric, I can hardly refuse, now can I?   Alright monks, daybreak!   Can you handle oars?"   They nodded.   "Well then, I might get something out of you yet!   Daybreak, don't be late!"

CHAPTER 41
Embarkation.

Botolph passed a fitful night, tossing and turning in his sleep, in his dreams and in his head, as his mind subconsciously contemplated the important steps he was taking: his first channel crossing; life in Gallia; becoming a monk; Eanswythe.

He thought he had been awake all night but then came properly awake with a start as Martha gently shook his shoulder. In her ever-homely way she fed and watered them both, made sure they had everything they needed, hugged them briefly and then pushed them out of the door with the inevitable two leather bags of goodies for the trip. Botolph turned to thank her but she was gone and he knew she would be weeping at the thought that she might never see them again.

Once back at the water's edge they could see the three vessels had been moved further offshore and were at anchor waiting for the tide to turn. Gloomy Eric appeared at the boys' side. "C'mon then," he said, "Let's get you aboard, there's a rowing boat here but it leaks a bit and I might have to take you out one at a time."

In the event they all managed to get aboard and Eric slowly and rhythmically rowed them out to their transport. A boy's grubby face appeared over the side and a rope ladder was thrown for them to board. They tumbled over the rails onto some nondescript items of cargo and Eric threw their leather bags of dunnage up after them. Loud snoring issued from under a cloth by the mast and, on searching, they found the source was a fetid open cavity smelling strongly of mead. Surrounding the noisy open mouth was something resembling a gorse bush, but which in fact proved to be the whiskers of their less-than-noble captain. Beside him, on the deck, was the real culprit in the shape of a half empty flagon of mead.

The sun was already climbing well above the horizon and the other two vessels were busily weighing anchor. Out of the corner of his eye, Botolph saw a movement in the bow and he started to study the rest of the boat and its cargo. The movement had come from a group of four slaves, shackled to each other and to their slavemaster who was in a similar state of inebriation to the skipper but quieter. The other cargo was a real mixture. Botolph guessed that some must have been speculative purchases and some specially ordered. There were jars of salt, animal hides and leathers, some ironware and fish. He turned as Luka spoke:-

"Well then Oh Clever One, what are we going to do? Are you going to wake him or shall I? No, I have a better idea. Where's that boy gone? Oi, boy, go and give the old man a shake!"

The boy looked wild-eyed in fright and shook his head and vanished into a hole under the cargo.

"Looks as if it's down to me then!" said Luka. Botolph thought he detected an element of glee in Luka's voice. Clearly the skipper held no terrors for him this morning. Botolph recalled the perverse pleasure that he had exhibited in the past when performing similar clarion duties.   The truth was that Luka shared a characteristic found in many people; he did not like being woken up himself but did delight in stirring others and today a determined Luka was about to get his own back for the previous day's interchange.

Subtlety was not his strong point. "Oi!" he shouted in the general direction of the gorse bush.

Nothing happened.   If anything, the snoring became louder.   "Oi!" he shouted again and, finding a shoulder, gave it a good shake.   Still nothing.   Botolph suddenly began to worry that perhaps the skipper was actually unconscious rather than merely being in a deep sleep.

"Now," said Luka "you will be my witness won't you Botolph my old friend?   I did try to wake him nicely but he resisted.   Now there's only one solution!"   He picked up one of the empty flagons and Botolph held his legs while he reached over the side and filled it with seawater.   Smiling gleefully he bore it triumphantly to the recumbent figure and upended it into the gorse bush.

A minor explosion came from beneath the blanket which erupted in the shape of animated arms and legs as the skipper's body regained verticality.   He only made it as far as the sitting position however and sat there shaking his head as a terrier does having caught a rat.

The head stilled.   The eyes opened.   They settled on Luka.   The gorse bush said "You!"   "YOU did that?"

Luka planted his feet apart and placed his hands on his hips in stubborn acquiescence and reflected that he seemed to be going through a period where everyone from Archbishop to Humble Sailor, seemed to address him in this way.   It seemed to him that being small was in some ways an advantage since his opponents did not seem to

315

expect offensive action and were doubly shocked when it hit them!

The skipper shook his gorse bush again, rose and gained his feet which started to stagger unsteadily in the general direction of Luka, his bloodshot eyes still staring at his adversary. Botolph decided the time had come for a distraction so said "The other boats have left."

"What's that?"

"The other boats left half an hour ago. Shouldn't we get underway?"

The staggering reorientated in his direction and the eyes stared at him in turn. "Ah! The other young monk! Boats left already you say?" The bush swivelled again as he looked towards the sun and his befuddled brain assessed its height above the horizon.

"Jesus Christ, we'll miss the tide! Boy! Boy! Where are you, you scamp? Why didn't you wake me? C'mon, get that sail started. You two, come with me and help me weigh anchor."

They accompanied him to the prow where he unlashed the hawse from the bits and took up the slack in the rope.

"C'mon youse two, do summint to earn yer passage. Heave! Heave! Heave! That's it, she's away, you haul her up tight while I go and steer. Boy! Get that sail right up now, we ain't got much wind."

Slowly the vessel turned and started to make some headway. The iron anchor clunked against the side and Luka held it while Botolph took a couple of turns around the bit. The skipper called Botolph aft to take the helm while he and the boy pushed past the slaves who eyed them sulkily and silently whilst the two seamen catted the anchor tightly against the prow. Once done, they heaved the leeboard down and before long the boat was dancing prettily across the waves towards a Gallia which was still hidden in the morning mist. The skipper took a swig from the flagon of mead and smacked his lips in appreciation. "Hair of the dog!" he said in response to Botolph's disapproving look.

"What's that mean?" asked Luka.

"Hair of the dog? Why, it's the expression we use when we've had a skinful. When youse had a good drink the night before and you wake feeling awful, the best thing you can do is to have another drink of the same stuff that caused the trouble. The hair of the dog that bit me! See?" he said triumphantly.

Luka didn't see at all but stored the expression away in his mind and determined to use it at an opportune future date. The next couple of hours passed pleasantly enough. The wind was on the prow and the sail was pulled in as tightly as it could be, forcing the boat over on its leeward side and pressing the water on the leeboard which was working hard to stop them slipping sideways to the north. It was not rough but the occasional wave slopped over the bow and the slaves did their best to huddle into a dry area. Botolph was uneasy about their presence. It had always seemed wrong to him that his brother humans could be bought and sold as mercilessly as any other merchandise. He sent off one of his silent prayers of thanks that neither he nor Luka had had to suffer this indignity ... yet! It could happen any day. Perhaps they were more likely to be captured in Gallia than in Britain. Still, it was too late to worry about that now.

"You sure we're going the right way?" said Luka. "We can often see the Gallia coast clearly from Folcanstane but there is no sign of it now."

"Ha!" boomed the skipper, "We have a saying that 'If you can see Gallia it's going to rain, and if you can't see Gallia, it's 'cos it's raining already!" and he slapped his thigh and laughed heartily as if it was the best thing he had ever heard.   Luka looked at Botolph and rolled his eyes then looked back at the skipper.

"So, it's not going to rain but when are we going to see Gallia?"

"Well, we are about halfway across now.   See that bumpy water ahead, that's the shallow ridge that runs down the centre of the channel.   Once we are over that we shall soon see the coast and ... Oh Christ No!"

Botolph and Luka jerked upright at the alarm in his voice, "What is it?"

"Fog!" he said.   "There's a fog bank rolling towards us.   I *hate* fog!   Look ... do you see it?"

He pointed ahead where a dark rolling line was extending ominously towards and around them;   moments later they were engulfed and could not even see the slaves at the end of the boat.

CHAPTER 42
Fog.

Hung over as he was, the skipper still broke into seamanlike action. The boy was taken off the steerboard which the skipper reclaimed for himself. The lad was sent to find some lengths of rope to join together to make a sounding-line. Botolph and Luka waited for their instructions which they guessed would soon come.

"How do you keep a course when there's nothing to look at?" asked Luka.

"Feel; instinct; and judging the wave pattern," replied the skipper. "Assuming that young varmint was sailing true when I took over, and I think he was, I reckon if I keep the same feeling coming through the steerboard as when I started then we are still going in the same direction. Can't really explain it, it's experience, but not one that I would choose to have to use, given the option which I haven't been!

Instinct! Gesoriacum is over there, I know it, I can feel it in my bones and that's the way I'll keep edging. Wave pattern! Well you can hardly see the rails, let alone the water, but when it clears a bit, I shall be able to tell by the wave pattern if we are going the right way.

And then there's still sight and sound of course. If it thins out only a little, I shall get a glimmer of light from where the sun is, and when we get closer to the shore we

319

shall smell it on the wind, feel it on the sounding-line and hear all manner of new sounds. So you two lads, get up there in the prow and pin your lugs back and let me know any changes you hear or see. Off you go now!"

The boys did his bidding and settled themselves one each side of the stempost, straining their eyes looking forwards into the mists of nothingness. There was still a reasonable breeze which kept the boat going nicely but showed no inclination to blow the fog away. They soon began to get cold with the dampness and Botolph went back aft and took a couple of animal hides out of the cargo and they wrapped themselves inside them and maintained their vigil, the wet fingers of the fog curling around their heads and streaking down their faces.

They could see nothing but the few feet of water ahead of them. They sniffed and smelt nothing but salt. They listened and heard nothing but the ripple of water as the prow cut through the waves. Botolph hoped that there were no other boats heading towards them. He then imagined the hard chalk cliffs and wondered how close they were and how much warning they would get before they slammed into them.

Suddenly a seagull, disturbed from its resting place on the water, took off vertically as the boat pierced the fog behind it.

Botolph and Luka had, long since, had the vision of the cliffs for which they searched imprinted in their minds and their overcharged anticipation mistook the vision of the seagull for the sheer white cliffs of expectancy.

They both shouted at once and involuntarily leapt backwards and fell over each other on the forepeak.

"What in Wotan's name's up with you two?" bellowed the skipper as they untangled themselves.

320

"Nothing," said Luka "Just a little misunderstanding" and, keen to avoid explanation, they sheepishly returned to their lookout positions and endeavoured to calm themselves.

Little happened for the next hour except that the fog thinned sufficiently for the skipper to get his bearings on the sun and it gave the boys confidence to know that they were at least going in the right direction. The wind dropped a little and they were obviously not making as much speed as previously. The skipper lashed the helm loosely, called the boy to him and handed him a small piece of wood to take up into the bow. When the boy was ready with his hand over the side, the skipper lashed the helm tightly, went over to the stern rails and shouted "NOW!" The boy dropped the wood into the water and the skipper muttered

"One little Roman, Two little Romans, Three little Romans, Four", and stopped as the wood swirled away into the fog behind the boat.

"What's all that about then?" Luka asked the boy.

"'E's worrit!" said the lad. "'E knows we left late, now the wind's dropped and 'e's worrit that the ebb's going to stop and the flood'll start and we'll never get to Gesoriacum this tide!"

"Oh, wonderful!" said Luka. "So what about the bit of wood?

"Speed! 'E's just working out what speed we're doing and if we're going to make it. It's my guess we won't and then, just mind my words, he'll break out another flagon of mead and drown 'is sorrows in that!"

"Even more wonderful" said Luka. "Here brother, the boy and I can keep watch here. Why don't you go back aft and keep an eye on the gorse bush?"

"Good idea," said Botolph, "shout loudly if you hear or see anything, this fog seems to blanket out all the sound."

Another half an hour passed.   The skipper had accepted Botolph's presence easily enough.   If truth be known he was glad of some company as his bloodshot eyes did their best to pierce the gloom.   He didn't talk much ... just a few words now and then ... and more to himself than to his companion.   During one of his silent periods there was a sudden call from Luka "Breakers, I can hear breakers!"

"Shit!" said the skipper, tensing.   "Boy!" but the boy already had the sounding-line over the side and was bringing it up again.

"Well, ... well, ... c'mon boy ... hurry up ... what've you got?"

"Six!," shouted the lad, hurling it out again, ... "Five!"

"Take the steerboard!" said the skipper to Botolph. He rushed up to the bows beside Luka and strained both his ears and eyes in the direction from which the sound of breakers came.   He looked down at the cutwater and saw they were only travelling at slow walking pace.

"Well there's one good thing," he said to Luka, "when we hit we are not going to hit hard!"

Luka was not consoled by these words.   He did not mind hitting a nice soft muddy or sandy beach but a vertical cliff face was not his favourite idea of a landfall.

The boy called again "No sounding".

"What do you mean, 'No sounding'?" bawled the skipper.   "Have you lost the sounding iron you stupid little ... ?"

"No, skip!" came the indignant reply "Here it is. We're in deeper water again!"

"Shit, shit and double shit! … that tide must be taking us north round Whitenose."

He leaned forwards again and sure enough could still hear the breakers but they were now further to windward.

"Oars!" he said, "Ship those two oars or we shall be up in Friesland before we touch the ground."

Luka helped the boy to get the larboard oar in place while the skipper prepared the steerboard one. Botolph did his best to keep the vessel sailing in the right direction, bearing in mind the slow progress they were making. The sun obligingly still broke through occasionally and at those times Botolph was aware of the skipper's critical assessment of the quality of his steering, but nothing was said, so Botolph assumed he was satisfied.

"I *hate* fog!" said the skipper again. "That sun's going down. It won't be long before we have darkness to contend with too! Where's that flagon of mead gone?"

"Who is going to row?" said Botolph, changing the subject. His distraction seemed to work and the skipper went down to the slavemaster and started to negotiate. All four slaves were stocky male Saxons and looked as if they could wield plenty of oar power. They were all chained together though and the slavemaster was reluctant to release them. The skipper pointed out that, if the boat did not make more forwards movement, there was a good chance they were all going to die anyway. Eventually a compromise was reached and the chain joining each pair was cut off and two slaves assigned to each side.

The vessel started to make more way but the light was beginning to fade. Dusk seemed to last a very short while; there was no moon and Botolph found himself alone in inky blackness on a rocking platform with absolutely nothing to guide his steering. He suddenly, for the first time, began to feel helpless and afraid. He tried to pray, but the words would not come; his praying mind had ceased to function. "God please help us and bring us all to safety," was all he could manage.

A shout came from the direction of the prow as Luka's sharp ears picked up the sound of more breakers. The skipper bellowed at the boy to get a sounding. From what Botolph could make out, the boy had tried and had found the bottom but could not tell the depth because of the darkness. There were more shouts and curses from the skipper and cries from the boy.

"Larboard, ... go larboard," shouted the skipper and Botolph pushed on the steerboard.

"Straighten up. Straighten up. Midships!" came the cry and Botolph heaved the helm back the other way. Their speed seem to be increasing now, but not because of the rowers or the wind, but Botolph felt they were in some tidal rip.

"Avast rowing!" shouted the skipper. "Get those oars inboard!" There was shouting and the sounds of scuffles, and then suddenly a bang as the hull hit the ground. The steering oar catapulted Botolph across the stern as the boat spiralled out of control in a semicircle and listed over onto her steerboard side.

CHAPTER 43
Stranded!

All went quiet except for the sound of water lapping the hull.   Botolph picked himself up out of the corner whence he had been thrown.   "Luka ... Luuuuka ... are you alright?"

"Yes, fine thanks" came Luka's cheerful voice, "I guess we've arrived then!   Welcome to Gallia brother."

Botolph grinned into the darkness.   "Are you there, skipper?" he called, feeling his way into the central part of the boat.   There was no answer.

"Boy?"

"Yes brother, I'm here" came the urchin's voice. Bodies were moving in front of him.   He identified the two slaves who had been operating the oar on the steerboard side and then fell over a crumpled body.

"Luka! Come here. Help me!"   Luka was soon at his side and they hauled the body up into sitting position. It was the slavemaster showing no sign of life.   There was little or nothing they could do in the darkness so they heaved him into a reasonably comfortable position and left him there while they searched the boat for the skipper.

Botolph called again.   Unsuccessfully.   They searched further and eventually found him in the larboard sluice.   He was covered in something sticky which Botolph

325

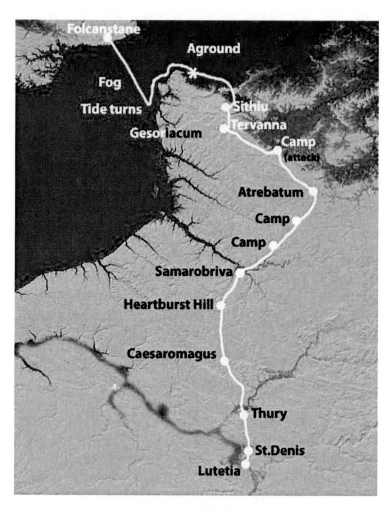

Fig. 8. Voyage and Overland Journey
from Folcanstane to Lutetia

guessed must be blood but he was at least breathing. Again they hauled him into a more comfortable attitude and covered him with one of the animal hides they had been using.   It was too dark to find where he was bleeding from, he was in God's hands now and any further repairs would have to wait until daylight.

"We'd better get that sail down." Luka suggested. They did just that, with the help of the boy who knew the ropes so well that, even in the blackness his nimble fingers soon had the spar down on the deck and the sailcloth scandalised.

"What's next?" asked Luka.

"Well," said Botolph slowly, "It must be about four hours before midnight now so it is long past high water and the tide will still be falling.   The question is whether our best action would be to leave the boat here and continue our journey by foot, or whether it would be wiser to stay where we are in the hope that the hull is undamaged and will float again on the next tide.   It sounds as if the water has nearly left the boat now.   Let's slip over the side and see if it's too muddy to explore."

"When you say 'Let's slip over the side', I suppose you mean me?" said Luka.   Botolph could not see his face but could guess what his expression was like.

"Certainly!" he replied "I am far too heavy.   God has made you nice and light and suited you admirably for just this sort of purpose."

"Oh, good, that was very nice of Him," said Luka resignedly.

Botolph and the boy found a stout rope and tied it around Luka's waist.   They then lowered him slowly over the sloping side until they felt the rope slacken.

"What have you got?" called Botolph.

"Wet feet!" came the reply.

Botolph chuckled. "No, you idiot, is it sand, rock or mud?"

There was some scrabbling around and stamping and then ... "Well it's not oozy. Quite hard in fact. A mixture of sand and pebble with just a bit of mud I would guess."

"Great. Well go and have a look round and see what you can find!"

There was some muttering and a few tugs on the rope as Luka disentangled himself and then nothing.

"Luka" ... Nothing.

Then, rather more loudly "Luuuka!" Still nothing.

"Now what?" thought Botolph. If I go down to find him, we'll probably both get ourselves lost, and the young lad will certainly not be strong enough to pull us back up. He leant out over the rail and shouted again at fullest volume he could manage: "Luuuuuuuuka!"

"Yes?"

He jumped as the voice came from under his chest.

"Is that you, Luka?"

"Well who else d'you think it would be stuck out on a Gallic mudflat in a thick fog in the middle of the night?"

"Right. What've you found?"

"Nothing. I really cannot see a thing out here and I cannot walk too far or I would never find my way back once I was out of range of your weak and paltry voice!"

Botolph ignored the sarcasm and said. "Well, you'd better come aboard again, but before you do, I'm going to lower the anchor, so that, assuming we refloat on the next tide, we won't go drifting out to sea again."

With the boy's help, the anchor was duly uncatted and lowered and Luka dragged it to the water's edge. He was then hauled back into the boat and they settled down to get some rest and wait for Divine Providence to bring daylight.

Botolph seemed to have just closed his eyes when there was a bang as a roller from the incoming tide hit the side of the boat. This made her shudder from stem to stern and she rolled upright for a moment and then fell back to her previous crazy angle as the water receded. Another roller hit them and the process was repeated. Then came another wave which both hit her and lifted her. She slewed round as she was deposited with a sickening thud onto a flatter piece of sand. Both boys tensed with each roll and listened for any sound of trickling water that might indicate that their beaching had holed the hull. There were so many noises of water however that a trickle from a leak would have been indistinguishable and they were both so tired that in a short while they fell asleep again.

An hour or so later Luka's awareness surfaced a little and he was vaguely aware of the boat now rocking gently to her anchor. He was warm and comfortable, and happy to delegate her care to Botolph's God and he drifted back into a fitful sleep.

It seemed only moments later, although it must have been several hours, when the boat spoke again as she gently touched the ground on the new falling tide. She gave a couple more bounces before she settled completely and this time, he was pleased to note, she lay completely upright on the sand.

He reasoned that they were completely safe now and that he was entitled to the comatose state that he craved so he turned over and screwed his eyes tightly shut in his determination to achieve his aim. He could hear a noise. He tried *not* to hear it. He really was not interested and did not want to know. He kept his eyes closed but could not help listening intently. What was it? He listened again. All seemed quiet but *something* had been stirring. He groaned inwardly and allowed his eyes to open and then squawked in alarm and shot out of his nest as a bloodstained gorse bush hovered over him. Botolph awoke too as the gap in the gorse bush tried to mouth a few words.

Dawn was just breaking although the fog was still present. The skipper's legs collapsed and the boys busied themselves with making him comfortable in the corner that Luka had just vacated. They could find no water to give him so decided that mead was the only answer and he seemed to appreciate this and closed his eyes again without saying a word.

Once again Botolph gloried in the miracle of daylight and took the opportunity to take stock of his surroundings. They were still blanketed by a thick cold clammy layer of fog but could see a couple of boat's lengths in all directions. There was still a foot or two of water under the hull but they were nicely placed in the centre of a wide channel. Botolph could see, on the edge of a nearby muddy ridge, the scar left where the vessel had grounded in the dark.

He turned away from the view and started to explore the boat further. Amidships, he found a plank with wooden slats that obviously doubled between a gangplank for runs ashore and a ladder for other purposes. He called on Luka's help and they heaved it over the side as the last of the water ebbed away. Both descended onto the sandy, gravelly river bed. Botolph listened: Nothing, except sea sounds. They climbed from the deepest part of the channel up the side of the bank and past the scar on the ridge until they reached the wide mud-sand top.

The fog relentlessly swirled around them as they followed the edge of the now-dry water course towards a white glimmer caused by the rising sun.

"What's that?" said Botolph, pointing ahead.

"A tree!" said Luka, "That's a strange place to have a tree."

As they came closer they realised that the fog had played one of its many tricks and that the tree was not as large as it had first appeared but was a branch, stuck in the sand to demarcate the edge of the sandbank.

"That's useful," said Luka, "I wonder if there are any others."

They walked on and sure enough, a few minutes later they came to another one.

"These would be fine for feeling your way up the channel on a nice clear day," said Botolph "but in these foggy conditions they are too far apart to be helpful. What we really need are a few more withies to plant along the bank. If we follow the rising ground there might be some trees at the river's edge."

"How long before the water comes back?" asked Luka.

"We should have at least a couple of hours," replied Botolph as they headed in the direction in which they hoped the shore would be, keeping the embryo sun to their left. They walked across flat sand for several minutes but there was no sign of any grass, let alone trees. Worse still was the fact that the ground did not seem to be rising so they could not be sure that they were walking in the right direction. They stopped and listened but only sounds of gulls and sea came to them.

"Not one of your best ideas," said Luka, "I think we ought to abandon this and get back to the boat."

"Yes, I think you're right," admitted Botolph and they turned back the way they had come, following the footprints in the sand. After a few minutes they came to a harder patch of gravel where the footprints were lost and very shortly afterwards, so were they. Somewhere high to the south-east, clouds had obscured the sun and eliminated that as a guide and the fog seemed to be conspiring with the other elements to compound the problems.

"What do we do now?" said Luka.

"Let's try shouting," said Botolph, so, cupping their hands around their mouths they, in unison called, "Skiiiiiiip!", to which, unsurprisingly, there was no answer.

"That's not going to work until we get closer," said Botolph, "C'mon, let's go."

"But we don't know if we are going in the right direction," insisted Luka.

"Well, any direction is better than standing here."

"I'm not sure that's true."

"Tell you what, let's offer up a quick prayer."

"Botolph! That's always your solution. How's that going to help us out here, right in the middle of nowhere, getting our knees wet praying?"

"Have you a better solution?"

"No."

"Right then, a quick prayer asking God for deliverance and asking him to tell us which way the boat is. We'll each close our eyes, turn round three times, kneel down, pray, wait for God's answer and then point in the direction we think he's telling us to go, and only then open our eyes! Alright?"

"If you say so," sighed Luka.

A couple of minutes later they opened their eyes to find Botolph pointing in one direction and Luka pointing at right angles to that. "Well, that didn't work then!" said Luka.

"Yes it did," persisted Botolph, "We'll split the difference. C'mon, we'd better get a move on or that water will be coming back again and we'll really be in trouble."

They half-walked and half-ran into the mist. After five minutes, Luka stopped.

"I think we're going the wrong way, we should be heading more to our right."

"If you think so, Luka. Off you go then, I'll follow, we are in God's hands now."

Luka trotted off with Botolph in pursuit. They had covered quite a distance and all seemed to be going well until Luka suddenly disappeared over an unseen edge. Botolph followed suit and landed on Luka's sprawling body.

"That's all we needed," groaned Luka, "now we are not only lost but covered in mud!"

"No we're not," said Botolph.

"We *are*!" insisted Luka, "- Just *look* at us."

"No ... Yes ... well, No ... What I mean is: Yes we are covered in mud, but No we are not lost. That was the edge of the river bank. All we have to do now is to follow it back to the boat." With that he scrambled back on top of the ridge and started running.

Luka was close behind him when they found the first withie and ran on. They were both out of breath and getting hungry when Botolph heard a new sound. He stopped too suddenly and Luka ran into him. "What's up?" said Luka.

"Can you hear that noise?"

"Oh Jesus Christ, it's the water coming back, the flood has started. We're going to drown!"

Botolph felt that now was not the time to reprimand Luka's blasphemy, so shouting "Quick, ... as fast as you can!" he ran on. His attention was caught by the sight of a stream of fast-flowing water filling the ditch beside them. For an eternity, it seemed, he had been running with his eyes focussed on nothing but the channel bank six feet ahead of him, looking neither right nor left as the ridge guided them back to where he fervently hoped the boat would be.

Suddenly there was a shout from behind him, "Fog's lifted!" and Botolph raised his head and saw with joy, the shape of the boat half a mile ahead, rolling as she started to float. His short-lived joy turned to horror as he looked around him and surveyed the desolate spot in which they found themselves. To their left at the end of the long flat bank of sand, some cliffs were just visible, but they were several miles away. Ahead and to their right was the open sea and that sea was roaring in over the flat sands as fast and as noisily as a galloping horse.

"Quickly!" he shouted and stretched his long legs into a sprint, but they were still a quarter of a mile from the boat when the water flowed over the edge of the ridge and in no time at all they were immersed up to their knees and unable to maintain any speed at all. The force of the water was incredible. Botolph looked behind and saw Luka struggling as the water approached his waist. Then, in a trice he was over and trying to regain his feet as the current washed him back the way he had come. Botolph gave up his boat-quest and turned back. As he reached Luka, he too stumbled and they clutched each other. Both were trying to stand, gasping for breath and coughing and retching in the spray. The water was deepening quickly, dragging at their legs and even Botolph found he could not stand. Their Priority was to maintain a hold on each other as they were buffeted by breakers which had gained in strength as they had already run a couple of miles across the flat sand. Now came a different sound over the roar of the surf. Botolph looked up and experienced a mixture of emotions as he saw a distant gorse bush driving his infernal boat down onto them. The prow reared over their heads and Luka felt sure they were about to be killed by the very boat that brought them there. At the last moment, the skipper pushed the helm over and then rushed to the rails where he and the boy leant over and grabbed the swimmers. Luka was the first to be pulled aboard and then Botolph's world spun around as he was propelled into the sluices.

There was no time for niceties and they were left there to disentangle themselves whilst the skipper jumped back to the helm and heaved on the steerboard as the boy in the prow strained his eyes for the next withy. Several times they hit the bottom and the boat faltered and twisted slightly as she broke herself free. The boys were none the worse for their dowsing and they stripped off and wrung the water out of their clothes before putting them back on again. The fog had gone but a westerly breeze had sprung up and the clouds were alternately obscuring and exposing the sun. The water had been very cold and both the boys' teeth were chattering.

They were now making good progress towards a cliff face that the skipper clearly recognised.

"Where are we?" said Botolph.

"Never mind where *you* are, just tell me where *they* are," said the skipper gesticulating into the bows.

"Who? Oh, the slaves?"

"Yes, the slaves!" mimicked the skipper in return. "What happened? Did *they* kill the slavemaster? Did they also try to kill me? Is that how I got this gash on my head? Why didn't they kill you? Did you help them to get away? Where have they gone?"

"No" said an indignant Luka, "they must have escaped while we were exploring. We had nothing to do with it. Poor devils, I don't envy them their freedom, out there in that water with shackles on. They would have been better to stay where they were. Anyway, do you know where we are or are we heading into oblivion again?"

"Well," said the skipper, stung by Luka's hinted criticism and accepting the change of subject, "It seems the tide turned early and we got ourselves swept around Greynose Point in the fog and then the last of the flood pushed us round Whitenose too. If I could have seen where I was going I could have got us at least half way up Sithiu river even though we would have been fighting the ebb. In the event, we was dumped on Caleton Sandbank which as you know to your cost is miles away from bleedin' anywhere.

If you look ahead of us you will see a break in the hills and that'll lead us over some shallow water to Sithiu, where I shall be very pleased to stay for a few days after this lot!"

"Sithiu?" said Botolph.   "So, what's of interest there?"

"Well, it's a small port," said the skipper, working the steerboard as they approached the hills, "nothing like as big as Gesoriacum where you *were* going and where I would have found it much easier to sell my cargo.   Still, this isn't bad and there won't be so much competition for my wares."

"Who lives there?" asked Luka.

"This whole area is inhabited by the Morini tribe. If you had made it over the sandbank, it would have been them as got you and it'll be them as gets those slaves if the sea don't get 'em first."

"Morini?" repeated Botolph.

"Yes, Morini. It means coming from the sea and these lands out here to the east of Whitenose, are all a mixture of marshes, bogs and sea. The Romans did their best to overcome the Morini, but they led them a right dance on the marshes; attacking and then dodging back over solid passageways that only they knew so that those soldiers who were brave enough to follow them ended up drowning.

"A bit like we did to Penda" Luka giggled as he turned to Botolph.

"They tried the same trick the following summer but the Romans were up to it this time," continued the skipper. "Not only that, but it was a drier year so the Romans won that battle. Look out, 'ere we come!"

The skipper leaned hard on the steerboard as the sail backed and fluttered and then, with a bang as the sail filled again, they shot through the gap that had opened between the two hillsides.

CHAPTER 44
Sithiu.

A calm and peaceful lagoon stretched before them. Tall grasses grew out of the shallowest water but a clear fairway led through the centre. The sail drew again and Botolph saw the rising hill of Mount Sithiu for the first time. As they came closer, a small wooden jetty became evident. The skipper steered towards this and the boy deftly lowered the sail at the last minute as the boat came gently alongside.

It was close to noon but there was no warmth in the sun and Botolph and Luka were shivering in their wet clothes. As the vessel touched the jetty, they jumped ashore and helped to make her fast.

"Pax vobiscum," came a voice from over Botolph's left shoulder. He turned to see a tall monk just a few years older than himself. Clearly Latin was going to be the language of the day and neither Botolph nor Luka had any problem with that; it was only their chattering teeth that hindered communication!

Brother Bertin was a tall skinny monk about five years older than the boys; he seemed keen to make friends. He was dressed in a white habit with a rope belt and heavy cowl which fell down his back and, Luka guessed enviously, might keep his shoulders nicely warm.

Bertin observed the boys' sodden clothes and, asking no questions, simply gave a beckoning wave followed by a quick "Venite!", and set off up the hill, glancing back to make sure they were following.

Luka jumped back into the boat and threw his and Botolph's leather bags onto the quayside and then leapt back after them. After a hurried thanks to the skipper and his boy they hitched up their habits and ran up the hill in the direction in which the tall monk was now disappearing.

He vanished into the trees and the boys caught a glimpse of his swirling figure as he ducked down and entered a large wooden hut from which smoke was curling through the thatch. By the time they arrived Bertin had come out again and was standing by the open door. He ushered them over to a central grate where the fire had recently been stirred into a blaze. They put down their bags and hovered as close to the flames as they dared, holding out their hands and then rubbing them as the feeling gradually returned. The fronts of their habits began to smell as the seawater-soaked clothes started to dry.

The interior of the hut was too smoky for them to be sure just how many occupants it had, but shadowy figures drifted to and fro. One such figure wordlessly handed each of the boys a clean habit. Without standing on modesty they helped each other haul off the still-sodden clothes and replaced them with the dry ones; it seemed no time at all before they began to feel human again.

Bertin reappeared and invited them to the refectory. Luka however had forged a relationship with a new-found friend called "The Fire" and he was reluctant to leave. Indeed he thought that he had never seen nor felt a better fire in the whole of his life. Food had always been a major interest to him though and so as Botolph and Bertin disappeared through the doorway, he fleetingly warmed his hands again and at the last moment quickly followed.

The refectory was a thatched wooden building rather similar to that which they had just left, but much bigger. It also had an atmosphere lightly pervaded by smoke which in this case the boys found to be homely rather than unpleasant. There was a central hearth upon which the logs were glowing healthily without any surfeit of flame or smoke. To one side was a large table around which sat a dozen monks of varying ages.

They stopped eating and looked up in expectation as Bertin brought the boys in. He announced the two as brothers from England on their way to Burgundo-Fara's Monastery. Leading them around the table he introduced them to two brothers called Mummolin and Ebertram and eight or nine others. The door opened again and an older imposing figure walked in.

"Well-timed Father," said Bertin. "Brothers Botolph and Luka, this is our Abbot, Bishop Audomar."

The bishop was a big man with a benevolent face pierced by penetrating eyes guarding a sharp nose atop a forked but greying beard. He offered his hand and, in turn Botolph and Luka knelt and kissed it and then rose again.

"Bless you my sons" he said in a soft and warm Latin burr, "and welcome to our humble gathering. Come, eat and then tell us the story of your journey."

Grace was said anew and the simple but welcome food and wine was shared around in silence as was their custom.

* * *

When the meal was finished, Bishop Audomar explained that he had been a novitiate at the Abbey of Luxovium in Burgundia . After he had been tonsured, his teaching ability was recognised and he became responsible for the tuition of three novitiates called Mummolin, Bertin and Ebertram.

"It was a sad day for me," he said "when my Abbot told me that the time had come for me to leave Luxovium and my pupils and come to this wilderness to bring Christianity to the land of the Morini tribe but it was a challenge I willingly accepted, since that is my calling."

Audomar told the story of his struggle to set up a monastery at Tervanna, some three leagues further south, and of all the setbacks he had endured.

"Then, a few months ago," he continued "three young newly-tonsured monks arrived at the abbey. And who do you think they were?"

"Hah!," said Luka, "Mummolin, Bertin and Ebertram!"

"Exactly!," triumphed Audomar. "They came in answer to my prayers and we have never looked back since."

"How did they help?" asked Botolph.

"Well of course the fourfold increase in teachers was the first advantage but being younger than me they could see that Tervanna was not close enough to the centre of the Morini tribe to be effective so while I looked after the abbey there, they started a new monastery here. We soon hope to build a newer and bigger monastery further up Mont Sithiu.

CHAPTER 45
Audomar.

Botolph and Luka were made so welcome that they were in no hurry to leave. Indeed Audomar did his best to persuade them to stay and join his commune. Botolph was tempted since the whole atmosphere seemed tinged with excitement and vitality but being single-minded by nature he was sure that Evoriacum was the place to which he was being drawn.

Audomar admired his conviction and asked what plans they had for the journey. He was stunned when the boys said that they supposed they would walk!

"You would not get ten leagues before you would be set upon by robbers, have the clothes stolen from your backs and your heads chopped off!" he said. "The locals hereabouts are very fond of chopping off people's heads, even if some of our brothers seem to be able to manage for quite a while without them."

Luka was suddenly all-attention. "How's that then?"

"Well," said the Bishop, "Gallia has been blessed with visits from a wide variety of saints for several centuries. The first four came when the Romans were still in occupation. They were the Saints Denis, Quentin, Lucian and Rieul who came to Gallia from Italy. Rieul

342

stayed in the south, Denis settled in Lutetia, Lucian went to Caesaromagus and Quentin came on to Samarobriva.

Denis was the first one to lose his head. He was a victim of his own success. The Parisi tribe in Lutetia converted so quickly to Christianity that the Roman Emperor became jealous and concluded that Saint Denis had more influence over the people than he did and so ordered his assassination. Denis was duly arrested and held while a Roman soldier chopped off his head. Once done, the story goes, Saint Denis picked it up and carried it with him for more than half a league before he finally died."

"How could he see his head to pick it up?" asked Luka innocently.

Audomar's paused and peered thoughtfully at him for a few seconds but saw innocence rather than insolence. "I wasn't there," he said drily, "but perhaps, even after it has been chopped off, you know instinctively where your head is."

"So what happened to Lucian and Quentin then?" asked Botolph.

"Well," replied the bishop warming to his theme, "I am sorry to have to tell you that they were both decapitated too! In fact Lucian had a couple of disciples with him called Maximian and Julian and their heads were chopped off at the same time as Lucian's so you can see why I don't want you two lads wandering about on your own in such territory as this."

"Don't you have any happier stories?" asked Luka.

The bishop was just considering this question when Bertin suddenly reappeared at his side closely followed by a man-at-arms.

Audomar stood "Pax vobiscum my son and welcome. What can I do for you?"

"Pax vobiscum Father, I bring you greetings from King Dagobert and ask that you will receive him and his entourage in two days' time."

"We shall be honoured," replied Audomar "but there are no Royal quarters here. If the king is planning on staying overnight he would be much more comfortable at the abbey in Tervanna."

"His majesty particularly wants to see the progress you are making at Sithiu but anticipated your suggestion and will be pleased to travel on to Tervanna afterwards."

The bishop turned away and walked outside, still chatting to the new visitor. A few minutes later he returned alone.

"The king?" said Luka excitedly.

"Yes indeed; in fact not one but *two* kings. King Dagobert is escorting his young son Sigebert around the courts of Austrasia. Sigebert is in fact *our* king but he is only eight years old. He has been king for four years but, in the latest peace, this is his father's first opportunity to parade him around his kingdom. It is always good for the people to see their sovereign."

"Sigebert?" said Botolph, his memory working furiously to recall where he had heard that name before. Then it came to him. Of course, old Blue-Eyes, the fisherman who had crushed his chest with his foot whilst poking his throat with a seaxe! Blue-Eyes had fought in Sigeberht's army, but that was *another* Sigeberht, Sigeberht of East Anglia. "Must be from the same tribal origin," he guessed silently. Luka had clearly forgotten.

"So what's his father king of?" asked Luka.

"Well, his father King Dagobert *was* king of all of this area. Being foreigners, you won't know, but this part of Gallia is made up of Austrasia, where we are now, Neustria which starts a few miles further south and Burgundia to the Southeast. The Austrasians decided that they wanted their own king so, although he was only four, Dagobert handed over the kingship to Sigebert."

"Ah, so Dagobert is now just king of Neustria and Burgundia ?"

"Yes but there is some talk of him handing those kingdoms to his other son Clovis."

"So how old is *he*?"

"He is still only a baby but that is the way kings seem to be doing things these days. Dagobert remains king as far as power is concerned but the populace are able to focus on the young princes as their leaders. Anyway, Dagobert is a great man and soon you will see him. In fact the sensible thing to do would be for you to join the king's party as he rides south."

"Vorroof!" said Luka.

There was the customary pregnant silence after this expostulation and Audomar peered intently at the young Anglo-Saxon. Botolph winced. He was becoming convinced that it was not just the unusual word that Luka used but it was the way that he said it. Somehow he always managed to get it piercing the silence like an arrow zinging into a tree. Was it the volume or the tone? Botolph could not make it out but it certainly stopped the old Abbot in his tracks.

Audomar looked questioningly at Botolph who instinctively shrugged, half apologetically, but then felt guilty about that. It was Luka's special word after all and really deserved no apology.　He broke the silence by awkwardly changing the subject.

"When will the kings arrive?" he asked.

"The day after tomorrow," replied the Abbot.　"If you *are* going to join the party then, you boys had better start getting ready and prepare some intelligent conversation."

* * *

Two days later, the whole community was abuzz with excitement.　The locals were looking forward to the prospect of some serious trading.

The boys went down to the quayside where they found their former skipper and his boy preparing for the royal visit with great enthusiasm.　The wharf, which had been virtually deserted when they had arrived, was now already thronged with people setting up trading stalls and showing off wares in the hope of making a killing.　The word of the kings' impending arrival had spread like wildfire and Sithiuans and Morinis from surrounding villages had crowded into the port.　They were eager both to buy and to sell and the hubbub of excited voices had reached the boys' ears well before they arrived at the dock. Ox carts could still be seen coming down the hill and 'trading between the traders' was well underway. Children and dogs were squeezing between people's legs and there were frequent commotions when an animal would escape and push its way through the crowd in a bid for freedom.　First came a squealing, grunting pig, closely followed by a puffing red-faced farmer's wife, and then from the other direction, a gaggle of geese.

Fig. 9. Austrasia, Neustria and Burgundia.

A bugle sounded in the distance and a host of eyes went to the top of the hill and a partial hush came over the crowd. It seemed to be a false alarm however and the cacophony of voices soon started again. Some minutes later however, came a second call and this time the upturned eyes were rewarded by the silhouette of a group of riders on the crest of the hill. Soon the rest of the entourage appeared over the brow and it was not long before the population of the quayside was doubled as the vanguard of the procession arrived. Soldiers pushed and cursed endeavouring to keep the crowds away from their monarchs and Botolph and Luka had their first view of King Dagobert and his young son.

Both were on horseback. Dagobert was in his mid-thirties, a tall handsome man with flowing locks and an elegant beard. By his side rode the eight-year-old Sigebert, at once chatting and smiling and acknowledging the inquisitiveness and adulation of the crowd. Behind them came more soldiers escorting a carriage carrying a royal lady nursing an infant. Botolph discovered later that this was Dagobert's second wife Nanthild and their two-year-old son Clovis. Behind them, the followers-on just kept appearing.

The royal party continued to swell the crowd as trading resumed around the water's edge. There was a disturbance to one side and Botolph realised that Bishop Audomar and his monks had come to welcome the king. At Botolph's insistence Luka dragged himself away from one of the sweetmeat tables and they pushed between the heaving bodies until they too formed part of the bishop's party.

At this point the two kings separated from the melee and dismounted. Their horses were led away and, with a handful of soldiers, the royals and the monks climbed the hill and entered the great hall. Here there was a chance for rest and refreshment, but not before the arrival of Nanthild and little Clovis, and the formality of prayers led by Bishop Audomar in thanksgiving for the king's safe journey thus far and for blessings on the meagre food and drink that was about to be provided.

The infant Clovis was becoming fretful and was led away to be fretful in solitude. His half-brother Sigebert looked as if he would like to join him but it was clear that Dagobert expected a more adult and statesmanlike approach from the eight-year-old.

Brother Mummolin was introduced to the king by the bishop with the words "... and this is the brother of whom I told you." Mummolin knelt and kissed the king's ring finger. The king looked down on him with interest and then bade him rise. They talked until it was announced that the food and drink were ready, whereupon Dagobert invited the young monk to sit by his side. Mummolin looked nervous but was soon put at his ease by the king who nevertheless persisted in asking him searching questions about the progress of the foundation.

All the while, more and more people were entering the great hall and the slaves were kept busy filling and refilling glasses, and providing food in response to shouts for service. Luka's attention was attracted by one particular individual. He nudged Botolph and whispered "Who's that?"

"I don't know," replied Botolph "but he certainly has a presence about him."

The man was tall with a rosy face and long fair curly hair. He had a noble way of walking and exuded elegance and authority. They watched him as he made his way

349

between the tables, smiling here and giving a kind word there. Clearly he was much beloved and respected by all those of the royal party.

A soldier touched his arm and guided him over to the king who rose and greeted him fondly. They held a fleeting conversation before the stranger was asked to sit between the king and Mummolin who then became engaged in deep conversation with the new arrival. All of this was watched in silence by Bishop Audomar from the opposite side of the table. The stranger finished his conversation with Mummolin and looked across at Dagobert and gave the briefest of nods. The king passed the same nod across to the bishop who rose and called for silence.

This took a while to achieve but once effected, the bishop, in his strong clear voice, announced that it was the king's pleasure that Brother Mummolin be consecrated Abbot of the new monastery at Sithiu, and that Brother Bertin be Prior. There was a murmur of approval and the meal continued as individuals formed a steady stream congratulating the new incumbents. A short while later silence was called for again as the royal guests prepared to leave to complete the last part of their journey to Tervanna.

Bishop Audomar was talking to the rosy-faced stranger and he beckoned Botolph and Luka over to join him.

"This is Eligius, King Dagobert's chief counsellor. He has agreed to let you join the kings' retinue and will do his best to ensure that you reach Lutetia safely. Thereafter further arrangements will be made for you to go on to Evoriacum."

Luka could not take his eyes off the counsellor's magnificent belt. It was made of the finest soft pale leather

and studded with gold and gemstones.   Furthermore it
was at Luka's eye level which made it even more difficult
for him to avert his gaze.

The counsellor looked down at him with soft brown
eyes to which Luka's were hypnotically attracted.   He
spoke with a regal air but in a way that Luka immediately
identified as 'caring'.   Suddenly Luka felt that he mattered
to this man, and yet, at the same time he realised that this
was the same with everyone to whom he spoke.   He
thought back on other 'holy men' that he had met: Abbot
Fursey, Prior Peter, Archbishop Honorius, they all had this
softness and benevolent attitude, but none as warmly as
this man Eligius.   Luka set to wondering if his magnificent
belt imbued him with magical powers and his imagination
began to run away with him until it was brought to a
standstill by Botolph's voice repeating "wouldn't we
Luka?"

"Ah, yes, certainly!" he replied, looking back into
Eligius's eyes and wondering what he had just committed
himself to.

Then there was another mad scramble to collect
their few belongings together, load them onto one of the
carts and then to go around and thank everybody for their
hospitality before they joined the end of the long procession
that snaked its way up the hill and out of Sithiu.

They walked through woody glades and then down
a hill before crossing a marshy valley and climbing up the
other side.   Being fit young men and, for a change, not
having to carry any baggage, they were able to walk faster
than most and were gradually making their way up the line
until they were not far behind the kings' party.

One contingent of soldiers had been denied the
festivities at Sithiu and had been sent ahead to Tervanna to

erect the tents and light the fires, so although the sun was beginning to settle onto the tops of the trees by the time the monastery hove into sight, it was not long before the horses were fettered and the encampment populated.

The boys had taken leave of their new friend Bertin and the recently-appointed Abbot Mummolin, but Bishop Audomar, and, of course, Eligius had all been part of the procession. The king and his family and nearest courtiers were provided with accommodation by the bishop. Botolph and Luka went to meet the brothers of the Tervanna Monastery and joined them for Vespers and then for Compline before they finally lowered their heads and slept the sleep of the dead.

CHAPTER 46
Night Camp

The next day they travelled south-eastwards from Tervanna towards the capital town of the next tribe down the line, the Atrebates. King Dagobert had sent his scouts forwards to find a suitable place in which to pitch camp for the night since Atrebatum was too far to travel in one hop. They passed through pine and oak forests atop a ridge and then the path led downwards and they were once again able to glimpse water sparkling in the distance. Both Botolph and Luka were enjoying the walk; the weather was mild enough not to get too hot and yet cool enough to prevent undue perspiration.

"There are a lot of us, aren't there?" said Luka. "Why are there so many people accompanying the king?"

"Well, I suppose that there is safety in numbers, for one thing," said Botolph stretching and craning his neck as he undertook a rough count of the party. He had to guess some numbers as the tail of the procession was lost to sight in the trees and then he had to add others like the two scouts that he knew had been sent ahead.

"About four score I should think," he said, "and I don't know how many mules and horses, about half as many again probably."

"That's a lot to feed," said Luka. "It is all very well when we visit a place like the abbey at Tervanna where

Bishop Audomar's staff can provide the fodder, but I assume the king is providing our food tonight."

"Yes, I am sure that is the nub of the problem," Botolph mused. "Not only does the king have to bring food with him but also tents and tables and cooking implements. Some of those are being carried directly by the mules, and other things are being carried in the wains. They take time and manpower to load and unload and to drive them during the journey. If one of the wooden wheels gets broken a wheelwright's needed to mend it; a farrier needs to be on hand in case one of the horses goes lame. I noticed that the king's horse has iron shoes."

"Yes," said Luka, "I noticed that. King Anna used to have iron shoes fitted to his horse too. Apparently, he originally used hipposandals to protect his horse's hooves, but they were unreliable and so he moved on to the iron ones."

"We used to make horse shoes in the Bloomery," reminisced Botolph. "There was a farrier who had a smithy somewhere to the west of us and he was a regular customer. More and more people seem to be using them now."

"None of the pack horses or mules have them though," rejoined Luka. "No doubt it is because of the cost. What about the king's bodyguard, do their horses have iron shoes?"

"I've no idea," said Botolph patting his friend's head, "you can make that your special project for the day."

"Hey-up," said Luka, "it looks as if we are nearly there, I can see the scouts' horses through the trees."

It was mid-afternoon and they had been travelling for five hours or so as they turned off the old Roman road and descended a rough slope to a grassy plateau bounded by what seemed to be an inland lake.

"You boys," called the captain of the king's bodyguard, "go and find the Captain of the Contubernium and make yourselves useful unloading the tents and getting them erected."

He moved on down the line, directing the men leading the mules, to the places where he wanted the tents unloaded and pitched.

"The who?" said Luka.

"I think he said the Captain of the Contubernium," said Botolph. "Not too sure what one of those is, but I guess he means the foreman of the tentmates. Let's go and find out."

Before long the plateau was inundated with people as the tail of the procession caught up with the front. There was shouting and swearing and laughing and crying and all the noises of a mass of people suddenly arriving in the same place at the same time.

Soon wood smoke began to pervade the air and was followed shortly afterwards by the smell of cooking. Botolph and Luka had kilted their habits to make for easier movement in the melee and decrease their likelihood of tripping over some carelessly placed implement. There were ten tents to go up so the boys offered their labour to the gang erecting the nearest one. Since they were not much good at anything else, they opted to help in manhandling the central pole and holding that straight whilst the more experienced workers concentrated on pulling out the material and fixing the edges.

Once they had finished their work on the first tent, they moved on to the next one but the central pole was already up. They could see what needed to be done at the edges though so they joined in with the stretching and pulling. "That was fun!" said Luka. "Next one then, over there," and they shot off to lend their further help.

Luka managed to strike up a brief conversation with one of the tentmates before they were again moved on to another tent, but he could at least confirm to Botolph that a contubernium was what they called themselves.

Within an hour or so the encampment was beginning to look fairly serviceable and the workers took their sweaty bodies down to the water's edge to wash the grime from their faces and hands.

"Ugh" said Luka in disgust, "it's salty! I was looking forward to some nice fresh drinking water."

"So it is," said Botolph, "and we should have noticed. Look, it's tidal. This must be part of the same sea that washed us into Sithiu."

They had to content themselves with splashing their faces a bit. "Fancy a swim?" grinned Botolph.

"I've had enough of that for the moment," said Luka, remembering how cold it had been when they had almost drowned on their arrival in Gallia.

"I thought you'd say that. C'mon, let's go and get something to eat and find out where we are sleeping tonight."

It was a very convivial evening, sitting around the embers of one of the cooking fires. One of the king's bodyguards was an accomplished singer and player of the lyre and he was duly commanded to entertain the royal party, singing the ballads of the king's forefathers. Together with others, Botolph and Luka left their fire and crowded around the king's group as night settled in.

Nobody heard the raiders.

One minute it was party time and the next minute there was a whinny from one of the horses and flashes of steel as the horsemen came out of the blackness, cutting and thrusting at anyone who stood in their way.

There were shouts and screams and blood-curdling cries as the royal party scattered in disarray. One of the horsemen came thundering towards the boys swinging his sword in an arc. Like a flash, Luka whisked out his seaxe, ducked under the sword and, unable to reach anything else, plunged the seaxe into the horse's belly as it passed. The horse's forelegs crumpled and the unbalanced rider pitched forwards towards Botolph who was standing a few yards further along the rider's original trajectory. The horse's fall propelled the rider directly at him and Botolph instinctively balled his hand into a fist and thrust it forwards as the rider fell towards him. To Botolph's horror there was a sickening crack as his victim's jaw broke and the next moment the rider was supine on the ground with Luka about to plunge his seaxe into his neck.

"No!" shouted a horrified Botolph, "he's unconscious anyway, let him be."

They turned to get back into the fray but it was all over as quickly as it had started. There had only been six raiders; two had been summarily despatched from this life by the king's bodyguard, three had been captured and Botolph's victim was out cold.

Luka found some rope and trussed the inert body's arms and legs together before he was then hauled into the group where his conscious compatriots were sullenly being "questioned" by the captain of the king's bodyguard.

"What's up with you?" asked Luka seeing his friend rubbing the knuckles of his right hand.

"My hand hurts," said Botolph ruefully.

"Not half as much as his jaw will hurt when he wakes up," said Luka laughing. "I didn't know you had a punch like that!"

"He fell onto my fist!" was Botolph's excuse.

"Oh yes?" said Luka. "From where I was standing your fist was moving towards him pretty fast at the time! Going to be a long confession for you tonight then Brother Botolph!" he giggled wickedly.

Extra guards were posted all round the camp. Miraculously nobody seemed to have been killed or seriously hurt. The magic of the singing had been lost however, so there was nothing for it but for everyone to put their trust in the extra guards that had been posted and repair to their straw palliasses in the tents.

"What were they thinking of?" said Luka in the morning. "Six of them, attacking a king's party that included goodness-knows how many bodyguards and other men at arms?"

"It's strange," admitted Botolph, "unless they were just opportunistic and hoped they might get something out of it."

"They did," said Luka "two dead, one broken jaw and four fresh slaves for the king to sell."

"Perhaps they did not realise the size of the party or who they were attacking? Perhaps they just heard the noise coming from the forest, came to investigate, thought they would muscle in on it and then ended up with a bloodied nose and a nasty surprise?"

"It's very odd," said Luka. "The guards were all in position, so why weren't they spotted before they got close enough to attack?

"Perhaps they took a path that did not pass close enough to the guard posts for them to be heard, or maybe they were already inside the ring when we arrived and we camped on top of them, or there again they might have heard us from a distance and decided to take a chance and just came in fast and recklessly! I don't know. Why don't you go and ask them?"

"I might just do that," said Luka.

CHAPTER 47.
From the Camp to Atrebatum.

It seemed to Botolph that he had hardly had his eyes closed for more than a few moments before he was cruelly dragged from the depths of a black sleep to the reality of a black tent, a fierce grip on his left arm and a voice saying "Move one muscle and I'll kill you!" followed by some more incoherent words. It was the incoherent words that brought reassurance out of incipient panic, but, obediently lying still just to be on the safe side, he said "Luka! Wake up! It's me, Botolph!"

In the blackness he sensed Luka release the grip on his arm and suddenly sit bolt upright. "What's the matter?" said Luka.

"Nothing," said Botolph, "You were dreaming and threatening to kill me."

"Nonsense!" said Luka accusingly. "You've just woken me up from a nice dream I was having about that servant girl with the blond hair."

"Go back to sleep," said Botolph.

The shape of Luka grunted and dissolved again. Botolph was relieved to find that he had turned away from him and was soon rumbling away peaceably.

Botolph must have followed his own advice because the next he knew was that it was first light and the camp was astir. Luka was still away in the land of slumber so

Botolph slid out from under his blanket, pushed open the flap of the tent, went down to the water's edge and splashed his face in the cold water. He licked his salty lips and turned back to the camp, resolved to find some fresh water to clear the taste of the night from his mouth.

He reached the tent as Luka came through the flap and stretched and yawned. "Morning brother!" said Botolph, "I trust you slept well?"

"Like a log," said Luka, "didn't stir once my head hit the hay."

"You don't remember threatening to kill me during the night then?"

"What? Me? Threatening to kill you? You must've dreamt it!"

"Oh, never mind," said Botolph, realising that he was on a fool's errand, "let's go and see if we can find some bread and water to break our fast."

"Maybe some eggs and ham too?" Luka agreed enthusiastically.

They joined the rest of the retinue who were making their way to the cooks' tent where the smell of newly-baked bread was mingling with the smell of recent logs which had been added to the early-morning fire. They joined the queue. Nobody seemed to want to catch anybody else's eye in case it meant they had to talk, so after a series of grunts and shuffles they reached the front of the queue and collected a couple of horns which they filled from a pitcher of water. They took a loaf between them and four boiled eggs and some slices of ham and made their way over to a grassy mound where they sat looking towards the sea and the rising sun.

Botolph broke the bread in two and gave half to his friend who dutifully bowed his head in readiness for

Botolph's rendering of the grace. Luka's amen was partly lost in his first bite into the still warm bread which he munched with vigour before pouring water from his horn to wash it down his throat.

He let out a gasp of pleasure. "My, that's good! What a wonderful life eh? Food fit for a king, good company, wonderful scenery, a good night's sleep, what could be better?" He slapped Botolph's shoulder with his left hand while his right hand reached for one of the eggs which he deftly cracked and, dropping the two halves of the shell on the ground, raised his knees and rested his forearms on them while he munched contentedly at the victuals.

Botolph smiled. He always enjoyed watching the enjoyment his friend took from the simple pleasures of life. He reflected that, for all his apparent irreverence, he mostly lived life as Jesus would have wanted him to and relished and appreciated every good thing about it.

They threw the last of the food down their throats and emptied their horns after it as the cry went up to help strike camp. Tossing the empty horns in the back of the cooks' wagon, they set to with a will and, within the hour, nine of the ten tents were safely stowed on the mules. The king's tent would not be struck until after the royal party had left.

The scouts were astride their horses and receiving their instructions from Eligius and they soon dug in their heels and urged their horses back up the hill whereupon they were lost to view as they turned past the trees.

By this time the bodyguards were mounted and their horses were snorting and pawing the ground, partly it seemed as a reaction to being disturbed and partly in their eagerness to be away. They moved off to the bottom of the track and the royal carriage was hitched to its two horses and led to wait behind them. Queen Nanthild came out of the royal tent followed by the wet-nurse Hwanna carrying Prince Clovis. Botolph noted how young and regal Nanthild looked. He felt an unexpected pang of something he knew not what, but then realised it was because she reminded him of Eanswythe.

She got into the carriage as did Hwanna and her charge and the bodyguards' horses started to move up the hill with the royal coach rumbling behind.

The king and Prince Sigebert's horses were waiting at the entrance to the tent and there was some delay before they both appeared and mounted and trotted off up the hill to join the royal carriage.

The contubernium immediately started to dismantle the royal tent and Botolph and Luka moved as if to go and help but they were turned away as the tentmates took pride in keeping the handling of the king's tent to themselves.

Behind them, Eligius and the other counsellors and priests were moving off. A couple of them were on ponies, half a dozen in a wain and others on foot. The boys joined on behind them as the centreguard and rearguard fussed about preparing their horses and trying to ensure that the contubernium party with the tentmates and their mules were ready to go. There seemed to be some delay which proved to be the farrier's party with the wheelwright and carpenter and spare horses that were wanting to push past and get moving. The captain of the centreguard was not having that though and insisted that everyone took their proper place. The farrier would just have to wait his turn.

The boys did not see anymore as by that time they were up the hill and into the trees but they had glimpsed the four prisoners from the previous night's skirmish, being shackled to one of the baggage wains.   Botolph was relieved to see that there were four walking prisoners so obviously his victim was still alive.   He wondered what had happened to the bodies of the two that had been killed. Presumably they had been buried near the camp.   He hoped one of the priests had given them a Christian burial, if they *were* Christians?   But there again, Christian or pagan, one could only do one's best for them in those circumstances.

"Sorry, what did you say?"   Luka had been chattering on about something at the periphery of Botolph's perception and he forced his attention back into focus.

"That fellow in front," said Luka, "the young priest leading the pony with the leather box on the saddle, what do you think that's all about?"

"No idea," said Botolph, "shall we see if we can catch up with him and ask?"

They increased their pace of walking and it was not long before they came alongside their quarry.

"Hello," said Luka and Botolph thought to himself how chatty and sociable his young friend had become; not at all like the surly bad-tempered misfit that he had first met in East Anglia.

"Hello," said the priest "You are the brothers from Cantwarebury aren't you?"

"That's right," said Luka "how did you know that?"

"I have heard much about Cantwarebury and its monks and college.   It is my ambition to travel there one day.   What's it like?"

"Well," said Luka, considering, and realising for the first time that he had experience and knowledge of a place that was so notable that other people might envy his having been there.

Suddenly he was lost in his own world and in that realisation. "Well now, there's a thing!" he said.

"What is?" said the young priest, puzzled.

"Well, that you want to go somewhere where I've already been!" said Luka.

The priest was not getting this at all. "I don't understand," he said.

"No, I don't suppose you do," said Luka softening, to Botolph's further surprise. Botolph stayed silent and just watched and marvelled as he seemed to see his dear friend and brother, suddenly growing up, right in front of his eyes, and wisdom and stature transforming his body. Botolph was sure that the young priest did not see any of this; how could he? He did not know Luka like Botolph did. He had not seen him fight his mental and physical battles. Botolph praised God and stayed silent as Luka continued:

"Cantwarebury is a wonderful place. But until you asked me I never saw that." He looked up, his face radiant, "It is full of knowledge and peace and the love of God. It is surrounded by green grass and lovely countryside with streams and rivers flowing round it. Saint Augustine's Abbey itself is quite large and is peopled by a mixture of amazing characters who treat you with love and compassion whilst leading you to knowledge and the way of Christ."

Botolph could hardly believe his ears now, as he thought back to the fights that Luka used to have with Brother Ivan in the Scriptorium. He became a little alarmed and looked closely at Luka to see if he was, as they say, 'diverting the water' but to his relief it seemed that Luka was being totally sincere.

Luka chatted away for ages to his new friend, giving vivid descriptions of his time in Cantium and offering encouragement and advice on how to get there and experience it for himself.

It became clear at last that Luka was coming to the end of his store of anecdotes about Cantwarebury and he finally came around to asking the priest about *his* story.

It transpired that his name was Marcus and that his home town was Saint Riquier but he had spent the last three years in the service of King Dagobert and travelled with him wherever he went. Luka remarked that it sounded like a very nice job. The young man replied that he enjoyed the travelling and living in court but did not relish the battles so much.

"Do you have to fight then?" asked Luka with increased interest.

"No, but I have to stay close to the king and look after the reliquary box."

"Ah, you're the Capellanu." said Botolph.

"I certainly am," replied Marcus.

Luka looked astonished. "How did you know that?" he asked Botolph.

"I was talking to Eligius a short while ago and he was telling me the story of Saint Martin's cloak and how it stays in the presence of the French king and it is the capellanu's job to look after it.

"Capellanu is really the old title for my office," said Marcus, "I'm usually called the Chaplain now."

"So where is it then?" said Luka, warming further to both the young priest and his job.

"It's in there," said the chaplain, pointing to the pony.

He leaned across and undid a couple of leather straps and, lifting up a cover exposed the filials of a silver casket.

"Is that the one with the cloak?" asked Luka.

"It certainly is; we don't carry saints' bones into our battles; this is the real thing and I can tell you that Saint Martin is still protecting us to this day. There have been many times when I thought the king and I were doomed to die but I hold onto the box and pray constantly to Saint Martin as the sound of the fight crashes around me and he always sees us through. There is no doubt of the cloak's sacred powers because it has never left the side of the Gallic kings during the past two hundred years and without such powers we would surely have lost it by now."

"Can I see it?" asked Luka.

"Nope. Sorry, I do not even have the key. Bishop Modegisile looks after that at Tours. Even the king has only seen the cloak once!"

"So what's the story?" persisted Luka.

"Well," said Marcus, "Two hundred years ago, Martin was a Roman soldier stationed in a town not far from here called Samarobriva.

He was about your age, and, before he left Italy had been well on his way to becoming a staunch Christian. His parents however were pagans and they forbade him to be baptised and, with the intention of breaking his link with the church, sent him off to join the Roman army.

It was one cold dark night when he was patrolling by the gates of Samarobriva that he noticed a shivering nearly-naked beggar huddling in a doorway. His first thought was to act like a dignified Roman soldier and he haughtily swung round and turned his back on him and tried to pretend he wasn't there. It was impossible for him to drive the sight from his mind however and he turned and, swinging his Roman cloak from his back put his foot on the hem, drew his sword and sliced the cloak in two. One half he pressed into the hands of the beggar, saying quietly, 'There is enough material here to keep us *both* warm tonight," and continued on with his patrol.

Later, when asleep in the barracks, he dreamt he saw Jesus wearing the torn half of his cloak and saying: "I was given this cloak by Martin, a Roman soldier who has never been baptised."

When he awoke he remembered his dream and decided to be baptised at the first opportunity. Later, his increasing devotion to God finally overtook his sense of military duty and he felt compelled to refuse to fight and so was discharged from the army. Ultimately he became a bishop and his cloak became one of our most precious objects. It is now carried by the king wherever he goes, particularly into battle; the rest of the time it stays with me in Lutetia."

"What's Lutetia like?" Luka veered off on a tangent.

"Quite a lively place really," came the reply. "We call it 'Lutetia Parisii' now, on account of the Parisii tribe who live there.

"What are *they* like?"

"Oh much the same as any other Frank. They are no different to the Morini or the Atrebates as far as I can make out. They all speak differently and only a few have Latin so most times I can't understand a word they say. They were here with the Romans, and when they left, most of the Parisii left too and the place became quite deserted. It was our great Christian King Clovis who decided to make his base camp at Lutetia and then the people started flooding back."

368

"Ah, that would have been Big Clovis then," said Luka.

"Certainly was," laughed Marcus, "He was a great man and we are looking forward to Little Clovis following in his great-ancestor's footsteps as far as wisdom and honour is concerned."

"Have you been to Atrebatum before?" asked Luka, mentally taking another tangential turn.

"Many times," came the reply. "The king is very fond of Atrebatum and visits as often as he can."

"Heyup," said Luka as they reached the top of a rise and found the royal carriage stopped in a clearing. The rest of the caravan soon arrived and the horses were watered and fed and the cooks busied themselves providing luncheon.

Marcus went over to join the other priests while Botolph and Luka took their food to the side of the track to enjoy it in solitude.

"This is the life eh?" said Luka.

Botolph laughed. "Well, we are certainly lucky to have fallen in with this crowd and had food and protection for our journey across Gallia. God must have wanted us to come this way, he is looking after us well."

"Amen!" said Luka, rather more clearly than usual.

An hour or so later when they were on the move again the boys were surprised by the soft voice of Eligius behind them.

"Do you mind if I join you?"

"We would be honoured, but surely you usually travel in style rather than walking with a couple of lowly brothers?"

"I like to walk, and travelling in style either means sitting by myself with only my thoughts to keep me company, or joining one of the wagons and either being bored by adults or pestered by children."

The last sentence he said with an increasing smile which sent the message that there were times when he enjoyed both. "Today, I want to stretch my legs and enjoy the company of two intelligent young men, so that perhaps their youth and intelligence may rub off on me!"

"I doubt that you are in need of any of our intelligence sire" said Luka, falling into the trap.

"Aha" rejoined the counsellor "so you concede that I might benefit from a portion of your youth!"

Eligius' comment brought instant laughter from himself and Botolph and slightly delayed laughter from Luka who took a little while to catch up with Eligius' wit.

This rejoinder put the boys at their ease and the journey passed more quickly as it became evident how much and how many people Eligius knew. Somehow he seemed to have been everywhere in the world and experienced every possible situation at least once in his life; yet he was interested in every aspect of the boys' lives from their births until the present day.

"This must be," Botolph reflected silently, "the way he is able to create his mystique of total knowledge. He has acquired the ability of living, not just *his* life, but the lives of others too. Not only does he have a phenomenal memory but he is clearly constantly pushing the boundaries of his knowledge further at every opportunity and this is why he is taking the trouble to talk to us now."

"... don't you think so?" said the white-bearded mouth below the twinkling eyes on Botolph's right.

Botolph paused before answering. "Sire, I must confess that something you said earlier had taken my mind away from the present conversation and the sin of inattention had prevailed.   I apologise.   What was the question?"

Eligius let out a great laugh and clapped Botolph's shoulder,

"Now that's what I like about a man," he said, "when he is totally honest and freely admits his sins when found out.   It was a matter of no importance ... but what had I said that had so caught your interest?"

"Both you and Marcus the Capellanu mentioned King Dagobert's love for Atrebatum.   Why is that then?"

"Well," replied Eligius, "one hundred years ago, our king, Clovis I was in great danger of being annihilated by the Alemanni tribe at a place called Tolbiac.   Clovis was half-interested in becoming a Christian but decided to put the new religion to the test by pledging his soul to Christ if he was victorious.

He won the battle by killing the chieftain after which the rest of the tribe surrendered.   The following morning he called them together with the intention of testing Christianity further by telling them that if they agreed to be baptised as Christians he would spare their lives.   To his astonishment their newly-nominated leader got his word in first and pleaded for baptism.   Seeing how easily the new religion was spreading, King Clovis became an instant convert and it was Bishop Vedast of Atrebatum who became his Christian mentor and friend.   Since then all King Clovis' successors have had a special fondness for the town."

"So, what relation is Little Clovis, who is with us today, to Big Clovis then?" asked Luka.

"Well, let us see, - he would be his great-great-great-grandfather I should think.   Either way, he bears the same name and I have no doubt that he will carry on the traditions of Christianity that Big Clovis, as you call him, started."

CHAPTER 48
Atrebatum

It was with educated eyes therefore, that the boys saw the city of Atrebatum on their arrival. After descending the Roman road into the city, they turned to their right and entered the remains of the garrison where Dagobert and his family were being welcomed by the mayor and shown to their billets.

It was still only mid-afternoon and there were no tents to pitch so Eligius insisted on taking them to visit the little chapel built by Saint Vedast and dedicated to Saint Peter.

They found it by returning to the path by which they had come and following it further down the hill and across a flat area before climbing again to reach the little church on the opposite bank. When they arrived they were astonished to find that King Dagobert had arrived first. His lonely figure was kneeling at the altar, receiving the Holy Sacrament from the local priest. They entered the chapel but stayed at the back and Botolph prayed his thanks for a safe journey thus far.

After they had finished their devotions the king approached them with a smile. "How do you like my ancestral cathedral then?" he quipped, gesturing at the tiny chapel.

"It is a noble place," said Botolph tactfully.

"Indeed it is but not as grand as I would have it be. If God spares me, I shall indeed build a great cathedral here in honour of the holy man who brought comfort and faith to my family."

"Saint Vedast," said Botolph.

"Saint Vedast indeed. His bones were interred in this very church but they have now been moved, together with his former bishopric, to Cambrai but it is my earnest wish that some day they will return here where they belong."

They left the chapel and wandered through the city streets where the locals stared with interest at the elegant group. The noble bearing of both the king and Eligius was outstanding and the youth of the boys in their simple habits made a great contrast. What could they be talking about? What could they have in common? As with any settlement they visited, there was great interest and delight at the influx of nearly a hundred people and the prospect of profitable trading. Grain and wool were Atrebatum's specialities and already the king's provenders were out about and busily bargaining for merchandise at a good price.

They gradually made their way back to the fortress which, Botolph noted, had seen better days. No matter for it was wellguarded.

On their return, the king was greeted again by the mayor and invited to meet with the leader and representatives of the Atrebati tribe who had come to pay homage. The boys peeled off to find themselves a quiet corner while the king and Eligius went to do their civic duties.

Later that evening, when they were called to supper in the Grand Hall, they found that eight members of the tribe had been invited too.

The leader, whose name turned out to be Commius, was a dark, stocky man with long unruly black hair which contrasted with his neatly-trimmed black beard. Eligius told them later that, like Clovis, Commius took his name from a famous ancestor who had led the tribe to great successes many years previously, even venturing as far as Britain.

When the meal finished, the boys retraced their steps to the quiet corner and thankfully bedded down for the night.

25th March 638
Onwards from Atrebatum.

The following day, unusually, Luka was first to wake. He said later that it was the cockerels crowing which woke him and made him think of eggs for break-fast. Though it was still dark they were quick to dress as they had learned that it was better to keep ahead of the game. As soon as there was sufficient light, the first of the travellers started to pour into the Great Hall to collect their supplies for the day. The scouts were promptly mounted and away and the royal family were even early that morning.

The town mayor and his party lined up to bid the king farewell and the familiar routine for departure was repeated as the group passed through the South Gate on the long road towards Samarobriva.

It was two campsites later and mid-afternoon before the walls of the city appeared over the last rise of the day's journey.

"That's a big city!" said Luka.

"It certainly is," agreed Botolph. "Apparently it is even bigger than the king's city of Lutetia."

"Ah, well there is the briva," said Luka pointing to an old stone bridge that led across to the city walls. "I guess it must be crossing the Samara river."

"Not necessarily," said Botolph. "The briva at Durobriva does not cross the Duro river!"

"Oh, Ha Ha," said Luka sarcastically. "It just shows that your mates the Romans weren't as logical as they liked to think they were."

"Just teasing," said Botolph. "I am sure you are right and that it is the Samara river that twinkles before us now."

"Do you think that's the gate where Saint Martin gave his cloak to the beggar?" asked Luka.

"I don't think it is," replied Botolph, slowly considering the question, "I have a feeling that Martin was guarding the gate of the city that leads to Lugdunum and that would be on the east side. We will ask when we get there."

CHAPTER 49
Samarobriva: The Vanishing Prince

The boys were soundly asleep that night on their beds of straw in one of the castillon's out-buildings in company with a gaggle of other hangers-on. First Botolph and then Luka were shaken awake. It was still dark but they were just able to make out the shape of Eligius as he put his finger to his lips and motioned them to come with him. They grabbed their leather sacs and followed, threading their way carefully through the mass of snoring slumberers.

Once outside the building, Eligius gathered speed and they hurried to keep up with him as he headed towards the king's quarters. Here they found King Dagobert with a few of his most trusted courtiers and the queen who, to their surprise, was sitting and sobbing uncontrollably.

Eligius led the boys directly to the king who, with a grave face, started to speak but then, unaccountably, seemed unable to do so and waved his hand at Eligius who assumed the duty of explanation. He beckoned them to a quiet corner where they could discuss the matter privately.

"Prince Clovis is missing," he said in a low voice. "The child was in his cot one minute and then, when his nurse looked again, he was gone! The queen is distraught. She had a dream two nights ago, in which her son was stolen by

377

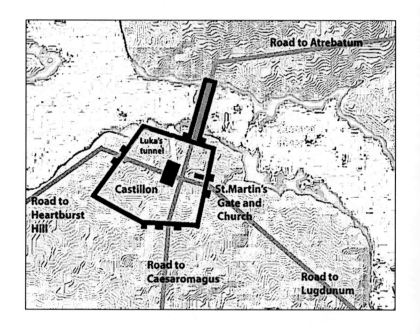

Fig. 10. Map of Samarobriva.

a group of wandering vagrants, and she now believes that is what has happened." "So why have only we been called?" whispered Botolph. "Why has the whole entourage not been awakened?"

"Apparently, in her dream, Queen Nanthild was comforted by a couple of young monks, not unlike yourselves, and it was at her command that you were woken."

"Is that all we have to do then?" hissed Luka, "Comfort her while everyone else goes off and apprehends the kidnappers?

"No," said Eligius "When I said 'comforted', I meant that they brought comfort to the queen by telling her that God had told them that her son was safe."

"Oh, and did they find her son in the dream?"

"Sadly she awoke at that point and we know no more."

"Great!" said Luka, throwing up his hands in despair, "she could have at least slept a bit longer so that we knew where to look! What are we supposed to do now?"

"Well," said Eligius "when I was commanded to go and wake you, I tried to point out that you were only the embodiments of figures that she saw in a dream and that you could not be expected to be able to help, but she would have none of it. She is convinced that you two are going to save her."

Luka groaned.

"Watch out" said Eligius, "here she comes."

Luka groaned again.

The young queen crossed from the other side of the hall, dragging a reluctant husband behind her. When she reached Botolph she sank to her knees and raised a pair of supplicative hands and a tearstained face in his direction. Botolph, horrified, looked down at her and then at the king who shrugged.

Botolph uttered a silent prayer and, sounding more confident than he actually felt, he raised the queen from her knees and said, "Fear not my lady, we shall find your son." There was a muffled squawk from Luka at his right elbow but Botolph continued:

"Sire, firstly you must send four search parties to check each of the roads which lead from the city; let them ride three leagues and ask if a child matching the prince's description has been seen.

Secondly, you must wake your whole retinue. Bring them here to the Great Hall and explain the situation and arrange for more search parties to scour the monastery buildings and grounds.

Thirdly, Abbot and monks must be asked to pray for Prince Clovis' safe return.

Fourthly, you must now lead us to Prince Clovis' cot and allow us to question his nurse there privately."

Luka's mouth was in the gaping position and he stared up at his friend wondering just where all *that* had come from and whether or not they were facing a monumental failure, the result of which might be both of them losing their heads.

Botolph's words had had an authoritative ring however and the king nodded to Eligius who strode towards the door of an anteroom.   He was followed by Botolph and the still-incredulous Luka, who kept giving violent shakes of his head as if warding off a mosquito; he was in fact hoping that he was having a nasty dream and that he would soon wake up.

Once he had left them in the company of Hwanna the nurse, Eligius quietly closed the door and returned to the king to help organise Botolph's prescribed search arrangements.

Hwanna looked terrified and tears were welling in her eyes as she looked up at her tall inquisitor. Luka had a pent-up question which ran along the lines of "Botolph! What are you *doing?*" but the greater part of the question had to remain unsaid since as soon as the word "Botolph" made it to his lips, his taller brother said, "Not now Luka, there is God's work to be done and I need your help".

Luka was mystified once more by this sudden change in the friend he had followed through thick and thin, and mud and water. Due to his leader's recklessness or inspiration (Luka had yet to decide which it was) they were already well-entrenched in this latest venture though, so after a moment's thought, Luka decided that there was nothing for it but to shut up and follow Botolph's lead again now.

Botolph had sat the young nurse down and she had found a cloth with which to dab her eyes. She was small and homely and a few years older than the boys. As they already knew, she performed the double function of looking after the prince and of being his wet-nurse.

"Now tell me," said Botolph authoritatively, "does Prince Clovis get very hungry for his milk or is he not a greedy baby."

A greedy baby it transpired he was and had last been fed just before midnight. It was now an hour or so before dawn and his next feed would be due shortly.

Luka could not see where this was leading but he found his eyes being drawn towards the attractive and ever-swelling bosom of the wet-nurse.

381

"Has this cot been touched or altered by anyone since the prince vanished?" asked Botolph.

Hwanna shook her head.

"The side is down, making it fairly easy for him to climb out.   Do you usually raise the side each night?"   She said she did.   "Do you remember raising it last night?" She said she did that too.

"It looks as if the latch might have slipped and the side fallen of its own accord.   Has that ever happened before?"

Apparently not.

"Has Clovis ever climbed out of his cot before?"

It transpired that he had and that the child was quite an adventurous little chap and was always, given half a chance, vanishing and hiding from his carers.

"So what do we have?" said Botolph, as they sat round in a group of three.   "An adventurous two-year-old who is awoken in the middle of the night by the sound of his cot side becoming unlatched and finds his freedom to roam."

"Or" said Luka, "a sleeping abbey, sleeping guards and a sleeping nurse and a brigand creeping through the Priory, stealing the baby and making off with him."

"We have not seen any brigands; there is no obvious reason, apart from the queen's dream, for a brigand to steal the prince; an intruder would not know where the prince was billeted; he would never have taken the trouble to lower the cot's side ... he could just have leaned over and removed the sleeping bairn.   No!   He is not far away, I am sure of it.   Come on, let's look."

Hwanna shook her head.   "I have looked everywhere in this room and in the adjacent rooms brothers," she said.   "He is not here!"

"It is not daylight yet" said Botolph, "and it is difficult to see every nook and cranny in a building like this, just by the light of these burning wall-torches. Soon we shall see better and that will help our search for him and the needs of his stomach will encourage *him* to start searching for *us*. Maybe there is a clue behind these wall coverings. Hwanna, you had better go back and tend your lady. *Your* presence may bring some comfort in the absence of your usual charge. Luka, you take this brand and I will take the other. Let us start at the cot and work our way in opposite directions around the walls, examining them and the wall-coverings thoroughly, until we meet again at the opposite side of the room."

Luka and his flame, casting gruesome silhouettes, slid off to the right and Botolph moved to the left, peeling back wall-coverings as he went and feeling the cold slabs of stone behind them. He came to a doorway and then to a corner and another doorway but decided against extending the search into other rooms until it was daylight. In any case, he just had the feeling that the young prince was closer at hand than that. He started to continue his exploration down the next wall and then realised that he had better discourage Luka from being diverted by any doorways he might find so, turning, he called "Luka".

Silence replied and there was no other burning brand in the room. "Luka," he shouted. "Luka," he shouted louder, hoping that his voice would carry into any adjacent room. There was still no reply. Botolph groaned and gave up his exploration of the wall coverings and followed round the wall of the room searching for his friend, or at least for signs of other doorways through which he might have gone. He found himself back at the cot.   There was no Luka and, more to the point, there were no other doors.

Botolph leaned on the wall and then sank to the floor close by the cot and went over the situation in his mind.   The bad news was that Luka had vanished but the good news was that he had vanished in a part of the room from which there was no apparent exit.   It was likely therefore that Prince Clovis had taken the same route. "Think, think, think!" said Botolph to himself, and then "Dear God, sweet Jesus, please help me to reason this thing out."

No great revelation came and so he obeyed his original exhortation and reasoned that a prince and a dwarf could not just vanish into thin air.   Wherever Luka had vanished from, had to be close to the wall and not in the middle of the room.   He must be out of earshot or he would yell back.   Botolph tried once more: "Luuukaaaa!"

Botolph stood and held up his brand and looked around the room.   The only item of furnishing that was present on the opposite side of the chamber, was a stone table, the thick top of which was set into the wall.   He went over to examine it more closely.   It was supported by a vertical slab at each end.   Botolph got on his knees and thrust the torch in front of him into a crack that appeared around the corner of one of the vertical slabs.   The smoke from the torch hit the roof of the confined space and bounced back into Botolph's eyes, momentarily blinding him and making him cough.   He rapidly backed out of the cavern into the clearer air of the main chamber, where with stinging eyes and clenched eyelids he rasped and coughed the smoke away.

CHAPTER 50
Luka's Triumph.

When Luka left Botolph, he did as he was bid and carefully lifted each of the wall coverings and probed the walls behind.   When he reached the table, he fitted neatly beneath the vertical slab, holding his brand low and to one side of him.   He too saw the opening adjacent to the horizontal slab and moved towards it feeling his way around the edge.   He squeezed his body through the gap and then pulled his brand in after him.   He was in a tall narrow chamber with a tunnel leading off to the left.   The brand was burning quite happily with its smoke apparently rising upwards so, he reasoned, there must be a supply of fresh air available above.   It occurred to him that he should go back and put Botolph in the picture but felt it would be more sensible to have a look at the tunnel first, and in any case there was no way that anyone as large as Botolph would be able to come and see for themselves.   As he moved forwards, he noticed the air change from the mustiness of the antechamber to a sweet fresh smell.   He inched his way to the edge of the tunnel which sloped downwards making the light from the brand useless.   His feet felt the edge of the floor start to angle downwards and he put his left hand onto the wall for support but he pulled it quickly back when, to his horror, he found it cold, wet and slimy.   The shock made him jump and the sudden jerk caused his feet to slide away from him crashing him backwards onto the stone floor. He inadvertently dropped the brand which extinguished plunging him into inky blackness. He felt his body slipping downwards and he scrabbled at the slimy stones, trying to prevent his downward motion but then he sensed his body going over a slippery ridge and suddenly he was on a helter-skelter tumbling down, down and down. He hit a corner and spun off to the right where he hit another corner and spun leftwards again and then, blessedly, he suddenly somersaulted out of the tube into some sort of dim daylight.

"Oomph!" he said as he landed, winded and then lay for a few moments collecting his senses. There was a childish chuckle from over his right shoulder and he turned to find the errant prince sitting cross-legged and contentedly building a pyramid out of a pile of stones.

Now Luka was always pleased to talk to people or animals who were smaller than he was and coming from a noble family he was not over-awed by royalty. He was then, the ideal person for this confrontation. Instantly regaining his composure and trying to give the impression that he always exited castles in this way, he swung himself round and perched similarly cross-legged on the grassy tussock which had broken his fall.

"Well, young Clovis," he said. "Here you are safe, well and as happy as a king. You have led us all a pretty dance!"

The prince grinned and handed him a stone. It was a round dusky-red pebble. Luka put it in one hand then in another and back and forth while the child watched, and then held out both fists for the child to choose. Of course the fist was empty, so the child pointed to the other one, but that also was empty.   Then Luka leaned over and plucked the pebble from behind Clovis' ear which brought forth another delighted chuckle.

"Come on," said Luka, "we cannot stay here enjoying ourselves all day.   We must get you back to your mother so that you can all break your fast together."

He stood and the little one willingly took his hand. They were in an area that, in a forest, would be called a "clearing" but this one had great fronds of tall weeds growing up around the edge of it.   A low canopy of root-entwined vegetation let in the early morning daylight and made Luka stoop as he led his new charge to the periphery. Here, there were even stronger roots creating a seemingly impregnable fence.   The height was just enough here to allow Luka to stand upright.   He let go the prince's hand and, perplexed, placed his hands on his hips while he ducked and dived scanning the barrier for an opening. Seeing none, he looked down again with a view to imparting more words of wisdom to his new charge, only to be hit with a feeling of panic as he found the wretched child had vanished again.   There was only one way he could have gone this time however and that was under the curtain of roots and leaves.   Luka dropped to his knees and thrust his head through the vegetation.   To his relief the first thing he saw was a grinning cherub sitting on its haunches expectantly waiting for him.   He grinned back and pushed, expecting the rest of his body to follow his head.   It did not.   His grin faded.   He pushed again.   The prison still held him captive.   He pulled his head back out of the gap.   How had the little chap got out so easily? Luka took his trusty seaxe and tried to chop away at the roots but they were as tough as his father's old boots and they were not going to give in so easily.   Inspired he then placed his seaxe right at the base of the foliage where it joined the damp pebbly ground. He sliced the knife along horizontally and felt that he was making more progress. He then lay down on his stomach along the length of the border and shuffled his body as close to the base of the curtain as he could. Placing his hands over his face to protect it, he then rolled violently against the edge, hoping that his back would break through the area previously weakened by his seaxe. He failed. He stood up and had another try with his knife, this time trying to ensure that the tougher strands were broken. He returned to his prone position and repeated the process. This time he was successful and he rolled out of his nest knocking into the waiting child. He lay on his back recovering and rubbing at the bleeding points on his arms where the palings had exerted their final attack. Prince Clovis jumped onto his stomach and sat there grinning at him.

"Come on then," Luka said for the second time. "Off you get and we will go and find your mother."

When he was allowed to sit up and see his surroundings, Luka found that they were down by the edge of the Samara river. They were actually outside the city walls and the coarse vegetation that had held them captive, climbed ivy-like up towards the battlements. To his right Luka could see the old stone bridge which they had crossed on their arrival at the city, so it was towards this that they made their way across the muddy stones that formed the edge of the river bed. The child at first hopped gleefully from stone to stone clasping Luka's hand to give himself stability. He would have fallen several times but Luka deftly hauled him upright and lifted his little body by one hand ensuring that the feet remained the nadir. After a while though, the little one's energy began to flag and he started dragging behind. Luka scooped him up and placed him upon his shoulders whereupon the young fellow's energy suddenly returned and he began to treat Luka like a horse, spurring him along with his heels and shouts of encouragement.

It was in this manner that they entered the north gate of the city and made their way back to the castillon. They arrived here at the same time as the mounts bearing King Dagobert and some men at arms, came out with a view to scouring the countryside. The crumpled figure of a still-weeping Queen Nanthild was standing by her husband's horse obviously in despair of ever seeing her young son again, when her eyes fell on the weird shape of the two-headed figure breaking through the morning's misty gloom.   The figure had congealed blood on its legs and arms and the upper head was squealing with delight and shrouded by what had once been a pure white nightshirt.

The king was first to react and he joyfully swung himself down from his horse and ran to his son, sweeping him off Luka's shoulders and running back with him to his queen, hugging and kissing him on the way as if there was no tomorrow.   The queen's sorrowful face that had at once travelled through disbelief and astonishment reached its destination of rapture as her beloved child was placed in her arms whereupon the tears started afresh.

Luka had, of course, been forgotten in all this but he continued to trudge up towards the crowd at the gate of the castillon, rubbing his shoulders and reflecting that, even at two years of age, a young prince becomes quite a weight after a while.

When he neared the group, the king turned again and asked "Where was he?   Where did you find him?"

"Down by the river sire," was the only answer Luka could give, whereupon everybody started talking at once and asking how he could have got there and what had made Luka decide to look there. Eventually the king said: "Right, everyone, this young hero can get cleaned up, and we will catch up with the gruesome details later. The most important thing is that my son is back.

Today will be a special feast day in celebration of Prince Clovis's safe return. We will not break our fast at the usual time but two hours later and then will start a feast day for you all to remember." The king nodded to Eligius who turned to confer with the Count of Samarobriva whose presence had also been summoned. There were questioning looks and noddings of heads and both the Count and Eligius strode off in different directions to set the wheels in motion.

Luka noted that Botolph was not amongst the crowd, so he pushed through the throng and ran back towards the princeling's chamber. He met Hwanna on the way and they entered the chamber together. Daylight was filtering into the room and Botolph's presence was not evident until Luka heard a scuffling sound coming from under the stone table. Legs resembling those of his friend were sticking out and squirming as the rest of the body wrestled with the problems of confinement. Luka tapped one of the legs.

"Who's that?" came a muffled cry.

"It's me, Luka!"

The legs stopped moving. But then went into a furious reverse as the body shunted back out of the cavity.

"Where did you get to?" said the tussle-headed smoke-blackened face of Botolph.

"Long story," replied the blood-smeared face of Luka.

Hwanna's guilt-ridden tensions collapsed, as did she, in a helpless fit of uncontrollable laughter.

CHAPTER 51
Explanation.

A couple of hours later saw hordes of people entering the Great Hall. Not only was the king's retinue present but the Count and all the civic dignitaries and their families were invited too. Tables had been laid outside and around the castillon and the kitcheners had had a fine old time trying to find enough food to keep everybody happy.

All the special guests, of which of course Botolph and Luka were two, were catered for in the Great Hall and they were joining in with the pushing and pulling and general scramble to get the choicest food from the tables. Suddenly the bodyguard who had played the lyre at the camp site, sounded a blast on a bugle and the king called for silence.

"We're never going to eat at this rate," grumbled Luka whose stomach was protesting at the two-hour delay.

"Before we start our meal," said the king, "I want to remind you all of the reason for it. Brother Luka, please come here."

Botolph nudged Luka and, reluctantly he put down the trencher he had just been successful in filling, wiped his rather greasy hands on the flank of his habit and made his way to the dais.

392

"My son was lost and now is found, thanks to Brother Luka and for this great service I give him this ring of thanks and friendship," and to Luka's astonishment, he slid a glinting gold ring from one of his own fingers onto one of Luka's.

"I know," he said, "that one day you will become a monk and then you will have to give up all your possessions, this ring included. You must do with it what you will. It is yours to give away, sell or keep, but the friendship and thanks of my family will always stay with you."

He raised his hands and again everyone clapped and cheered. Luka finally overcame his confusion and embarrassment and bowed to both king and crowd.

"Now," said Dagobert, "let us all enjoy this special repast and you boys come and join us at the royal table and explain just how you solved this mystery."

The table was laden with bread, eggs, cold meats and fruit. Luka claimed possession of his chosen items and was just about to take his first bite of a hunk of fresh bread, when the booming voice of the king said: "Well then Brother Luka, tell us what happened."

Luka put down the bread and closed his mouth, took a deep, somewhat remorseful, breath and said: "Well, Botolph had convinced me that the prince had not been abducted, so we agreed to look around the chamber to see if there was a way out. He went one way and I went the other, looking behind the tapestries which lined the walls. It was when I came to the stone table, which was set into the wall, rather like an altar, that I found the hole." He paused for breath and took a swig from his drinking horn and went to pick up the piece of bread, but all eyes were on

393

him so he capitulated and placed it to one side again and continued with his story.

"Well," he said, "the Good Lord in his wisdom has made me of a similar stature to the prince," and then, warming to his subject and thinking it was worthwhile to risk adding some humour, he added ruefully "which makes me ideally suited to go on baby-hunting expeditions!"

From Queen Nanthild there issued a great peal of laughter which was echoed by everybody else and the king slapped his thigh! This gave Luka the chance he needed and he grabbed the bread and ground his way into it before the laughter died down. As the silence returned he poured some more liquid after it and continued.

"So, I was able to remain standing upright and squeeze through the same crack that young Clovis had squeezed through previously. I found myself in a small darkened chamber and started to feel around, half-expecting to find him sitting in the dark, or dead, or trapped." Luka risked another mouthful of bread.

"The chamber smelt damp and there must have been some water dripping in there, because before I knew it, I had slipped on the edge and was tumbling down some sort of chute. I tried to grab an edge to stop myself falling but it was hopeless and then suddenly I reached the bottom and there was the prince looking as contented as a calf!" The company tittered.

"The main problem then," continued Luka, "was getting out of the infernal cage of roots and stems that were trapping us." To some alarm, he suddenly brandished his seaxe: "Fortunately, my trusty friend here saved the day, and it is really him you should be thanking sire!" and he bowed once again to laughter and clapping.

"But" said the king, turning to the Count, "what do you know of this quick way out of the castle that my son took?"

"Well sire," returned the Count, "nobody here to my knowledge knew that this passageway existed. I myself have looked under this table this morning and to all intents and purposes it looks like any other table and shows no signs of concealing an exit. No adult of normal size, with apologies young man," Luka graciously bowed his head, "would be able to have the advantage of investigating it. But this building was constructed over the old Roman amphitheatre, and I suspect that what has happened, is that that part was either not finished properly, or was left open for some purpose and has been long since forgotten. Brother Luka's tumbling flight was therefore down the slope of the old amphitheatre and maybe if he had done the same thing a couple of hundred years ago in Roman days, he might have found that his arrival was on the stage in front of 15,000 people!"

There was more laughter which Luka acknowledged and nodded to through a mouthful of eggs and meat.

"Well," said the king, "the important thing is that we are all happily reunited now, so eat up everybody and let us enjoy our day of rest before moving on tomorrow."

CHAPTER 52
Samarobriva to Heartburst Hill

They left Samarobriva by the West Gate and followed the river southwards up into the hills. It was a pleasant morning and the boys were happy to be on the move again. Luka had enjoyed the praise but it was wearing a little thin now and he yearned to return to normality. Botolph was bemused by his colleague's developing emotions but accepted them for what they were.

Eventually they came to a fortress where the river divided. Here they followed the bank around to the left until the tributary became narrower and a sturdy wooden bridge took them across to the foot of the hills.

They had climbed plenty of hills before, but this one just seemed to be a struggle. It was no steeper than its predecessors, nor was the pathway any narrower but for some reason it seemed to be hard-going. Even the mules kept stopping and as the day wore on people started to become irritable.

They reached the summit by mid afternoon and the king in his wisdom decided to call a halt and to pitch camp for the night.

Once the tents were up and they had eaten, Botolph and Luka made their way to the highest point and looked down the river valley back towards Samarobriva. It was a magnificent view as the vivid glow from the setting sun turned all the countryside pink.

"It fills your heart with joy, doesn't it?" said Botolph.

Luka nodded slowly. "Reckon they ought to call this 'Heartburst Hill"; it nearly bursts your heart getting up here and then your heart nearly bursts again with the wonder of it all!"

Botolph laughed and put his arm around his shoulder and they contentedly made their way back to the camp and a peaceful night.

30th March 638.
From Heartburst Hill to Caesaromagus.

The next day everyone seemed well refreshed and in better frames of mind. Striking camp went smoothly and they were soon trundling down the hill and into the valley that leads to Caesaromagus which was the capital town of the Bellovaci. The tribe had turned out in force and gave their king and his young progeny a great welcome. Indeed Botolph remarked to Luka that as a project to help the populus warm to their sovereign, Dagobert's strategy seemed to be working very successfully.

The boys were introduced by the king to Eveqcomte Bishop Radingus, who, to their surprise, welcomed them warmly in an Irish lilt. It came as a pleasant relief to Botolph and Luka to be able to avoid speaking Latin for a while.

It transpired that, as Eveqcomte, the bishop enjoyed a mixture of secular and religious authority that gave him great power. This power was increased even further by the proximity of his see to the king's palace in Lutetia. The bishop had spent a lot of his life in Alamania where he had achieved many successes in spreading the word of Christianity.

"They tell me you have also lived as a hermit," said Luka.

"To be sure I have," he replied, "and a wonderful life it was too; communing with nature and taking what God offered and being able to spend hours and hours in undisturbed prayer."

Luka stayed silent and the bishop smiled and placed his hand on Luka's shoulder. "Not the sort of thing that suits everybody my son," he said, reading Luka's mind. "It is something you have to be called to and I feel that when my work is done here, I may well be called back to the ascetic's life again. I shall welcome it."

"But," said Luka, "here you are rich and powerful and have everything you could possibly need."

"Exactly" said the bishop, "and that is why, to be closer to God, I have to give this up and revert to being like a little child and coming into this world with nothing.

And to tell you the truth," he went on, "I am not sure where most virtue lies. I shall have a much quieter life living as a hermit than living as Eveqcomte, so sometimes I wonder if the discomfitures of my position here are more virtuous." He sighed. "It needs a lot of prayer."

31st March 638.
From Caesaromagus to Thury.

The following morning as the procession was assembling ready for departure, the boys were standing near the king when the scouts rode up to him.

"Where to tonight sire?" one said. "Do you think we can make Lutetia today?"

"When we arrive in the capital, I want us to be in fresh condition not totally exhausted," he chided. "No, we will stop at Thury Meadow tonight. It's a good site for a camp and there are plenty of traders to cater for our needs so that we can enter Lutetia in style rather than as a rag-tag of foot-worn peasants!"

"Right, my lord," laughed the scout, "Thury Meadow it will be. May we have your permission to depart now, so that we can make sure you are well provided for?"

"Yes," said the king, "away you go and with any luck we shall see you again shortly after noon."

Away went the two horsemen and, once the king and queen had taken their leave of Bishop Radingus, who had just finished officiating at the office of Prime, the rest of the procession started its slow rumble out of the gates of Caesaromagus.

"I am sure that both the king and the queen are eager to be home again," said Botolph to Luka, "and it seems to me that even Eligius has had enough of travelling!"

"Can't see why we don't just push on," said Luka.

"Well, I can see Dagobert's point; a triumphant arrival in Lutetia would help to inspire the Parisii."

"What's going to happen to young Sigebert," I wonder, "now that he has been shown off. Will he stay in Lutetia or be parcelled away to his own kingdom?"

"I've no idea," said Botolph, "I cannot imagine that Queen Nanthild would be keen to see him go. I understand his traditional capital is the town of Mettis."

"Everyone's going home then," said Luka, "except for us, and we still have many more leagues to go before we make our destination."

"Do you know?" said Botolph, "In a funny way, I feel I'm coming home too."

"How on earth do you make that out?" said Luka. "We're hundreds of leagues away from anywhere that either of us could call home!"

"It's not that sort of home really," said Botolph. "You know that board game we play where the square you start on is called 'home' and you have to get back to that each time before you can win any tokens?"

"Yes," said Luka, cautiously.

"Well, that's the sort of home I mean. I feel a sense of destiny, of arriving somewhere solid and secure which will be the foundation for our futures; where both of us will gain strength and wisdom."

"Vorroof!" said Luka teasingly, pricking Botolph's bubble of hope.

"Don't you Vorroof me, you ignorant little dwarf," he said lunging at him. Luka neatly side-stepped and ran off with Botolph in hot pursuit. They dodged in and out of the mules and horses until Luka tripped and Botolph grabbed him and ruffled his hair.

They sat up grinning just as the king and Eligius passed on horseback.

"They *are* still boys then?" said Dagobert.

"It's good to see," said his wise counsellor.

They travelled down a shallow valley and a couple of hours later climbed an escarpment from which they could see another valley with a wide river winding through it. The track descended a gully and came out onto a flat marshy area bordering the river. The two scouts came

400

cantering along a solid causeway which had been built over the marsh and, confirming that all was ready on the other side of the wooden bridge, they led them to a busy and colourful town nestling between two hills.

The traders and townspeople of Thury Meadow joyfully welcomed the king and his family as they made their way to the field prepared by the scouts. The tentmates were soon hard at work and Botolph and Luka, who were now used to the routine and had acquired certain skills in the erecting of the cumbersome beasts, set to with a will.

"Last time I s'pose," said Luka.

"Yes, I reckon it will be a long time before we join a king's party and become unofficial contubernia again!"

"I'm quite sorry in a way. It has been fun and, to tell you the truth, I quite enjoy spending overnight in camp rather than being stuck in some of the draughty or smoky halls we have had to endure."

Botolph agreed and once all the tents had been erected, they strolled back into Thury to see what it had to offer. They passed an open-fronted hut with a table stacked with fresh-baked bread. Luka struck up a conversation with the miller's buxom daughter who seemed fascinated by his miniature stature and twinkly eyes. He promptly made a point of twinkling them rather more than usual and she offered them a couple of rather tasty-looking bread rolls. There was a language difficulty as she spoke no Latin and the boys were trying to convey the message that they had no money when the burly miller appeared at his daughter's shoulder. He looked less than happy and was not at all impressed by Luka's twinkly eyes, so Luka abruptly switched them off.

The boys started again but the miller was having none of it.   He was not at all interested in wasting time trying to communicate with two monks if there was going to be no money at the end of it.   He started waving his arms about and shouting, so Botolph caught Luka's eye and they decided it was time to beat a hasty retreat out of the shop into the crowded thoroughfare.

They could hear the shouting continuing as they immersed themselves in the crowds and were washed down the street.   There were stalls selling materials and clothes and grain and sweetmeats and animals and slaves and spices and vegetables and meats.   But Luka had the taste of the buxom daughter's fresh buns in his mouth and he was having difficulty in thinking about anything other than food.

"We can't buy anything anyway," he said.   "C'mon, let's go back to the camp and get something to eat, I'm starving to death here!"

So they turned and retraced their steps but, being in deep conversation, did not notice that they had once again come into the view of the miller until his shouting recommenced.   Some instinct made Luka start to run and Botolph followed suit whereupon the miller immediately started a chase, threateningly waving a wooden staff and still ranting and raving as he ran.

"This is ridiculous," panted Luka.   "What have we done to him, he must be stark staring mad."

"I don't know," said Botolph "but let's not waste time thinking about it, he's getting closer.   Run faster!"

Either the miller gave up or the boys outran him. The shouting was soon lost in the distance and they were puffing well when they reached the security of the camp. Luka did not hesitate but went straight to the cook's tent and helped himself and Botolph to a horn of mead and asked the cook to bring them some bread and cheese while they found a comfortable place to sit and eat.

An hour or two later the whole company were called to supper to which the king had invited the mayor and aldermen of Thury. Botolph was talking to one of the aldermen and telling him the story of their escape from the clutches of the miller.

The alderman laughed, "Aah, pfff, 'e is alwez like dat," he said. "I can tell you for one thing that 'e doesn't like monks and for anuzzer, that 'e alwez suspects that strangers have evil designs on his daughter. For a third thing, 'e is a greedy miser and nevaire will 'e give anyone anything free! Forget 'im!"

"I will," said Luka, "and his daughter, to whom," and he preened himself a little and stretched to his full height, "my intentions were entirely honourable!"

Botolph laughed at the caricature, as did the alderman and the rest of the evening was spent in excessive eating and drinking and joyful socialising.

The following morning held a different atmosphere as everyone knew that it was the final stage of their journey. Sore heads and tender stomachs following the previous evening's festivities made the company break their fast cautiously. Once all the tents, with the exception of the royal one, had been struck, they lined up for departure.

The scouts were sent on ahead with instructions to prepare Lutetia for a royal homecoming and the cavalcade set out from the meadow and along the base of the hill heading to the southeast. The track ran through a valley and then wound up through some woods ascending a tor but avoiding the steepest part by snaking around until it started to drop down the other side.

Soon they came out of the trees and onto a plain and Luka could see some huts in the distance. They passed a farm with some children playing and a pair of oxen being led by a young boy whilst the farmer tended the plough that they were drawing.

The ground then took on a different appearance and it was clear that to either side of the slightly-raised roadway, the land was soft and marshy. The track became busier and a competition started to develop between who was going to give way to whom. Naturally a king's party would normally be granted precedence and the wains would move to one side but certain of the gallic farmers were reluctant to observe these niceties and remained stubbornly in the fairway. Shouting matches developed between the bodyguards and the drivers of some of the wains and violence was but narrowly avoided.

A tall hill could be seen ahead and to the left of it the city was gradually coming into view. "Martyr's Mount!" said the young Capellanu with whom they had again fallen into company.

"Is that special then?" asked Luka.

"That's where Saint Denis was beheaded by order of the Roman Emperor," said the Capellanu.

Just then it became clear that the vanguard of the procession were leaving the main track. Led by King Dagobert and his young son, the horses were heading towards a magnificent chapel on the left hand side of the road. "Saint Denis' Shrine," said the Capellanu. "This is where our great saint's body lies."

"Ah," said Luka, "I remember Bishop Audomar telling us that, after his head was sliced off, he walked for half a league before he finally died."

"Well," said the Capellanu, "I would not like to come into dispute with Bishop Audomar but if Saint Denis started at Martyr's Mount and finished here it would have been twice that and just over one league is not bad for a headless saint!"

"The king and prince dismounted and, leaving their horses in the care of the ostlers, they led Queen Nanthild and the rest of the royal party into the chapel.

They were welcomed at the door by a priest, and as many who could, squeezed inside the building. Botolph and Luka were right at the back but they both suddenly gasped when they saw the rich beauty of the shrine.

Wherever they looked there was gold, silver and jewels. Everything sparkled and dazzled.

"What a magnificent end to a wonderful journey," said Botolph.

"Vorroof!" replied Luka, otherwise lost for words as, open-mouthed, he gazed above and around himself.

Their attention became focussed as the priest led the prayers of thanks for a safe journey and the exhortations to Saint Denis to bless the entourage on their future travels. The sacrament of Holy Communion was taken and the boys performed their own devotions. Once the service was concluded they were at leave to once again take interest in their surroundings.

"That must be the actual tomb," said Luka, pointing to where a marble ciborium, decorated in jewels and gold, formed a canopy over a marble slab surrounded by golden apples.

"But did you see the altar?" replied Botolph. "What a magnificent structure. Just look at that circle of gold and silver axes supporting the roof of the altar throne. Where would you find a craftsman who could make such a fantastic structure?"

"I am glad you like it," said a soft and familiar voice behind them. They turned to find the elegant form of Eligius behind them. He had clearly positioned himself purposely in such a way that he could observe the boys reaction.

"Like it?" said Luka. "I have never seen anything so beautiful in my whole life."

"A fitting tribute then, for Bishop Denis, the patron saint of our city, would you think?" said Eligius.

"A fitting tribute indeed," said Botolph, "but who is the person who could design and make such a thing?"

"Ah," said Eligius, "I must admit that I had a hand in it."

"You made this?" said Luka.

"Quite a lot of it, yes," replied Eligius. "You see I was originally trained as a goldsmith and, a few years ago, King Dagobert expressed an interest in turning Saint Denis' shrine into something really special."

"You certainly did that," interrupted Luka.

Eligius smiled a little patronisingly but then continued "I always loved my trade. It gave me great satisfaction to take a piece of gold, a metal which of course has great intrinsic value, but then to be able to mould it and shape it and turn it into a piece of artwork that increased its value one hundredfold. That all used to give me so much pleasure. When our king asked me if I could help him to transform the bishop's shrine, I jumped at the chance. And now, I get the greatest pleasure of my life when I am able to watch newcomers like yourselves admire and wonder at the humble work we have done."

The king joined the talkers. "Like it?" he said to Luka. "Wonderful sire," was his reply. It crossed Botolph's mind that he might have aimed his question at Luka on the basis of being sure of a positive reply. It had already occurred to Botolph that there was some conflict between the church vows of poverty and the opulence of such an edifice as this.

CHAPTER 53
Arrival in Lutetia.

The two kings remounted their horses and the group, refreshed both spiritually from the Holy Sacrament and bodily by horns of water that had been passed around, made their way out of the grounds of the holy sepulchre. They passed a small cluster of habitations before they reached Martyr's Mount but after that they came across no more huts between the mount and Lutetia itself. They travelled across the last of the marshy ground and the boys watched, fascinated, as the city grew before them.

It seemed, Botolph thought, an idyllic setting for a king's residence. A pretty island with the security of strong walls and water encircling it. The fortifications were a mixture of wood and stone and Luka noted with approval a number of boats tied up to a jetty and others, no doubt plying some sort of trade, moving to and from the city. A cluster of waving citizens stood at the beginning of a long wooden bridge which led through the already-opened gates into the island-city. The noise from the horses' hooves changed from the crunching sound they made on the causeway to a dull clopping on the wooden bridge. This then became a clatter as the horses gained the flagstones and cobbles of the town.

The crowds waved and cheered and Dagobert and Sigebert acknowledged them graciously. Queen Nanthild waved from one side of the carriage and Hwanna held Clovis up on the other side at which the crowds roared their approval.

The road bore round to the right and the procession shortly came to a stop outside the royal palace. Before long the riders had all dismounted. Some of the bodyguard were being welcomed fondly by families they had not seen for several weeks. The royals all disappeared into the palace and Botolph and Luka seemed to have been forgotten. In fact, Botolph was quite relieved that this part of their journey had come to an end. His feet were blistered and his armpits and various other parts of his body had been chafed by the rough material of his habit. He glanced down at Luka who was probably also struggling but, as usual, showed no sign of it.

Eligius appeared, nodded a greeting and made as if to move on. He seemed to think better of it however and turned back.

"Where are you two going to sleep tonight then?" he asked.

Luka shrugged and Botolph said, "We were just wondering the same thing."

"Come with me," said the kindly courtier and led them into the palace. They had already collected their leather sacs from the ox cart so they wasted no time in chasing after the striding figure and soon discovered that they were to be guests in his private apartments for the next few days.

2nd April 638.

The following day had been decreed by the king to be a public holiday and for the boys it was a day for rest and recuperation. Eligius joined them as they broke their fast and asked them what their plans were.   Botolph replied that they wanted to push on to Evoriacum as soon as convenient.

"Yes, I was afraid of that," said Eligius.

"How do you mean?" said Luka.

Eligius side-stepped the question and instead said: "It might be tactful to include the monastery at Meaux in your itinerary."

"Why's that?" asked Luka.

"Well, the Abbot, Bishop Faro, is Burgundo-Fara's brother and it would be the right thing to call on him first. Be a little cautious of him though, for he has had an interesting history."

"In what way?" asked Luka, his ears ever-alert at the suggestion of scandal.

"Well, there was a time when he and his brother Chagnoald came very close to murdering their sister Burgundo-Fara, your future Abbess.   She is called *Burgundo-Fara* because her father Chagneric came from Burgundia .   He was chancellor to King Theudebert who, you might remember Botolph, was the grandfather of your friend the Abbess Eanswythe!"

Botolph reeled slightly and blushed.   If Eligius noticed, he gave no sign but continued:

"When young Fara was of ten or eleven summers, the family was visited by an Irish saint called Colambanus. As was his habit when visiting, the saint blessed the whole family individually but when he came to Burgundo-Fara he left his hands on her head for a while as if receiving a message from God. He drew back and looked at her saying "You, my child, will have a long life and become a great saint in the service of Christ.   As soon as he left, the poor child became afflicted with a mystery illness and soon seemed close to death."

"So much for the predictions of Irish monks," muttered Luka to Botolph.

"Sorry Luka, what was that?" said Eligius.

"Nothing important sire, please carry on."

"Well, her father summoned another monk called Eustasius and he led the prayers for her recovery. The little girl's father, Chagneric, had been rather put out by Columbanus' original predictions, since he had been looking forward to marrying Fara off to a rich nobleman. If she became a nun he was going to lose a lot of money. That said, he loved his daughter very much and certainly did not want her to die. In desperation he vowed that if her life were spared he would do his best to ensure that she devoted the rest of her life to God. From that day onwards she made a good recovery."

"Eustasius did a good job for the Irish saint then?" said Luka.

"Well," said Eligius, "I am sure the saint had no doubt that her life would be spared. Anyway Botolph, all seemed to be set fair until one day your friend Eanswythe's grandfather, King Theudebert, came to Chagneric with the proposal that Fara should marry someone whom he was trying to cultivate in his attempt to become King of all Gallia. Chagneric was pleased about this because it meant he would be in funds again so he promptly started making the marriage plans. Are you with me so far Luka?"

Luka's eyes were fixed on those of Eligius and there was no doubt that he was totally with him.

"Well Burgundo-Fara, was having none of this. She had made up her mind to be the bride of Christ and she was not about to be forced in any other direction so she ran off and hid in the nearby church of Saint Stephen. Her father was furious and her brothers, Faro and Chagnoald chased after her and burst into the church. They grabbed her with the intention of hauling her out and dragging her home but she dug her heels in and a tremendous argument followed, during which she swore she would never marry. They gave her the option of 'Marry or Die' and she, being the headstrong girl that she was, opened her arms and said "Kill me then". One of the brothers picked up an iron candelabra and was about to do just that when his arm was grasped from behind by the monk Eustasius who had arrived at that propitious moment."

"What? A *Bishop*, about to kill his *sister* in a *church*?" broke in Luka.

"Ah, well Faro had not at that stage actually been made bishop and the local customs have always been very severe in this part of Gallia. If they had have killed her, there is no doubt that they would have been absolved of all sin by the local community since their indignation would have been seen as being righteous."

"What?" said Luka again.

"Never mind," said Botolph. "Go on Eligius".

"Fortunately Eustasius managed to quieten the situation down and restored the young lady to her father who was well-pleased to see her back and very glad that his two sons hadn't managed to kill her.

He was so remorseful that he honoured his previous promise and provided her with the land at Evoriacum so that she could build the fine monastery that you will shortly be joining."

"Well there's a happy ending," said Luka.

"How long ago did all this happen?" asked Botolph.

412

"Burgundo-Fara was fourteen at the time and she must be in her early thirties now. Her brothers have both been bishops for nearly ten years so the monastery would be about eighteen years old."

Eligius's story made the boys look forward even more to the prospect of meeting this redoubtable Abbess.

Luka was not too sure that meeting up with Bishop Faro was such a good idea though. He was uncertain how he would feel about him. Bishops were meant to engender respect. Luka thought that the first thing he might want to do would be to kick him firmly on the shins.

Botolph had similar worries. Partly about Luka's reaction which he was correctly assessing, and secondly because of his own feelings. Perhaps it might be more diplomatic to avoid the confrontation; find some excuse. He would pray about it.

"King Dagobert will be holding a feast to celebrate his successful tour," said Eligius. "Sadly he cannot do this until Lent is over, so he is going to combine it with the Easter festivities in a week's time. He has however, specifically asked me to persuade you both to stay and join him as his special guests."

"Oh," said Botolph, "we were really hoping to be able to press on straight away to Evoriacum."

"Yes," said Eligius, "I guessed that that would be how you felt, but there is more to come I am afraid."

"What's that then?!" said Luka.

Unusually for him, Eligius looked a little uncomfortable and he shifted in his seat before answering: "Queen Nanthild has been so inspired by her visits to monasteries throughout the kingdom, together with the stories you have told her of the nunneries of Eanswythe and Ethelburga in the province of Cantium, that she has in mind to build a monastery here in the name of young Prince Clovis. The king has approved this and we are about to start discussions on the very subject. Queen Nanthild has specifically asked that you join in with the meetings and give us the benefit of your opinions."

The boys were silent; partly in confusion with regard to their plans being thwarted and partly in astonishment that their opinions should be sought.

"I am afraid that you do not really have much choice," Eligius continued. "The king would not be pleased if you chose to continue your journey straight away. Look at it this way, you have had the king's protection for the past two weeks and eaten at his expense. Staying on for a few more days will balance that out and enable you to enjoy even more of his hospitality. I am sure you will not regret it and your contributions towards the monastery's design will forever give you the king's ear."

The boys were stunned into silence. Suddenly they were experts in monasteries.

"I suppose he's right," said Luka later. "We *have* visited and lived in an awful lot of seminaries. The one at Sithiu and the others we have already visited in Gallia to name but a few."

"Seminaries," mused Botolph at his use of the word. "Seed-beds for growing clergy. That is the business we are in. We are like migrating birds, not fully-fledged ourselves and yet carrying the word of God with us and dropping these seeds wherever we go in the hope that they will germinate and produce more monks who will spread more seeds and thus the story of Christ will grow."

Luka was uncharacteristically silent at this philosophising. Instead of making one of his usual quips, he just said "Hmm".

414

Botolph was pleased.

At last, he felt that Luka was beginning to see the point in all this.

Here they were, being asked by a king and queen for *their* advice.

They would have some hand in the building of a new monastery.

That monastery was to be in the *capital* of Gallia and it would bear the little prince's name.

Yes, Botolph was pleased, he was *very* pleased.

THE END OF THE BEGINNING:

THE END OF "YOUNG" BOTOLPH,

THE BEGINNING OF "BROTHER" BOTOLPH

AND THE MAKING OF "PRIOR" BOTOLPH.

Glossary

Abbey	A building inhabited by a religious institution of monks or nuns governed by an Abbot or Abbess.
Amblethuys	Ambleteuse near Boulogne, France.
Apuldre	Appledore near Tenterden, Kent.
Atrebatum	Arras, France.
Austrasia	Ancient part of Northwest France (Fig. 10).
Beltaine	Celtic festival held on 1st May. Devoted to the god Bel and involved the lighting of fires.
Beodricsworth	Bury St.Edmunds, Suffolk.
Beorgh Asc	Burwash, East Sussex.
Bloomery	Strictly a primitive type of furnace used in the Iron Age but in this book is the fictional name of a Saxon village in the Weald devoted to iron-making.
Bourn	A stream.
Burel	Natural undyed wool. Varies in colour between white and brown.
Burgh Castle	Near Great Yarmouth.
Burgundia	Ancient part of Southeast France (Fig. 10)
Caesaromagus	Beauvais, France. Stronghold of the Bellovaci tribe.
Caleton	Sands off that part of the coast of Gaul which eventually became Calais.
Cantium	Kent. A province in England.
Cantwarebury	Canterbury. Known in Roman times as Durovernum Cantiacorum and later as Burh. Although the latter would have been the correct choice of name for Botolph's time, I have chosen not to use this in order to avoid confusion between Burh and Burgh in East Anglia. Occupied **by** Roman forces until c.400 AD when they were recalled, after which little is heard of the town until c.590 AD when Ethelbert became king. By the time Augustine arrived in 597 AD via Ebbsfleet on the island of Tanatus, Cantwarebury had become well-established again. In this book, a

I

	monastery/abbey under the control of Archbishop Honorius and Prior Peter.
Capellanu	The guardian of reliquaries.
Celts	Celts were polytheistic animists. That is to say that they had many gods and goddesses and also venerated deities existing in aspects of nature such as streams and trees.
Coenobium	A religious institution of monks or nuns following a communal rule of life.
Colneceaster	Colchester, Essex.
Contubernium	Roman term for "Tent erecting party".
Convent	From Latin "Convenire" meaning "To come together". A religious institution, usually (but not necessarily) consisting of nuns.
Cnobersburg	A monastery near Great Yarmouth, under the control of Abbot Fursey and, in this book, Prior Matthew.
Dofras	Dover (also at other times called Dubris).
Ebon's Island	Ebony, Kent.
Eveqcomte	Special title for the Bishop-Prince of Beauvais.
Evoriacum	The name of Faremoutiers before Fara's death.
Faremoutiers	Moûtiers (in the Albertville region of France) was the capital of the Ceutrones, a Celtic tribe of Gaul. The town was previously called "Monasterium" and the two names became interchangeable. Thus "Faremoutiers" and "Marmoutiers" represent Fara's and Martin's Monasteries respectively.
Folcanstane	A nunnery under the control of Abbess Eanswythe. Dedicated to Saints Peter and Paul. Generally known as a Nunnery but could just as properly be referred to as an Abbey. The first such institution in England.
Francia	That part of Gaul populated by the Franks (following the collapse of the Western Roman Empire).
Fyrd	A militia band called to fight in times of danger

Gallia	Gaul. A large area comprising the southern part of the Netherlands, Belgium, part of Germany, France and northern Italy subject to constant alteration of sovereignty.
Gesoriacum	Boulogne. Also known as Bononia and Itius Portus.
Greynose	Cap Gris Nez, France.
Gippeswic	Ipswich.
Hide	Originally a parcel of land of a size suitable for supporting a family and its dependents. Later a specific size of 60 to 120 acres used for assessing taxes.
Heartburst Hill	Crevecoeur in France.
Hrofsceaster	Rochester, Kent. Also known as Durobrivae.
Imbolc	Celtic festival held on 1st February. The spring festival dedicated to the goddess Brigid.
League	Three miles (the distance a man or a horse could walk in an hour).
Ligugia	8 km south of Poitiers, France.
Liman	A bay or harbour (the Turkish language still uses the same word). In the 4th century, the Celts used this word for an "elm-wood" or "marshy" river. Before that time, the word may have been used to describe the whole Romney Marsh area when it was a lagoon.
Liminge	Lyminge. A village in Kent which took its name from the tribe who lived by the Liman (see above). The site of England's first mixed-gender Monastery (under the control of Abbess Ethelburga).
Longseaxe	A large Saxon fighting knife.
Lotha's Croft	Lowestoft
Lundwic	London. As mentioned in the Pronounciation Section, the "c" here is pronounced as "ch". Thus "Lundwich" or "LundCity". When the City became large and divided into two, Lundwic became "Ealdwic" (or "old" city) which eventually became the more familiar "Aldwych". During

	Roman times, the capital was called "Londinium" and this name was used for many centuries after the Romans left, but "Lundwic" was in common use in Botolph's time.
Lugdunum	Lyon, France.
Lughnasadh	Celtic festival held on 1st August. Dedicated to the three-faced god Lugus.
Lutetia	Paris. Originally the home of the Parisii tribe.
Luxovium	Luxeuil, Burgundia, France. Site of monastery, founded 585 by the Irish monk Columbanus. Became one of the largest and most important monasteries in Gaul.
Manigfual	Cnobersburg sailing vessel. (Name "borrowed" from Frisian legend)
Mettis	Metz, Northeast France. Important Roman city.
Mile	A Roman mile was 1,000 paces, i.e. 1,000 "yards".
Minster	Any large church originally connected to a monastery.
Mithras	God popular with Roman military between 1st and 4th centuries
Monastery	From Greek "Monos" meaning "Alone"; a religious institution living in seclusion from secular society and bound by religious vows. Usually (but not necessarily) consisting of monks.
Neustria	Ancient area of Western France (Fig. 10).
Niwendenne	Newenden, Kent.
Novitiate	A person who has entered a religious order but has not yet taken their final vows.
Nunnery	A religious institution consisting of a community of nuns.
Ox Island	Isle of Oxney.
Portus Limanis	A Roman port near Lympne, Kent. Functional c.130-350AD. Site of Studfall Castle.
Priory	A religious institution governed by a Prior. Sometimes subordinate to an abbey.

IV

Prior	The deputy head of a monastery or abbey, ranking directly below the Abbot. In certain religious orders the Prior is the actual and only head of the community.
Rhee Wall	Raised land-wall on Romney Marsh, running from Appledore to New Romney. Origin controversial but may be Roman.
River Limen	A stream, running along the northern edge of Romney Marsh, consisting of a tidal saltwater creek at its eastern end and a narrow freshwater tributary from the River Rother at its western end.
River Rother	A river running from the Weald to the Marshes of Rumniae. The river's name was not in fact acquired until the later middle ages.
Sandgap	Sandgate, Kent.
Samara River	River Somme, France
Samarobriva	Amiens, France. City where Saint Martin gave half his cloak to the beggar.
Samhain	Celtic festival held on 1st November. Starts at sunset on 31st October and finishes at sunset on 1st November. The day when spirits of the Otherworld become visible. Generally hoped to be the day of the first frost after the harvest has been gathered in. The first day of the new Saxon year. Customarily a place was set for the dead at the Samhain feast and the night was notable for the telling of tales of ancestors. A westerly door or window would be opened to invite the dead to attend. A candle would be placed nearby to guide the spirits home. The time to take stock of supplies, in terms of both grain and cattle. Decisions to be made how many and which animals are to be slaughtered. The bones of bonefires. Once these were alight (often two bonefires side by side) the rest of the village fires were extinguished and then re-lit from fire taken

	from the bonefires, thus re-establishing a bond between the villagers. People and livestock walked between the bonefires as a symbol of purification.
Scrip	A leather pouch typically carried by a pilgrim.
Seaxe	A Saxon fighting knife.
Sithiu	Saint Omer, France.
Sixmile	Hamlet on Stone Street, Kent, six miles from Canterbury, and also six miles from Portus Lemanis, Folkestone and Ashford.
Stade	A name of ancient derivation used in southern England for "quay" or "strand".
Stone Street	Roman Road between Canterbury and Portus Lemanis, Kent
Tanatus	Isle of Thanet, Kent. The royal base chosen by Hengist and Horsa, 455-488, and probably subsequently by Octa and Eormenric. "Thanatos" was a minor Greek God; the daemonic personification of death.
Tenetwaraden	Tenterden, Kent. (Thanet-men's forest den).
Tervanna	Therouanne, France.
Thury	Meadow Town near Beaumont-sur-Oise.
Thwart	A structural crosspiece in an open boat. Used as a seat.
Tonsure	The partial shaving of the head to leave a "halo" of hair to indicate membership of a monastic order.
Venta Icanorum	(Also, later, Norwic) Norwich.
Whitenose	Cap Blanc Nez, France.
Wic	Suffix meaning "Trading Station".

Appendix.

Slaves.

In Botolph's time, slaves were often the descendants of Britons who, years previously, had been taken by raiding Saxons who subsequently settled in the country. From then onwards they and their offspring would be bartered as the mood took their owner. In times of famine and severe hardship, a husband or wife might find that their only hope of survival lay in choosing *voluntary* enslavement. In such circumstances they were known to sell their families and/or themselves into slavery. Slaves were ubiquitous, even being found in religious institutions.

The value of a slave was set at one pound which was the price of eight oxen. This was the price that anyone who killed a slave would be expected to pay to his aggrieved owner. There was no law against anyone killing their own slave. Owners had to treat the acquisition of a slave with caution since they became responsible for their actions. The dress of slaves was however indistinguishable from free people but they were expected to do all the heavy manual labour and anything that was remotely unpleasant. It was within the right of an owner to grant a slave his freedom. This was usually done at a holy place or at a cross-roads, symbolising, for the newly-freed person, his or her right to choose their own pathway in the future.

Topography

The topography of the maps figured in this book is innovative. Most maps found in literature that is concerned with the seventh century feature coastlines following twenty-first century shape, or are medieval maps drawn several hundred years later, or are hand-drawn estimated topographies based on such medieval maps.

The maps, featured in this book, have been generated using data received from space shuttle technology. This data has then been modified (using specialised software) to bring the water levels up to where they would have been in the seventh century. I would urge you, the reader, to spare a little extra time to study the maps closely. I hope you will be able to appreciate the exciting vision of the land as it once was, - revealed by the tricks of modern technology.

Sadly the demands of printing decreed that my beautiful coloured maps be converted to monochrome so they will have lost a little of their lustre.

King Dagobert and his counsellor Eligius (also known as Saint Eloi).

In about 1786, over 1,000 years after his death, a poem was written called "Le bon roi Dagobert". This eventually became a nursery rhyme which is still familiar to most French schoolchildren.

The original purpose of the poem was to poke fun at the aristocracy in order to further the causes of the French Revolution. King Dagobert is portrayed as a bumbling selfish fool who relies heavily on Saint Eloi to get him out of many scrapes.

The twenty-two verses of the poem refer to the same King Dagobert whom I hope we have grown to know and love in the preceding chapters; it must be clear then that these libellous accusations are quite unfounded. I attach just four (liberally translated) verses for your amusement, together with one example in the original French:-

VIII

Le bon roi Dagobert.

Le bon roi Dagobert
A mis sa culotte à l'envers ;
Le grand Saint Éloi
Lui dit : Ô mon roi!
Votre Majesté
Est mal culottée.
C'est vrai, lui dit le roi,
Je vais la remettre à l'endroit.

The king wrote some verse,
But the rhymes were bad and worse,
The Arch Saint Eloi
Said "Oh mon roi!
Leave some other smelly swine
To write for you the awful rhyme."
"Good idea" said the king,
I'll get *you* to write the thing.

The good king Dagobert
Went hunting in Antwerp.
The Arch Saint Eloi
Said "Oh mon roi!
You do seem left
Quite out of breath."
"It's true" said he, "I am a bit",
"I've just been chased ... by a rabbit!"

The dogs owned by Dagobert
By spots became "covaired"
The Arch Saint Eloi
Said "Oh mon roi!
To get them sound
You must have them drowned."
"Oh well, if that's what's to do,
You 'd better drown yourself too!"

The pretty queen of Dagobert
Took a lover, - Oh so fair.
The Arch Saint Eloi
Said "Oh mon roi!
You are cuckold
I'm reliably told."
"It's good," (to him said the King),
"My father was the very same thing!"

IX